W hat happened?" Hrym sa
"I'll explain later," Ro
get *away*." Away, and off the island as soon as possible.

Someone slammed into Rodrick in the mist, knocking him to the ground and nearly sending Hrym spinning from his grasp. Nagesh loomed over him, frost hanging in his beard and in his eyebrows. How had he pursued them? Hrym's fog turned the ground where it touched so slick it was impossible to walk without falling, which should have covered their escape from any foot pursuit. But this was an island of mystics, and anyone with Nagesh's level of authority doubtless had hidden resources. If he could read minds, maybe he could also run nimbly across ice too.

The advisor bent down toward Rodrick, reaching for his throat. Rodrick swung Hrym wildly, the blade sinking into the man's face—

Or, rather, it should have. Instead, the edge *bounced* off, leaving a thin line like a shallow razor cut. Nagesh howled as if he'd received a much more grievous injury, and his features *flickered* again—but this time, instead of returning to normal, they changed utterly.

Where a darkly handsome human head had been a moment before, there was now an immense serpent's head. Nagesh's true face was covered in gleaming dark scales, the eyes black and shining, his mouth a maw that opened to reveal a pair of curving fangs as long as Rodrick's forefingers. When he cried out, it was a discordant hiss of sibilants. He reached for Rodrick again, and something was *wrong* with his hands, the fingers curling the wrong way, the palms where the backs should be . . .

The Pathfinder Tales Library

Called to Darkness by Richard Lee Byers
Winter Witch by Elaine Cunningham
The Wizard's Mask by Ed Greenwood
Prince of Wolves by Dave Gross
Master of Devils by Dave Gross
Queen of Thorns by Dave Gross
King of Chaos by Dave Gross
Lord of Runes by Dave Gross
Pirate's Honor by Chris A. Jackson
Pirate's Promise by Chris A. Jackson
Beyond the Pool of Stars by Howard Andrew Jones
Plague of Shadows by Howard Andrew Jones
Stalking the Beast by Howard Andrew Jones
Firesoul by Gary Kloster
The Worldwound Gambit by Robin D. Laws
Blood of the City by Robin D. Laws
Song of the Serpent by Hugh Matthews
Nightglass by Liane Merciel
Nightblade by Liane Merciel
City of the Fallen Sky by Tim Pratt
Liar's Blade by Tim Pratt
Liar's Island by Tim Pratt
Reign of Stars by Tim Pratt
The Crusader Road by Michael A. Stackpole
Death's Heretic by James L. Sutter
The Redemption Engine by James L. Sutter
Forge of Ashes by Josh Vogt
Skinwalkers by Wendy N. Wagner
The Dagger of Trust by Chris Willrich

Liar's Island

Tim Pratt

A TOM DOHERTY ASSOCIATES BOOK
New York

PATHFINDER TALES: LIAR'S ISLAND

Copyright © 2015 by Paizo Inc.

Maps by Crystal Frasier

A Tor Book
Published by Tom Doherty Associates, LLC
175 Fifth Avenue
New York, NY 10010

www.tor-forge.com

Library of Congress Cataloging-in-Publication Data

Pratt, Tim, 1976–
    Liar's Island : a novel / Tim Pratt.—First edition.
        p. cm.—(Pathfinder tales)
    "A Tom Doherty Associates book."
    ISBN 978-0-7653-7452-3 (trade paperback)
    ISBN 978-1-4668-4264-9 (e-book)
1. Magic—Fiction. 2. Swords—Fiction. 3. Travelers—Fiction. I. Title.
    PS3616.R385 L53 2015
    813'.6—dc23

                                                                2015015071

Tor books may be purchased for educational, business, or promotional use. For information on bulk purchases, please contact the Macmillan Corporate and Premium Sales Department at 1-800-221-7945, extension 5442, or write to specialmarkets@macmillan.com.

First Edition: August 2015

Printed in the United States of America

0 9 8 7 6 5 4 3 2 1

For Heather and River. There's a circle around us.

Inner Sea Region

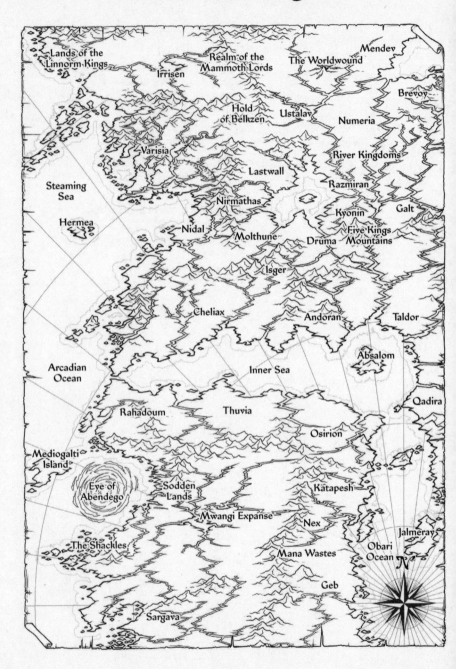

Jalmeray

Obari Ocean

Tiger's Eye
Monastery

Padiskar

Gho Vella

The Pure Temple
of the Maharajah

Grand
Sarret

Veedesha

River Sald

Niswan

Kaina Katakka

Prada
Hanam

Sêgang Jungle

N

1
Cornered

Kresley was head of the little lord's household guard, a position that seldom required more than standing around looking good in a polished breastplate at interminable balls and occasionally kicking priests, beggars, or solicitors who somehow made it past the lord's gates back out into the streets of Absalom. Today, unfortunately, he'd been sent on an errand that was really more the province of the city guards . . . but the little lord wanted it handled personally, because the city guards were interested more in the law than in allowing the lord to exact a terrible revenge.

Kresley cleared his throat and tried once more to do it the easy way. "Rodrick! Come out! None of us want to see blood spilled." This gray street in a rough part of the city had probably seen plenty of blood spilled, though the predominant scent was actually urine.

"Especially our blood," muttered Haverford, a grizzled veteran with a long scar down one cheek who'd been hired onto the household guard because he'd once saved the little lord's cousin from getting a crossbow bolt in the face on one battlefield or another. Haverford was fond of wine and didn't respect Kresley's authority at all, even though Kresley's breastplate always *far* outshone Haverford's own.

Kresley, Haverford, and three other men—and the wizard, but Kresley didn't want to think about the wizard; they weren't the sort of people you wanted standing *behind* you, because what if one of their spells went off by accident?—were arrayed in a loose semicircle before an abandoned storehouse in the Coins. The wizard had tracked their quarry this far, through the winding streets of Absalom, and there was no doubt they'd found their prey, and that he was trapped. Kresley had scouted for other exits, and this door was the only way out, since the storehouse was built right up against the similarly dilapidated buildings around it on all sides.

But the thief, Rodrick, wasn't acting like he was trapped, and showed no interest at all in giving himself up. Kresley wasn't keen to bash his way into a building full of who knew what, through a door only large enough to admit one man at a time, against an enemy who'd had time to set traps or an ambush.

Especially *this* enemy. Kresley had seen the damage done by Rodrick's sword, the holes blasted in the little lord's wall, ragged gaps still rimed with frost. He knew the wizard was here to take that icy advantage away, but what if the man's magic *missed*?

The front door of the storehouse was even hanging askew, practically an invitation to enter, which surely meant some terrible preparations had been made beyond. Kresley had never served in any organized military force, but he knew attacking an enemy on prepared ground was harder than kicking a beggar down the little lord's front steps.

"Why don't you come in?" Rodrick called, voice muffled. "It's nice in here. Plenty of room. We can sit and chat."

"If we have to come in after you, there will be violence!" Kresley said. "Give yourself up, and it will go easier on you!"

"I see," Rodrick called, but his voice seemed to come from farther away. What was he *doing* in there? "So, if I come out, you won't harm me?"

"That's right!"

"But you'll take me back to the little lord, who will harm me?"

"He . . . hasn't told me his plans for you . . ."

"Oh?" Rodrick's voice was bright, and now sounded closer. "He could want me for anything, then. Perhaps I'm to be guest of honor at a feast, or he wants to play a game of towers. Sit with me and sip brandy by the fire and discuss the peculiarities of Osirian funeral rites or the philosophies of the Mammoth Lords, just us, two men of the world. I suppose that's the sort of hospitality he offers thieves? Though to be *accurate* I'm not a thief at all, because I was discovered before I had a chance to steal anything. The indignity of fleeing the palace—of running from *you*—isn't that punishment enough, especially considering I made no profit off this endeavor at all?"

"You did get your wages for serving as security at the ball," Kresley said. "Those are ill-gotten gains." Why was he arguing with the man? Oh, yes: Because it was better than rushing someone who had a magical sword. Or indeed any kind of sword.

"Are you claiming I didn't provide adequate security?" Rodrick sounded outraged. "Was the dance floor attacked by hordes of ravening demons? Did ogres overturn the punch bowls? Did a bugbear eat the goose liver off a rich man's plate? Were the musicians torn apart by werewolves? They were not, and I'm sure my presence made all the difference. I gave good value for those meager coins."

Haverford spat and, to Kresley's surprise, spoke up loudly enough for Rodrick to hear: "The little lord paid you for your loyalty, thief. Just for one night, but you took the coin, and you made the deal, and so were bound by it. You betrayed him, and a man who'd betray another is no man at all. Treachery's a worse crime than theft."

"Oh, in *that* case, I'll be right out," Rodrick said. Something clattered, and someone else inside the warehouse swore.

Kresley frowned and leaned over to Haverford. "Is that . . . is there someone else in there? Does he have an accomplice?"

"It's the *sword*." The wizard rolled his eyes. He was fat and robed, but he wasn't old, and didn't look like a proper wizard at all, being entirely beardless. "You know, the whole reason I'm here? The reason this Rodrick was hired to provide security at the ball in the first place? He's just a man, but that Hrym is a wonder. A talking sword of living ice."

"I knew about the ice," Kresley muttered. There'd been something about the sword talking, too, but he'd dismissed it as exaggeration. The sword certainly hadn't said anything back at the little lord's manor house.

"I can also sing!" the second voice called. He—it?—sounded jovial and curmudgeonly all at once, like a drunken grandfather at the wedding of a relative he didn't like much.

"No, Hrym, don't sing!" Rodrick cried. "We want them to *leave*, not die!"

Kresley pinched the bridge of his nose between his thumb and forefinger. He was getting a headache, and this street really did smell like every cat, dog, and vagrant in the Coins used it as a latrine. "All right. This is nonsense. We're going in. Rodrick, this is your last chance—"

"Oh, well, if you really want to die, I can't be blamed," Rodrick interrupted. "But I have to wonder if you've thought this through. Say one of your men manages to get a sword into my neck before Hrym freezes him solid. What have you accomplished, really? You can kill me, but you can't kill *Hrym*. He's a sword. And a magical one, at that—you can't even melt him down. Believe me, many have tried."

"I daresay the lord would be pleased to have a . . . a talking sword . . . to add to his collection."

"Ha! You don't want *this* sword." Rodrick's laugh was booming and hearty. "He's cursed, you know."

Kresley blinked. "I . . . what?"

"My sword. Ooh, look, a magical sentient sword of living ice, everyone's always so impressed. But, yes: he's cursed. Cursedly cursed."

"You have, by all accounts, traveled with this blade for many years," Kresley said. "In what way is it *cursed*?"

"What? Look where I am *now*," Rodrick said. "I'm about to be murdered by a bunch of household guards, of all things! Hrym's *obviously* cursed. It's just a slow-acting curse."

The wizard sighed. "The sword isn't cursed. Are we going to stand around here much longer? It's only, I've got plans."

"Cursed or not, the very idea of Hrym languishing in your master's collection disgusts me!" Rodrick said. "Hrym thrives on open air, long roads leading to nowhere in particular, and a general life of adventure!"

"I wouldn't mind resting on a pile of gold coins somewhere cool and dry, actually," Hrym said. "If anyone's asking me. Which no one ever does."

"Honestly!" Rodrick said more loudly. "Doesn't the thought of such waste, of turning a majestic creature like Hrym into an ornament—doesn't it sicken you, Kelso?"

"It's Kresley," Kresley said automatically.

A long pause. "If you say so. I'm sure you know best. But your confusion about your own name aside, doesn't it trouble you? The way your lord and master keeps such wonders—none as wondrous as Hrym, but still, quite wondrous—locked up, out of sight in a vault, made useless? Is it any wonder I wanted to take a few of them away with me? Those relics deserve to be appreciated, not kept sealed away for one rich man's pleasure."

"You were just going to sell them," Hrym said. "And for sums only another rich man could afford."

"Yes, true, but I was going to sell them to *several* rich men, to sort of spread the joy around, you see."

"I get the sense that Rodrick isn't taking us very seriously." Haverford looked Kresley up and down. "I can't imagine why."

"Fine," Kresley snapped. "Men, let's go in."

"The first man who comes through that door," Rodrick called, "will be frozen into an ice sculpture of himself. The process is *generally* fatal, but at least you'll make a beautiful decoration at your own funeral."

"Don't worry about it," the wizard said. He muttered something and made a series of complex gestures. He stepped forward, tapping each man briefly on the back of the neck. "There," he said. "Protection from ice, cast on all of you. Go forth and do whatever it is people like you do. As you should have ten minutes ago."

"Protection from ice won't help if they've got traps set up in there," Haverford muttered.

The wizard rolled his eyes again. "I wouldn't worry about it. This Rodrick probably hasn't had to think his way out of a problem since he first got his hands on that sword. This building, it's just an old storehouse, not an armory. They might try to push a pile of crates on top of you, but otherwise I wouldn't fret."

"Did someone out there say 'protection from ice'?" Hrym said.

"You're still a *sword*," Rodrick said. "We can, you know . . . cut them. Stab. What have you."

"But you're no swordsman," Hrym said. "No offense, but if it's just you against, what, three of them?"

"Four!" Haverford called, and drew his blade. "Five, counting our illustrious leader." Now he was smiling. "Things are looking up. These are the sort of odds you like, eh, Kelso?"

"Kresley," Kresley muttered. But, yes—he did like these odds. He considered sending Haverford in first, in case there *were* traps, but the man would look at him with even more scorn than usual if he did that. Kresley strode forward and kicked the door off its hinges. The interior of the storehouse was visible in light streaming through the dusty skylights, and the space was almost entirely barren, apart from a few cobwebbed shelves near the back.

Rodrick stood in the center of the space, sipping from a flask and holding a crystalline longsword that shimmered like diamonds and sent up faint curls of icy vapor all along its length. Rodrick lifted the sword, and a blast of white wind spiraled toward the door. Kresley winced and closed his eyes, but apart from a cool, damp breeze, he felt nothing, and when he opened his eyes, Rodrick was making a face like he'd bitten a lemon.

Haverford shouldered in, followed by the other men. The wizard seemed content to wait outside. "How bad of a beating do we put on him before we drag him back to the little lord?" Haverford asked.

"Medium bad," Kresley said. "Feel free to break his arms and hands, but leave the legs and feet—otherwise we'll have to carry him the whole way back."

"You *are* cursed, Hrym," Rodrick said.

"*You're* cursed," the sword replied, voice emerging from the empty air in the vicinity of the blade. "Oh well. It's been a while since I was owned by a nobleman. As I recall, they hardly ever sleep in ditches or haystacks."

The guards advanced.

They were quite surprised when a djinni appeared before them in a swirl of mist and wind, rising nearly eleven feet tall, its lower body a swirling funnel of air, its upper body that of a muscular dark-skinned man, with a very solid-looking scimitar gripped in each hand.

"You will not harm this man," the djinni intoned, dust and filth swirling around in its whirlwind. Kresley stepped back, and even Haverford retreated a few steps. Kresley looked at the sword in his hand. He considered dropping it so the creature wouldn't mistake it for a threat.

"Ha," Rodrick said from behind the genie. "You didn't expect that, did you, Kelso? I can summon djinns. Djinn. Djinnis? One of my many skills."

"No it's not," Hrym said. "You've never even *seen* a djinni before. The plural is djinn, by the way."

"Shh," Rodrick said. "This is a marvelous opportunity to embellish my already considerable legend."

Kresley swallowed. "Ah . . . wizard? Do you . . . is there such a thing as . . . protection from . . . djinn?" He stole a glance through the open door and saw the wizard running away as fast as his sandaled feet could take him.

"Guess not," Haverford said, and ran away too, followed by the other guards.

Kresley waited a moment longer, as befitted his position as head of the household guard, and then he ran away as well.

2
Summoned

After a long silence, broken only by the susurration of the djinni's whirlwind body, the creature slowly rotated until it faced the fugitives. "You are Rodrick and Hrym."

"Hmmm," Rodrick said. "What do you think, Hrym? Do we admit anything? Is this thing going to kill us?"

"It could kill you, maybe," Hrym said. "I don't see how a man who's half wind can possibly hurt me."

"I mean you no harm," the djinni said.

"Oh. That's reassuring." Rodrick held up Hrym's glittering blade, putting the length of enchanted ice between himself and the djinni. He was frankly overawed at the presence of the immense magical creature, but he'd had a lot of practice pretending to be bored and unimpressed—people hardly ever expected you to steal things when you looked totally bored by them—so he hid his surprise well.

The djinni's vortex had picked up bits of trash from the store-house, and scraps of paper and ragged bits of leaf swirled where its legs should have been, an effect that made the thing seem less monstrously inhuman, though not by much.

"Thank you for scaring off those . . . oh, let's say 'muggers,'" Rodrick said.

The djinni stared at him impassively, and Rodrick resisted the urge to clear his throat, duck his head, shuffle his feet, or run for his life under the unmoving onslaught of its gaze.

"How do you know our names?" Hrym said.

Excellent question, Rodrick thought. If he hadn't been halfway to soiling himself with fear he might have asked it himself.

"I was sent to deliver a message," the djinni said. "The thakur of Jalmeray requests the pleasure of your company at his palace in Niswan."

"I understood some of those words," Rodrick said. "Notably 'pleasure' and 'palace.'"

"Jalmeray," Hrym said. "You mean that island off the coast of Nex? With all the monasteries and tigers and so on?"

"Ah," Rodrick said. "The place where those fighting monks study, isn't that right? I hear they'll take anyone who shows talent. You just have to go there and pass some kind of test, where you punch an efreeti in the face, outdrink a marid, spank a djinni—things like that. Then you get to join a House of Perfection and live on rice water and regular beatings for years while you learn how to punch a man's heart out through his back, or kill someone with your pinky finger. Never saw the point, myself, as a sword is just as effective, and you don't get blood on your fingers unless you use it wrong."

The djinni was not noticeably amused. "Jalmeray is a wondrous island, the westernmost of the Impossible Kingdoms of the Vudrani."

"And this thakur you mentioned is, what? The king?"

"In essence," the djinni said.

"Hmm. I don't owe a foreign king any obedience—"

"Oh, because you're so obedient to *local* kings," Hrym said.

Rodrick shrugged. "Local kings tend to have local soldiers who can compel obedience, though, so I walk a bit more softly around them, you have to give me that."

"This king of Jalmeray sent a djinni," Hrym said. "The one standing right here. You remember. Look at him. He's got a scimitar in each hand, and when he kicks you, you get kicked with a *tornado*. You want to disobey him?"

"I will not compel your attendance," the djinni said. "You are invited guests. A ship leaves the docks tomorrow at first light, the *Nectar of the Gods*, and there is a berth for you if you wish to board. Whether you accept the invitation or not makes no difference to me."

"All right, fair enough, but can you give us a *hint*?" Rodrick said. "Does this thakur want to hire us to do something unsavory? Marry me off to his ugliest granddaughter to bring some fresh blood to the family line? Give me a medal for some act of heroism that's temporarily slipped my mind?"

The djinni still didn't look amused. Rodrick might give up trying soon at this rate. "I cannot say," the creature replied. "But for a man from the barbarous lands of the Inner Sea to be granted an audience with the thakur is a great honor."

"Honor doesn't fill my belly, or my purse," Rodrick said.

"Mmm. If you proved hesitant, I was instructed to offer this incentive." The djinni sheathed one of the scimitars—sheathed it where, or in what, exactly, Rodrick couldn't see, but that was supernatural creatures for you—and reached into the swirling vortex beneath its waist. Its hand reemerged holding a small leather bag, which the djinni tossed to Rodrick.

The bag clinked endearingly, and a peek inside revealed the warm yellow glow of gold, coins stamped with multi-armed women and elephant heads and roaring tigers.

"That is merely a taste of the wealth that awaits you," the djinni said. "If you come to Jalmeray, and reach an accommodation with the thakur, you may well leave the island with your own weight in gold."

"Every time someone says that," Rodrick said, "I wish I were a great deal fatter." He made the coins disappear almost as neatly as the djinni had made his sword vanish. "We will consider the thakur's kind invitation. Do convey my thanks."

The djinni turned to smoke and vapor, and Rodrick was briefly buffeted by a strong wind as the creature disappeared into or merged with or rode away on currents of air.

"That was unusual," Rodrick said once the wind had died down. "Even by our standards."

Hrym briefly pulsed with red light and giggled, the sound of a demented child who was also probably possessed, and Rodrick winced. A skylight overhead cracked, but fortunately didn't fall in. He aimed the blade away from him, toward a dusty corner of the warehouse, and a few icicles shot forth from the sword, smashing into a shelf and knocking it over with a clatter.

The sword had spent some time the previous year in close proximity to an imprisoned demon lord, and Hrym had the ability to soak up sufficiently powerful ambient magic. He'd picked up some kind of demonic taint, which so far hadn't proven *too* deleterious—he didn't seem compelled to slaughter innocents for the sheer joy of spreading chaos, at any rate—but he had these little . . . episodes. *Fits*, Rodrick might have called them, if Hrym had been human. More and more, though, Hrym giggled horribly, and pulsed with red light, and when that happened, chaos and disorder seemed to spread. Vases broke, chandeliers fell from the ceiling, food rotted, wine turned to vinegar. And those were just the *atmospheric* effects. Lately the giggles had been followed by outbursts of icy magic, like lethal spasms.

One such demonic fit had ruined their attempt to break into the little lord's vault the night before. It was such a *good* plan, too—look tough, get hired to do security at the ball, slip away to the basement, freeze the guards watching the vault, turn the locks to ice, smash them open, steal the wonderful relics within, get on a ship before the little lord even noticed the theft, sell the loot to a not-terribly scrupulous fence named Skiver in Almas, enjoy ill-gotten riches, etc.

But Hrym had one of his fits just as Rodrick was creeping toward the vault, his titter and the attendant *crack* of a roof beam breaking neatly in two overhead alerting the guards to their presence in time to yank a cord that set an alarm bell to ringing somewhere up above. Worse, Hrym had fired off spears of ice, seemingly as involuntarily as Rodrick loosing a sneeze, blowing holes in the wall and ceiling above and calling even more attention. They'd escaped and tried to make their way to the ship bound for Almas anyway, but the little lord's men were there, and they'd pursued Rodrick and Hrym relentlessly through streets until they ended up here in the Coins.

The worst part—all right, one of the many bad parts—was that Hrym wasn't even aware of his condition. He had no memory of his giggles, or the chaos, or the ill-timed bursts of ice magic. As far as Hrym was concerned, the guards had just noticed them when they were sneaking up on the vault—it was pure bad luck.

Rodrick hadn't yet figured out how to tell Hrym he was demon-tainted. After all, who among us doesn't have some little quirk or another? But the fits were becoming more frequent, and violent, and Rodrick was considering the appalling prospect of finding a priest and asking for help.

"Did you hear something?" Hrym said.

Just your terrible giggle and aura of destruction. "A shelf fell down, or something. Everything's busted-up and broken in here. No surprise really."

"Hmm," Hrym said. "So. Do we get on the ship and travel to a faraway land?"

"There are pluses and minuses." He put Hrym in the sheath at his belt, ignoring the sword's protest—walking around the Coins with a naked blade, especially that blade, would draw too much of the wrong kind of attention. "Pluses include that whole weight-in-gold thing."

Hrym's voice was muffled by the sheath, but audible. "Minuses include the fact that no one gives you your weight in gold without expecting you to work for it."

"I do hate work. But being in close proximity to my weight in gold might provide the opportunity to steal it, thus getting the gold without doing the work."

"How much gold would that *be*, anyway?" Hrym asked. "In terms of coins, I mean. Gold is awfully heavy, so it might not be so many, and you know I like to rest on a good bed of coins. He'd better not pay you in gold bars—they're not nearly as comfortable to sleep on. Why *aren't* you fatter, anyway?"

"However much it is, it's certainly more gold than we have now, by quite a large margin. Also, I've never been to Jalmeray. Could be interesting. All djinn and monks and tigers and temples in high mountains. And, hmm—women who dance around wearing nothing but scarves, and translucent scarves, at that. Am I remembering that right?"

"As always, you're a keen student of cultural matters," Hrym said.

"I suppose I should see if I can find a map. Perhaps read a book. No, no time for that—but perhaps I should *talk* to someone who's read a book." He turned a corner and walked along the back of a warehouse, past stacks of empty crates piled up twice the height of a man—or once the height of a djinni, apparently.

"A *whole* book?" Hrym said. "I don't think we know anyone who's gone quite that far."

"True." Rodrick paused in the mouth of an alleyway. Had he heard the scrape of a boot on stone back there? He drew Hrym and whirled, blade outstretched. He was quite good at the drawing-fast-and-whirling bit, as it made quite an impressive display; it was the parts that usually came after—actually trying to kill someone with a sword—that he'd never been much good at. Luckily, Hrym's ice magic made him lethal at a distance.

Except against these two. That buffoon Kelso and the other guard, the old one with the disreputable mustaches, approached with blades drawn. "What now?" the old one said, and grinned. "Gonna summon your djinni again?"

3
Inner and Outer Seas

I can only do that once per day, alas," Rodrick said. "You'll have to settle for ice in lieu of wind."

"The wizard's magic still protects us, blackguard," Kelso said.

"Did you just call me a blackguard?" Rodrick said. "I don't think anyone's ever called me that before. I'm not saying you're wrong, exactly. I don't know the exact definition of the term, but I get the gist, and it might be accurate enough. I'm just saying, it's unusual." He sighed. "So, fine. You've got protection from the cold. But do you have protection from *gold*?" Rodrick jingled the bag of coins he'd gotten from the djinni. "I'll give you this if you go away and leave me alone."

"You'd better only be offering them your share," Hrym said. "I do not approve of this plan."

"You think we can be bought so easily?" Kelso's virtuous jowls quivered in outrage.

"You? Perhaps not. But your friend here has the look of an old veteran, and in my experience, soldiers are practical. Take the gold, and tell your little lord you couldn't find me. Everyone wins."

"Better plan," the grizzled guard said. "We beat you bloody and take the gold *anyway*."

"Damn," Rodrick said. "Some old soldiers are entirely too practical. Another way, then." He waved Hrym toward a stack of crates, unleashing a torrent of icy wind that knocked the whole pile down, tumbling crates smashing into Kelso and the old guard and driving them to the ground. They groaned, not badly hurt, and started to climb out from under the wreckage, but Rodrick played Hrym across the broken mass of crates until they were a fused and frozen lump of ice-locked wood, with the guards trapped underneath. The old guard had gotten his head free from the pile, and he glared at Rodrick as he struggled futilely to escape the crates pinning him down.

"At least you won't be too cold under there," Rodrick said. "Until that spell you've got protecting you wears off, anyway. Then . . . brr."

"I've reconsidered your offer," the guard said. "I'll take the gold."

"I like you," Rodrick said. Feeling cheerful about his prospects, he flipped a coin through the air, making it land an inch from the soldier's nose.

He sauntered away. Nobody could saunter like Rodrick. He didn't even have to practice it anymore. It just came naturally now.

"That coin you threw away is coming out of your half," Hrym said.

"I'll be sure to make a note in the company accounts."

They didn't dare go back to the inn where they'd been staying before the job, in case the little lord sent more men looking for them, so they spent the evening loitering in shadowy alleyways with the other thugs and drinking in the sort of anonymous grog-holes down by the docks where no one would even bother to look around if they heard someone being axe-murdered at the next table. An hour before dawn Rodrick stumbled out, Hrym hidden away in a plain sheath at his belt, and went in search of the *Nectar of the Gods.*

The docks of Absalom, the City at the Center of the World (depending on how you defined "the world," admittedly), were bustling with activity even at such an inhospitable hour, all shouting sailors and grunting dockhands, crates and coils of rope and buckets of pitch, and the ever-present smells of salt and sweat and fish.

"Is it possible to wake up with a hangover when you haven't actually gone to sleep?" Rodrick mused aloud, but Hrym didn't answer. He asked a harried-looking clerk of a woman if she knew where the *Nectar* was berthed, and got a mumbled reply and a slightly more helpful gesture in the right direction.

The ship was medium-large, flying an unfamiliar flag that Rodrick assumed was that of Jalmeray, even though it didn't have a monk or a tiger on it. (He really did wish he'd learned a bit more about the place. Knowledge wasn't as good as wealth, but it was useful.) The crew seemed to be all dark-skinned men and women dressed in practical sailing clothes—billowing trousers and the like—and most were at least a head shorter than Rodrick.

I think I'm going to stand out in Jalmeray, he mused, which made the idea of subtly strolling into the country and stealing a few things less likely. There were advantages to being a noteworthy stranger in town, too, though. There was always an angle to work, if you looked hard enough.

He strolled toward the gangplank, and a middle-aged Vudrani woman wearing a broad red sash above her trousers came down and put a hand on his chest to stop him. She looked him up and down. "Do you need some assistance?" She wrinkled her nose. "Perhaps a helping hand back to the vat of rum you climbed out of? Or is it empty by now?"

He yawned. "You can point me toward my stateroom. At least I assume it's a stateroom, since I'm to be an honored guest of the thakur."

She stepped back, frowned, and then shouted something in a language Rodrick didn't recognize at all, but suspected would become familiar (if not comprehensible) if he made it to Jalmeray.

Rodrick's hand moved to Hrym's hilt, just by way of taking reasonable precautions.

Another woman, this one ten years younger but with the swagger of authority and rather more earrings than the first, arrived and looked Rodrick up and down. He looked her up and down, too. She was lean and athletic, with short hair and dark, merry eyes. Not his usual type, which tended toward softer, more rounded women . . . except for her eyes. He liked those eyes. "You are Rodrick?" she said.

He bowed as extravagantly as he could, given his continued drunkenness and the wobbliness of the gangplank under his feet. "I am."

"You're drunk."

"I hope no one promised you I'd be sober. I didn't get that part of the message."

"Let me see the sword," she said. "So I know you are who you claim to be."

Rodrick considered objecting that such a display would prove only that he had Rodrick's *sword*, not that he was Rodrick himself, but then realized he'd be arguing against his own interests, which was seldom a wise policy. He shrugged and slid out a foot of Hrym's length, the crystalline blade glittering in the light of the lanterns and sending up streamers of vapor.

The woman's demeanor changed entirely. She opened her arms wide and smiled, showing off a gold tooth, which Rodrick gathered was traditional for sea captains of all nations. You probably got hit in the mouth with swinging mizzenmasts and such all the time at sea, so a certain amount of decorative dentistry was to be expected. "I am Saraswati, and this is my ship. This is my first mate, Pia." The older woman still glared at him, but now she gave a grudging nod. "Where are your bags? I'll have someone help carry them."

He had a pack full of extra clothes and a bedroll and other useful things, but it was all back at the inn, which the little lord's men were doubtless watching. He'd stolen most of it, anyway, so the loss didn't sting that much—he could steal most of it again easily enough. Except for a very special cloak he'd acquired during his adventures up north last year, which had both practical and sentimental value. He would be bitter about losing that when he sobered up. "No need. I thought I'd travel light. Just a man and his sword and, ah, his wits. And so on."

"Hmm," Saraswati said. "A man and his sword and one set of clothes, anyway. I'll reserve judgment on the wit until I see some evidence of it. Pia, when you have a moment, see if we can find another shirt and some trousers for him. The pants might be a bit short for you, but the voyage is warm this time of year. Welcome, Rodrick. I've got to make ready to sail, but Pia will show you to your berth."

She started to turn away, and Rodrick touched her shoulder. "Just out of curiosity, do you happen to know why the thakur wants to see me?"

Saraswati gave him a long look, then whistled. "You're going to see the thakur *personally*? I knew the summons came from his staff, but I didn't realize . . . No, I don't know why, and I wouldn't expect to. I was told that if a man named Rodrick showed up this morning with a sword that looked like it was made of ice, I should make him comfortable, get him safely to Niswan, and then send word to the palace. We don't have any clothes here suitable for a meeting with the thakur, but I'm sure they can take care of that at the palace, if they want you to look remotely reputable. Though perhaps you're meant to be an object lesson on the savage disreputability of the denizens of Absalom?"

"I'm Andoren by birth."

She shrugged. "You all seem much the same to me."

His national pride was the least of his many prides, so Rodrick just shrugged, and the captain departed. Besides, he'd barely known where Jalmeray was, so it would be hypocritical to disparage the captain's lack of geographical distinction. Rodrick tried to only be hypocritical when there was money in it.

The first mate beckoned and led him onto the ship, which seemed much like the other seagoing vessels he'd had the pleasure to board in the past, which wasn't that many; more often he traveled on river craft, if he went aboard ships at all. The crew members ignored him with the same disinterest possessed by underpaid and overworked people everywhere. Maybe these strange and exotic Vudrani wouldn't be so strange after all.

The mate led him belowdecks, into space sufficiently cramped that Rodrick had to duck his head. "You'll be staying in my quarters," Pia said, and Rodrick winced. It was never a good idea to inconvenience someone you'd be stuck with on the small world of a ship for . . . how long? He had no idea how far it was to Jalmeray. He really should have tried to find that hypothetical person who'd read a book about the island, but there had been a notable shortage of reputable scholars in the grog shop, so the failure wasn't really Rodrick's fault.

"I'm terribly sorry to displace you, perhaps we could share . . ." He trailed off when she opened a wooden door, revealing a space the size of a fat man's coffin, with a sea chest (locked, of course, not that locks usually gave Rodrick much trouble, if it came to that), a narrow bunk that folded down from the wall, and a tiny table. The table was crowded by a two-foot high bronze idol of a many-armed woman, holding aloft various small objects of doubtless great religious significance, surrounded by seashells and small piles of salt. That's right—the Vudrani were supposed to have hundreds or thousands of gods, weren't they? He hoped there wouldn't be a quiz. "Then again, I suppose sharing it would be a bit tight."

She shrugged. "I'll take the second mate's room, and his is nearly as big as mine, so I don't care. The third mate's the one who'll be angry with you. He's been bumped down to sleeping with the regular crew on deck or in a rope hammock." She pointed at the idol, then at the chest. "Don't meddle with my things. If you do, I'll know. We probably can't kill you, which is what we usually do with thieves, but if you only keelhaul someone a *little* bit, they usually live."

"The captain has even better quarters, I suppose?" Rodrick said.

Pia snorted. "We're to treat you like an honored guest, not like the thakur himself. Don't get above yourself. The captain's giving me a little slice of her own share of profits for my trouble, anyway. She figures the inconvenience of ferrying you around is worth it to show the folk in the palace she's reliable and accommodating. She thinks there might be some opportunity in it for her." She sniffed. "The captain says you can dine with her tonight, if you wash the stink off first. For lunch you can settle for the same rations the crew get. At least they're fresh, us being straight out of port. In the meantime, well. You're not confined to quarters or anything, but try not to get in the way."

She went off, and Rodrick closed the door, not bothering to hook the little latch—it wouldn't keep the door shut if anyone *really* wanted to come in, though it would probably keep the door from flying open every time they crested a wave. He drew Hrym, who sighed contentedly, like a man released from a cage, and set the blade down on top of the sea chest.

"You mind if I get some sleep?" Rodrick said. "I have a date with that hangover I mentioned."

"Fine, fine, just scatter some gold on the chest for me to rest on, would you?" Hrym had been a dragon in a past life, sort of— it was complicated—and was never happier than when he rested atop a heap of treasures, though Rodrick could usually provide only a very modest hoard.

He moved Hrym to the bed. "Didn't someone threaten to keel-haul us once before?" Rodrick shook out a handful of gold from the bag, scattering it on the chest, and then put Hrym on top of the coins. He knelt and examined the lock on the sea chest, just out of professional interest, though he didn't touch it.

"Mmm. Last year, when we were trying to find that magical key. I don't think anyone *threatened* it, exactly, but the subject came up."

"Keelhauling. Is that the one where they put you on a rack and attach your hands and feet to things and stretch you out until your bones break?"

"No, that's just called the *rack*," Hrym said. "Keelhauling is when they tie a rope around you and—"

"Oh, right. Throw you overboard and drag you along underneath the ship, scraping you against the barnacles on the hull, and drag you back up the other side. And if you didn't drown, they beat you and then do it all over again. It's coming back to me now. People must get *bored* at sea, to think of doing something like that." He sighed and stood up. There was probably nothing he wanted in the chest anyway, and it would be a shame to let mere habitual larceny ruin his chance to reach Jalmeray and get his own weight in gold.

He stretched out on the bunk—hardly the best bed he'd slept in, but a long way from the worst, insofar as it *was* a bed, and not a ditch full of leaves or the stone floor of a dungeon cell. He felt the ship jerk as it left port, and settled into sleep as the voyage began.

Rodrick woke some unknown time later—there was still daylight in the tiny porthole, so he hadn't lost the whole day—and sat up with a groan. His head was full of thunder, his mouth was dry, and he was simultaneously ravenous and nauseated.

"Sleep well?" Hrym said. "I don't know how you could with all the snoring you were doing. How a noise like that doesn't wake you up is beyond me."

"The sleeping was fine. It's the waking up that's proving difficult." He stretched as well as he could in the confines of the cabin, then blinked. His battered knapsack was resting on the floor, tied closed, along with his bedroll and lantern. "Are those my things?"

"Apparently a djinni delivered them," Hrym said. "Fetched them from our inn, though how it knew where we were staying, I couldn't say, and don't like to think about. I told the crewman to leave it there. You were sleeping like the dead. Only the dead are quieter."

Rodrick opened up the pack and dug through it. Spare clothes, a couple of knives, and the usual odds and ends—and, down at the bottom, his most valuable possession: a cloak of the devilfish, which would transform him into the eponymous vile, tentacled, and hard-to-kill sea creature if he donned it and gave the right command. That cloak was a great comfort to have on a ship, as such things had a distressing ability to sink with all hands lost, or so he gathered. Rodrick had owned some other wondrous items, once, but he'd sold them for enough to live like a lord for a few months. They'd been good months, but maybe a little boring, if he was being totally honest. The good months were followed by some hard ones, but that was the life he'd chosen—feast alternating with famine. At least this way he got the feasts. Most honest men had to settle for a steady diet of famine.

He was rather cheered, having his possessions back. Who knew djinn were so considerate? "Want a breath of fresh sea air?"

"I'm happy here."

"Too bad. I don't want to leave you unattended." He scooped up the scattered coins, counting to make sure none had rolled away during the voyage, though this ship was large enough he barely felt it sway.

"I was *using* those."

"I'm not going to leave the gold unattended, either."

"No one could take it—or take me, for that matter—without me freezing them into a lump of ice. I may not be able to move around without your help, but I can protect myself and my hoard just fine."

"Just *yesterday* we ran into a wizard who used magic to render you powerless."

"Hmph. I wasn't powerless. My power was fine. It just didn't *work* on those men. But we took care of them anyway."

Rodrick put the refilled coin pouch away and picked up Hrym. "Yes, but I'd rather you not knock holes in the boat fighting off thieves. Look, I'll wear the sheath on my back, and you can freeze yourself to the outside of the scabbard so you can see, all right?" Wearing a longsword on your back was generally not a clever thing to do—reaching over your own shoulder and drawing a four-foot-long blade from a sheath strapped to your back was logistically impossible for most people, and even if you had comically long arms, it was a good way to accidentally cut off your own ears—but with Hrym stuck to the outside of a scabbard and unfreezing himself at will, it worked all right, and looked impressive, too. They often traveled that way when they weren't trying to keep Hrym's wondrous nature hidden, though the freezing and unfreezing tended to destroy the scabbards after a while. Rodrick kept meaning to look into buying them in bulk, but he usually just stole a new one when the old one fell apart.

Once he got the sword belt arranged across his chest and Hrym froze himself in place on his back, Rodrick ducked through the door and went up the steps to the deck. The sunlight dazzled him briefly, but he was good at adjusting to new environments quickly—it was one reason he wasn't dead yet—and soon he was taking in a vast view of . . . nothing much. Ocean waves on all sides. No krakens or dragon turtles or pods of—he shuddered—gillmen. (He had nothing against gillmen, particularly, except the only one he'd ever met, Obed, had been a demon cultist who'd tried to murder him, so there were bad associations.) Just water and waves and a few crew members doing obscure but strenuous things with rope. The captain was at the bow, standing by the traditional big wooden wheel, but Rodrick's attention was caught by a woman standing in the stern, wearing something like an embroidered white robe, but the cloth was wrapped around her in some complex way—women's magic. She had a ruby stud twinkling in her nose, her hands outstretched over the water, and she was breathtakingly beautiful, with a hint of lushness under all that cloth.

Rodrick strolled her way, and she turned her head before he got within five feet. Her eyes were dark, her lips full, her smile knowing. "You're new," she said.

"I'm Rodrick. I came on board this morning. I'm taking passage to Jalmeray."

"How fortunate, as that is where we're going, if She Who Guides the Winds and the Waves so wills. I am Tapasi."

"Ahhh," he said. "A priest, are you?" That wasn't necessarily bad news. Not all priests were celibate, after all. Some, in fact, showed their devotion to their deities by being very much the opposite. There was always hope.

She nodded. "I serve my god, and pray for good winds and gentle waves."

"Better to have the gods on your side than against you," Rodrick said, though in truth, he preferred to avoid them altogether. He leaned on the railing and looked at the white wake trailing off behind them.

"Are you a godly man?"

"Ah. Not particularly. Nothing against the gods, mind you, just haven't ever felt the call. I'm not familiar with your goddess. I've heard of your Irori, but most of the gods of the Vudrani . . . we don't hear about them much where I'm from. Is it true you have thousands of gods?"

"If not more. It is said that every crossroads, every heap of stones, every bend in the river has a god in our lands. Most are very small gods, though, with limited spheres of interest and influence. She Who Guides the Winds and the Waves is more prominent on Jalmeray than in our homelands, as we are an island nation. In fact, your people worship my god under another name—you call her Gozreh, though you revere her male aspect as well. Many in our homeland do the same, but to some of us, combining two perfectly sensible, focused gods into a conglomerate with multiple areas of concern seems needlessly complicated."

Theology was a bit beyond Rodrick's realms of expertise or interest, so he decided to steer the conversation toward more useful areas. "How far away is Jalmeray, anyway?"

She cocked her head. "The island is some eight hundred miles from Absalom. The journey is closer to nine hundred, in truth, as we must divert around Stonespine Island when we pass from the Inner Sea into the Obari Ocean."

"Ah. That's . . . a long way." It was a good thing the djinni had brought his clothes. "How long will it take?"

"The best part of a month. Perhaps as few as twenty days, if the winds are generous. Do you often embark on journeys without knowing how long they will take?"

"I received an invitation to meet the thakur in his palace. I wasn't doing anything more exciting, so . . ." He shrugged. "It seemed an opportunity for adventure." Preceded by a great deal of boredom. Maybe some of the crew diced. Maybe Tapasi diced. Maybe she did other things.

She shaded her eyes and gazed off into the distance, then made a concerned sound. "I think you may have an opportunity for adventure sooner than you thought. A ship is approaching at speed, and it flies the flag of Nex—and below that, a banner with a symbol of the Arclords." She pointed to a flapping flag, inscribed with the symbol of an eye inside a triangle.

"Is . . . that bad?"

She stared at him. "Do you know nothing of the history of Jalmeray?"

Rodrick just shrugged. "I know there are monasteries, and the requisite monks, and it's supposed to be very beautiful, but . . ."

"The Arclords of Nex settled on Jalmeray, long ago. But they were not the rightful owners—they were, I think you would say, squatters? The Vudrani returned to take possession of the island, and had to drive the Arclords away. The battle was ferocious, but the golems and other constructs of the Arclords were no match for the bound elementals and genies of the Vudrani. Ever since the expulsion of the Arclords, relations between that faction and our people have been . . . strained. They don't dare attack us directly, but if they see an opportunity to make one of our ships disappear, well. There are always accidents on the sea."

"How long ago did this falling-out happen?"

"Since the Vudrani returned to Jalmeray and drove the Arclords into the sea?" She considered. "Two thousand years, more or less."

"That's a long time to hold a grudge," Rodrick said. "Do the Arclords really still really—"

There was a distant *thrum*, and a huge stone splashed into the water some distance behind them, blasting a gout of water forty feet into the air.

"Oh," Rodrick said. "I suppose they do."

4
Cabin Boy

The usual sort of chaos reigned on the deck. The captain and first mate were shouting orders, sailors were scrambling to and fro tugging on ropes and tying some knots while untying others for doubtless excellent reasons, and the priest beside Rodrick raised her hands and began to chant, or pray, or something.

Rodrick stepped away from her, because you never knew with priests. She might summon a spirit of water to smash the other vessel, or she might start shooting lightning out of every orifice, or do something else he couldn't even imagine. Supposedly some priests could turn water into wine, but he'd never been near one who shared such a useful ability with thirsty bystanders.

They were under attack, and his cloak of the devilfish was in his cabin below. Wasn't that always the way? He could scamper down and grab it, just in case the ship went down, but disappearing belowdecks was no way to impress a pretty priest.

Instead, he drew Hrym and pointed him toward the approaching vessel, which had grown from a speck to something recognizable as a black-hulled ship with a vast mainsail. "The Arclords are the ones with a third eye in their foreheads, aren't they?"

"Sounds right," Hrym said. "There probably isn't one of them on the ship, though. They're grand high so-and-sos. I imagine they have the usual lackey scum to do their dirty work."

The approaching ship wasn't loosing its catapults anymore. It seemed unlikely they'd only brought along one heavy rock, though. He supposed the first shot had been to test the range, and it was found wanting. They'd paused from launching projectiles in order to concentrate on closing the distance, and once the range was better, they'd doubtless try again.

Rodrick sighed. "Well, Hrym? Should we earn our keep?"

"I don't see how this is *our* problem. We aren't from Jalmeray. We don't have any quarrel with the Arclords."

"The fact that we're on a ship the Arclords intend to fill with holes, which will then fill with sea water, which will then fill with drowned sailors, might be grounds for a quarrel."

"It's not as if *I* can drown," Hrym said. "And I can make an ice floe for you to use as a lifeboat, if it comes to that."

"True. But as much as I'd enjoy sitting soaking wet atop a sheet of drifting sea ice, I don't think you're considering all the potential drawbacks. I could drop you in the confusion, and then you'd sink to the bottom of the sea, there to stay for all eternity—"

"I'd wrap myself in a cocoon of ice, and float to the surface, and eventually the currents would take me to shore, where someone would find me. I'd be fine."

"More likely a gillman would find you," Rodrick said.

A flash of red light illuminated Hrym's blade, and Rodrick winced, expecting cackling and chaos, but it was just a mild pulse of the demonic. "I don't much like gillmen," Hrym said. He had the same reasons Rodrick did.

"Oh, they're not *all* devotees of evil who want to use your powers to free demon lords and set them loose upon the world. I'm sure many of them are perfectly nice. Of course, Obed's cult probably has connections among many of the cities or tribes or whatever it is gillmen have—"

"Fine," Hrym said testily. "Let's do *work*. What do you want me to do?"

"The mainsail could be amusing. Can you do it from this distance?"

"I'll manage. Point me in the right direction."

Dark clouds were gathering, either by coincidence or because of the priest's incessant chanting, and a strong wind was blowing them fast away, which didn't help much, since the Arclord ship had the same wind and was apparently better designed to take advantage of it. They were close enough now that Rodrick could make out the individual crew members standing on the deck. Some of them were brandishing swords. But none of them looked as impressive as *his* sword.

Rodrick extended Hrym out over the railing, pointed the end of his blade directly at the pursuing ship's mainsail, and smiled as Hrym unleashed a torrent of icy wind. The temperature in his immediate vicinity plunged, but Rodrick was used to cold by now, and holding Hrym protected him from being damaged by the sword's own magical effects.

The enemy's sail began to turn white, then blue, as sheets of ice built up on the canvas, the mast, and the crossbeams. The sailors ran around in pointless terror as the weight of ice on the mainsail became too great to support. The mainmast cracked with a sound like a branch snapping, but a thousand times louder, and the sail—transformed into an immensely heavy hammer of solid sheet ice—smashed onto the deck with sufficient force to break the wood. The ship listed hard to port, though it didn't quite capsize, and sailors leapt into the sea in terror—always an amusing sight, as long as they weren't doing it on a ship you were on.

Tapasi stopped chanting, and the dark clouds began to dissipate. She stared at Rodrick. He grinned, shrugged, and replaced Hrym on his back. He turned to find the entire crew staring at him, and the captain came forward, the sailors parting to let her through.

"So," she said. "*That's* what your sword does."

"Among other things. I hope I didn't overstep my bounds. I was just trying to be useful."

"I heard it talk," Tapasi said. "The sword. It speaks!"

"Of course I talk." Hrym's tone was peevish. "Why is everyone so surprised when I talk? What's so great about talking, anyway? Loads of idiots can talk. Even kobolds talk. Lots of things talk."

"Ah," Saraswati said. "But not swords. Usually."

"She's got you there, Hrym," Rodrick said.

"Maybe they can talk, and choose not to. Maybe they just don't have anything to *say*. You can't prove otherwise."

"I am pleased to hear your voice, at any rate, sword," the captain said. "You've both saved us a great deal of trouble."

"Also possibly a great deal of drowning," Hrym said. "Feel free to reward us handsomely. Gold is always appreciated."

"Don't mind him," Rodrick said. "We're happy to help."

Saraswati suddenly turned, glaring at the crew, who responded as if she'd cracked a whip, all of them racing back to whatever obscure acts of seamanship they'd abandoned.

"Why don't you go speak to the navigator, Tapasi?" the captain said. "She wanted to see if you could do anything about some weather she's worried about." Tapasi bowed her head and went on her way.

Once they were alone, Saraswati said. "I don't have much in the way of spare gold, but I'll see if there's another way to demonstrate my gratitude. Join me in my rooms for dinner tonight?"

"Of course. Should I bring Hrym? He enjoys intellectually stimulating conversation, but some other activities tend to bore him, and when he's bored, he often provides a running commentary he intends to be humorous, though I rarely find it so."

Her lips quirked into a smile. "Do you mind if we leave you alone for an hour or two, master Hrym?"

"I insist," Hrym said. "I'm *so* glad I don't have a squishy meat body. Pleasures should be cold and clean, like gold."

Saraswati chuckled, sketched a salute, and then strolled back toward the bow. Rodrick watched her walk, giving particular attention to the movement of her rear end in her tight breeches. Lush and round women weren't the only kind he found appealing, and enthusiasm went a long way, too. "Mmm. If all acts of heroism were rewarded the way I expect this one to be, I might engage in them more often."

"What did you even *do*? You pointed me at a boat! I did everything, and you get all the credit, as usual. The world is horribly biased against swords in favor of swordsmen."

"It was my idea to freeze the mainsail. I know you. You would've just buried the deck in ice and frozen all the sailors."

"Yes, and it would have worked fine."

"Ah, but it wouldn't have been as *funny*."

Hrym grumbled, but ultimately had to concede that Rodrick's argument was unassailable.

"That was pleasant," Saraswati said, and Rodrick *mmmm*ed in a contented way, gazing up at the beams on the ceiling of her cabin. "Pleasant" wasn't quite the ringing endorsement he liked to hear from women he'd just bedded, but perhaps she was merely prone to understatement. That had to be it.

Saraswati slid out of bed and back into her clothing, Rodrick watching with interest, since he wasn't sure he'd see her naked again. He'd been with women from all over Avistan, an Osirian, a woman whose parents had hailed from the Mwangi Expanse, a couple of half-elves, and, on one occasion, a gnome, though he couldn't remember much of that night very well. But he'd never been with a woman from the Impossible Kingdoms. Her dark skin and the blue jewel in her navel aside, he found her much like most of the other women he'd bedded: altogether wonderful.

In his own opinion, Rodrick had never had a bad relationship with a woman. This was likely because he seldom had relationships with them at all. Having *relations* with them was an entirely different matter, of course, and some such experiences were better than others, but after the days of his awkward teenage fumblings, they were rarely *bad*. He'd discovered over the years that two people, with good will and a sense of mutual adventure, could almost always manage to have a nice time together.

Of course, some of the women became inexplicably annoyed with him in the hours or days afterward, when he didn't behave the way they'd hoped, but he couldn't be blamed for that.

"Are you going to sprawl in my bed all night?" Saraswati looked at him pointedly from her seat on the little chair by the fold-down desk.

"I don't have anywhere else to be, Captain, but if you'd like me to make myself scarce, I'll obey. You've been sufficiently welcoming in all other ways that I won't be offended."

She snorted. "No, it's fine. Stay a bit. Might as well see if you're equally adept at the conversational arts."

"If you don't mind an ignorant traveler . . . Would you tell me a bit about Jalmeray?"

She wrinkled her forehead. "What, do you want a history lesson?"

He waved his hand. "Nothing so dry. Just . . . practical matters. Will I need a warm coat? Is there a local delicacy I absolutely must taste? Is there some forbidden act I'm likely to blunder into, causing murderous offense? Will the thakur expect me to bow, or kneel, or kiss his ring, or will I be eviscerated ritually if I touch his shadow or look directly upon his face?"

She shook her head. "We aren't savages, Rodrick. The Vudrani civilization is ancient and sophisticated."

"Savagery is relative, my captain. They do things routinely in Cheliax that would make an Andoren's blood boil, but to the Chelaxians, they're not savage acts at all. In my travels, I've learned not to make assumptions."

She leaned back in her chair and looked at him thoughtfully. "It's not as if I've *met* the thakur, you know. By all accounts, Kharswan is a polite and thoughtful man, a scholar and lover of poetry and music, with rich and refined tastes, as you might expect. He spends most of his days writing and dallying with his wives—"

"Wives? Plural?"

Her lips curled in a smile. "Surely you've heard of the harems of the Vudrani nobles? I understand they're the subject of much fevered speculation, and are frequently if inaccurately described in a particular class of literature favored by the depraved legions of the Inner Sea."

Rodrick had perused the occasional lavishly illustrated volume once or twice in his time, and nodded. "Harems. Yes, that rings a faint bell. Is it really forbidden for a man to look upon the thakur's wives?"

"To look upon them? No, though they don't go out much. Touching them, however . . ." She shook her head. "I can't imagine there's any woman so beautiful that you'd pay *that* price just to touch her. You're really going to the palace? I feel I've just had a premonition about how you're going to die, Rodrick."

"I am a paragon of restraint. At least, when the alternative is death." Sleeping with noblewomen, and surely the wives of the more-or-less king of Jalmeray counted as nobles, was always fraught. He much preferred serving girls. They were just as fun in bed and didn't bring nearly as much trouble with them. "I take it the thakur's not a despotic sort of ruler, then? No beheadings for breakfast or the gentle swaying of public hangings to lull him to sleep?"

"No, not at all. The thakur hardly runs anything, not directly. Oh, in theory his word is law, but when it comes to actually governing . . . The Maurya-Rahm—you would think of it as a sort of parliament or legislative body—does that. There are many powerful factions in that group, with influential mystics, leaders of monasteries, and nobles all vying for power. Everything seems to stay in balance well enough. Jalmeray is a prosperous place."

"So the thakur is just a figurehead, then?"

"I wouldn't go *that* far. If the thakur said someone should have their legs broken, and then be carried high into the air and dropped into the sea—for instance, someone who tried to seduce one of his wives—his will would be done without question. He just doesn't make such demands, usually. I've heard rumors that he's adept at subtly setting prominent people against one another, to maintain the balance of power, and keep any one faction or individual from growing too strong. He is by all accounts a master diplomat."

Drat, Rodrick thought. A man skilled at manipulation. That was supposed to be Rodrick's territory. Then again, it wasn't always too hard to trick a trickster; they often made themselves vulnerable by thinking they were immune to being deceived. "Do you have *any* idea why he'd want to summon a swordsman from Andoran? Even one as widely famed and accomplished as myself?"

"I hope this doesn't puncture the balloon of your self-regard, but I'd be very surprised if a whisper of a rumor of your fame has touched the shores of Jalmeray. If I had to guess . . . it will be something to do with your sword. No offense, but of the two of you, Hrym *is* rather the more remarkable."

"Oh, really?" Rodrick slid out of bed and stood up with his usual grace. He was blessed with a naturally good physique and had marvelous balance and reflexes, and supposed he actually could become a decent swordsman if the need ever arose, though the thought of doing all that *training* was loathsome. Other physical acts, however, were more interesting.

Saraswati glanced down, then up at his face, smirking. "Really? Again? Already?"

"Oh, well. I just wanted to point out that Hrym isn't more remarkable than I am in *every* respect."

5

Over the Obari Ocean

The rest of the voyage was pleasant enough, at least until the disaster at the very end.

The crew continued to treat Rodrick as a conquering hero, and Hrym appreciated the awe he inspired. Tapasi was still good for a conversation, seemingly interested in every aspect of his life—keeping all the lies he told her straight was an interesting challenge. Unfortunately, any hope he'd had of seeing what she looked like underneath her flowing acreage of wrapped silk faded quickly. She fled every time she noticed Saraswati looking at the two of them, and no one else on the ship was willing to try to steal him away from the captain, either, no matter how much he might like to be stolen, so he reluctantly became a one-woman man. He got a bit bored, as usual when he dallied with the same woman for more than a night or two, but it was better than nothing at all, and he thought he hid his lack of interest well. He was good at faking almost anything.

They only stopped at a port once, to drop off cargo at Sothis, a bustling city in Osirion. They didn't stay there long, only half a day, but Rodrick appreciated the chance to stretch his legs on solid land, and let himself goggle about like a tourist, marveling at the distant peaks of pyramids and the strange black dome of some immense building—it looked like a giant beetle's carapace; foreign architecture was so strange—at the center of the city. The air was noticeably warmer than it had been in Absalom, and they were still

far north of Jalmeray, so the island itself must be sweltering. He
ate candied dates and almost got pickpocketed in a crowd before
returning to the ship. Perhaps he'd go back to Sothis for a longer
trip someday. It seemed like a rich place.

There were no more attacks by Arclords or more prosaic pirates
on the journey, though they did witness a battle about halfway
through the voyage. They passed by Stonespine Island, a sort of
miniature mountain range rising from the sea, which Tapasi told
him was nominally controlled by the nation of Katapesh, but
was mostly infested by hyenafolk, aside from the busy slaver port
of Okeno. As they sailed east to move around the island, he saw
ships near the island joined in battle, heard the booms of offensive
magic, and saw one ship burning. "What's going on over there?" he
asked Tapasi. "Is it something we need to worry about?"

"You don't recognize your own countrymen?" She sounded
amused. "They don't fly flags of your nation, but it's an open secret
that the ships of the Eagle Knights harry the shores of any nation they
can reach that keeps slaves, and try to set the poor wretches free."

"The Gray Corsairs." Rodrick watched the battle until the ships
receded into invisible distance, feeling a little spark of national
pride. He didn't have much use for Eagle Knights—they had far
too narrow a view of the law, and the advisability of following it—
but he didn't much like the idea of slavery either. Apart from being
a terrible thing to do a person, there was the fact that slaves didn't
have anything worth stealing, and thus reduced Rodrick's pool of
potential targets.

When he wasn't lounging on the deck or dallying with
Saraswati or gambling with the crew, Rodrick was overcoming
his natural inclinations and reading books borrowed from the
captain's library. He'd had high hopes upon first noticing the
captain's small stock of volumes, because the Vudrani were said
to have elevated lovemaking to an art form, with the sum of their

knowledge contained in a sacred instructional volume—certainly
Saraswati had suggested a few approaches that were entirely novel
to him, one or two of which had given him muscle strain—but
most of the texts on her shelf were nautical or historical in nature,
without a diverting erotic woodcut to be found.

The most interesting thing he'd found was a book of the
Vudrani equivalent of fairy tales, and he was learning all sorts of
interesting things about garudas and rakshasas and other creatures
of legend. Legend, at least, where he was from; Tapasi said they
were all too real in her homeland.

He also hoped to gain some insight, through the stories, into
the Vudrani cultural mindset, which seemed to favor placidity,
languor, and equanimity punctuated by sudden violence in the
face of betrayal, dishonor, or violation of social mores. There
was one element of their culture he'd heard about vaguely, that
he confronted again and again in the texts, and that offended
him deeply as an Andoren: the notion of "castes," or social classes
you were born into. Some were born to be merchants, some to
be warriors, some to be princes, and some to shovel dung, and if
that was your station, there was no changing it: you'd earned that
position, it seemed, in some past life, and if your present life was
unpleasant, you just had to suffer through it as best you could in
hopes of being reborn a bit higher up the ladder next time.

Rodrick had been born into a family that was far from rich,
though they didn't go hungry; his parents were hardworking and
honorable people, oddly enough. From those fairly humble begin-
nings he had, through guile and wit and luck, convinced the world
he was a warrior of moderate renown. To think he might have been
stuck tending pigs or tanning leather or laying roof tiles for his
entire life, just because that was his *caste*, was a terrible thought,
and he'd complained about it to the captain.

She'd just shrugged. "Do you not have princes where you're
from?"

"Well, yes, but—"

"Can a tanner become a prince? Do the sons of hostlers generally become ship captains, or the sons of turnip farmers goldsmiths? Or do they instead tend to follow the paths of their fathers? Do the rich not stay rich, and the poor poor?"

"All right, admittedly, in *practice* there's not all that much ebb and flow of social status, but it's *possible*. You can break with tradition."

"Our people can do that, too, at least on Jalmeray. They can abandon their family and their name and take a ship to Absalom or Andoran or Taldor and become whatever they wish. But most of us take comfort in knowing our position. I never doubted what I would be: a trader on the sea, just as my mother was, and her mother before her. I never had to doubt, or wonder, or suffer silly dreams that would breed only disappointment when they failed to come true."

"Fine," he said, "But you've got a *ship*, don't you? What if your caste had required you to scrape barnacles off the ship instead? Or to dig latrines?"

"Then I would have even more incentive to lead a just and noble existence, in hopes that in my next life, I would be reborn in more pleasant circumstances."

"You really believe in all that?"

She chuckled. "Reincarnation? Of course. Life is a wheel. We go around and around."

Rodrick was unsure how he felt about the whole subject of reincarnation—would being reborn as, say, a worm be better or worse than being judged for his actions in life by Pharasma, the goddess of death? At least he could try to charm Pharasma, or repent sincerely on his deathbed, when he probably *would* feel pretty contrite, as he always did right before he had to face a judge at any level. Reincarnation! How odd.

He decided he just had to accept a certain fundamental disconnect in their worldviews. He couldn't help but push a *little* farther, though. "But suppose someone is born into the dung-hauling caste who has a brilliant mind for, say, planning elaborate parties? Or someone is born into the scholarly class but has vast natural talents for soldiering or organized violence?"

"The former will doubtless throw the best dinner parties ever experienced by his shit-shoveling brethren, and as for the latter—anyone can attempt to enter the Houses of Perfection. Mostly the warrior caste try for those positions, it's true, but the monks are . . . flexible about such matters. There are some who oppose the whole caste system, who say we should be ordered by the gods alone, to rise and fall as our abilities dictate, and not by the opinions of other men and women. But they are a small group of malcontents, and a few radical philosophers. Most of us believe the gods *do* order us, by making sure we are born into the appropriate roles."

"Mmm," he said. "I won't argue with you, but I do know I would have made a *terrible* swineherd."

"It is fortunate for you that the gods chose to let you be born in Andoran, then, instead of in a more civilized kingdom."

"Am I such an unlettered brute? You don't seem to mind my company."

She rolled him onto his back. "Oh, well. Sometimes a woman likes a bit of a savage in her life."

Rodrick sat up in bed—he'd slept in his own, for once, because Saraswati had needed to make some final preparations for their arrival in Niswan. He yawned, stretched, and scratched himself. They were supposed to make landfall today, and to his surprise, he was almost sorry the voyage was ending. It had been a pleasant respite, and soon he'd have to find out what the thakur wanted him for. Something glorious but not too strenuous, he hoped. "Care to take the air, Hrym?"

"I keep telling you, I don't *breathe*," Hrym said. "I'll just stay here on my gold, thanks." Rodrick never bothered to take the coins with him when he left the room anymore. The crew held him in sufficient reverence after the assault on the Arclord ship that he wasn't afraid of theft, and if anyone did try, Hrym was right—he could freeze them where they stood, and Saraswati wouldn't even blame him.

"If you're sure. Last chance to stroll about on deck, probably."

"Of course I'm sure. Uncertainty is for you fleshy types." The sword sounded cranky, but not demonically so. He'd had only one fit during the entire journey, not long after they left Sothis, and it had just been a flash of red, a titter, and a surge of disorder making everything on Pia's shrine fall off the table, which was easily remedied. He'd spurted out a small cloud of freezing fog afterward, but it quickly dissipated. Maybe the sea air was good for Hrym's condition.

Rodrick had almost discussed Hrym's problem with Tapasi half a dozen times—he'd never talked so much to any cleric in his life, and she might have useful advice—but he was reluctant to let anyone know they were on a ship with a magical sword that had unpredictable destructive tendencies. Guest of the thakur or not, sharing the captain's bed or not, they could find themselves stranded on a rock somewhere if news like that got around.

Rodrick shut the door behind him and went up the stairs to the main deck. The members of the crew he'd become friendly with greeted him warmly, and he smiled and waved. The Vudrani weren't a bad sort, though they liked their fish spiced so heavily he could barely taste it for the burning on his tongue. The crew members were at least all fairly terrible at dice, always a welcome quality in new friends. Or else they let him win most of the time because he'd saved them from the Arclord ship—either way, his purse was fattened, though the copper and flecks of silver didn't look like much next to the gold the djinni had given him. At least he could spend those lesser coins without Hrym moaning about how Rodrick was stealing cushions from his bed.

The captain was up on the foredeck, giving orders, and though she glanced at him and smiled, she seemed too busy for him to wander up and bother her just now. She took her work as seriously as she took her play, an approach to life that Rodrick found at least half baffling. The first half, mainly.

He stood on deck, gazing back toward Absalom and the whole of the world he'd known before. You'd never know there was anything in that direction but more water.

"You're looking the wrong way," Tapasi said, tapping him on the shoulder. "Turn around, and take in your first view of Jalmeray.

6

Impossible Islands

Rodrick turned and stared, because where before there had been only open water, there was now a smudge of land, like a mountain range rising from the water but vastly larger than Stonespine, some peaks capped with snow and others crowned with clouds. He leaned on the rail and stared. Were those islands full of gold for him, or danger, or both?

"Jalmeray." Tapasi stepped up to the railing beside him. "The kingdom of the impossible. The jewel of the Obari Ocean." She pointed toward smaller bits of land jutting out of the sea between them and the peaks of Jalmeray proper. "We will navigate around the small islands—Grand Sarret, and Veedesha, and Kaina Katakka—and then dock at Niswan, near the mouth of the River Sald."

"Does anyone live on those smaller islands?" Rodrick said.

"Grand Sarret is still occupied. It's home to the Conservatory."

That sounded familiar to Rodrick, perhaps from one of the same books (with the exotic woodcuts) where he'd read about harems. "Isn't that where, ah, courtesans are trained?"

Tapasi snorted. "You couldn't be more transparent if you were made of ice, like your friend the sword. Do you hunger for company softer than that of our good captain? The Conservatory does train men and women in the arts of seduction, yes, but those fortunate enough to study there also learn music, cooking, and courtly arts. The graduates are welcomed in all the palaces of the

Inner Sea for their wisdom and wit, and they often serve foreign courts as advisors. Some are even royal consorts."

"Ah," Rodrick said. "So it's a school for spies, then."

Tapasi frowned at him. "I have never heard it described as such."

"Naturally. Wouldn't be much of a spy school if everyone *knew* it was. But it stands to reason, don't you think? Why spend all that time teaching people how to seduce and recite poetry and hobnob with nobles, and send them out to posts in the various kingdoms, unless you expect them to report their secrets back to your thakur—or, I suppose, his spymasters?"

"Some believe in studying beauty and art and other such matters for their own sakes, Rodrick. Not everyone is so cynical as you."

"I haven't met many kings or queens, or rajahs or thakurs for that matter, but I have a hard time believing any of them are *less* cynical than I am—at least, not if they expect to live very long. I don't suppose we can stop off at the Conservatory for a bite to eat?" And perhaps he could help the courtesans-in-training practice their budding skills. Surely they had to train, not just on each other, and maybe they wouldn't charge much. You could get your wounds treated more cheaply by apprentice chirurgeons, after all, than by those who'd proven themselves in the profession. He was aware that a courtesan wasn't *exactly* the same as a prostitute, but the distinction had always seemed exceedingly fine to him.

"Unless that sword grants you the power of flight, no. Grand Sarret was once home to the Maharajah Khiben-Sald's harem, and he chose the location because it's so inaccessible. The entire coastline is composed of sheer cliffs, and it's difficult to reach the school by means other than magic."

Hrym was capable of lifting Rodrick to great heights, by conjuring stairs of ice or lifting him on a rising pillar of the same, but it wasn't the most comfortable mode of travel, and was rather conspicuous besides. The Conservatory would be an interesting place to see, and if it really were crawling with spies, there might be things inside worth stealing . . . not state secrets, of course, because Rodrick knew better than to dabble in politics, but spies often had marvelous weapons, and you could always find a buyer for those.

"And the other islands?" They were closer, now, and Grand Sarret did indeed present a sheer face of rock with little to indicate any life at all atop its heights. The island to its south was smaller and, if anything, looked even less inviting.

Tapasi shivered and pointed to the southern island. "Kaina Katakka. For a long time that island was a sort of . . . refuge . . . for the original inhabitants of Jalmeray, those who did not wish to live under the rule of the maharajah." She glanced at him sidelong. "You remember what I've told you about the history of Jalmeray?"

He shrugged. "The broad outlines, anyway. The Vudrani came, and ruled for a long time. Then they left, and the Arclords moved in and took over. Then the Vudrani came back, and kicked the Arclords out, and you've all been here ever since."

"Simplistic, but not wrong," Tapasi allowed. "Incomplete, though. The great maharajah did not simply settle on this island. He traveled from the Impossible Kingdoms in the east to the shores of the continent Garund, to the city of Quantium. This was some four thousand years ago, and the maharajah brought with him a fleet of one hundred and one ships. The Vudrani were all but unknown in the Inner Sea then, and the maharajah became friendly with the great wizard-king Nex, ruler of the country that still bears his name, though he has long since departed this world. As a gesture of friendship, Nex granted the maharajah dominion over Jalmeray, and his people made it their own, erecting temples and monuments, and calling djinn and efreet and other creatures to help shape the island's environment more to their liking."

Gesture of friendship, Rodrick thought. Ha! You didn't give a visiting noble dominion over part of your territory out of *friendship*. He wondered what Nex had gotten out of the arrangement. Ah, well, who cared? Ancient history. "And then the maharajah left?"

Tapasi shrugged. "He was only ever just visiting. The maharajah had a great and searching intellect and a vast curiosity about the world. He sailed home with his people eventually, and the wizard Nex left his own throne, vanishing from this world, and chaos reigned in his absence. The Arclords ruled in Nex's name for a time—they are descended from Nex's own household servants, or claim to be—until a shift in power saw them exiled. They took up residence on Jalmeray, because it is close enough to Nex to influence matters there, but far enough away to be easily defended from their enemies on the mainland."

"Ah, so they scuttled off to this island, and then the Vudrani came back and kicked them out. Golems and homunculi against elementals. You told me that much."

She nodded. "Nex did not give Jalmeray to the maharajah as a *loan*—it was a gift, and gifts are forever. Those who returned to Jalmeray were descendants of Khiben-Sald, and they had a rightful claim. The *only* claim. Imagine if you returned to your ancestral home and found it full of vile squatters who claimed they *owned* the place, merely because they'd resided there without being rooted out for some time? You would ask them politely to leave, and if they did not . . ." She shrugged. "You would resort to the sword. Or, in our case, summon storms to wreck their fleet and elementals to drive them away."

"You drove the wizards into the *sea*?"

"Not all of them. We're not savages. We left them a single ship. They were happy to leave, by then. Those who could cram themselves aboard."

"But they've resented you a bit ever since. Hmm. I suppose I can see why they attacked us after we left Absalom."

"Relations are strained to this day, yes." She shook herself. They were passing between Grand Sarret and Kaina Katakka now, and she gestured toward the latter. "Of course, in the arguments between the Arclords and the maharajah, the natives of the island always suffered, whether they took sides or tried to stand apart."

Rodrick nodded, keeping his face expressionless. "Of course Jalmeray didn't actually belong to its natives, because they didn't have a great wizard-king or a maharajah to say so. They just lived here."

Tapasi noticed the dig, but didn't argue, just shrugged, her mouth downturned in sadness. "They were simple people, I'm told, who fished and hunted and lived largely in peace, until we arrived. They fought against us, but what use are fishing nets and spears against the power of Nex and the maharajah? Those who were unwilling to join our society when we took over were graciously allowed by the maharajah to relocate to Kaina Katakka, where we left them alone. The maharajah liked having them there, I understand."

"Of course. A sort of human zoo." The island looked to be mostly barren rock, dotted with what might have been ruined buildings, or just unusually shaped heaps of stone. "It looks very inviting."

"It was lush, once, I understand. When the Arclords came to take over Jalmeray, they did not leave the natives in peace. They killed them all, scouring the island with magic and leaving it in ruins. A haunted place, now, used only by those smugglers brave enough to ply their filthy trade despite the ghosts."

Aha. Smugglers. That was useful information. You never knew when you might need to escape a place quietly, and smugglers would often move people as well as stolen goods, if the price was right.

As they left those islands behind, another appeared to the north. "That's Veedesha, you said?" The more he knew about this place, the better he'd be able to turn things to his own advantage.

"Yes. It was once a great port, and honestly is a better natural deep-water port than Niswan, but the thakur chose to make Niswan the center of power, and Veedesha was all but abandoned. There are still ruins of the great buildings, but they are infested by beasts or used as the lairs of bandits or worshipers of some of the . . . less sociable gods. Few go there now—all the treasures were long since moved to safety, or else looted."

"That's it for islands, then? Apart from the Conservatory, I can't say I feel even a passing desire to visit any of them."

"No," Tapasi said. "There is one other island large enough to merit mention. Gho Vella, off the northwestern coast, on the far side of the island. It is an accursed place."

"In what way?"

"Do you know of lepers?"

Rodrick nodded. "Ah. Yes. A terrible contagious disease, so those who have it go off to live by themselves, among others of their kind. Gho Vella is a leper colony?"

"In a manner of speaking. There are great magics on Jalmeray, and great sorcerers and wizards and mystics, many of them pushing the boundaries of what magic can do. Sometimes there are . . . mishaps. I knew a woman once who was working with elementals, and she became cursed by a permanent cloud, pouring rain on her endlessly, and shooting jagged lightning at anyone who came too close. She was not well liked, and either no one could cure her, or no one cared to, so she had no choice but to go into exile. I heard of another man who laughed at a wizard, for what reason who can say, and the wizard cursed him so that he vomits up tiny venomous frogs whenever he tries to speak. There are other such poor souls, who cannot live in normal society, and many might choose death as their only release, but instead the philosophers known as the

Curse Shepherds see them safely to Gho Vella, where they can live among the other outcasts in whatever peace they can find."

Rodrick shivered. He thought about Hrym, and the demonic taint that made him flash red and lash out sometimes. Was Hrym cursed, now, as he'd half-joked, half-threatened with that fool Kelso? Would Hrym have to be put away someday, if his condition worsened, on an island where he couldn't harm anyone? Rodrick hated to think of it, though with a sufficiently full bed of gold, the sword himself might not mind much. "So I should watch my manners, then, if I don't want to find myself spitting up newts."

"You are an invited guest of the thakur! None would dare harm you." She paused. "Unless the thakur brought you here to *do* you harm, and even then, it would be the harm he specified, and no other. You truly have no idea why you were summoned?"

"None at all. I'm curious to find out."

"And you will, soon. You can see Niswan, now."

Rodrick shaded his eyes, peered out, and grunted despite himself. He'd seen Absalom, and Almas, and other great cities, but nothing like Niswan before. The land itself seemed harsh, rocky and wave-battered, but that land was embellished lavishly, like a spiked gauntlet decorated with jewels. The harbor was large and crowded with ships of all sizes, but they looked like bath toys against the city rising beyond, the mouth of a vast wide river cutting through the cliffs. Gleaming pagodas in silver and gold and bronze rose in tiers upon tiers, silk banners streaming from their heights, and the streets between the towers were deep red stone, dark as blood in places, glittering like rubies in others. Spires rose here and there, impossibly high and delicate, and there were squares dominated by statues, some of the stonework immense enough that Rodrick could make out details of their shapes even from this distance, depicting figures with many arms and sometimes the heads of fanciful beasts. Things flew among the high spires—wizards? djinn?—under their own power, or on wings made of light, or floating on what looked for all the world like carpets. Rodrick had seen magic before—indeed, he spent his days in the company of a wondrous relic of a bygone age—but never used so openly, so profligately. Niswan had spellcasters the way the Coins had pickpockets.

The sound of cracking wood somewhere below their feet suddenly interrupted his sense of wonder.

Rodrick and the priest stared at one another, wide-eyed. "Was that . . . the *hull*?" she asked.

7

City of Pagodas

The crew shouted, though not as loudly as their captain, and Tapasi leaned over the railing to look for damage.

"What happened?" Rodrick said. "Did we hit a rock?"

She shook her head. "There are no rocks in the harbor. The elementals cleared them all centuries ago." She leaned out even farther and pointed. "Look there, cracks in the hull!" Several nearby sailors heard her and clustered around the rail to look.

Rodrick reluctantly leaned over himself, and saw two dozen cracks, most thin but several as big as a fingerwidth, long and jagged, showing blackness. The cracks were above the waterline . . . but there could be more below that he couldn't see. As he watched, some of the cracks widened, the wood groaning. If the boat wasn't taking on water already, it would be soon. Something about the cracks was strange, though. They didn't quite look right—

Oh. For one thing, the wood was splintered *outward*, as if some force had struck the hull from within.

And for another, the cracks were radiating out from the spot where Rodrick's cabin was. That was bad for a big reason and a little reason. He shouted the little reason—"My gold could fall into the sea!"—and then raced belowdecks, shoving past the crew who got in the way and thudding down the tilted ladder, tearing open the door to his cabin. The cracks grew wider as he watched, and some indeed extended below the waterline. There was enough seepage to provide a steady trickle of seawater into the room, and he splashed through growing puddles as he entered.

Bits of the first mate's shattered shrine were floating in the water, as if it had been struck with a hammer and then scattered by a wind, but Hrym was still resting on the chest atop the gold coins. The blankets on the bed were shredded, like they'd been attacked by a flurry of knives. Or struck by a blast of icicles.

That was the big reason. Hrym must have had another of his fits, his episodes, his *bad turns*, and this time, his icy eruption had struck the hull hard enough to splinter the wood. If Rodrick didn't move quickly, this fit could end with this ship on the bottom of the harbor.

He rushed to the sword's side. "Hrym, what happened?" He picked up the weapon, alarmed at the threads of flashing red in the blade, but the color vanished a moment after his hand touched the hilt.

"Wha?" Hrym's voice was vague, distant. "I was—was I— what's going on?"

"There are cracks in the boat," Rodrick said. "Well, they're cracks *now*. I'm pretty sure they'll be holes soon. I don't want to be on a boat full of holes, Hrym."

"Oh," Hrym said. "Let's fix them, then."

Rodrick pointed the sword toward the cracks, and a wave of cold swirled out from the crystalline blade. The sea water on the floor froze first, and the ice crept up the water toward the cracks, sealing them by freezing the very water they were letting in. Ribbons and streamers of ice crawled across the network of cracks until they were all sealed with patches of shimmering magical ice. It was pretty, in a way. Not that Rodrick expected the captain to think so.

The wall groaned, the sudden cold making some of the wood contract, but the ice held, less prone to cracking than the nonmagical variety. The broken bits of the shrine and the book of Vudrani fairy tales he'd been reading were all partially encased in ice on the floor, but at least they weren't on the bottom of the sea. Rodrick wondered how narrowly they'd averted disaster—how soon those cracks would have become holes, and those drips torrents—and was glad he didn't know more about the breaking point of ship hulls. Sometimes ignorance was a balm to the troubled mind.

"It seems you've saved my ship again, Rodrick."

He turned to see Saraswati standing in his doorway, the first mate goggling behind her, and Tapasi not far behind. Rodrick gave the captain a smile and took a deep bow. "Always a pleasure to—"

"I *am* curious about what damaged my ship in the first place, though. There are no rocks we could have run ourselves onto, and no creatures of the sea that could do that kind of damage, at least not this close to the harbor." Her voice was as cold as Hrym on his worst day.

"Iceberg," Hrym said suddenly. "They form, sometimes, great jagged rocks of ice, just floating along, and they've sunk many ships."

Saraswati frowned. "Icebergs? In the Obari Ocean? This isn't the northern Steaming Sea!"

"What else could it be?" Hrym said, irritable as an old man jostled early from his nap.

Saraswati shook her head. "I don't know. I know that ice is just a patch, and it will cost more than I'd like to pay to fix the hull permanently." She looked at Rodrick thoughtfully.

"You know," he said, "it strikes me as unfair that I shouldn't pay *anything* for my passage, even as a guest of the thakur. Please, let me thank you for your hospitality and kindness on the voyage." He scooped up a generous handful of coins from the chest, ignoring Hrym's squawk, and pressed them into the captain's hands.

She looked at the coins, then at Hrym, before grunting. "You clearly have no idea how expensive it is to fix a ship."

Rodrick smiled blandly. "Since the damage was done while you were in the service of the thakur, surely he'll be happy to reimburse you for any costs above and beyond my contribution?"

She gave him a long look, and Rodrick suspected she was trying to decide whether to try for the rest of his gold. He clearly wasn't going to part with it willingly, though, and since he was holding Hrym, he didn't think she'd try it by force. She shook her head, and didn't look at Rodrick again before disappearing above, followed by her mate.

Tapasi leaned in the doorway. "This is all very strange." She gazed at the lacework of ice on the hull. Maybe she thought it was pretty, too. Rodrick felt she was something of a kindred spirit, though it was possible he just felt that way because he wanted to see her with no clothes on.

"I thought Jalmeray was famed for its strangeness?"

"Not this kind of strange. Well, no permanent harm done. Would you like to go above and watch as we come into the port? I think the captain wants you off her ship, but I'm grateful to you for saving us, and would enjoy more moments of your company."

Rodrick quickly packed his few belongings and slipped Hrym into the scabbard at his waist, hesitating only a moment as he did so. If the sword had another fit, would he blow holes in *Rodrick*, ones that couldn't be so easily patched? A terrifying thought. But the fits didn't usually come one right after another. He had to admit that ignoring his friend's problem was no longer a viable strategy. Jalmeray was supposed to be full of scholars from the Impossible Kingdoms and all over the Inner Sea as well. Perhaps one of them would know of a cure. But what if the only cure involved Hrym's destruction? People looked at him and saw a sword, albeit a wondrous one, but to Rodrick, Hrym was a *person*—indeed, he was more of a person than many of the more conventionally people-shaped persons Rodrick had met.

He went upstairs, pouch in his pocket jingling with gold—albeit less than before, wasn't that always the way—pack on his back, sword on his hip, ready to go forth and seek his fortune again, ideally before Saraswati figured out for sure that Hrym had damaged her ship. He didn't think she'd do anything drastic, not when the thakur wanted to see him, but having an enemy in a foreign land was never a good idea, and enemies who'd once been friends were the worst. A double handful of women he'd slept with had turned into implacable enemies over the years, and he had no desire to increase that number.

Luckily, Saraswati was busy shouting commands as the crew bustled about. He joined Tapasi at the railing near the bow and watched in wonder as a water elemental glided into view, shaped vaguely like a fat human, big as an ox. The churning, wave-tossed water before them turned smooth as fine glass, and the elemental gestured, seeming to shepherd them in. A sudden strong current bore the *Nectar of the Gods* toward an open berth, where it was soon nestled among other ships. Members of the crew jumped from the deck and began tying ropes to wooden posts and doing other maritime things.

"I must go to the temple and make gifts to She Who Guides the Wind and the Waves in thanks for our successful journey." Tapasi squeezed Rodrick's arm in a companionable way. "It has been . . . interesting knowing you, Rodrick. Perhaps we will meet again, if you survive whatever use the thakur has for you."

"Cheerful," he muttered as she walked away.

"So it *wasn't* interesting knowing *me*?" Hrym grumbled. "I'm far more interesting than you. Infinitely. Categorically."

"You weren't very sociable on the voyage. I'm sure if she'd been exposed to your charms she would have liked you better than me."

"Possibly," Hrym said. "She seemed like a fairly sensible woman, after all."

The captain strode across the deck toward them, and Rodrick put on his best smile. Saraswati stood before him, hands on her hips, glaring, then reached out and put her hands on his shoulders, pulling him close for a kiss as deep as any she'd given him in her cabin. She looked into his eyes, afterward, still holding his shoulders. "You made the voyage interesting, I'll give you that much."

Interesting. Two women had called him that in the space of minutes. It wasn't his favorite adjective—he preferred "dashing" or "irresistible" or "virile"—but it was better than "treacherous" or "cheating" or "bastard." Except "bastard" wasn't an adjective, was it? Did he mean "bastardly"? "Bastardish"?

"You made the journey into a voyage of delights, Saraswati. If you'd like, I'll see if I can wrangle an invite to the palace for you, perhaps a seat at a feast—"

"May the gods preserve me!" she said. "No, leave me out of your entanglements, please. The gold is recompense enough for the difficulties you brought along with you." She frowned. "Is your sword . . . safe? For you, I mean? There are no icebergs in this harbor, Rodrick."

"I'm perfectly safe!" Hrym said. "Unless I don't *want* to be. I don't know what put a hole in your boat, but it wasn't me."

Saraswati's eyes widened a bit at Hrym's voice, which was rather loud and emphatic, but she kept her gaze on Rodrick.

"We'll be fine, Captain. I hope the repairs go smoothly, and, ah, may the wind and the waves be kind."

"Yes, yes. Get off my ship. I'm told there's a man from the palace waiting for you on the deck, and he doesn't look like a servant, so best not keep him waiting."

A representative of the thakur, then. Rodrick was glad he'd dressed in his best shirt and breeches—a shame the cuffs of the latter were damp from swirling seawater, but it couldn't be helped. He started toward the gangplank, walking with as much swagger as he had in him, hoping to give an impression of arrogant nobility

that was spoiled only slightly when Saraswati swatted him play-
fully on the rear.

He'd expected Jalmeray to be terribly hot, but it was actually
quite temperate, cool ocean breezes taking the bite out of what
heat there was. The docks didn't even smell bad. Most of the
people bustling around the harbor wore flowing garments in
light colors, with silk appearing as often as linen. Billowing trousers and vests embroidered in jewel tones were common on the
men, some of whom wore turbans, while the women were a more
varied sort, some wearing veils and robes that covered nearly all
their skin, others wearing what seemed little more than arrangements of innumerable diaphanous scarves. Several women had
rings in their noses, as some of the female crew had, and many
people had numerous earrings, men and women both, along
with bracelets and necklaces of gold and other precious metals.
Rodrick wondered if they dressed according to caste, or the gods
they worshiped, or merely personal whim. What skin he could see
ranged from coppery to almost black, and he thought he must be
the palest person in Niswan, at least here on the docks. One of
the tallest, too. As he'd suspected, this would be a difficult place to
remain anonymous, so if he did anything villainous, he'd better do
it so subtly he wasn't noticed.

One man stood at the end of the gangplank, the flow of
people working and walking parting around him, as if he were
surrounded by an invisible armed guard. Who knew? Maybe he
was. Many elementals could be invisible if they chose, couldn't
they?

The man's mustache and beard were black and carefully
groomed, his eyes dark and piercing. His vest was embroidered
in golden thread, and the arms crossed over his chest bulged with
muscles accentuated by golden armbands. He looked quite a bit
like the djinni who'd summoned Rodrick, though he had legs in
those billowing white trousers instead of a vortex of wind.

He inclined his head a fraction. "I am Nagesh, an advisor to the thakur. On his behalf, I welcome you to Niswan." From the fierceness of his countenance, Rodrick had expected a harsh voice, but it was smooth as oil, and the man smiled ingratiatingly, though his dark eyes never changed. He gave a slight bow, which Rodrick returned as naturally as he could manage. He'd always been adept at picking up local customs. Part of the tendency toward helpful camouflage that probably wouldn't be so helpful here, where he stood out so much physically.

"I'm Rodrick. And the fellow on my hip is Hrym."

"May I . . . see him?" Nagesh said.

"If I won't get in trouble for drawing a sword here." There were some cities where showing bare steel (or bare enchanted ice) would get you arrested.

Nagesh waved his hand, unconcerned. "No, no. Many of the most dangerous people in Jalmeray have no need of weapons, and can defeat your armored knights of Absalom with their bare hands—the Houses of Perfection are very thorough in their teachings. We do not worry about the display of weapons on the streets, as long as you don't seek to threaten our citizens."

Rodrick reached down and drew Hrym from the scabbard, displaying the blade in all his glittering glory. "Say hello to the nice man, Hrym."

"Hello, nice man," Hrym said.

"The stories are true," Nagesh murmured. He bowed again. "I am honored to meet you, Hrym."

There'd been no mention of honor when it came to meeting Rodrick, but he was used to being outshone by his more sparkling companion. He put the sword away, though Hrym squawked at being sheathed again. Too bad. Rodrick had a pack on his back, and he wasn't going to walk around holding an obviously magical blade in his hand, no matter what this advisor said. "Nagesh, I was humbled to receive the thakur's invitation. I can't imagine why he went to such trouble to bring me here. May I ask the purpose of this summons?"

"All will be explained when you meet him. If you are tired from your journey, I can have you taken to the palace in a litter. Unless you'd like to see a bit of the city first? Many find it worthy of attention."

"I wouldn't mind the chance to walk on solid land for a while. Bobbing around in a litter might be too much like bobbing around on a ship, and I've had enough of that. If there's no hurry, that is."

"The thakur will receive you this evening. There is time to walk, and rest, in the meantime." He gestured for Rodrick to follow, and began moving along at a brisk pace.

"You speak the common tongue of my homeland very well," Rodrick said, falling into step beside him. "The crew on the ship does, too. Is it spoken widely here?"

"Not by everyone, no. Those who sail must be able to trade with those they meet, of course. And I have spent enough time abroad to learn several languages. Many at court speak only the tongues of the Vudrani, and though the thakur knows your speech, he prefers our own; he says yours is ill-suited to poetry. Here." He reached into a pocket and drew out a silver chain with a dangling medallion, etched with the face of a figure with two eyes, one nose, and four mouths, all open. "This amulet will aid your understanding, and allow you to speak the most common of our dialects."

Rodrick slipped it over his neck. He'd used translating magics before. "Can you comprehend me?" Nagesh asked, and apart from a faint echo of unintelligible speech, he sounded as clear as before.

"I can."

Nagesh grunted. "Your accent is not perfect, but it will serve."

"To be serviceable is my greatest aspiration."

The man frowned at him, but Rodrick just kept blandly smiling. Something about the man rubbed him the wrong way—perhaps just his excessive dignity, which Rodrick naturally wanted to puncture.

The streets were winding, which helped offset how steep they were, and soon they'd left the docks behind. The broad red avenues were lined by shops selling rugs and fine pottery and herbs and weapons and clothes, but also by temples, which ranged from tiny one-monk places squeezed into alleyways with only a bronze statue and an offering plate, to gilded pagodas as big as palaces, with ranks of monks spinning prayer wheels or chanting. Even the servants sweeping the streets here wore ornaments of gold, and in all the place smelled of wealth as no other city in Rodrick's experience ever had. Even if he assumed Nagesh was taking him on a path deliberately chosen to highlight the glories of Niswan, it was impressive.

They paused at a square where several men and women dressed in flowing white moved together in unison, bowing and twisting and kneeling and bending and standing on one leg and reaching up toward the sun, following the motions of a leader who hummed a repeating syllable endlessly.

"An exercise to strengthen the body and focus the mind," Nagesh said. "Perhaps you could try it during your visit. Many find it very restful."

They continued on, but Rodrick paused soon after at another open square, this one full of bare-chested men in yellow trousers and women dressed similarly, though they had on tight, midriff-baring tops of the same yellow. They tumbled and whirled about as adroitly as any acrobat Rodrick had ever seen, but this wasn't just a display of balance and athleticism: they were *hitting* each other, or trying to, and grabbing one another, flinging and rolling and springing up to strike again, legs and fists in a flurry of motion. An old woman with a long stick stood atop a short stone pillar, occasionally shouting instructions or insults or—very rarely—praise.

"They are from the Houses of Perfection?" Rodrick said.

Nagesh shook his head. "No. The monasteries are elsewhere. These students are far more raw, though the best of them will doubtless seek entry to the monasteries in time."

Rodrick could only shake his head in wonder. They all looked sufficiently formidable to him. He could only imagine what the students at the monasteries—let alone their masters—could do. He followed Nagesh again, this time along a street steep enough that every step made his calves burn, which abruptly leveled out into an open-air market, scores of tables set up under canopies of silk and coarser cloth. Not as fancy as the shops they'd passed before, but bustling with activity, noisy with hawkers shouting about the quality of their wares, which encompassed everything from fine cloth to handmade brooms to mouth-watering skewers of grilled mushrooms. The air was a riot of smells, all wonderful. Rodrick realized he hadn't eaten anything since dinner the night before, and Nagesh seemed to take note of his sniffing.

"You are hungry? There will be a feast at the palace, but in the meantime, perhaps one of these humble places serves something suitable." He strolled along a row of booths devoted to cookery, passing by several that seemed more than adequate to Rodrick, offering bowls of stew and lumpy potato cakes and plates of curious yellow rice and bits of fish in sauces that were creamy or red and so spiced they made his eyes water just from catching a passing whiff. There were other non-Vudrani people here, he noticed, some as pale as himself, many with Taldan coloring, others who might have been Osirian, and even a devilkin, doubtless from Cheliax, with bluish skin and tiny horns, arguing with a seller of delicate glassware about a price. A blue-eyed woman with short blonde hair, dressed in dark leather from head to toe, eyed him intently for a moment before disappearing down another row of tents.

"This will do." Nagesh stopped at a booth that seemed no different from any other, except for the unusually long line of people waiting before it. Nagesh ignored them all and walked to the front, and the person already standing there in mid-order bowed and moved away. Nagesh took no notice of their deference, and the round-cheeked man at the booth smiled widely while wringing his hands in what Rodrick took as an unconscious sign of worry. Did that mean Nagesh was known as a dangerous man, or merely a powerful one? "How may I be of service?"

"Two of the kebabs, and two lassis."

The man bowed, then skewered chunks of mushroom and grilled onion and some yellow fruit on wooden sticks as long as Rodrick's forearm and handed them over, followed by wooden cups full of something orange-yellow and sweet-smelling. Rodrick sipped his carefully, and his mouth filled with creamy sweetness, redolent with some strange fruit—it was like a pudding, but lighter. "Delicious!"

Nagesh nodded gravely and turned away from the booth, not bothering to pay. Rodrick wondered if he had an account of some kind with the cook, or if the thakur's advisors simply got to eat free. Being powerful had its perks.

He took bites of the mushroom, grilled and lightly spiced, and felt his energy come surging back as he matched pace with the advisor. They passed out of the market square, and he saw the blonde in dark leathers again, watching him from the top of a wall up the hill, this time. She was more severe than pretty, but any woman who showed such interest was worth a second considering look—alas, she hurried away again when she noticed him looking. Perhaps she was captivated by his handsomeness, but if so, why not give him a smile? If he'd had Hrym on his back, he would have assumed she was staring at that, but with him hidden away in a scabbard . . . She was probably just gaping at the fellow foreigner, or perhaps she recognized Nagesh's rank and wondered why he was walking with a swordsman wearing saltwater-stained trousers.

"This way." Nagesh beckoned, turning down a narrower street, and they marched uphill again, emerging on yet another level stretch—this was a city of tiers, it seemed. This area was even more full of temples—seemingly nothing but—with an open square dominated by a pair of those towering statues, one a man holding aloft great spheres that glowed with inner light, one a woman whose eight outstretched hands all held real dancing flames, blue and red and white and yellow.

"Welcome to the High-Holy District," Nagesh began, but before he could expound on its virtues someone nearby screamed, and a horse someone had apparently doused in lamp oil and set on fire came bolting out of a side street, running straight for Rodrick.

8

Palace of Gardens

Without thinking, Rodrick drew Hrym, and a wall of ice grew in front of him, ten feet high and ten feet wide. The flaming horse—no, it wasn't a horse on fire, it was a horse *made* of fire—struck the wall and disappeared in a billow of steam. Rodrick stumbled back, sword held before him, looking for further attacks, but nothing came. A pale man in dark robes hurried out of the same side street the horse had come from, looked at the ice wall, gasped, looked at glowering Nagesh, and gasped again. He bowed so low his forehead almost touched his knees, at the same time holding up his hands, palms turned toward them. "I'm sorry, I'm sorry, it was an accident—"

"Fool," Nagesh said curtly. "Begone, and don't loose your abominable magics in public again." The man backed away, bowing as he did, until he disappeared back into the street he'd come from.

"That was . . . unusual," Rodrick said.

Nagesh thumped the ice wall with his knuckles and looked at the sword. "You acted quickly."

"I don't like fire," Hrym said.

"Mmm, I understand. How long will the wall last?"

"Magical ice melts slowly," Hrym said. "It could stand for days, or . . ." The wall abruptly began to sag, rivulets of water running down the slope toward the street they'd trekked up, and in moments only a thin scrum of ice and a puddle remained. "I can make it go away."

"Why did that man throw a burning horse at us?" Rodrick said. "Or are horses made of fire an everyday hazard here?"

Nagesh made a sound of disgust. "His name is Kaleb. He claims to be a conjurer, an illusionist, and a pyromancer. I believe he is a sorcerer, whose bloodline is somehow touched by fire. I met him briefly when he performed at a feast in the palace, eating fire and juggling balls of flame and the like. He came here to lean how to master elementals, and had sufficient natural ability—and gold, until he ran out—to convince some of our wizards to teach him. Apparently he has not yet achieved the mastery he sought. Though I've never seen anyone convince a fire elemental to take on the shape of a horse." He shook his head. "He is of no consequence." Clearly attempting to recover his equanimity, Nagesh stood straighter and gestured toward the statues. "As I was saying—this is the High-Holy District. There are temples, as you see, to some of our gods, and also many scholars, clerics, and mystics, from across the breadth of the Inner Sea. Ice witches, Kellid skalds, Osirian priests, wise women from the Mwangi Expanse who chew strange roots and see visions, and many others beside. Wizards, too, of course. There is more knowledge within this quarter than in all your great cities combined, I would wager."

Rodrick would have been more interested in the High-Stakes Gambling District, if there was such a place, but he made appreciative noises anyway, keeping his eyes open for more flaming horses, occasionally turning his eyes skyward to watch the figures flying overhead. Most of the people he'd seen in the skies from the ship originated here, it seemed, borne aloft by magics. Some of them really *were* sitting on floating carpets. They must be worth a fortune, assuming they'd fly for anyone. You could smudge a bit of dirt on one and roll it up and transport it in a cart of ordinary secondhand rugs and no one would even notice it . . .

They continued walking for a while past temples and statues. Men and women prayed, or sat cross-legged in meditation, or leaned over tables scowling at scrolls, or bowed and chanted, or played games with stones on boards, or argued in booming voices about subjects that were incomprehensible even though the medallion of tongues let Rodrick understand the words.

Eventually they moved out of the High-Holy District, this time walking up a broad avenue lined by tall poles with flapping banners alternating with trees laden with sweet-smelling white blossoms. "The palace." Nagesh gestured grandly, and Rodrick didn't have to fake his appreciation this time.

The thakur's palace was made of white marble, mainly, but there was no end of gold, too, ornamenting the fluted towers and delicate archways. They walked up the broad steps, Nagesh nodding to guards who were armed with scimitars but probably didn't need anything more than their bare hands to deter unwelcome visitors. They stepped through an open archway and into a vast courtyard, full of bubbling fountains and low benches, roofed by trellises of vines. Many of the benches were occupied by young Vudrani men and women dressed in flowing silks and countless jewels, some reading, some laughing, some trailing their hands in the water of the fountains and looking appealingly pensive. Servants—themselves dressed as finely as lords and ladies Rodrick had seen in other lands—circulated among them holding trays and pitchers, bowing and gliding.

"Are these courtiers?" Rodrick said.

"These are mostly the sons and daughters of members of the Maurya-Rahm, those who govern and advise the thakur. This is a favored gathering place for those youths blessed with powerful families. They come to see and be seen, to further the fortunes of their families or to make their own connections."

"I can see why they congregate here. It's a beautiful place."

A faint disturbance in the air passed by, blowing Rodrick's hair, and he stepped back.

"Do not be alarmed," Nagesh said. "It's just a djinni on some errand. They are all bound, here, and serve."

Bound genies as servants! It was not entirely surprising, as he'd received a djinni as a messenger himself, but to have beings of such legendary power pass by without arousing any comment from the locals . . . This truly was a strange place.

Nagesh continued, leading him to a set of golden doors, these guarded by men holding spears, though the weapons looked more ornamental than functional. Still, a spearhead of gold would gut you as neatly as one made of steel if driven in with sufficient force. The guards opened the doors so smoothly that Nagesh didn't even have to break stride, and Rodrick followed on his heels.

He'd expected to enter the palace proper, but instead, they stood in a garden, larger than some farms Rodrick had seen. Everywhere fruit trees flowered, and paths wound among them, perfumed by blossoms of every shape and hue. Songbirds fluttered and filled the air with music, and there were more fountains, stone wrought to look like trees and vines and branches. There were fewer people here, but he caught glimpses of some, older than those in the outer courtyard and even more richly dressed, walking in pairs or alone on distant paths. An earth elemental passed by on an adjacent path, a mobile statue of immense size, and no one paid it any attention. They probably had creatures like that as groundskeepers here.

"These gardens are not so fine as the thakur's own at the center of the palace, but they are pleasant enough," Nagesh said. A servant—Rodrick could tell because he was only dressed as richly as a Taldan noble—with a shaved head appeared, bowing low. "I must take my leave of you now, Rodrick, and Hrym. This man will show you to your rooms. You will be honored guests at a feast tonight, and you will meet with the thakur afterward. In the meantime, please rest, or explore the palace."

"I get free run of the place, then?" Perhaps Rodrick's larcenous reputation hadn't preceded him.

"There are some areas you may not enter, but they will be . . . clearly marked." Nagesh bowed and turned, strolling away.

"Lead on, my good man," Rodrick said.

The servant didn't speak, just bowed again and gestured along a pathway.

Rodrick followed the man, asking one or two questions, but the answers were brief and factual. Sometimes servants were useful gossips, but apparently not this one. They left the gardens and entered a grand hall with an actual roof over it, though the place was so full of statues and more fountains and plants in huge pots that the transition from garden to interior seemed gradual. The floors were polished marble, the walls decorated with friezes depicting gods and strange scenes, one or two familiar from his reading of Vudrani fairy tales—a woman with a scimitar confronting a tiger-headed rakshasa, a man wearing a snow-capped mountain on his head like a crown, a monkey with a scepter, a tower of those strange creatures called elephants standing on one another's backs.

The servant pointed out doors that led to baths, other gardens, the library, the dining hall, and many more places, and finally bowed and pointed to a wooden door in an archway. "Your room." He opened the door, and Rodrick stepped inside.

"This is fit for a—" he began, but the servant was gone. "King," he finished. "Or at least a prince. Maybe a duke." He drew Hrym and gave him a look. "Don't you think?"

"I've known kings who lived in worse places," Hrym said. The room was huge and round, with a bed big enough for five people, several well-cushioned armchairs, low tables holding books and bits of statuary, lamps both conventional and alchemical, tapestries depicting scenes like those from the friezes in the hallways, and a washbasin next to a fountain that bubbled endlessly. Doors filled with glass panes stood open, white curtains drawn back, giving access to a balcony that was larger than the best room at an Andoren inn. A table on the balcony held bread and fruit and a pitcher of something that proved to be very fine pale wine.

Rodrick leaned Hrym against one chair on the balcony, then dropped into another, poured himself a second cup of wine to savor, and sat looking out at the gardens below and the high wall beyond. "This is acceptable," he said. "Don't you think? We've landed on our feet quite nicely. I mean, I have. You don't have feet."

"We don't even know why we're here yet," Hrym said. "You think it's going to be all free wine and garden views?"

"You never know. We *did* save the world from the depredations of a demon lord, you know. Saraswati told me about something called 'karma'—the idea is, if you do something good, good things will happen, and if you do something bad, bad things will happen, with no tedious waiting around to be judged in the afterlife first. Maybe this is our just reward for our virtuous acts."

"Ha. I think our bad actions still outnumber our good. Maybe, at best, we've achieved neutrality."

"Here's to neutrality," Rodrick said, and poured a third cup of wine.

Rodrick woke with a start, slumped on the balcony, to find a shaven-headed servant bedecked in gold clearing his throat loudly.

"He's been doing that for five minutes," Hrym said helpfully from the other chair. "I told him to smack you on the side of the head when you wouldn't wake up, but he refused."

Groaning, Rodrick looked into the wine cup, which held only dregs, and then into the pitcher, which was in a similar state. Oh well. It had been very good wine. Most of the day had passed, it seemed, the sky tinged with colors as bright as those of the silk banners that fluttered over Niswan, all violets and oranges and reds as the sun set beyond the gardens.

The servant bowed. "May I help you prepare for the feast?"

Rodrick rose to his feet. He hadn't been asleep long enough to develop a hangover, so that was something. After picking up Hrym he followed the servant back to his rooms, and from there out into the hallway and toward the baths. The opulence there was a fit for the rest of the palace: marble columns, dizzyingly high ceilings, friezes on the walls of people bathing in rivers and waterfalls, and the pools themselves, tiled in pale blue, one cold and still, one warm and still, and one hot and bubbling, but apparently magically, and not because it was boiling. Each pool was big enough for a dozen people to bathe without jostling one another, though no one else was there. "Does everyone in the palace bathe here?" he asked.

"This bath is for guests such as yourself."

So much for the hope of seeing a few Vudrani women dressed in nothing but flowing water. Rodrick bathed, enjoying the warm pool and the cold, letting the servant scrub his back with a sort of rough sponge on a stick, and declining the array of oils, perfumes, and unguents offered while he toweled off. He wrapped himself in a robe and went back to his rooms, where another servant was laying out a suit of clothes in the local fashion: loose white trousers, silk shirt, embroidered vest, and shoes that were more like slippers, all of the finest cut and cloth. A golden scabbard lay on the bed, too, studded with sapphires, rubies, emeralds, and diamonds. "Hrym!" he called. "They have a fancy scabbard for you!"

Hrym, still leaning against the chair on the balcony, said, "You know I don't like being cooped up in those things. I can't even *see*."

"Hrym, the thing is literally made of gold. Or at least gilt—I suppose if it were pure gold it would be abominably heavy. But still: you could rest *inside gold*."

A pause. "I suppose that might be all right, but you have to take me out when we get to the feast. I like to see what's happening."

If the servants found the conversation strange, they didn't give any indication. They must be used to even stranger things than a talking sword. Rodrick glanced at them. "So are these things gifts, or loans?" The servants blinked at him, and he sighed. "Do I have to give back the clothes and the scabbard and things when the thakur's done with me, or do I get to keep them?"

"They . . . are yours, of course, sir," one said, a man with a curiously high-pitched voice. "We would not give any guests clothing or gifts that had been used by another." He shuddered delicately at the very idea.

"Excellent. The thakur's hospitality is justly famed." The jewels in the scabbard alone would make this trip worthwhile, even if there were no other riches to be had on this little expedition. He put Hrym on the bed while he dressed, buckling on the bejeweled sword belt that held the empty scabbard. "If you'd wait in the hall, gentlemen? I'll be right there." The two servants exchanged glances and the slightest of frowns, so Rodrick said, "I need a few moments to pray to my own gods. It's important to do so before a meal."

They seemed to understand reverence, because they bowed out and shut the door. Rodrick picked up Hrym and went out to the balcony, just in case the servants were listening at the door. "Well, old friend, here we are. I try not to worry too much about momentous events that are off in the future, because they may never arrive—the ship could have gone down with all hands on the voyage over, or we could have been eaten by leviathans, and then all that worry would have been wasted. But it seems quite likely we're going to end up at a feast soon, and will be at some point in the presence of the thakur, who will presumably tell us what we're *doing* here. I find the immediacy of that prospect a bit alarming. Don't you?"

Hrym harrumphed. "What are you suggesting? If we tried to go for a stroll in the garden in the general direction of the front gate, we'd probably be herded back like sheep, with djinn as the shepherds. I wouldn't want to fight my way out of this place. You drank the wine and put on the clothes—they've paid for you, so we might as well find out what they think they bought. Besides, it could mean more gold."

"I just wanted to take a moment to recognize the gravity of the situation. Usually when authorities want to see us, we make a point of running *away*. But perhaps I'm nervous for nothing. I just hope they don't mean to marry me off to someone. Maybe word of my prowess as a swordsman has spread, and they want me to audition for a place in a House of Perfection."

"Or to put me in the hands of a halfway competent swordswoman, to see what *she* could do with someone as wonderful as me," Hrym said.

Rodrick sighed, rising, then slid Hrym into the golden scabbard, where he fit perfectly. "I'm capable of facing reality. I know it's more likely they're interested in you than they are in me—or that they're interested in me mostly because I am presently your wielder, and the only person you can be trusted not to freeze into a lump of magical unmelting ice."

"Oh, good. I'm glad you can admit that. I didn't want to say anything, because I know your feelings are delicate." Hrym's voice was muffled but perfectly comprehensible.

Rodrick frowned and put his hand on Hrym's hilt, realizing something. "Wait. *You* never got an amulet to let you understand the languages these people are speaking, or to make them understand yours. How are you communicating?"

"Hardly anyone talks to me *anyway*, it's very rude, but as for how . . . well, they make as much sense to me as any of you humanoid creatures do, and I suppose I can make myself understood. I must have picked up their tongue somewhere." Hrym had potent magical properties of absorption—he'd gained his ice powers by stealing them, over the course of long years, from an ice dragon, and had picked up a demonic taint after a much shorter period of time in proximity to a demon lord, so maybe at some point he'd soaked up other abilities as well. His memory was fragmented, though perhaps not so badly as he claimed, and there were depths in Hrym that were hidden from Rodrick, and possibly even from Hrym himself.

"Hmm. You're full of surprises, but I'm glad I don't have to play translator for you. Speaking of voices, though, did you hear that servant? He could sing the soprano part in a choir."

"He's a eunuch, Rodrick."

Rodrick blinked. "What, you mean someone cut his . . . particulars . . . off?"

Hrym snickered—not the creepy demonic titter, but his more usual crass indication of amusement. "You male humanoids are so attached to your reproductive organs. Even you, though as far as I can tell you never have any intention of reproducing, at least not intentionally."

"I enjoy going through the *motions*, though," Rodrick said. "Why would they unman the man?"

"I don't know much about the Vudrani, but I know it's not uncommon in their culture to do that to servants. Cut off that part of a boy before he starts to become a man, and he's made more reliable in various ways, or so it's generally believed. Do *you* always think with your head, Rodrick, or do other parts of you sometimes make the decisions?"

"I have made some choices based on suggestions from my lower regions that, in retrospect, were unwise. Cutting them off seems a bit extreme, though."

"Humanoid carnal relations are baffling and disgusting to me, of course, but I gather some men in power feel better if their women are attended by men who can't, ah, compete with their masters in certain respects."

Rodrick made a disgusted face. "I suppose it makes a sick sort of sense. I've never demanded faithfulness from any woman, myself. It's true I'm frequently dishonest, but asking for *that* would be downright hypocritical. It's not as if the eunuchs have their tongues and fingers removed, though, so it seems a half-measure at best . . . I'd worry about a eunuch revolution, personally. I can't think of many things that would make me more likely to go into a frenzy and try to kill someone than having *those* cut off."

"Do the cutting early enough and they don't know what they're missing," Hrym said.

"Poor bastards. I mustn't *tell* them what they're missing. There's nothing sadder than a weeping servant."

He slid Hrym back into the scabbard and strode out into the hall, toward destiny—or, at the very least, a free meal.

9
The Thakur's Proposal

The servants, moving fast without ever exactly running, led Rodrick through the palace to yet another gorgeous hall of marble and columns, this one full of long tables made from exotic (by Inner Sea standards, anyway) wood, with chairs carved so delicately they seemed constructed of lace. There were scores of people in the room, most already seated, a few standing and mingling in little groups, the women in scarves and veils, the men in loose pants with broad sashes, except for those in monk's robes in various hues, doubtless denoting their religious and martial affiliations.

Rodrick was fairly adept at reading the composition of a crowd of nobles in most of the kingdoms back home, but his ignorance of Vudrani ways limited his capacity here. Who were the true powers here, and who were the strivers? Was it even worth his while to know? He picked up a tall fluted glass of something bubbly from the tray of a passing servant—another eunuch, he suspected—and took a sip.

"Ah, good, you've arrived." Nagesh appeared at his elbow and gently herded him toward one of the tables. "You will be seated not far from the thakur's table, beside one of the teachers from the Monastery of Untwisting Iron—your mutual interest in weapons should make conversation pleasant."

Rodrick smiled instead of groaning. Was there anything more tedious than talking about the merits of various sorts of swords? Clearly magical swords of living ice were best, but when he made that point, it was seldom well received. He was surprised, when he reached the table, to find an elaborate sword stand beside his chair, made of silver and gold.

"For Hrym," Nagesh said, and Rodrick couldn't contain a grin. Lots of people preferred to pretend that Hrym was just a sword, however remarkable, and it was nice to see his partner treated with respect. He drew the sword, perhaps a bit too hastily as the room rapidly went silent, heads turning to look at the man holding a few feet of glittering magic in his hands. He raised his other hand in a wave, gave his most rakish smile, and set Hrym point-down on the stand beside his chair.

"Mmm. This is all right," Hrym said. "Make sure you get to keep this stand, too. It's not as good as resting on a big pile of gold coins, but it's better than being propped up against a wall."

"There's the thakur," Nagesh murmured, and Rodrick looked where he gestured. At a table raised a little higher than the others, a dozen Vudrani even more richly dressed in silks and jewels than the rest—presumably important members of the Maurya-Rahm—surrounded a figure seated in the center. The thakur was on the early slopes of his later years, and had a grandfatherly aspect, all smiles and nods, with laugh lines around his eyes and mouth. His clothing was relatively simple, but impeccably made, his beard perfectly trimmed and iron-gray. His eyes seemed to catch Rodrick's, for a moment, and those eyes were *sharp*, dark and intent and all-seeing despite his smiles. Not a man Rodrick would choose as a potential mark for cheating, so he hoped he wouldn't be forced to try.

"I will come for you after the meal," Nagesh said. "In the meantime, enjoy."

Nearly everyone else was already seated, so Rodrick took his place and turned to Hrym. "So that's the thakur. Hmm."

"What?" Hrym said. "Why are you talking to me? Broaden your horizons, man. Good evening, my lady. Doesn't the thakur lay on a lovely feast?"

A woman of middle years, dressed in drapes of glittering white cloth, was seated beside Hrym, and looked startled when the sword spoke, edging away in her chair. Undiscouraged, Hrym continued to speak, in a sonorous and gracious voice, complimenting her diamond-and-gold jewelry and comparing her pale garment to the beauty of glittering high snows on mountain peaks. She responded cautiously at first, but gradually became more enthusiastic, until the two were discussing jewelry with the intensity of two aficionados starved of conversation with fellow devotees.

Who knew the curmudgeonly old sword could be charming? He'd certainly never bothered to show that side of himself to his wielder. Rodrick took the hint and turned in his own chair, nodding with a bland smile to the iron-faced man wearing dark orange robes beside him. The man looked Rodrick up and down frankly, frowned, and said, "You are a swordsman?"

"In my own modest way," Rodrick said.

The monk grunted. "We train with swords, a bit, but mostly we teach our students how to take them away from men who don't know how to fight without blades in their hands. Take a sword away from a swordsman and what's left is often barely a man, and can be beaten by any student halfway through his first year." With that, the monk turned in his own chair and began speaking to a vastly bearded man beside him, chattering about preparations for something called the Challenge of Sky and Heaven.

Rodrick looked to the seat across the table from him, but it was unoccupied, though a plate and silverware waited there. Ah, well. Who wanted to socialize anyway? Rodrick concentrated on the wine and food which regularly appeared before him, delivered by smoothly gliding servants. Every dish was strange, with an emphasis on flatbreads, yellow rice, heaps of green vegetables, and spiced fish in strange sauces of cream or peppers. No proper meat at all as far as he could tell, no beast or fowl, just seafood, and little enough of that. A peculiar people, but it all tasted good, even if none of it touched his appetite the way a rare steak or roast lamb reliably could. The wine was odd, too, honey-sweet or strangely spiced, but more than palatable. There was entertainment, with graceful dancers on a stage, followed by acrobats (one of them winked at him, he was sure of it, and when he saw the way she bent all the way over backward and grabbed her own ankles, he was more than happy to give her a broad smile in return). Then came someone playing an instrument that was a bit like a lute with an absurdly long neck, full of twangy atonalities. Not to Rodrick's taste, but it would be a boring world if we were all the same, he thought.

Partway through the meal a young woman arrived, with the largest, darkest eyes he'd seen here yet, and dangling earrings in geometrical shapes the eye could not quite follow, shapes that were repeated on the silken cloth of her loosely cut blue dress. He'd heard of cloth-of-gold, but surely this was cloth-of-magic, illusory and shifting. She seated herself in the empty chair across from Rodrick, and a servant appeared immediately to fill her plate and goblet. He thought he recognized the woman from the palace courtyard full of noble youths, but he'd passed through so quickly it was hard to be sure. Her presence at this banquet was enough to tell him she was either someone important or related to someone important.

Rodrick smiled at her, even though he might as well have been smiling at the moon for all the response he got. Her sharp, foxlike face was pretty, despite a certain ferocious quality in her expression, as if she were replaying the details of a recent argument in her mind. She finally noticed Rodrick looking at her, and after a glance that seemed to measure and weigh him to the inch and the ounce she looked over at Hrym, then nodded as if she'd received confirmation of some horrible prognosis. When she spoke, it was in his own language. "So you're the mysterious swordsman. Your arrival has been on everyone's lips."

Instinct almost made Rodrick say something like, "I wish I could be on *your* lips," but while that might get him a laugh and a blush in the right tavern from the right woman, this one could be a fighting monk or a mystic or a political leader, despite her apparent youth, so he stepped more lightly. "My name is Rodrick, my lady. I don't think I'm all that mysterious. To me, Jalmeray is the land of mystery."

"It's all a matter of perspective, I suppose," she said. "My name is Kalika." She looked at him in that assessing way again. "As long as you're here, you might as well help me practice your language. I've traveled a bit to the Inner Sea, with my father. Shall we talk of places we've seen until we find one we have in common?"

She seemed very interested in the legal systems of various countries, a subject on which Rodrick was moderately well informed, having had brushes with said legal systems on a few occasions (a fact he glossed over). With just a bit of steering, he moved her toward discussing the best places to eat and drink in various of the great cities, a subject much more to Rodrick's liking. He gave up his few attempts to flirt after they were neither rebuffed nor encouraged but simply ignored, as if he hadn't said anything at all. In truth, the woman never exactly warmed to him—Kalika seemed to have a core of ice, something else Rodrick was moderately knowledgeable about—but the dinner conversation was at least diverting.

He made a habit of trying to find people's buttons or handles, attitudes or opinions or outlooks he could manipulate if need be, but she gave him almost nothing he could use. Not that he expected to embroil anyone here in a confidence game, but it was useful mental exercise, and frustrating that she had such impenetrable reserve. One thing his conversation with Kalika made clear: despite Rodrick's sense that everything here was strange and exotic, *he* was the exotic one in this company, and his essentially Andoren attitudes toward everything from peacekeeping methods to slavery to good citizenship struck her as bafflingly wrongheaded when they weren't merely amusing. All a matter of perspective, indeed.

After a course of some sweet fruit on a bed of white rice, and thick syrupy dessert wine that must have been made from honey, Nagesh touched his shoulder. "If you and Hrym would accompany me?"

Rodrick looked to the high table, and saw the thakur was gone. Aha. The moment of truth, and consequences.

"Must you take him away, Nagesh?" Kalika said. "He was just telling me the most amusing things about the so-called Eagle Knights of Andoran. Do you know, when I heard of those knights as a little girl, I thought they must be garudas wearing armor, from their name?"

"Fascinating, Kalika." Nagesh's voice was as dry as ash from a fresh fire. "Alas, our guests have more pressing business than enter- taining you." Rodrick could see immediately there was no love lost between these two, and naturally wondered what the cause of the tension was, and if he could somehow exploit it to enrich himself—but that wasn't why he was here. With luck, he'd find out soon why he *was* here.

"Forgive me." Rodrick gave Kalika a bright smile. "Perhaps we'll talk again."

"If your mysterious business with Nagesh allows you any freedom, perhaps we will."

Rodrick rose, swaying only a little—those wines were decep- tively strong—and half-bowed to the older woman still deep in conversation with Hrym. "My lady, forgive me, but we have matters we must attend to." He lifted Hrym from the golden stand and slid him into the jeweled scabbard, ignoring the sword's muffled protests, then followed Nagesh's lead through the tables toward a small door at one end of the hall.

"That Kalika. Is she someone important?"

"She thinks so," Nagesh said. "But her greatest distinction so far was being born to important parents."

"Some people have all the luck. I suppose we're going to see the thakur now? Still no hints for me? It would be nice to have some idea what I'm walking into."

"I will say only that if you do as the thakur asks, you will become a very rich man."

"I like being rich, but there are some things even gold won't buy."

"This is true," Nagesh said. "But when gold will not do for payment, I have found that blood will often suffice."

That certainly sounded ominous, but before Rodrick could answer they reached an arched doorway guarded not by men but by genies: a djinni with a swirling lower body, and an equally towering, horned, mostly man-shaped creature with crimson skin that Rodrick assumed was an efreeti. The air in the hall wasn't disturbed by the djinni's whirlwind, and the efreeti's presence didn't seem to raise the temperature, but Rodrick had no doubt they could unleash the forces held within their bodies at any moment. Nagesh swept past them as if they weren't there at all, and Rodrick stayed close behind.

They entered an open-air courtyard, small by the standards of some other gardens in the palace, but if anything even more lush and fragrant. They moved among fountains and creeping vines and heavy blossoms until they emerged into a little paved square. The thakur sat in a folding chair of canvas and wood before a spindly desk, a bound book open before him, scratching with a quill, pausing occasionally to look up at the nearly full moon, then writing again.

Nagesh waited with seemingly infinite patience, and Rodrick tried to do the same, taking the opportunity to look at the moon in the clear sky, too. Except, it wasn't all that clear—there was a disturbance in the air some feet over the thakur's head. Ah—another djinn, doubtless standing guard in case the outlander decided to draw his remarkable sword for reasons other than conversation.

After no more than three minutes, the thakur put down his pen, closed the book, lifted his gaze to Rodrick, and smiled. His eyes were just as piercing as before, but the smile seemed genuine to Rodrick, who was something of a connoisseur of artificial expressions of friendliness. "My apologies for keeping you waiting. I have been working on this poem for some time. The gods finally presented the right lines to me, and I wished to put them down before they slipped away."

Rodrick bowed low. "You need never apologize to me, Your Majesty. I am humbled by your hospitality. Truly, your island is a land of incomparable wonders."

The thakur nodded as if Rodrick had stated the obvious. "Yet you carry with you a wonder that does not have a match here. May I see . . . Hrym?"

Rodrick glanced at the djinni overhead. Drawing a sword in the presence of an absolute monarch, even one who liked writing poetry about the moon, struck him as a dangerous act—but then, so was disobeying said absolute monarch. He pulled the sword out slowly, and held it at a deliberately non-threatening angle. The moonlight was caught in Hrym's crystalline facets, making the length of the sword appear to glow.

"Remarkable," the thakur said. "May I hold him?"

Rodrick cleared his throat. "I have no objection, Your Majesty, but I cannot presume to speak for Hrym."

The thakur raised his eyebrow. "Indeed? Very well. Hrym, may I take you in my hand?"

"It's been a long time since I've been held by something resembling a king," Hrym said. "I'd appreciate the change."

Rodrick suppressed a snort, half-bowed again, and presented the sword to the thakur, hilt-first. The thakur rose and took the sword in his hand, then stepped a little distance away and flowed easily into a series of sword forms. The specific moves were unfamiliar to Rodrick, doubtless a Vudrani martial style, but the thakur's grace and comfort with the blade were obvious despite his age. He was surely a better swordsman than Rodrick himself, though that wasn't such a high bar. "Your balance is impeccable, Hrym," the thakur said. "Is it true, what I've heard, about your other properties? That you possess a mastery of cold that can rival that of an ancient white dragon?"

"I'm made of ice," Hrym said. "I'm good at doing icy things. Much more convenient than a dragon, too. I don't think Rodrick would get very far with a white dragon hanging from his belt."

Rodrick chuckled, and even Nagesh's beard shifted enough to reveal a smile.

"May I have a demonstration?" the thakur said.

"Let there be snow," Hrym said, and thick flakes began to fall. The invisible djinni was made more visible by the way the snow fell around it, revealed in negative space. Within moments the entire garden was covered in a layer of white. A mound of snow rose up into a half-sized statue of the thakur himself, holding a sword aloft, making the old man exclaim in delight. Hrym had done the snow-sculpture trick once or twice in the past to help Rodrick impress women.

"I could make a wall or dome of ice," Hrym said, "but they'd muck up your garden a bit. As for my other powers . . . they aren't good for company. Blasts of ice, freezing fog. Good for discouraging bandits on the road, but I wouldn't risk them in your presence."

The thakur chuckled, then tossed the sword in the air, caught the hilt in a reverse grip, and handed it back to Rodrick. The warm air was already melting the snow around them into slush, but the statue remained standing, and would for some time—magical ice didn't melt as quickly as the ordinary stuff.

"I am impressed," the thakur said, returning to his chair. "Nagesh, tell them my proposal."

Nagesh bowed, then turned to Rodrick. "The thakur would like to buy this sword—"

"No, no." The thakur shook his head. "Forgive him, Hrym, for discussing you as an object, and not an individual—he speaks without thinking."

Nagesh's expression tightened, and for a moment his features seemed to shift—his nose flattening, his eyes growing larger and darker, his mouth widening and teeth sharpening. It was a fleeting impression, one Rodrick was willing to blame on the moonlight, but it was still hard not to take a step away from the man.

"I wish to take Hrym into my service," the thakur said. "I realize this will be a great inconvenience to Rodrick, as Hrym aids him in his ongoing quest for fortune, and so . . ."

Nagesh took his cue. "And so the thakur, in his generosity, offers you jewels and gold, more than enough to see you in comfort for the rest of your life, so that you need seek your fortune no further."

Rodrick nodded. He wasn't entirely surprised. This wasn't the first time he'd been offered a king's ransom for Hrym—though it *was* the first time an actual king had done the offering. "It's a very kind offer, and I appreciate your concern for my financial security, but as I've said before, I cannot speak for Hrym. I carry him, but he is not my property."

"What do you want to do with me?" Hrym didn't bother to hide the suspicion in his voice. Many had sought to hold him in order to pursue personal wars or fulfill dreams of conquest, but those were not Hrym's aspirations.

"I have a dear friend, a distant cousin, who is a rajah in our homeland," the thakur said. "We visited one another often as children, and have remained in contact ever since, writing long letters. This rajah is a collector of rare and wondrous objects—far more than I am myself—and I occasionally send him such interesting relics of the Inner Sea as pass through my hands, since his collection is mostly items from the Impossible Kingdoms and Tian Xia.

He considers treasures from your lands particularly fascinating. He keeps me supplied with the finest literature from across our homeland, sometimes even commissioning works from noted poets written for my eyes alone, and I confess that we sometimes try to impress one another with the quality of our gifts. I have developed something of a reputation, I am told, among those in the Inner Sea who deal with ancient artifacts from lost times, and a certain class of trader knows to send me letters offering me items of special interest, as I pay well for them. Word reached me of a wonderful sword." He inclined his head. "A sword of magical ice, that speaks. A sword that perhaps dates back to the time of the Shory Empire."

"My memory doesn't go back that far," Hrym murmured. "At least, not reliably. But I don't doubt it's true."

"My cousin is visiting this island, due with his ships and his retinue in a fortnight, and it will the first time I have seen him in more decades than I care to count. To offer him the companionship of someone as astounding as yourself, Hrym . . ." The thakur's lips quirked in a smile. "He would have a difficult time offering me a gift more impressive than *that*, and the thought of his delight upon seeing you would delight *me*. I worried that a sentient sword might resist such an offer, fearing that you hungered for blood and conquest, but I have heard from my sources that you resemble a dragon not just in your powers, but also in your predilections . . . ?"

"He means you like to lay around on piles of gold, Hrym," Rodrick said.

"I do like that," Hrym said. "Who wouldn't? If I took up with this rajah, I wouldn't be dragged off to kill anyone, shoved in a sheath, taken all over the countryside on campaigns?"

"You would rest upon a stand of gold, upon a *mound* of gold, if that is your preference, in a place of honor. Indeed, once my cousin hears your voice and discovers you have such a wit—and that you speak our language!—I suspect he will be happy to converse with you on matters of wealth and history. It will be a life of comfort, Hrym, if you agree to my offer."

"That . . . is very generous, Majesty," Hrym said. "And most tempting, I must say. May I have some time to discuss it with my partner, and consider?"

"Of course. I know it is a momentous choice to make. Could you decide in, oh . . . two days? Only because I will need to make arrangements for a different gift if you are not amenable."

"That should certainly be sufficient, Majesty."

The thakur nodded. He brushed a bit of snow from his desk and smiled. "Nagesh, bring them back to me in two days' time, and I will hear their answer. Until then, extend them every courtesy." He cocked his head. "Tomorrow is the Festival of Ten Thousand Flowers, a day of holiness and celebration for our goddess Arundhat, bringer of blossoms and sweet scents. You should go into the High-Holy District and elsewhere to experience the event. I often wish I could move among the people freely, to celebrate with them."

"We look forward to it, Thakur." Rodrick bowed again.

"I will see you back to your rooms." Nagesh guided them away, down a slushy path. "Do you need anything tonight? A woman? Two women? Or do you prefer boys?"

"A most gracious offer, but I think sleep will suffice for plea- sure tonight." As he grew older, Rodrick more and more lost his taste for sleeping with women who were bought and paid for— where was the sense of accomplishment in *that*?

Nagesh guided them back toward a familiar hallway and then bid them goodnight. Rodrick went to his room, made sure the door was shut securely, and propped Hrym on his golden stand, which some helpful servant had brought into the room after dinner. He sat on the floor beside his friend and said, "So," in a neutral tone.

"So," Hrym said, in a near-identical tone.

"Quite an offer. Life of luxury."

"Like you've been promising me all this time," Hrym said.

"And have intermittently provided."

"'Intermittently' is the right word," Hrym agreed. "This offer. It's not a bad deal for you, either. You could set yourself up as a country lord. Or just try to burn through the coin in your usual hedonistic excess—sounds like you'd die of old age before you ran out, though."

"Yes, indeed," Rodrick said. "So. Do you want to go? Live with this rajah?"

A long pause. "Do you *want* me to go?"

Rodrick sighed. "I know it doesn't come naturally to us, but *one* of us has to speak honestly and risk being mocked. I suppose I'll do it. No, Hrym. I don't want you to go. I know we don't always wallow in luxury, but we . . . we work well together. I spent months upon months chipping you out of a prison of ice. I hope you know what you mean to me. That said, I know you love gold, and if you'd like to be a pretty ornament in a rajah's palace in Vudra, I won't blame you."

"That rajah would think he owned me, Rodrick. The thakur says he understands I'm my own person, but in the same voice, he speaks of me as a *gift*. Like I'm an object."

"I'm sure he'd speak of giving a flesh-and-blood person as a gift, too. They have slaves here, or the next worst thing." Like most Andorens, Rodrick found the idea of slavery offensive, and it was even worse, here, since they made some of their lowliest servants into eunuchs. Those eunuchs probably blamed themselves for being born into the wrong *caste*.

"It *is* a lot of gold, though," Hrym said. "If we said no, we'd both be giving that up. I suspect the thakur would be nice enough if we refused, but we'd be on a ship back to Absalom or some other port not much richer than we were when we left. Are we fools to refuse?"

"When I think of us, Hrym, I think of a . . . sort of circle, drawn around us. You and I are inside the circle, and so we're the ones who matter. Everyone else—*everyone*—is outside the circle."

"What do we do with people outside the circle?" Hrym said.

"Leave them alone, mostly," Rodrick said. "Sometimes drink with them, sometimes dice with them, sometimes travel with them." He reached out and touched Hrym's hilt. "But if they've got something we want . . . we *rob* them."

"So we're going to rob the thakur, then," Hrym said. "Come up with a scheme to steal from the ruler of an island nation full of wizards, mystics, fighting monks, and deadly elementals."

"No one," Rodrick replied, "can say we're not ambitious."

10
Festival of Flowers

A festival of flowers is nice enough," Rodrick said. "But wouldn't a festival of wine, women, and dice be better?"

"I'm sure the Vudrani have gods for all those things, too," Hrym said. "They've got thousands of the things. I hear in some places in the country over there, the gods outnumber the people."

Rodrick strolled through the streets around the High-Holy District, a fat purse jingling in his pocket, sipping another of those creamy-sweet concoctions he'd had the day before. The people of Jalmeray knew how to put on a festival. Invisible creatures overhead kept up a steady light rain of fragrant blossoms, which swirled away back to the heavens before they could accumulate in quantities sufficient to impede progress or commerce. Priests in robes in all the hues of a wildflower meadow danced and chanted and made offerings, and there were heaps of fruit free for the taking in front of many of the temples. Pretty girls with flowers in their hair danced by, along with laughing men with blossoms woven into their beards, and children with floral crowns. There was a great deal of music, though it was too dependent on reed flutes for Rodrick's taste, and he stood for a while watching a parade composed of immense levitating flowers bobbing in midair, the buds opening to reveal men and women dressed in leaves and vines inside, waving to the crowd and tossing out sweets and coins.

"They should be careful they don't attract enormous bees," Hrym said. Rodrick had the jeweled scabbard on his hip, but

Hrym was frozen to the outside of a more functional leather scabbard on Rodrick's back, so he could take in the sights. They were both in good spirits, having come to an agreement about how to proceed, and as far as they could tell, they weren't being spied on by any agents from the palace, though it was possible the watching eyes were just very subtle. They had to find local help, of course, but the festival was a great excuse to wander the streets and poke into various alleys and byways.

In early afternoon, Rodrick ducked into a tea shop that also sold flatbread and some sort of succulent bean paste for a bite, and found just the man he'd been looking for sitting at a table in the corner, peering sullenly into a cup. Rodrick clapped him on the back, startling the man and making him yelp, then dropped into a chair opposite him. "Kaleb, isn't it? We met yesterday. You had a horse." Rodrick drew Hrym—the conjurer watched the blade with wide eyes—and leaned him against the wall, point-down.

Kaleb swallowed. "I'm sorry about that. Elementals are tricky to control, if you don't get the forms exactly right they'll break free—"

"Think nothing of it. I thought the flaming horse was an impressive piece of work, before it tried to run me down, anyway. You didn't *deliberately* try to kill me." Rodrick leaned on the table, making sure his biceps bulged, and put on his toothiest, most menacing smile. "Then again, you did endanger my life by accident. I don't suppose you want to make it up to me?"

The man—who was quite thin under those robes—tried to straighten up. "I can conjure fire. Do you really want to threaten me?"

"Hrym?" Rodrick said.

Kaleb yelped and released the cup before him as it was covered in a thin sheet of ice, the liquid inside freezing solid. After a moment, the cup itself cracked, loud in the silence.

"I have a magical sword of living ice," Rodrick said. "I don't worry about fire. At best, your magic and Hrym's could fight each other to a standstill, which would leave me free to beat you over the head with a chair. Who do you think would get the better end of *that* interaction?"

Kaleb wasn't cowed yet. "Try causing that kind of trouble here, or anywhere in Niswan, and the thakur's men will clap you in irons—"

"Do you think *that's* likely, Hrym?" Rodrick said.

"Can't say I do," the sword replied.

Kaleb flinched at Hrym's voice. "It *talks*?"

"He not only talks, he has things to say I actually care to hear. A remarkable property, and an increasingly rare one. We are in Niswan as invited guests of the thakur—didn't you notice we were being shown around the city by one of his chief advisors?"

"I . . . Yes. I recognized him from the palace." Another little flare of defiance—maybe the fellow *did* have some fire elemental ancestry. "You see? I've been to the palace too."

"I heard. As a performer. Did they let you eat in the kitchens? I quite enjoyed the dancers and acrobats at the feast held in my honor last night, but I suppose a fire-eater would have been amusing, too." The bit about "in my honor" was stretching it a bit, but it seldom hurt to seem more impressive than you were. "Anyway, if it came to blows, I suspect my word would carry more weight than a penniless conjurer's. Or do the pockets of your robe bulge with free festival fruits because they're your favorite food, and not because that's all you can afford to eat?"

Kaleb hunched down in his seat. "What do you want?"

That was probably enough stick. On to the honey. "I want to give you money." He reached into his pocket and drew out a glittering ruby the size of his thumbnail and put it on the table. He'd pried the jewel off the scabbard that morning, and had already bought a glass gem to replace it so it wouldn't be apparent that he was chopping up the thakur's generosity for parts. "That would buy you rather a lot more tutoring in the mystical arts, wouldn't it?"

"I assume it's not a gift?"

"You could call it a gift. Assuming you were inspired to give me a gift in return. Are you truly an illusionist as well as a pyromancer?" Nagesh had said so, but Rodrick needed to be sure.

Kaleb nodded. "I was trained as an illusionist in Absalom. It's not my true passion, but I'm quite capable."

Rodrick nodded. Something was bothering him, and in a rare burst of candor, he decided to simply ask. "If you're so talented, why, precisely, are you so *poor*?"

Kaleb sighed. "In Absalom I could make a nice living, it's true. But here? Throw a stone and you'll likely hit a wizard. Though I don't recommend performing the experiment—wizards don't like being hit by stones. The well-established locals, the famous names of ancient standing, get all the worthy work on the island, leaving me to pick up what I can here and there. Moreover, I came here to *learn*, to discover magics that are all but unknown in the lands around the Inner Sea, and good teachers cost money. I came here with a chest of gold. A few months back, I was reduced to selling the chest for food."

"I see." Rodrick liked dealing with people who were desperate for money—their rates were so reasonable, and they seldom asked awkward questions. "I've seen your skill with fire. How are you with ice?"

Kaleb frowned. "What did you have in mind?"

"I'd like to make a replica of Hrym here. Can you enchant a sword to make it into an exact copy of him?"

"Not *exact*—it wouldn't have your sword's ability to ruin my cup of tea. But I could make a sword look like it—him—and maybe generate a bit of cold, too, to make the copy more convincing. I could even make it capable of uttering a few simple phrases, though nothing you could have a conversation with. More like talking to one of those parrots you see sometimes."

"That would be fine. Hrym's conversation tends toward the non sequitur anyway."

"I never liked the look of walruses much, I must admit," Hrym said, as if by way of demonstration.

"Okay." Kaleb dug into his robes and pulled out a well-chewed nub of pencil and a scrap of parchment. "Here. Write down a few examples of the sort of things he'd say."

Rodrick did so, then handed the paper back.

"I'll need to buy a longsword to use as a base," Kaleb said, "and some other components, so there will be expenses—"

"Take them out of the ruby." Rodrick flicked the jewel across the table, and Kaleb scrambled to scoop it up. "I'll give you another when it's done. I need the sword by tomorrow morning. Oh, and while you're at it, work up an illusion to make Hrym here look like an ordinary longsword. Nothing too fancy, something good but practical."

"And you want this by *tomorrow*? I'd have to work through the night!"

"You'd better order some strong black tea, then, to help you stay awake. Good. That's settled. Don't think of running off with the advance payment, or I'll have Hrym freeze your blood the way he did that tea. And if you fight him off with fire, well, I can always hit you with that chair we talked about."

"I do what I say I'll do." Kaleb was all haughtiness now that he had a ruby in his pocket.

"Excellent. I do as well. Don't tell anyone about this commission—it's a surprise for a friend. Now show me where you're staying, so I know where to pick up your work in the morning."

The conjurer led them down through the steep streets, out of the High-Holy District. Rodrick wasn't convinced that Niswan had any "bad" neighborhoods, considering how richly even the slaves were dressed here, but this was the closest he'd seen—the gilt on the buildings was chipped, bits of paper and rubbish occasionally marred the red stone walks without being swept up by djinn or eunuchs, and there were a lot more non-Vudrani faces than usual.

"The foreigners' quarter," Kaleb said, making a face. "In the worst part of the Harbor District. We are, of course, welcome to take rooms wherever they're available—but they only seem to be available right around here. I think the Vudrani like to keep us where they can find us. They still talk about how 'mainlanders' will try to move into a place that doesn't belong to them if it's left unattended for a moment, as if the occupation by the Arclords happened just last week. On the other hand, there are a couple of places here where you can get decent food and wine like they have back home, and hear people speak familiar languages." He stopped at a narrow building three stories tall and opened the front door with a key. "I'm on the top floor. I should get to work if you're really coming back tomorrow morning."

Since the man's key had opened the door, Rodrick felt fairly comfortable that this was actually his real home, and not a trick. It was always possible he'd take the ruby and flee without doing the work, which would be inconvenient, but Rodrick thought the man really did want to finance his studies further. Life was full of risks and chances, but this one didn't strike Rodrick as too big a gamble.

Rodrick strolled around the foreigners' quarter, pausing at a couple of cafes and wine shops that had outdoor tables, but they were populated by scholarly types talking animatedly about ancient history or scribbling notes. A couple of discreet inquiries about where a man might find a dice game eventually led him to a staircase that disappeared belowground. "Sorry, Hrym, it's in the scabbard with you. The sight of you would distract the honest, simple souls down there."

"I bet the rajah wouldn't shove me in a scabbard."

Hrym unfroze himself from the outside of the leather scabbard, and Rodrick slid him inside the golden sheath. He wished for a mirror—he needed to look just right, rich yet not entirely reputable—but you couldn't have everything.

The steps were cracked and unswept, and the basement room at the bottom—calling it a filthy rum-pit would be giving it too much credit—had the combination of darkness and muttering sullen occupants he'd hoped for.

There were Vudrani here among paler faces from the north side of the Inner Sea, but their clothes were less rich than those he'd seen elsewhere, their eyes more narrowed, or else their smiles were too wide and their jewelry too flashy. Every city had places where unsavory types gathered, and Rodrick always felt at home in those. He sidled up to the bar and asked for an ale—"Something that tastes like it was made on my side of the Obari Ocean, if possible"—and the bartender slid him a tankard. Rodrick laid a thick gold coin on the bar. "Drinks for anyone else who wants them until this runs out, too."

The bartender, a woman who looked like she had a touch of orc in her ancestry, raised one eyebrow and said, "That starts with me, then." She poured herself a shot of something from a bottle she took down from a very high shelf. Some of the others overheard his offer and crowded around, muttering thanks and looking at him frankly or sidelong depending on their natures.

"You're new here," a Vudrani man with an oiled beard said, ordering a glass of some bright-red cordial on Rodrick's coin.

"I am," Rodrick said. "I heard of the wonders of Jalmeray and thought I'd come see them for myself. I must admit, the place is nice enough. I might pick up a few souvenirs to take back home, if I can find the right ship to carry me back."

"What kind of ship might that be?"

"One where the captain doesn't inquire too closely about who I am, or what I'm carrying with me. Only because I value my privacy, you see."

The fellow stroked his beard. "A man like me might know a man who has a ship like that."

"There could be coin in it for someone who points me toward a helpful captain." He sipped his ale, which was terrible, but it was always terrible in places like this, in every country Rodrick had ever visited. "Of course, someone who thought to take advantage of my good nature might not get gold, or silver, or even copper. They might get paid in steel instead." The man frowned, and Rodrick sighed. "What I'm saying is, if you try to cheat me or lure me somewhere to steal my purse, I'll put a sword through your neck."

The man's expression smoothed out. "Ah, of course. That's just good business sense. I could . . . make a few inquiries. Though that takes time, and effort . . ."

"I'm not showing you the color of my coin on a promise," Rodrick said. "Order another drink on me and call that your advance, all right?"

The man nodded slowly. "Meet me back here this time tomorrow?"

"That works. If you have a friend with the kind of discreet ship we talked about, bring him. We might have things to talk about, and I'll pay for his time, and a finder's fee for you."

The man bowed and slid away, disappearing up the stairs. More risks. Maybe the man was an informant working for the thakur, but if so, Rodrick would just claim it was a misunderstanding— he was only trying to arrange passage home to avoid infringing further on the thakur's hospitality, he had no idea he was talking to a criminal, let alone a man who knew *smugglers*—and hope his charm would see him through. It had done so often enough before. He wasn't entirely sure he'd need a smuggler's help getting off the island, but he wanted to have access to transportation that wasn't arranged by the thakur's people, just in case. Better to have the contingency in place. Such plans had saved him more than once.

He finished his drink and went back upstairs, continuing to saunter through the streets, getting a feel for the city, and coincidentally figuring out the most efficient route to get from the vicinity of the palace down to the docks. When Hrym complained, Rodrick drew the blade and froze him to the outside of the scabbard on his back. After a few minutes, Hrym said, "Someone's following us."

Without breaking stride, Rodrick said, "Dangerous thug? Sneaky agent of the palace? Terrifying djinn armed with scimitars? Street urchin with aspirations to purse-snatching?"

"Woman dressed in leather," Hrym said.

"Ooh," Rodrick said. "That sounds promising."

11
Collector

Rodrick was walking in a residential district, all beautiful homes of stone and jewel-toned glass surrounded by low ornamental fences, with front yards decorated with statues and fountains and shrubs grown in fanciful shapes. After Hrym told him they were being followed, Rodrick continued on, taking a couple of right-hand turnings into narrower streets, then hurrying up a set of stairs to a small courtyard with a few stone benches and a statue of a man sitting on a bull playing a flute (the man was playing the flute, not the bull). He leaned against a wall, Hrym in his hand, and when a woman dressed all in black leather with short blonde hair reached the top of the stairs, he said, "Hello. You've followed me all this way, so I assume you want something?"

She narrowed her eyes, looked around—including upward, as if on the lookout for lurking djinn, which was a bit pointless since they could become invisible—and moved to put a bench between herself and him. Reasonable behavior when facing a man with a sword. "I saw you go into that tavern, but I wanted to speak to you somewhere more private. I was just . . . waiting for the right moment to approach you."

She wasn't pretty, exactly, though that could have been a side effect of her permanent scowl and the short hair, which wasn't particularly flattering on her. She was at least a head shorter than Rodrick, maybe a year or three older, and she looked like the kind of person who'd stick a knife in anyone who tried to steal a kiss; people who dressed mostly in black leather were generally trying to cultivate an air of unapproachability and menace, in his experience.

"Why do you look familiar to me?" he said. In truth, he'd remembered her instantly. He hadn't seen so many black-clad blonde women on this island that he couldn't keep them straight. She was the one who'd been watching him in the streets, when Nagesh was taking him to the palace, but there was no reason to let her know how observant he was. Rodrick made a point of letting people assume he was lazy and unobservant, when he was really only lazy, and even then only about certain things.

"I can't imagine." She met his eyes and lied with a straight face. He could respect that.

"Mmm, a strange woman, so captivated by the sight of me that she stalks me through the streets. It's understandable. I'm very compelling."

She stepped over the bench and sat down. "We might be able to help one another."

He didn't sit, but he did put Hrym away. "I can be very helpful, with the proper incentives. What did you have in mind?"

"You're staying in the palace, an invited guest of the thakur. He's even met with you personally, I understand. That grants you access to places that not many foreigners can reach."

Aha. He was on the inside, and someone wanted his help with an inside job. He wasn't opposed, in theory, but there were some suspicions he needed to voice first.

"By that accent you're trying so hard to disguise, you come from Nex," Rodrick said, and was gratified when the woman's eyes widened. Possibly a misstep, but he couldn't help showing off a little, and maybe it would keep her off balance. He'd met a few people from Nex in Absalom, and knew the flavor of their voices. "I understand some powerful factions in Nex have . . . disagreements with the rulers of Jalmeray." Let the woman think he had a complete and complex understanding of the political situation, rather than just the brief history sketched out for him by a biased priest on the passage across the sea. "If you see me as an opportunity to hire a killer inside the palace, I'm afraid I have to decline. For one thing, I never take on work that is certain to end in my own execution, and for another, I'm not an assassin at any price."

The woman looked around again. "I am well aware of your limitations." She raised one eyebrow and regarded him coolly. "You aren't the only one who knows things, Rodrick. I made inquiries with some friends of mine back home, and learned all about you."

"Not all, surely. I'm a complex man."

"He's not that complex," Hrym said.

The woman ignored the sword. "You're a thief, and a confidence trickster. The fact that you aren't more notorious speaks well of your abilities—most people think you're an adventurer, notable only for the sword you carry. Speaking of, just how many times *have* you sold that wondrous blade of yours?"

"Oh, once or twice. Hrym is very popular, but somehow he always finds his way back into my hands." The first scam he and Hrym had ever pulled together was enchanting an ordinary sword to look like Hrym and selling the fake as the real thing. It was still a reliable fallback job when they couldn't come up with a better scheme. People seldom complained about being duped, though obviously *someone* had, if she'd heard about it. Usually no one liked to admit they'd been played for a fool, which was a great help when it came to providing tricksters with job security. He wondered if she might tell the wrong person about that detail from his background and spoil his plans with the thakur. Probably not; the thakur was unlikely to give an audience to a woman from Nex, or take a message from one too seriously. Still, it might be better to keep her happy. "So it's theft you want, then? I haven't been given the keys to the thakur's private vaults, alas. What do the Arclords want to steal from the palace that *I* could reach?"

She hissed at him. "Speak softly! Don't mention the . . . those particular lords, here, if you're wise. Jalmeray has decent relations with Nex as a whole, but that . . . particular faction . . . is not looked upon fondly on these shores. Yes, it's true I'm from Nex, but I'm here for my own reasons, not a servant of *those* particular wizards."

"Fine, then what do you, personally, as a private individual, want me to steal? Please tell me it's the jewel from the navel of the thakur's prettiest wife—that would be an enjoyable challenge."

She smiled. "Mmm. It would be, wouldn't it?"

Rodrick blinked. This was a more interesting woman than he'd initially supposed.

"But, no. Nothing so . . . adventurous. Or as likely to end with your messy death. I have not come to Jalmeray for jewels—you can find jewels anywhere. I'm here because I love knowledge."

Rodrick grunted. "Knowledge can be nice. Like knowing where a chest full of gold is kept, and how well it's guarded. Or knowing a secret a rich person would rather *keep* secret—that can be useful knowledge. I'm not an intimate of the thakur's, though. I don't imagine he'll tell me anything that could be used as blackmail."

"You misunderstand me. I'm a collector of old things, forbidden and forgotten knowledge, and there's something in the palace I'd like very much for you to collect on my behalf. The thakur has a great library, and in that library there are thousands of scrolls. I want one of them. As a guest in the palace, you have access to the library, yes?"

Rodrick nodded slowly. He'd paid more attention to the parts of the tour that involved the dining room, and the gardens, and the baths, and the long gallery with precious works of art (including some statues small enough to fit into a pocket without making much of a bulge)—but yes, there'd been a library, too, with tall wooden doors carved with the image of a serenely smiling woman with four arms, holding book and pen and scroll and lantern in her many hands. "I do."

"If the scroll in question were to make its way to me, I'd be grateful, and by grateful I mean extremely generous with coin."

Rodrick considered. "Is it likely to be guarded?"

She shook her head. "I doubt the scroll has even been glanced at in centuries. No one will notice if it goes missing. When the Vudrani returned and took the island from the . . . former inhabitants . . . they destroyed most of their works and monuments and buildings, but the Vudrani revere knowledge, and so many of the scrolls and books were kept, stored in a dusty corner of the library, where they've remained ever since. Back home, I came across a very old manifest, listing items that were lost in the emergency evacuation of this island, and while most of the books and scrolls are either uninteresting or exist in duplicate form elsewhere, there's one rare item that would be a crowning addition to my collection. I did some research and found out where the items are housed, and came here in hopes of talking my way into the library as a scholar, but the thakur is very particular about letting foreigners into the palace." She looked him up and down and muttered, "Even though he let *you* in. Why did he do that, anyway?"

"I think I'll keep my business to myself, thanks. We were talking about *your* business. I'm not opposed, in theory, but finding one particular scroll in a vast array of jumbled documents . . ."

She leaned toward him, suddenly eager. "In that, we are lucky. The records I've seen say the scroll was stored in a very distinctive case—I can give you a description. And if you can't find it . . ." She shrugged, doing her best to look like it was a matter of no consequence. "Then I will be disappointed, and you will be unpaid."

Rodrick stroked his chin. It seemed like just his sort of job— low risk for a decent reward. If he'd been asked to steal documents from the thakur's desk, he would have assumed there was some greater intrigue at work, and refused—he was even less willing to be tangled in politics than he was to commit an assassination—but something that could be taken from a library even *he* could access wouldn't be that valuable, would it? He'd met a few collectors in his time, and they were fanatics about the strangest things—particular bits of porcelain from certain places made at certain times, or tiny carvings by artists who'd died a long time ago in impoverished obscurity, or, indeed, very old books and scrolls, sometimes in languages few could be bothered to read anymore.

Which wasn't to say he believed the woman. Safest to assume everyone was lying at all times. But he could take her stated story as a place to begin. Besides, it wasn't as if he couldn't look at the scroll before whisking it out of the palace. If it appeared to be something more than a historical curiosity—if it were labeled "Incantation to Expel the Vudrani from Jalmeray and Usher in the Return of the Arclords," say—he could always change his mind and slide it back onto the shelf.

"What's your name?"

She smiled. "You may call me Grimschaw."

"All right, Grimschaw. Why don't you tell me exactly what I'm looking for, and exactly how much you'll pay me to steal it?"

"Care to come to the library with me?" Rodrick said when they were back in their rooms at the palace. No one seemed to pay any attention to their comings and goings, which meant they were either trusted or considered unimportant or being followed very subtly indeed. The first two were fine with Rodrick, and he couldn't do anything about the third, so no use worrying about it.

"You dragged me through the streets and made me talk to assorted villains all day," Hrym grumbled. "Put me down on a pile of gold. Unless you're planning to take this scroll by force?"

"I wouldn't like to try to fight my way out of this palace," Rodrick said. "If a librarian so much as glares at me, I will walk away and consider it a sign from one of this island's ten thousand gods that my pilfering is not to be."

"Why did you agree to do this, anyway?" Hrym said. "We'll get a trunk full of gold from the thakur. Just the jewels in that scabbard could set us up nicely back home. The money this Grimschaw is offering is nice for the effort involved, but it hardly compares."

"If all goes well, yes, we'll be rich in two days' time. But things could still fall apart on us, and if they do, won't you be glad I took this other job?"

"No. It's a pointless risk. Admit it. You just *like* stealing."

"It's good to do what you love. And, yes, fine, we don't *need* this job, but it seems so easy, and it's hard for me to leave coin lying in the street when all I have to do is bend over and pick it up. Even if I'm caught with the scroll, I'll just say I took it from the library to read because it looked interesting. Oh, you mean things aren't supposed to be removed from the library? Sorry, savage foreigner here, my mistake, please forgive me. We're engaged in a high-risk, high-reward venture right now, and I'm happy to offset that a bit with a low-risk, moderate-reward venture."

"Also a woman asked you to do it, and you like to impress women."

Rodrick made a face. "Grimschaw? I'd sooner kiss a jar of pickles."

"She's a human female. What's the problem?"

"My standards aren't *that* broad, Hrym. She looks like she'd bite anyone who came too close."

"I don't understand at all. You fleshlings all look the same to me." For just an instant, his blade pulsed red, and Rodrick winced. Yes. Once they had this gold, he would seek out a holy man. Maybe not on Jalmeray—they might need to leave in a hurry—but as soon as they landed wherever they ended up, he'd find help for Hrym's . . . condition, however much it cost.

"Yes, well, you're only attracted to gold," Rodrick said lightly. "I wouldn't expect the nuances of my romantic desires to be comprehensible to the likes of you."

"Have fun in the library. Don't accidentally read a book, it might make your head fall off from the unaccustomed weight of knowledge."

Rodrick placed Hrym on the bed, atop a liberal scattering of gold coins. Hrym liked the fancy sword stand, but still preferred to rest like a dragon atop a hoard.

Gnawing his lower lip in worry over that red flash, Rodrick went out into the hall. He wished he'd been able to determine some pattern in Hrym's outbursts—it would be convenient if a flash of red were reliably followed by an explosion of ice and a noted surge in bad luck and general disaster exactly ten minutes later. Or not convenient, obviously, but *manageable*. The nature of demons was chaos, though, so it was too much to hope a demonic taint would present itself with any regularity. As long as Hrym could avoid another outburst of boat-wrecking proportion for a few more days . . . Maybe he should have told Hrym what was happening to him, let him know about his condition. But what was the point? The knowledge could only upset Hrym. Why make Hrym feel bad, when the sword couldn't do anything to prevent his outbursts? Better just to find someone who could help them, as soon as possible. Surely the problem could be cured. Demons could be banished.

Rodrick found the library again without any difficulty. Paying attention to the ins and outs of places, especially places potentially full of treasure, was something he did automatically. He pushed open the tall wooden doors with ease and stepped into the library.

If you liked books, he supposed this would be a sort of heaven—it was certainly a cathedral to knowledge. The floor was all polished marble tiles, and shelves towered halfway to the fifty-foot ceiling, where globes of magical light gently bobbed, casting a bright, even illumination. Some of the shelves held bound volumes, and others had cubbyholes for cased scrolls. Tall ladders on wheels allowed access to the higher shelves. Long tables of dark wood accompanied by straight-back chaired dotted the vast space, each with an alchemical lamp, and overstuffed chairs were placed here and there throughout the room for more comfortable reading.

A male servant, dressed in a vest embroidered with silver, appeared from between a pair of shelves with a book tucked under one arm. He approached Rodrick with rather less deference than most of the servants here showed. "You are Rodrick," he said. "A guest of the thakur. I did not realize you were a scholar."

"Nothing so grand," Rodrick said. "But I do like to read occasionally. I thought I might find a volume and take it back to my room, if that's all right?"

The librarian bowed. "Of course, sir. I would be happy to assist you in finding something suitable."

That was no good. "Oh, there's no need, I'm happy just to browse a bit."

The man frowned. "There are upward of one hundred thousand volumes and scrolls in this library. The chance of stumbling upon something you'd like to read by mere happenstance is low. Won't you let me guide you? Are you looking for histories? Biographies of great figures? Tales of adventure? Or books with . . . intriguing woodcuts?" He didn't quite smirk on that last suggestion, but Rodrick thought he wanted to.

"I will confess my great limitation," he said. "I can read only Taldane, the common tongue of the Inner Sea. This medallion the thakur was kind enough to provide allows me to converse with you, but not to read your language."

The librarian nodded. "That does rather simplify things, as most of these volumes are in Vudrani, or other tongues. We do have a small collection of materials written in your language, though many are very old, and the syntax might be a bit challenging."

"I like to challenge myself occasionally," Rodrick said.

"In that case, come along." The man led Rodrick through the library, deep into the stacks, where shadows gathered. The place should have smelled dusty, but it didn't, just clean. The djinn were excellent housekeepers. The librarian snapped his fingers, and a mote of light broke off from one of the bobbing globes above and drifted down to hang about ten feet off the floor. The small light, about the size of a human head, followed them and illuminated their passage.

In a far corner, ten shelves stood off to one side, a little island of literature, and one armchair stood in a corner beside a low table. There was, incredibly, a bit of dust here. Clearly this part of the library was not a priority. "It's all a bit of a jumble, I'm afraid," the librarian said. "Most of these books and scrolls were on the island when our people returned, though some newer volumes in your language brought by travelers have been shelved here, too, over the years. I think there was some attempt made to organize it, once upon a time—there's a row of books on natural philosophy, and here are a few cookbooks, if you can call what the people of Nex do 'cooking.' But none of it has been properly inventoried yet."

The Arclords had been driven off Jalmeray long centuries before. If the books they'd left behind hadn't been inventoried "yet," they likely never would be.

"There aren't any . . . dangerous volumes, are there?" Rodrick said. "Jalmeray is famed for its magic, and I've heard that some books used by wizards and mystics can be dangerous to handle."

"No, no. Any volumes or scrolls with magical qualities were separated out long ago. Those volumes are kept somewhere else, under proper guard."

Well, that eliminated one concern of Rodrick's—that he was being sent to fetch a scroll of dangerous magical lore.

The librarian went on. "These are no more dangerous than any other book—though any knowledge can be dangerous, in the wrong hands."

"Someone armed with those cookbooks might commit a crime against the appetite, for instance," Rodrick said, and the librarian chuckled.

"Quite. There's not much danger of encountering radical knowledge here. Some of my fellows from the Impossible Kingdoms consider those who live around the Inner Sea to be unlettered barbarians. I can only say that my work would be much easier if they *were* unlettered. Instead, they produce a great many written works . . . but of mostly dubious quality." He peered at a shelf. "It looks like this is where we put most of the old maps, too. Their literature is bad enough, but the cartography is worse. The Taldans produce these obsessive, detailed maps, merely describing what anyone can see at a glance from the back of a flying carpet. And they rarely ever harness the powers of elementals and djinn to simply remake the land into more useful shapes. It's bewildering."

"Yes," Rodrick said. "It certainly demonstrates a shocking failure of imagination."

The librarian seemed to realize he was, in fact, *speaking* to one of the Inner Sea's barely literate barbarians, and he had the good grace to look embarrassed. "Indeed. I should return to my work, but I'm sure you'll find something here to keep you occupied. The books are very old, but they've been magically preserved, so I don't *think* any of them will crumble in your hands. The light will stay with you until you leave. If you need anything, just shout."

Rodrick thanked him, and made a show of perusing the shelf of histories until the librarian was well out of sight. Then he began a more systematic search, groaning when he reached the shelf full of jumbled scrolls—the section of unimaginative cartography the librarian had decried. Most of the scrolls appeared to be maps and navigational charts, none of it particularly interesting. Finally, he found a scroll wrapped in stiff waxed paper shoved way in the back—but a tear in the paper revealed a glimpse of black wood beneath. Aha. Someone had hastily attempted to disguise this scroll case, and Rodrick was always interested in things that people tried to hide.

After glancing around to make sure he was unobserved, he tore the rest of the paper away. The wooden scroll case he revealed was about ten inches long, made of black wood, both ends sealed with blobs of pale wax. There were symbols carved along the sides of the cylinder—wavy lines, spirals, an open eye.

The librarian said there was nothing magical here, but the case certainly *looked* like it contained something occult. The case was sealed, presumably unopened for centuries. Rodrick used his thumbnail to break the wax seal, then slid out the single sheet of rolled parchment inside. It was very old, yellowed and tattered, but when he unrolled it on the table, it was still legible. The scroll was, in fact, a map—at least mostly—drawn in dark ink, sketched with hasty lines that were too thick in some places and too thin in others, but the shape of the isle of Jalmeray was recognizable from charts he'd looked at on the ship during his voyage to the island.

On the southern part of the island, there was a drawing of a triangle, with an eye inside. That symbol was familiar, though he couldn't place it exactly; at a certain point, all occult symbols and runes and sigils started to look alike, stars and eyes and geometric shapes, all terribly fraught with meaning, and all terribly boring. A few barely legible lines were written at the bottom of the map, disconnected phrases including: "southern edge of the jungle," "three hours to walk from the sea," "east of the old temple," and "marked by the sign of the eye." There was a drawing of something, a column or an obelisk, decorated with spirals, wavy lines, and another eye.

Ah, well. Rodrick had seen things like *this* before.

This was a treasure map.

12
The Wicked Counselor

I found this book, *An Account of a Journey to Tian Xia*—is it all right if I take it back to my room?"

The librarian looked up from the shelf he was organizing and laughed. "As long as you remember it was written by a fool and is filled with more nonsense than truth, of course. It has a certain humorous value as a historical curiosity, and is certainly readable enough. Hmm. It's not a particularly valuable item, but I would ask that you not remove it from the palace. Bring it back when you're done, or leave it in your room when you depart the palace, and a servant will return it to me."

"Absolutely." Rodrick smiled and left the library. Those loose, billowing trousers were good for something—he had two scroll cases hidden in his pant legs, shoved partway down in his boots, and he was fairly sure they weren't noticeable. Possibly the librarian would have let him walk out with those, too, but it was better if no one knew he had them, since they wouldn't ever make it back to the library.

Back in his room, he took the scrolls from his pants and tossed them on the bed. "Well, Hrym, this is interesting indeed." He took out the map and spread it on the table, lifting the sword to let him take a look.

Hrym groaned. "A treasure map? *Really?* Didn't you have enough of hunting treasure when we were in Brevoy? Delving into dungeons and being attacked by bandits and chased by yetis and menaced by swordsmen? Look, it even says there's a *jungle*. Why would we ever want to go into a jungle?"

"I don't propose to *hunt* for the treasure, Hrym. This scroll is so old, who knows if there's even anything hidden away under this obelisk anymore? No, I have a better idea."

"That idea isn't 'sell this to the nice woman as promised,' then?"

"We could do that. Or." He took the other scroll case, opened it, and removed the parchment inside. "This appears to be a shipping manifest. 'Eighty barrels of flour, twenty barrels of smoked pork,' that sort of thing. I propose we put *this* parchment in the fancy black scroll case, seal the ends so it looks unopened, and sell *that* to our collector. I'm sure she'll be disappointed when the contents aren't what she'd hoped for, but we'll make sure to get paid before she has a chance to discover the problem, and even when she does, what can she do? It's not *our* fault her information was inaccurate and led her to a worthless bit of nonsense, after all. We did the job we were paid to do. Then, when we're back in Absalom, or wherever we're going, we'll sell the map to some treasure hunter. I'm sure Skiver up in Almas knows some fools who'd pay good money for a reason to come to Jalmeray and poke around in the tiger-filled jungles. Why sell something once when we can sell it twice?"

"That should be the motto on your family crest," Hrym said. "Hmm. It's not a terrible plan, at that."

"That's high praise coming from you, old friend."

Rodrick hid the scrolls away, then summoned a servant—there was a rope you pulled to call for help, it was most convenient—and asked for a tray for supper, unless the thakur wanted the pleasure of his company . . . ? No? All right then.

Rodrick sat on the balcony and read from the book on Tian Xia in the fading light, and soon there was a knock on the door. Rodrick opened it, and was surprised to see Nagesh there, holding a covered tray.

"That's service, to have your meal brought by the thakur's advisor."

"I thought I might join you for the meal, if you like?"

"I'd love the company," Rodrick lied. He took the tray and led Nagesh to the balcony, the advisor pausing to say hello to Hrym before joining Rodrick at the small table. Rodrick put down the tray, took off the covering, and gasped.

The plate held roasted potatoes, a bloody-rare steak so large it overspilled the sides of the plate, fresh rolls of crusty bread, and mushrooms that smelled like they'd been sautéed in the juices of the meat and some wine.

"I heard you were strolling in the foreigners' quarter today, and thought you might be nostalgic for the food of your homeland. We seldom eat meat here, but I found a nice steak and a cook willing to prepare it."

Rodrick didn't let his smile falter. "This is marvelous." How much did the man know about his activities? "When I was out enjoying the festival, I ran into that conjurer—Kaleb, I think his name is? He wanted to apologize for unleashing that horse on us, and took me on a bit of a walking tour."

"I fear his neighborhood is not the most beautiful part of the city."

Rodrick waved that away. "The meanest street of Niswan is a palace compared to some of the places I've seen in Absalom and beyond. I did stumble into the wrong sort of tavern when I was looking for a cup of ale, though. I just wanted a cool dark place, and someone directed me down a set of stairs . . . well, I had to buy drinks for everyone in the place to generate enough goodwill to get out without someone trying to rob me."

The advisor laughed politely. "Surely, with your sword, no one would dare?"

"Ha. Some of that lot would try to steal Hrym himself from me. I kept him sheathed down there, anyway. I didn't think the thakur would appreciate me causing a commotion in his city."

"You are correct in that. The thakur does love order." The advisor leaned forward and closed his eyes. "I confess, I developed a taste for meat when I was studying abroad. Might I have a bite?"

Rodrick cut him off a generous slice of the steak—honestly, it was too rare for his taste anyway, practically still mooing—and offered it on a fork. Nagesh took a bite, eyes closed to enjoy the flavor, and again, for just an instant when he chewed, his mouth seemed . . . *different*. Wider, somehow, his teeth more like fangs. Rodrick suppressed a shiver. Was the man something other than he seemed? A magician as well as an advisor? That wouldn't be surprising, really. Throw a rock, hit a wizard, as Kaleb said.

Nagesh handed back the fork. "Delicious. Might I inquire, have you considered the thakur's offer?"

"Hrym and I have discussed it. We're still weighing our choices. We're both overawed by the thakur's generosity, but . . . we've been together a long time, and have gone through a lot together. We have until tomorrow night to decide, don't we? We'd both like to sleep on it for another night. Well, Hrym doesn't exactly *sleep*, but you see what I mean."

"Of course." If the lack of commitment bothered Nagesh, he didn't show it as he rose. "I'll leave you to your meal in peace. Feel free to walk out and enjoy the city again tomorrow, if you like. I'll look in on you about this time tomorrow evening—we'll see the thakur, and perhaps you can dine with me again, more formally."

"I look forward to it."

Nagesh departed, and Rodrick shut the door after him, then went to sit on the bed beside Hrym. "There's something strange about that man. I'd swear, for a moment, he had fangs."

"You're probably imagining things," Hrym said. "Or maybe he's a vampire."

"Nagesh and I walked together in the sun, Hrym."

"Oh. Maybe Vudrani vampires are different."

"You're very comforting."

"I strive to be so."

"I'm going to go take a bath. I want to think."

"I thought we'd done all our thinking already? We have a plan—we just have to execute it."

"Did you have to say 'execute,' Hrym?" Rodrick rose. "Enjoy your gold. I'm sticking you on that stand and taking the bed for myself when I get back. We've got too many errands to run tomorrow morning, and I need my sleep."

"Feeble fleshling," Hrym said, but fondly, so it probably wasn't the demonic taint talking this time.

Rodrick woke with a gasp to a room baking with heat, flames flickering in his peripheral vision. "Fire!" he shouted, and tried to rise and flee, but something was holding him down—a long golden rope was wound around his body and the bed itself, pinning him in place. He struggled, and the rope tightened like a serpent's coils. Some sort of magic was afoot.

Turning his head in panic, he saw a figure sitting on the edge of the bed. The man leaned forward, and was revealed as Nagesh, face flickering in the flames. "Nagesh? What—"

Rodrick turned his head further, trying to find the source of the fire, and discovered the light came from a fiery creature—an elemental?—shaped like an immense toad, crouching in the corner in front of Hrym on his stand. There were sizzles and hisses as Hrym's icy aura interacted with the elemental's flames, but they weren't outright fighting—that would have torn the entire room apart and killed Rodrick and Nagesh both, so fire and ice were behaving themselves, for now. The only reason Hrym would hold back would be for fear Rodrick would be hurt if he didn't. Rodrick shared that fear.

Once again, Nagesh's face seemed to shift into contours that were somehow inhuman, but in the darkness and mystical firelight, everything looked unreal and flickering. "I understand you need time to think over the thakur's proposal," Nagesh said, patting Rodrick's cheek with force just short of a slap. "I am here to aid your thought processes. You will accept the thakur's very generous offer."

"I am completely persuaded," Rodrick gasped. "I will tell the thakur we agree at this very moment, if you wish."

"I'm not finished. There's a bit more to the arrangement than we discussed earlier. Your friend Hrym will be presented to the visiting rajah, as planned . . . and at the earliest opportunity, Hrym will kill the fool. Spikes of ice through the eyes, freezing his blood in his veins—the precise method doesn't matter. The killing should be simple enough—the rajah will never anticipate an attack from a gift given by the thakur's own hand."

"How about I put a spike through *your* eye?" Hrym said.

"Perhaps your magics would be sufficient to kill me, Hrym," Nagesh said, not taking his eyes off Rodrick. "If that is the price of my service to the thakur, so be it. But my pet elemental will see your friend consumed by fire. You should have never let us know how devoted you were to one another, Rodrick. Weakness is to be exploited. After we give you to the thakur, Hrym, we will keep Rodrick in the palace as an . . . honored guest. And hostage to your good behavior. If you serve as we require, Rodrick will not be harmed. If you attempt to resist . . . my elemental can be summoned again. Or a more mundane servant loyal to me—there are so many—could poison Rodrick's wine, or simply put a knife in his back. But if you are obedient, there is no reason to fear. Once the rajah is dead, you will both be spirited out of the palace and put on a ship sailing away from the island, with all the riches you were promised and your partnership intact. How could our offer be more generous?"

"You could leave out the part about murdering a stranger." Rodrick winced as the rope around his chest tightened further.

"Do you understand what is required of you?" Nagesh's voice was pitiless and dry.

"Absolutely," Rodrick said. "Nothing has ever been more clear." He smelled something he dearly hoped was not his own hair singeing.

"Do you understand, too, Hrym?"

"I'm not deaf," Hrym growled from the stand in the corner. "Get this burning toad away from me."

"Marvelous," Nagesh said. "You did strike me as reasonable creatures." He rose and strolled out of the room, his elemental following after him briefly before disappearing in a cloud of roiling smoke.

Moments after the door shut, the rope holding Rodrick loosened and went slithering toward the open balcony doors, vanishing into the night.

Rodrick heaved himself from the bed, gasping, and went to the fountain to splash cool water on his face and hair. He sank down on the floor beside Hrym.

"So," Rodrick said. "Obviously we're not going to do *that*."

"You mean take part in a plot to murder a rajah of the Impossible Kingdoms? No. I think I'll pass."

"Glad we're in agreement. That simplifies matters. We've bought ourselves some time by letting him think we'd cooperate, at least."

"What good does time do us?"

"Haven't you heard that old joke? I'll even adapt it for our present environment. A man was caught sleeping with one of the thakur's wives. The man was dragged before the thakur, and knew he would surely be sentenced to death. The thakur asked if he had anything to say in his own defense. The man said, 'I am a very wise man. My death would rob you of a great opportunity. You see, I possess secret knowledge.' 'What kind of secret knowledge?' the thakur asked. 'I have the power to teach a monkey how to talk,' the man said. The thakur thought that sounded amazing. He said, 'How long will it take?' 'Oh, I could do it in ten years, Great Thakur,' the man said. 'I will give you one year,' the thakur said. 'If the monkey has not learned to talk by then, you will be executed.' 'I understand, Great Thakur,' the man said, and was set free. The next night he was in bed with the thakur's wife again, and she said, 'Is it true? Can you truly teach a monkey to talk?' The man said, 'Of course not, but I just bought myself a year of life. Anything can happen in a year. I could die. The thakur could die. Or the monkey could learn how to talk.'" Rodrick paused. "You aren't laughing."

"I'm a talking sword. Do you think a talking *monkey* would impress me?" They sat in silence for a moment, then Hrym said, "The thakur seemed like a gentleman. Do you really think that nice old man wants to use me as a tool of assassination?"

"I don't think you get to be the ruler of an entire country by being a nice old man," Rodrick said. "I think it's possible he's involved, but it does seem a little overcomplicated. Surely the thakur could just sink this rajah's ship and blame it on the Arclords, or something."

"Not without enlisting other confederates," Hrym said. "We're outsiders, and if we agreed to this plot, no one would have to know the plan except for us and Nagesh, which makes it much easier to contain. Even if we said anything, tried to warn someone, who would believe us, as savage strangers from a barbarous land?"

The more Rodrick thought about this, the more of a morass it became. "Right. So they arrange to kill the man, then blame the outlander and his evil sword. The very fact that we're outsiders makes it plausible. All very neatly done. But it works better if we *don't* escape to tell a different tale, doesn't it?"

"Oh, the offer to let us sail away on a ship full of gold is nonsense," Hrym said. "It would be a total waste of gold. No, you'll be executed, and I'll be tossed into a vault somewhere, surrounded by fire elementals boiling away my ice so I can't avenge you. That's true whether this is truly the thakur's plan or Nagesh's own plot."

"We can try to get the thakur alone . . ." Rodrick said slowly. "Tell him that Nagesh explained the whole murder plan, and we have some follow-up questions. If the thakur *isn't* part of the plot, he'll be glad we warned him, and he can protect us from Nagesh. And if it really is the thakur's plan . . . we'll have to figure out where to go from there. Whether we could find a way to warn this visiting rajah, or something. It would be tricky with Nagesh watching us, as he surely will, but maybe—"

"Rodrick. You're thinking like, I don't know what—a paladin, maybe. Why don't you think like a thief? Are we interested in rooting out corruption in Niswan? Getting into the middle of either an assassination plot or some kind of power struggle between the thakur and one of his chief advisors?"

"Ah. No. Not particularly."

"What are our goals, then?" Hrym said.

"To get off this island alive, without having to murder anyone in the process, ideally with a lot of gold."

"So let's figure out how to do *that*," Hrym said.

"We could . . . just flee. Arrange passage with the smuggler we're probably meeting tomorrow, and go at the first opportunity."

"Nagesh will be keeping a close watch on us already, won't he? Surely he thinks we might run."

Rodrick nodded. "Yes. That's true."

"I think our best hope is to play along," Hrym said. "And run away when he doesn't *expect* us to run away."

"In that case . . . I don't suppose it changes our plans much, really. We were going to pass off an enchanted longsword as you, sell the fake to the thakur, then get our gold and flee. We should just . . . flee a bit more rapidly, now, before Nagesh has a chance to murder me." He frowned. "How can this possibly not change our plans? Shouldn't this change everything?"

"Don't grow a conscience now, Rodrick. It would be inconvenient. And it *does* change a few things. For one thing, we'll *definitely* have to arrange our own way off the island now. That's no longer contingency, it's necessity."

"I don't suppose we'll ever see that chest of gold the thakur promised me, either. We'd have trouble carrying it out of here, anyway, fleeing from assorted armed men and elementals. Nagesh really wants us to sit around, knowing he's *watching* us, for almost two weeks while you wait for this rajah to arrive so you can kill him? Even if we didn't mind being assassins, how *dull*. I'd never be able to stand it." Rodrick sighed. "It's just as well I took that small commission from Grimschaw, isn't it? And we've got that jeweled scabbard. This trip won't be a total loss." How could it be so painful to lose a large quantity of gold he hadn't even *received* yet? Somehow, it was. "I doubt Nagesh—or the thakur, if he's involved—will give up his plan to kill this rajah, though, just because we slipped away. They'll find some other way to see it done."

"Leave a letter somewhere with a warning for the rajah, if you feel that bad about it," Hrym said.

"The problem with *that* is knowing where to leave the letter. How can I possibly know who to trust?"

"That's easy. I can trust you, and you can trust me, and that's it."

"True enough," Rodrick said, though when he thought of how Hrym pulsed with demonic light sometimes, it did unpleasant things to that trust.

13
Errands

When they left the palace, they were trailed by a eunuch, fortunately, and not a djinni or an efreeti. The man tried to be discreet, but Rodrick had been followed many times by men far more skilled, so he ducked down an alley, and then another alley, and then doubled back, and in no time he'd lost the man, without seeming to do so on purpose. Nagesh himself might be skilled at intrigue, but his operatives were not equipped to follow Rodrick.

Unless this was the *obvious* tail, to draw attention away from a more subtle one . . . Rodrick didn't let his dismay show on his face. Of course, that was it. Nagesh assumed he was an idiot—or just counted on him to underestimate the Vudrani. But they were an ancient empire, with many servants skilled at stealth and spying, and Nagesh was highly placed in the thakur's court. Rodrick wasn't sure what the man's job was, apart from "advisor"—for all he knew, Nagesh was the thakur's spymaster. He'd surely have legions of skilled operatives, and magical ones at that. Thus, the purpose of the bumbler following them was to let Rodrick *know* he was being watched.

Why, a lesser man might have quailed at the idea.

They went to Kaleb's house, pounding on the front door until the conjurer appeared to let them in. He was unshaven and red-eyed, but looked triumphant. "Come in, come in."

Rodrick and Hrym trailed him up the narrow stairs, past the closed doors of other tenants—ones less inclined to explore the cause for frenzied knocking, apparently. The interior here was musty, and Rodrick commented on it.

"We don't have legions of eunuchs or bound elementals to do our cleaning for us around here. The people in this house are scholars, students of the arcane come to Niswan to learn what we can—but we're not wealthy, or supported by academies. Most of us spent everything we had to get passage to this island and secure a place with one of the masters who's willing to teach. There's not a lot left over for maid service." He stopped at the top floor landing, unlocking a door and ushering them in.

The space beyond was surprisingly congenial, with lots of windows letting in light, and enough of those open to keep the room from smelling like the place where dust went to die. There was a good-sized fireplace, clearly made for a much bigger space, an indication that this top floor had been chopped into smaller apartments long ago, which was proven by the ugly plaster wall on one side, contrasting with the beautiful stone of the exterior walls. Flames danced in the fireplace with no apparent source of fuel, an obvious advantage of being a pyromancer.

Kaleb moved a pile of books off a rickety chair beside a table that doubled as a workspace and a dining area and gestured for Rodrick to sit. Rodrick complied, looking around at the shabby furnishings and bottles of powders and books, books, books.

Kaleb put a bare longsword on the table—plain, but not noticeably rusty or bent—along with various pouches and vials. "If you could put your sword beside this one? They should touch, if possible."

Rodrick drew Hrym and rested him on the table, the edge of his crystalline pommel touching the burnished bronze of the other sword. Kaleb bent over to examine Hrym, his nose so close it nearly touched the blade, and Rodrick had a sudden imagining— so strong it nearly seemed a vision—of Hrym pulsing red and shooting out spikes of ice, tearing the conjurer's head off.

But there was no flash, and Kaleb grunted, then straightened and opened a drawstring pouch. He reached inside, taking out a pinch of powder like gold-colored salt, and scattering it along Hrym's length.

The crystalline blade changed color, turning to gleaming steel, the change creeping down Hrym's length and altering as it went. The pommel and hilt changed, too, until they matched the workmanlike grip of the longsword beside it. The two weapons might have been twins.

"Are you all right?" Rodrick said.

"I suspect I'm uglier than I'd like, but I feel fine," Hrym said.

"Good work, conjurer. And the other sword?"

Kaleb nodded, muttering to himself as he sifted a handful of bluish sand from another pouch onto the sword. Its steel turned to glittering ice, and its hilt and grip altered to resemble Hrym's. The swords might well have just switched places. Rodrick reached out and touched the false Hrym's blade, drawing his finger back quickly. The blade was cold, and felt like ice instead of steel. "Good, you got the tactile element right, too."

Kaleb nodded, scowling. "Yes. The alterations will last forever, unless someone takes steps to reverse the spell."

"It's impressive work. You should be proud of yourself. Why so glum?"

"Making a lasting illusion of this complexity is . . . a bit outside my level of expertise. I had to purchase scrolls—don't worry, I bought them from someone discreet—and it took a goodly portion of the jewel you gave me. I should have asked you to pay my expenses, too."

"You certainly could have *asked*," Rodrick said pleasantly. "How about Hrym? Is his disguise likewise perfect and permanent?"

Kaleb shrugged. "I doubt I could suppress his cold if I wanted to, but I also doubt anyone will grab your sword's blade and notice. It—he'll—look like an ordinary longsword until you choose to change him back." The conjurer passed over a small vial of bluish sand. "Pour this on his blade, and it will remove the illusion."

Rodrick prodded the fake ice sword. "Does it talk?"

"Try it," Kaleb said.

"Ah . . . hello, Hrym." Rodrick felt like an idiot talking to an ordinary longsword, even if it did look like his friend.

"What? Can't you tell I'm trying to rest? Leave me be." The new sword perfectly matched Hrym's gruff and curmudgeonly tone.

"I don't sound anything like that," the real Hrym complained.

"It has a couple of other phrases," Kaleb said. "But along similar lines, things to discourage further attempts at conversation. Now, about the rest of my payment." The fire in the hearth grew brighter . . . and then stepped out of the fireplace, taking on the form of a small wolf.

"There's no need for that." Rodrick reached into a pocket and drew out a diamond, even larger than the ruby had been, and tossed it to Kaleb, who caught it deftly. "Don't suppose that longsword came with a scabbard?"

The conjurer held the diamond up to the light, peering at it, then nodded to himself. The wolf climbed back into the hearth, curled up, and became just a fire again. "Hmm? Oh. Yes. I don't have any use for it." He gestured to a scabbard and sword belt of sturdy leather dangling from the back of a chair.

Rodrick strapped the plain scabbard onto his back and sheathed Hrym there. "All right, old friend. You're living a secret life now. Keep conversation to a minimum." He took the fake Hrym and slid it into the jeweled scabbard on his hip. It would be good not to get the two weapons confused.

"Stop moving me around so much," the fake sword complained. "Where's my bed of gold?"

"He's captured you to perfection, Hrym."

"Your mother was a butter knife," Hrym said.

Kaleb snorted.

"Sentient sword insults," Rodrick said. "There's really nothing else like them." He started for the door, then paused. "Remember, this transaction never occurred. If anyone asks why we spoke, we were just reminiscing together about Absalom and complaining about Vudrani food, and you were kind enough to help me find a new sword. Right?"

"For what you paid, if you wanted me to say we were lovers, I wouldn't refuse."

"I don't think that will be necessary, but the enthusiasm is appreciated." He went downstairs, out onto the street, and the eunuch was there, pretending to carefully study a tile mosaic beside a fountain. Rodrick walked directly up to him and said, "Hello there, haven't I seen you in the palace?"

The man seemed torn between running away and lying, and so just stood there, saying nothing.

Rodrick patted the weapon at his hip. "I'm giving up my old sword soon, so I made arrangements to buy a new one. I just don't feel complete without a blade on my hip. Will you be following me to my next stop? I've got a powerful thirst, and I've only found one place in Niswan that serves the kind of ale I like."

"I—ah—regret that my duties—ah—""

"Of course." Rodrick patted him on the shoulder. "Pleasure running into you. I'm sure I'll see you later." The eunuch hurried away, but Rodrick doubted he'd go far. He was more concerned about spies he *couldn't* see.

Next he went to the nameless subterranean bar. Rodrick doubted they were being watched there. A place like that could hardly function if it didn't have measures in place to prevent invisible spies from crowding in.

His friend with the oiled beard was waiting at the darkest corner table with a middle-aged Vudrani woman who showed not very many teeth when she smiled. "I'm captain you-don't-need-my-name, of the good ship none-of-your-business," she said. "I understand you might want to book a trip off this island."

He slipped their mutual friend a few coins and thanked him. "Before you go, remember the value of discretion," he said.

"He won't tell anyone about our business," the captain said. "He knows my work thrives in secret." The man nodded, gave them both wide smiles, and slipped away.

"Then let's discuss that business," Rodrick said.

"I won't transport people who are unwilling, and that includes unconscious or stuffed in a trunk," she said. "Mostly I deal in bringing imports from the Inner Sea region, a bit cheaper than average because I have an arrangement with the authorities who handle the import tax. I do send ships that way, though, and occasionally they carry freight in that direction as well. You can be that freight, but not if you bring trouble down on me."

"I don't expect any trouble," he said. "I'd just rather travel without anyone knowing what ship I'm on, and with someone who won't remember me after the voyage, if anyone comes around asking."

"So you mean to cause trouble, but to be clear of it before anyone notices. Well, I don't object, as long as none of your trouble splashes on me. When do you want to leave?"

Rodrick figured he'd be handing over the sword tonight, and would then be closely watched by Nagesh's people—he was the hostage guaranteeing Hrym's cooperation, after all—so he'd have to escape that surveillance, get out of the palace, make his way to the docks . . .

They agreed on a time in the deep dark middle of the night, and decided the smuggler would wait for him until just before dawn—Rodrick figured if he hadn't made it by then, he wouldn't make it at all.

"I'll need a deposit now," she said, "and the balance to be paid the moment you appear before me on the docks. No getting halfway out to sea and having you say, 'Oh no, I've misplaced my purse,' understand? You don't set foot on my deck until the coins are in my hand."

"I'm offended by your insinuations," Rodrick said. "Don't I have a trustworthy face?"

"Be as offended as you like, as long as you pay."

Once those arrangements were concluded, Rodrick got back on the street. The eunuch was there again, this time half-hiding behind a small tree. Rodrick waved merrily, and the man ducked down farther.

Rodrick glanced upward, looking for a disturbance in the air to indicate a genie's presence, but he saw nothing. Which didn't mean there *was* nothing. Djinni could become invisible. They could be anywhere. The idea of being watched constantly was unpleasant, but it just meant he needed good cover stories, and he came up with *those* as a matter of course.

"Last errand of the day," Rodrick said, walking along with Hrym swinging on his hip. He darted through a few doorways, down a few alleys, up a few streets, and soon contented himself that he'd left the trailing eunuch hopelessly confused and far behind. Ditching him might be pointless, but doing so was a matter of pride. He hurried to the small courtyard where he'd confronted Grimschaw yesterday, and sat on a bench, humming to himself and running mental scenarios, considering possible complications and the consequences and his own potential reactions. He thought they'd get away with everything, barring unforeseen catastrophe—maybe not as rich as he'd wished, but alive, and better off than they'd been when they arrived in Jalmeray.

Grimschaw appeared, sidling up in her skulking manner, which was far more suspicious than just walking up to them directly. She sat on the bench beside him, without looking at him at all, and said, "Do you have it?"

Rodrick reached into the leather bag on his shoulder and drew out the black scroll case, the wax carefully melted to make it look as if it had never been unsealed. "Is this the one?"

Grimschaw stared at the case like a lecherous man at a serving girl's bosom. "Yes. Give it here."

He slid it back into the bag. "Gold first, please."

She reached into a pocket and drew out a leather purse, passing it to him. He opened it up, peered at the glint inside, shook it around a bit to make sure it wasn't rocks or lumps of lead under a layer of coins, then weighed the bag in his hand. It seemed right for what they'd agreed on. He handed her the scroll case and rose. "Nice doing business with you."

"Yes. Most satisfactory." She stared at the case as if she wanted to crack it open then and there. Rodrick did not wish to be in her presence when she did so.

"You might want to put that away," Rodrick said. "Speaking as a thief, if I saw *anyone* staring at something as intently as you're staring at that, I'd assume it was something worth taking, and try my luck."

She nodded quickly and tucked the scroll away. Without another word, she rose and scurried off toward the steps.

It was always possible she'd duck into the first alley and crack open the case and discover the contents were less than she'd hoped, so Rodrick hurried in the other direction, back toward the palace.

In the High-Holy District he saw the eunuch walking ahead, disconsolate, head down, and patted the man on the shoulder again, making him jump. "It's all right, I was just meeting a woman, and didn't want you lurking around. I'd hoped she might be good for a bit of—well, the sort of fun I gather you're not equipped for anymore. Barbaric practice, I've always thought, no matter how lovely it makes your singing voice. I hope you can forgive me?

I know you were just doing your job. Listen, if you don't mention to anyone that I gave you the slip, I won't mention to anyone that I noticed you following me. All right?"

"Yes," the man said, voice nearly a squeak. "Yes, that might be best."

They parted ways at the outer garden, the servant rushing off to make his report, no doubt. Rodrick made a point of strolling through the garden, pausing to chat with various beautiful youths, complimenting them on the majesty of their country and the wisdom of their leaders and offering other such empty fripperies. He walked through the hallways of the palace, whistling to himself, and returned to his rooms.

Nagesh was there, standing in a corner, arms folded, glaring as they came through the door. "Have you been there long?" Rodrick said. "I hope you at least brought something to read. Waiting menacingly in a corner can be very tiring."

The advisor stalked forward. "I've come to remind you of your duties, and of the consequences of refusing—"

"Yes, yes, fine. This posturing really isn't necessary. I'm prepared to hand Hrym over, and he'll do as you've asked. But if we're going to commit this assassination for you, we're going to need payment in advance, and in rather larger quantity."

Nagesh sneered. "You expect me to trust you with coin, now?"

Rodrick sighed. "You had me followed all over the city. I wouldn't be surprised if you put me under guard tonight."

"You remember my fire elemental?" Nagesh chuckled. "It will indeed watch over you while you sleep. Or while you lie awake in terror."

"Just so. Do you think I'll be *more* likely to escape if I'm carrying a chest full of gold? In my experience, that kind of weight limits opportunities for stealthy departures. We don't need to be adversarial, Nagesh. Surely you have some sense of the kind of people Hrym and I are. We're not defenders of light and righteousness—we're pragmatic opportunists out for personal gain. What I mean is, we're *professionals*. Treat us as such, and let us get on with the job."

Nagesh smiled, grin like a sickle blade. "No. You get nothing from me until the work is done. Do not think you can make demands of me." Nagesh spat at Rodrick's feet. "You're just tools. Don't forget that."

Oh well. It was worth a try.

"I will come to collect you soon," Nagesh said. "I can tell you're trying to plot escape—don't bother. It's impossible." He stalked off.

Rodrick considered taking a nap, but he was too keyed up. He wanted to go over the plan again, but Hrym told him he was being an idiot. It wasn't complicated, after all, and it was a trick they'd played countless times before. There were confidence men who specialized in the goldbrick scam, selling golden bars that were really lumps of lead with a thin layer of gilt, and this was a simple variation on that venerable ruse. What could go wrong? Escaping Nagesh's elemental guard later tonight would be the only real problem, and Hrym could trap the creature in a shell of magical ice with ease, since it wouldn't expect Rodrick's battered old long-sword to have such powers.

Rodrick settled for standing on the balcony, looking at the gardens, thinking about escape routes. The key would be to neutralize the fire elemental, then stroll out of the palace as if he had every right to do so, as he'd done for the past days. From there, a brisk walk to the docks, and *away*.

A servant brought him an evening meal, and Rodrick ate just enough to keep his strength up. After eating, Rodrick strapped on the jeweled scabbard—which glittered just as impressively as before, though a few more of its jewels had been removed and replaced with glass by a jeweler who seemed to understand the need to raise funds while keeping up appearances—and sheathed his "new" sword, actually Hrym in disguise, in it. The fake Hrym went into the plain scabbard on his back. He sat and waited, running contingencies through his mind, until Nagesh opened the door. "Come," he said.

Rodrick joined him in the hallway, where Nagesh put a hand on his chest. "Wait. May I take a look at Hrym?"

With a shrug, Rodrick drew the false sword from its place on his back.

Nagesh drew a slim ivory wand from his robe and touched it to the sword, which shimmered, and returned to its original form, revealing itself as an ordinary longsword.

The advisor clucked his tongue. "A nice try, Rodrick. I'm sure such little deceptions work well on oafish country lords out in the provinces, but you must have realized such a switch couldn't work *here*."

"Of course not." Rodrick fought to keep his voice level. "I was just . . . testing you."

"We will call it a childish prank," Nagesh said. "Just your funny Inner Sea sense of humor."

"What?" Hrym said. "I can't see, what's happening?"

"Nagesh noticed our little joke," Rodrick said levelly. "He turned the sword we disguised to look like you back into an ordinary length of steel."

"Oh," Hrym said. "Well. We can't help being hilarious."

"I'm glad you didn't try it in front of the rajah. He might not have found it amusing. May I?" Nagesh held out his hand, and when Rodrick tried to give him the plain sword in his hand, the advisor *tsked*. "Not that. We must restore Hrym to his proper glory."

Rodrick drew his friend from the jeweled scabbard, and Nagesh touched him with the ivory rod, too, dispelling the magic and breaking the spell. "Might as well switch scabbards," Nagesh said, helpfully holding the longsword while Rodrick sheathed Hrym on his back, then handing the other sword back so Rodrick could place it in the scabbard on his hip.

"How did you know?" Rodrick asked. "Really?"

"My boy," Nagesh said, "You're a terrible liar. I could see it in your face. I know about your little theft in the library, too, but don't worry, I don't care if you want to sell some useless old scroll to a collector. The librarian assures me there was nothing of value in the area you explored."

I'm a terrible liar, am I? Rodrick thought. The hell I am. Either there's been an invisible djinni hovering above my shoulder since I got to Jalmeray, or this bastard can read minds.

He concentrated. *Nagesh was sired by goats, he stinks worse than Chelish cheeses, and his beard looks like a rat curled up on his face and died.*

Nagesh turned his head, scowling, and looked as if he wanted to speak, but didn't.

Boo! Rodrick thought, and the man sniffed and looked away.

Mind-reading. Marvelous.

They walked in silence through the palace, Rodrick thinking furiously. They had two weeks to work something out before Hrym would be expected to murder this rajah. Rodrick could ask to spend time with his old friend the sword, and they could come up with . . . with *something* . . . He stopped himself before those thoughts went too far. Nagesh wore a faint smile. How did you plot against someone who could read your mind?

You couldn't. You had to act impulsively. Rodrick was good at improvising, but was he *that* good?

Eventually they reached the same inner courtyard where they'd met with the thakur before. The old man was there, writing poetry again beneath a glowing ball of magical light. He lifted his head when they appeared and smiled. "Gentlemen. So pleased to see you. Have you considered my offer?"

Rodrick bowed formally. "We have."

"I see you have a new sword on your hip," the thakur said. "May I assume this means you've decided to let Hrym go?"

Rodrick nodded. "Hrym and I have been together for a long time, and he was reluctant to leave me, but I convinced him this was the best course. We each want the other to be happy, after all, and I believe he'll be better off as a treasured companion for your friend the rajah than he would be traipsing around the world with me, earning a living by our wits and our strength of arms. Isn't that right, Hrym?"

Hrym said, "Oh, yes. Can't wait."

The thakur rose and approached, reaching out to clasp Rodrick's hand. "I appreciate this greatly, Rodrick, and recognize what a sacrifice it is for you. Gold and jewels are no replacement for friendship, I know, but I hope the riches I give you will at least ease the pain of your separation."

"I'm sure it will," Rodrick said.

"Nagesh? See that Rodrick is compensated as we discussed. Rodrick, you are welcome to stay in the palace for as long as you wish, or Nagesh can arrange passage for you to any port in the Inner Sea."

Ha. As if Nagesh would let him go, even if he *had* pulled off the deception. "I will be delighted to accept your hospitality a bit longer. Opportunities to visit Jalmeray are rare and precious."

"Quite so," the thakur said. "Hrym, are you ready to go with me?"

No choice but to go along with it for now. Rodrick reached back and put his hand on his old friend's hilt.

Then Hrym giggled, a long, demented trill of laughter that began low but gradually intensified in volume until it echoed throughout the courtyard, an unmistakable outburst of madness.

14
Enemies Abound

Rodrick thought quickly, and what he thought about was survival. When Hrym's demonic taint made him giggle and titter, it was inevitably followed by an outburst of power, with random chaos or a destructive surge of icy magic or both.

True, as long as Rodrick's hand was on Hrym's hilt, he'd be shielded from the effects of any ice magic, but as the guards they'd dropped a load of crates on back in Absalom had learned, there were dangers other than being harmed by the ice directly. Hrym was currently in a scabbard strapped to Rodrick's back, and if he shot out a torrent of ice in that state, the scabbard would shatter, driving shards into Rodrick's body. Escaping this situation would be quite difficult with wooden shrapnel severing his spine. He swiftly drew Hrym free.

The next split-second decision he needed to make was where to point the sword. Aiming Hrym at Nagesh was tempting—let the wicked advisor be buried in ice, it would only make it easier to escape—but the man was standing next to the thakur, and there were at least two reasons Rodrick didn't want to risk killing the ruler of Jalmeray. For one, it was possible he was innocent, and that the plot to murder the visiting rajah was all Nagesh's doing. For another, killing or even injuring a king would inevitably lead to greater problems in the future, like being pursued by an entire vengeful nation.

So Rodrick raised the blade high overhead, pointing skyward. Hrym giggled again, and then a cone of swirling ice shot into the air overhead. There was a long, silent moment, and then fist-sized stones of ice began to rain down.

"Assassin!" Nagesh yelled, and shoved the thakur to the ground, shielding him with his body. A disturbance in the air overhead resolved into a djinni, glaring and armed with scimitars, descending in a fury.

"Rodrick!" Hrym shouted. "We're being attacked!"

There was no time to close his eyes and groan. Hrym had no idea what he'd done—from his point of view, they were just in the midst of a mysterious hailstorm, being set upon by armed guards. Rodrick swung the sword toward the djinni, and Hrym obliged by letting out a rush of icy wind powerful enough to send the djinni spinning away through the air. "Cover our escape!" Rodrick shouted.

A thick, freezing fog precipitated out of the air around them, shrouding everything in icy mist. The fog was wonderful at hiding them, and holding Hrym protected Rodrick from the chilling effects of the cloud and the slipperiness of the ground, but now he had to stumble blindly in what he hoped was the right direction to escape the garden.

"What happened?" Hrym said. "Why did that djinni attack us?"

"I'll explain later," Rodrick said. "Right now we need to get *away*." Away, and off the island as soon as possible.

Someone slammed into Rodrick in the mist, knocking him to the ground and nearly sending Hrym spinning from his grasp. Nagesh loomed over him, frost hanging in his beard and in his eyebrows. How had he pursued them? Hrym's fog turned the ground where it touched so slick it was impossible to walk without falling, which should have covered their escape from any foot pursuit. But this was an island of mystics, and anyone with

Nagesh's level of authority doubtless had hidden resources. If he could read minds, maybe he could also run nimbly across ice too.

The advisor bent down toward Rodrick, reaching for his throat. Rodrick swung Hrym wildly, the blade sinking into the man's face—

Or, rather, it should have. Instead, the edge *bounced* off, leaving a thin line like a shallow razor cut. Nagesh howled as if he'd received a much more grievous injury, and his features *flickered* again—but this time, instead of returning to normal, they changed utterly.

Where a darkly handsome human head had been a moment before, there was now an immense serpent's head. Nagesh's true face was covered in gleaming dark scales, the eyes black and shining, his mouth a maw that opened to reveal a pair of curving fangs as long as Rodrick's forefingers. When he cried out, it was a discordant hiss of sibilants. He reached for Rodrick again, and something was *wrong* with his hands, the fingers curling the wrong way, the palms where the backs should be.

Rakshasa! Rodrick swung the sword again, and Nagesh shied away, clearly wary of receiving another cut, however minor. Rodrick had read of such monsters on the voyage to Jalmeray. They were treacherous and vicious, masters of illusion who infiltrated human society in the guise of mortals and sought to sow discord and chaos for their own gain and the love of destruction. In their true forms, they had had the heads of deadly animals, and backward-facing hands, and dreadful claws, and were masters of terrible magics, which apparently included mind-reading and an annoying level of durability. They were nothing Rodrick had any desire to tangle with, but discovering Nagesh was a monster at least made him more confident the thakur wasn't part of the plot to murder the rajah. Maybe if Rodrick could talk to the thakur, tell him the truth—

Nagesh's features blurred and became human again, and Rodrick scrambled to his feet, pointing the blade at the advisor. The rakshasa dove away, the main strength of the icy blast missing him, but it caught his legs, encasing them in ice. At least he wouldn't be chasing them anytime soon. Rodrick ran again, as hard as he could. Being chased by a king's advisor was one thing. When the advisor was a legendary monster, that was another, far worse thing.

"Did that man turn into a *snake*?" Hrym said.

"Not a man. A monster." Rodrick burst from the garden into a hallway, fortunately deserted. Now what? He still had the jeweled scabbard and the useless longsword at his waist, but the treasure map, and the gold they'd made from Grimschaw, and his wonderful shapeshifting cloak, were all back in his room. Did he dare retrieve them? It *was* probably the last place Nagesh would expect him to go, but if the alarm were raised . . .

Doing anything was better than standing around mired in indecision, so he ran down the hall toward his room. The only way he knew out of the palace went past there, anyway, and it wouldn't take long to duck inside and grab his bag. He passed a couple of servants on the way, but they didn't try to stop him, just looked startled at his headlong rush. The thakur might be slowed by the fog, and his djinni guard too, but it was only a matter of time before the defenses were roused. Rodrick *might* be able to fight his way out of the palace with Hrym in his hands, but he didn't want to try. Enough fire elementals could overwhelm Hrym's ice magic, and there were no shortage of such creatures here.

He reached his rooms and burst in, snatching up his pack and turning to rush back into the hallway . . . and only then noticed the toadlike fire elemental squatting beside the door. Waiting, no doubt, to begin his duty keeping Rodrick hostage to ensure Hrym's cooperation. Seeing him with a blade in hand, the elemental rose up, swelling in size, its flames flickering intensely, until it towered almost to the fifteen-foot-ceiling. Horns blossomed from its head, and it became less toadlike and more like some immense devil.

Rodrick swung Hrym at the creature, and a flurry of white ice filled the room, but hissed and turned to steam before it touched the creature. Gouts of fire poured from its mouth and outstretched hands—when had it grown hands?—but a wall of ice formed between Rodrick and the elemental, saving the swordsman from being roasted where he stood. Magical fire met magical ice, and the wall streamed with water. The elemental strode forward, pounding on the ice wall, and it grew over the elemental and formed a dome, enclosing the creature.

"That dome would put out a normal fire," Hrym said sourly. "Not enough air in there to sustain that kind of burning for long. But elementals burn forever, and it will break out soon."

Indeed, the dome cracked under one of the elemental's hammerlike blows, and Rodrick stumbled back, pack dangling from his free hand. He shrugged it onto his shoulder and turned toward the balcony. The elemental and the dome of ice thoroughly blocked his preferred exit, so the only way out was into the gardens. He rushed to the rail and looked down. It was only ten feet or so to the ground, and if he aimed right he'd land in a bush, hopefully one without any thorns—

While he was steeling himself to vault over the railing, Hrym sent out a torrent of ice, and a ramp of smooth white coldness stretched from the rail to a point midway through the garden. Rodrick groaned and climbed onto the slide. Walking down the ramp would be slower, so he just tightened his grip on Hrym and let gravity take hold. He slid so rapidly he ended up on his back, watching the starry sky overhead whip by, until he hit the ground with his feet, spinning sideways and falling off the ramp.

"Very dignified," Hrym said. "Now *run*."

The palace had finally been roused. There were shouts behind him, and the roar of inhuman voices, bound djinn and efreet and more, all being sent to find him. He ran for the nearest wall, raising Hrym before him. "Make a door," he said.

The bolts of ice that Hrym shot forth made the wall first crack and then shatter, and Rodrick stepped through the ragged hole, kicking bits of stone turned to icy shards out of his way.

He paused a moment to get his bearings. They were in a narrow street, palace wall on one side, a wooded hill on the other, part of the forested land that lay outside the city. Turning back to the hole in the wall, he saw figures moving in the garden, including one towering creature of flame, and he had Hrym seal up the hole they'd made with a patch of ice like they'd used on the ship, but thicker.

Rodrick ran for the hill. The slope was gentle at first, but soon became steeper, and he sheathed Hrym so he could grab onto saplings and bushes to haul himself up. At one point he fell and rolled halfway back down the hill, the ordinary longsword's hilt snagging on a bush and getting torn from the jeweled scabbard in the process. Rodrick paused to look for the sword, then decided it wasn't worth the effort—he couldn't sell it for much anyway, and it was extra weight he didn't need to carry. The most important thing now was to get *away*.

Disappearing into the forest was likely his only option, and he was glad when they reached a thickly wooded ridge. "We've got to get to the docks," he muttered. "Which bloody way is it?"

The sounds of pursuit followed them up the hill. Rodrick groaned and rushed in the opposite direction. Getting away from an angry mob was more important than making his rendezvous with the smuggler, who wouldn't be in position for hours yet anyway. Rodrick ran through the dark forest, tripping on every third root, being smacked in the face by branches, and doubtless leaving a path even a blind man could follow. At least his enemies would suffer from the darkness, too, and the trees all around might keep him from being spotted by any djinn soaring overhead. Off to his left, he saw two horned giants seemingly made of fire, and angled away from them. At least he could see the efreet coming.

When the trees began to thin and the ground beneath him became more stony, he came to a terrible realization. Efreet could probably become invisible, just like djinn, so *why* had they let themselves be seen?

He cursed. Because he was being herded, obviously. He stopped short at the edge of a stony cliff, looking down fifty feet to dark water below. He'd reached the edge of the island, or else a cliff overlooking the River Sald, he couldn't be sure—his sense of direction was too muddled. Rodrick looked over his shoulder. The efreet, and who knew what else, were coming, trees going up like torches around them, and he was out of room to run. He put his hand on Hrym's hilt.

"Rodrick," Hrym said from the scabbard, "I have no interest in a heroic last stand. Would you put on that hideous cloak already?"

"Hrym, you're a genius."

"I have a memory, anyway."

Rodrick slid his pack off his shoulder and began scrabbling inside it, drawing out the disgustingly slick length of the cloak of the devilfish. He'd stolen the cloak—or maybe inherited it—from a sorcerer of his acquaintance, but it worked just fine even for those with no particular knowledge of magic. He understood that cloaks of dolphins or manta rays were more common, but that sorcerer had possessed a perverse streak a league wide, and had preferred to shapeshift into something more alarming. Rodrick awkwardly shouldered the pack again, then threw the cloak on over it, fastening it closed at his throat. Just as the first efreeti emerged from the trees, wielding an axe of fire—which seemed like overkill, but perhaps it was just preparing to meet Hrym—Rodrick leapt from the cliff.

The water came at him very quickly. He hoped there weren't jagged rocks hidden just below the surface. Oh well. Better to be dashed to pieces than burned alive. Probably.

Halfway down, he put the cloak over his head, and his vision shimmered. He knew what he looked like, now. He'd seen others make the transformation. The hood closed around his face, the cloak's ragged hem thickening and elongating into seven tentacles, bristling with hooks and suckers. His upper body and head merged into something like an immense egg, with huge white eyes in the center—he was seeing through them, now, and the world was very bright by moonlight, because those eyes were made to suck up every scrap of light in the depths of salty seas. He shouted as he fell, and the voice emerged from the maw at the center of his seven tentacles, a mouth ringed with horrible teeth. Devilfish were at least somewhat intelligent, and could speak, not that he wanted to talk to anyone just now. Hrym and his other possessions were encompassed in the transformation, luckily, though he wished he'd kept Hrym loose, to swing around in a tentacle, maybe.

He hit the water tentacles-first with a terrible impact, stunning him, but devilfish were far hardier than humans, and soon he rolled and slipped beneath the surface. He spun, looking up through the water, and saw flickering flames at the top of the cliff. Would they assume he was dead, and leave him be, or would water elementals be sent down to look for him, and to recover his body?

No, he was being foolish. They probably didn't care about his body, but they *would* care about Hrym. Rodrick might be presumed dead, but a fall into cold water from a height wouldn't harm a magical sword, and Hrym was far too valuable to leave on the bottom of a river.

It *was* the river, he knew—something about the currents and the depth told him it wasn't the sea, speaking to his devilfish senses—and that meant it would lead to the docks if he just followed it down. He twisted his body, flicked his tentacles, and began to speed through the water, moving far more quickly than a human could swim. He was tempted to make for the sea and just try to swim to the far shore—how far was Nex, anyway?—but he didn't have superhuman stamina, or an infallible sense of direction, and the thought of being lost in the lightless depths of the Obari Ocean was horrifying. Besides, there were things in the oceans more dangerous than devilfish, and he didn't relish being some sea monster's prey.

Anyway, he had a ride off the island. All he had to do was reach the docks and hide in the shallows until it was time to the meet the smuggler, and then he could escape Jalmeray and get on with his life. Or try to. The thakur might hold a grudge, but Rodrick would unquestionably be safer with an ocean between them.

Eventually Rodrick noticed ships above, and moved closer to the surface, finally finding the pilings of a pier and nestling there in the water. No reason to become human again until he needed to. He settled down to wait until the appointed hour, absentmindedly snatching up small fish and shoving them into his mouth with his tentacles. Raw fish, eaten fins and eyes and guts and all, were actually quite delicious, at least in this form, and he needed to keep his strength up.

In the dark of the night, Rodrick dragged himself onto the rocks beneath the pier with his tentacles, then transformed back to his human form. He kept the slick cloak on, though, with the hood up, just in case he stumbled upon an agent of the thakur or Nagesh— the former would likely want him captured, but since he'd discovered Nagesh was a rakshasa, the advisor would probably want him killed. The cloak's ragged hem made him look like a beggar. That was fine. He could be a beggar. Beggars wouldn't be attacked on sight. With luck, everyone thought he was dead, and he could meet the smuggler and be away before anyone realized differently.

"Hrym, are you all right?"

"I've been better," Hrym said. "What *happened* back at the palace? Why did the thakur's djinni attack us?"

Rodrick sighed. He'd kept this secret too long, but things were dire enough now that truth actually seemed like the best option.

"Hrym, I didn't mention this before because I didn't want to alarm you, but you've been . . . unwell. For a while."

"What are you talking about? I'm a *sword*. I don't get filthy fleshling diseases."

"I know, but . . . this is different. All those months you spent next to the demon lord in the Lake of Mists and Veils . . . it affected you."

A long silence, and then Hrym said, "Bugger. I soaked up some of his demonic essence, didn't I? Just like I soaked up these ice powers from that white dragon so long ago."

Rodrick had expected disbelief or rage. This was better than either one, so far. "I think so. At first it was just the occasional flash of red light in your blade. Then you started talking to yourself, sometimes, without seeming to realize it. And giggling. Lately, the flashes and the giggles and the mutters have often preceded . . . more violent outbursts, and destructive coincidences, like shattered lamps or cracked roof beams. I'm sorry I didn't tell you earlier—I didn't want to worry you, and at first I hoped the problem would go away on its own. When I realized it was getting worse, I thought we'd take the money we made from the thakur to hire a priest to try and cleanse you."

"I see. I'm the one who nearly blew a hole in the hull of that ship, then?" Hrym said.

"Ah. It seems so."

"Did I . . . did I ruin the job at the little lord's manor back in Absalom?"

"I'm afraid so. I know, I should have told you—"

"It's true, you should have." Hrym's voice rumbled with annoyance. "I'm not a child to be protected from the truth—I'm older than *you*, by orders of magnitude. Didn't it ever occur to you that I might have some ideas about how to solve this problem?"

"Do you?"

"No," Hrym said. "But you should have asked."

Rodrick sighed. "You had no awareness of it happening, and you couldn't help yourself. I didn't want to make you doubt yourself, or blame yourself, or worry, when the fits couldn't be helped. I was hoping to fix you soon. But I'm beginning to think the taint in you, the demonic chaos, has begun looking for opportunities to cause the most damage. Or else we're just stupendously unlucky."

"You kept me by your side, though," Hrym said. "Even after I put your life in danger, and more than once. You never cast me aside, even though I really *am* a cursed blade, now."

"Of course not. There's a circle drawn around us, remember?"

After a moment, Hrym said, "I forgive you. But don't keep secrets like that from me again. I always tell *you* when you have some horrible affliction, such as your face or your voice or your bearing. Do me the same courtesy."

"Consider it done. Shall we find our smuggler and say farewell to Jalmeray?"

"Not a moment too soon. The climate doesn't agree with me. Too hot. And we need to find a cleric immediately once we reach kinder shores. I want this taint *out* of me."

Rodrick clambered from beneath the pier and went up a set of stone steps to the docks. The area wasn't deserted—places like that never were entirely, regardless of the hour—but the activity this late was nothing compared to the thronging bustle he'd seen on his arrival to Niswan. He moved among the laborers and sailors without drawing any undue attention, cloak hiding his face and his jeweled scabbard. Before long, he'd reached the appointed place, a crumbling pier at the far north end of the harbor, suitable only for small craft. The smuggler he'd met in the basement tavern was there, sitting on an upturned barrel, a small boat bobbing beyond her in the water.

"Oh Captain," Rodrick said. "I've come for our ride."

She started and stood up, eyes darting left and right nervously, then nodded. "Of course. Please. Come, board the ship, we should hurry." She moved down the pier toward the craft, but Rodrick didn't follow.

Damn it. The smuggler hadn't asked to be paid before letting him onto the ship. She hadn't been nearly so trusting at the tavern. "The gods are against us, Hrym," he muttered. "All ten thousand of them."

"What do you mean?" Hrym said.

Rodrick didn't answer, just turned and walked—he didn't run, not yet—away from the dock. Maybe he was overreacting, and walking away from his one reliable way off this impossibly irritating island, but—

A net landed on his head, sending him stumbling forward and tangling his limbs.

15
Buyer Beware

Cursing, he managed to wrestle Hrym loose and sliced through the ropes holding him, but by the time he was free the smuggler was shouting, "He's here, the assassin is here!" and there were men with torches and swords pouring from the ship to come after him. The man who'd flung the net over him took one look at Hrym and ran away, but the rest kept coming.

The smuggler might have little respect for the thakur's laws when it came to import/export dues, but she was apparently patriotic enough to report an assassin's attempt to escape, or else she'd just been offered a reward. Possibly both. People were complicated, after all.

Without being asked, Hrym produced another cloud of freezing fog, though it seemed less thick than it had been at the palace—was Hrym getting tired, or were there limits to how much he could gush forth in a day? The attackers—whether they were mercenaries, palace guards, or just good citizens, Rodrick didn't know—went slipping and sliding wildly on the rime-slicked ground as the fog froze everything it touched, and he and Hrym fled.

They emerged from the cloud of icy fog, but didn't stop running. Rodrick's cloak flapped around him, and he considered veering off and diving back into the water, but where would he go from there? He could try to steal a ship, but a craft small enough for him to handle himself would hardly be sufficient for crossing the ocean, and there was still the small matter of his total lack of navigation skills. Maybe he could get his hands on a flying carpet, somehow, or make his way to that haunted island off the coast and hope to find a less scrupulous smuggler there, or—

"Bastard!" a woman shouted, and something struck him across the chest so hard his legs flew out from under him and he landed on his back, groaning. A boot hit him in the ribs, and he rolled over to get away, then scrambled to his feet.

Grimschaw stood, all in black leather, holding a black-hafted spear. At least she hadn't stabbed him. The point looked wicked.

"I don't have time for this," Rodrick growled, swinging Hrym in her direction.

She shoved the spearpoint under his chin. "Don't point that thing at me, or I'll spear your larynx. You *stole* from me, you scum. Give me the scroll. The *real* scroll."

Retaining his bluster with a mob after him and a spearpoint at his throat was challenging, but Rodrick managed. "Our business is *done*, woman, and if you don't like what you bought, that's hardly my fault. Get out of my way, I need to *go*—"

"When I realized you'd *robbed* me, I started watching the palace, thinking you'd come out eventually, but then chaos broke loose there, and I heard rumors that the outlander with his icy sword had tried to kill the thakur. You maniac! I knew you'd come to the docks to escape the island, so I waited for you here. You can go on your way as soon as you give me what's *mine*."

Rodrick could have thrown himself backward away from her spear and simultaneously blasted her with ice . . . but he was in such dire straits that an enemy who only *threatened* to kill him was the closest thing he currently had to a friend. "Grimschaw, let's say I've got this parchment of yours. What's it worth to you?"

"You've already been *paid*."

"Yes, but my rate has changed. If you can get me safely off this island, I'll give you the map."

"You'll— Map. You said it's a map."

"You weren't expecting a map?"

"I . . . expected a coded letter. A cipher. But a map . . . a map makes sense, if time was short . . . I could just kill you, and take the map."

"If you so much as nick him, I'll fill your heart with spears of ice," Hrym said. "Rodrick might die, true, but it won't do you any good."

Grimschaw eased off on the spear a bit. "You . . . you impossible . . . I have no wish to get tangled in your crime. You're a fugitive! What kind of lunatic attacks a king in his palace?"

Why did she have to be so obstinate? "I have no incentive to help you, Grimschaw, so I suggest you provide one for me. If the thakur's people take me, your map will end up back in their library again, only this time, they'll *know* it's there, and you won't have such an easy time stealing it again."

She ground her teeth. "Fine. I may be able to help. Or know people who can."

"Marvelous. Where's your ship?"

She shook her head. "Not here. I don't have a ship at the dock. My friends are camped elsewhere on the island."

"That's fine. I don't find Niswan particularly hospitable right now anyway. But we need to *go*."

Grimschaw turned on her heel and stalked off, away from the docks, toward a narrow red stone street. Rodrick hurried after her, sheathing his sword. Soon they reached a plain wooden cart, suitable for a humble farmer, with a deep-chested workhorse hitched to the front. A few crates were loaded in the back, but there was room for him to ride, maybe hunched down, if not entirely out of sight. "A carriage would be better," he said. "Something where I wouldn't be quite so visible."

She glared at him, then reached into the back of the cart and touched the floor. There was a click, and a board rose up on concealed hinges, revealing a space inside that Rodrick would probably fit into, if he contorted himself properly.

"Oho," he said. "You're a bit of a smuggler yourself."

"A *collector*," she said. "Some things just need to be collected more discreetly. Get inside. Hurry, before someone notices you."

It was possible she'd deliver him to the thakur for a reward, but she seemed to genuinely want the map more than anything else, so he climbed into the cart. She closed the lid over him, sealing him into the darkness, and something scraped above him. She was probably moving crates over the lid, to conceal the trapdoor . . . or prevent him from climbing out. Well, whatever made her feel better. He could always blast his way out with Hrym if need be, or use his cloak to transform into a devilfish—even seasoned wood would be no match for those mighty thrashing tentacles.

"She's not too fond of us, is she?" Hrym said. "It's a shame she's our only hope."

"You work with the resources you have."

"Fair enough, but it's a bad situation when the only resource you have is a person who wants to murder you and loot your corpse."

Rodrick yawned. The flight from the palace and subsequent adventures had exhausted him, and he hadn't been able to sleep while lurking in the harbor in devilfish form. "I'm going to sleep, Hrym. You take first watch."

"Oh, certainly. I'll be sure to wake you if I see anything of note in the midst of this complete darkness. I'm sheathed, you idiot."

"It's a bit tight in here for me to snuggle up with your bare blade, Hrym. You have ears. Or, if not ears, some kind of auditory sensory apparatuses. Use those."

Being cramped in the hidden compartment of a cart wasn't as pleasant as sleeping in the guest quarters at the palace, but he'd suffered such precipitous changes in circumstances before and lived through them. Rodrick pulled his cloak around himself more tightly and went to sleep, exhaustion outpacing worry for once.

Rodrick woke, tried to roll over and stretch, and banged his knuckles and elbows on the cramped wooden confines of his box. His cramps had cramps. Things weren't so black anymore, at least—there was sunlight filtering in through cracks in the trapdoor above him and on both sides. The cart bounced unpleasantly along some rough track—that jostling was what had awakened him—and there was no sound but the rumble of motion. "How long was I asleep?" he asked.

"Some hours. We were stopped twice and the cart was searched, with soldiers standing right in the wagon bed, but they didn't notice the hidden compartment. I think Grimschaw might have handed out a bribe or two. We left the city behind some time ago, I suspect. I heard birds singing recently. Have I mentioned I hate the countryside?"

"Not since the last time we were in one." He thumped his fist against the cart, making a loud knocking sound. "Grimschaw! Let me out of here!"

The cart stopped, and someone climbed into the back of the cart. "Quiet, you fool." She'd never been overly friendly or complimentary, but any vestige of civility she'd possessed was gone now. Ah, well. It was understandable. He didn't usually spend time with people he'd duped after the duping was done.

"I'm afraid I need to relieve myself, and I'd rather not do it in this box."

She hissed in frustration, but the crates moved away, and the lid creaked open. Rodrick climbed out in stages, stretching his arms overhead, rolling his head on his shoulders, and sitting on the floor of the cart with his legs still in the compartment, massaging his thighs to work out the pins and needles. "I know what it's like to be buried in a coffin, now," he said. "I think I'll take cremation."

"I'd be happy to throw the first torch on your pyre," Grimschaw said, and her expression gave him no doubt that she meant it.

Rodrick looked around. They were on a track in the woods, more or less, though the trees weren't the sort he was used to—this was closer to jungle than the forests of the lands north of the Inner Sea. The path they traveled was largely overgrown, and it meandered away to the east. "Where are we?"

"The outskirts of the Segang Jungle. It's a sort of . . . nature preserve . . . adapted over the years by Vudrani druids. They filled it with plants and animals from the Impossible Kingdoms, a bit of wilderness from their homeland transplanted here."

"Perfectly safe, then?" Rodrick said. "Just one of the thakur's gardens on a larger scale?"

She shook her head. "Not at all. It's full of wild things, and deadly things, and there are always rumors of various forbidden— or at least frowned-upon—cults operating from the depths of the jungle, in forgotten temples or hidden shrines."

The map in Rodrick's pocket probably indicated one of those temples, unless he missed his guess. It would be very amusing if they marched right past the place marked on the map on their way to freedom. He'd have to enjoy the joke privately, though; he didn't think Grimschaw would appreciate it. "Sounds like a charming place to visit."

"I've traversed it successfully before. We could travel around the jungle to reach our destination, but it would take longer, and I'm sure you're as eager to be rid of me as I am to be rid of you. It's not trackless waste inside. There are still druids tending the plants, maintaining the magics that let some of them grow in what would be an inhospitable climate, and there are several hunting lodges, too. Wealthy foreigners like to come here, and pay exorbitant fees to go on 'traditional Vudrani hunts,' stalking wild creatures that are exotic by their standards. They're surrounded by armed guides, of course, so they're in no danger. We'll be in rather more peril, but that sword of yours should keep us safe."

"I'm ready when you are," he said. "I think I'll ride *outside* the box this time, though."

She shook her head. "We'd have to abandon the wagon and proceed on foot soon anyway. We might as well start now." She took a pack from the driver's seat and strapped it on her back, then unhooked the horse from the wagon. It stood patiently until she swatted it on the rear, and then it turned and trotted back along the track.

"Think it'll find its way home again?" Rodrick said.

She shrugged. "The jungle can be awkward to traverse even on foot. With a horse it would be impossible. Someone will find the beast and consider it a gift from the gods. Unless it strays from the path. Then it will be eaten, I'm sure, and some predator will count its own blessings. There are always other horses. Come."

As they walked, the jungle grew deeper, and soon they were enclosed by stands of towering trees wrapped with vines. They moved through verdant ferns and around clumps of mushrooms in virulent greens and oranges, past fallen logs rapidly being turned to soil by rot, with the click and buzz of insects and the calls of strange birds providing music of a sort. The air was thick and moist and smelled of vegetation and the strange perfumes of alien flowers.

Grimschaw had something more than a knife and less than a sword in her hand—she called it a machete—and she used it to slash a path when the vines and branches before them were too thick to proceed otherwise. Rodrick swung Hrym a few times in similar fashion until the sword complained of the feeling of sap on his blade, and after that, he settled for following in Grimschaw's wake. The devilfish cloak was a bit warm, but he kept it on, because it protected him from being lashed by branches. He liked having a potential weapon Grimschaw didn't know about, too.

Something rustled in the trees off to the left, then subsided. "Ah." Rodrick said. "You mentioned predators. What sort of predators?"

She shrugged. "Dire tigers, big cats the size of ponies. Venomous plants, some of them capable of uprooting themselves and walking around. Lizards bigger than horses that spit acid. Birds so immense they can, and do, feed on those lizards. Snakes big enough to swallow you whole. Insects that would love nothing more than to burrow inside you and lay eggs. Other things, I'm sure."

"Perhaps we could invest in a few of those armed guards you mentioned." Rodrick kept Hrym in his hand, though the weight made his wrist ache. Grimschaw had inspired a higher-than-usual level of vigilance in him.

Grimschaw shook her head but didn't stop walking. "You have the equivalent of an ancient white dragon in your hand. I think you'll be fine."

"Your confidence is—"

Something as big as a man blurred out of the trees and smashed into Grimschaw, driving her to the ground. At the first impression of orange fur and black stripes, Rodrick thought it was a tiger—he'd seen pictures and heard them described, though he'd never seen one in the flesh—but this thing crouched over Grimschaw's fallen form like a person, and when it lifted its head to look at Rodrick, its eyes were intelligent.

Rodrick was also fairly sure ordinary tigers didn't wear pants.

16
Jungle Manners

Rodrick pointed Hrym at the beast. "Can we kill this cat-man without hurting Grimschaw?"

"Precision," Hrym muttered, and a single arrow of ice shot forth from the end of the blade.

The creature somersaulted away smoothly, the icicle embedding itself harmlessly in a tree beyond. The thing bounced to its feet and lifted hands made monstrous by claws. Its eyes flickered past Rodrick, and something like a smile twitched across its bestial face. Rodrick spun, slashing out with Hrym, sending forth a fan of icicles that caught an approaching tiger in the throat, dropping it in a heap of blood and meat mere feet from where Rodrick stood.

The cat-man—it must be some kind of weretiger—howled as the big cat died.

Rodrick turned back to face his enemy, putting his back to the nearest tree so he couldn't be taken from behind. Except tigers were just big cats, and cats liked to climb trees, didn't they? What was to stop him from being taken from *above*? He raised the sword again, but the weretiger dove into the trees and vanished.

"You can't hide from us," the creature said, voice full of catlike hiss but still intelligible. Rodrick swung Hrym to point in the direction of the voice, but when it spoke again, it came from a different direction. "The archaka will have you. He hopes to kill you himself, but we are permitted to take your legs, your arms, your eyes. The rest of you will be food for a rakshasa. It is a great honor."

What was an archaka? Rodrick didn't know. But that mention of a rakshasa—the creature must have been sent to hunt him by Nagesh.

Grimschaw groaned and started to sit up, and in the moment Rodrick glanced at her, the weretiger struck, leaping from conceal-ment to take him from his blind side.

Just because Rodrick wasn't looking didn't mean Hrym wasn't, though, and the sword sent forth a spiraling cone of ice that caught the weretiger's midsection and sent it flying backward. By then Rodrick was looking in the *right* direction, so he had a good view of Hrym conjuring bands of ice to pin the creature to the ground. It writhed and struggled against the shackles, but couldn't break the magical ice. "Good," Rodrick said. "Now we can ask it—"

Grimschaw howled, leaping upon the weretiger much as it had leapt on her, slashing with her machete until the beast's throat was a ruin. She remained crouched atop the corpse, breathing hard, staring down at it.

"—a few questions, I was going to say." Rodrick sighed. "That was intemperate, Grimschaw."

She turned her head and stared at him with such hatred that he took a step back. "What questions could this abomination possibly answer?"

Ah. She hadn't heard it speak to him, apparently. Maybe it was better to let her think this was an attack of opportunity, and not someone sent to pursue a fugitive.

Grimschaw was still talking. "The jungle is full of dangers, and there's no need to *interrogate* those dangers. As for this thing . . . It attacked me. It *dared*. And after it knocked me down, it didn't even kill me! It ignored me. Me!"

"It didn't kill you because I pinned it with ice," Rodrick said. "You're welcome, by the way."

"Technically, I was the one who sprayed the ice," Hrym said. "Give any thanks and financial gratitude directly to me, please."

"It treated me like I wasn't a threat at all," Grimschaw said. "Such an insult could not be borne!"

What a baffling woman. "Of course," Rodrick said. "You can't go around letting people *slight* you. No one has manners anymore. Do you murder people at dinner parties if they use the wrong fork?"

"This is no dinner party."

"Really? I hadn't noticed." Rodrick froze Hrym to the sheath on his back, then knelt by the tiger. There was a medallion around its neck, etched black metal on a dark chain. The symbol inscribed on it was unfamiliar to him: a circle, its inner circumference lined with many triangles pointing toward the center. It looked like the stylized representation of a leech's mouthparts. Rodrick shuddered.

"Look at this, Grimschaw. Do you think it's the emblem of some cult? Worshipers of some Vudrani god or another, I mean?"

Grimschaw scowled, cleaning the blood from her weapon on the fallen creature's striped fur. "Very likely. They have thousands of gods. I can't be expected to know all their ridiculous beliefs."

Some scholar and devotee of secret knowledge she'd turned out to be. Rodrick felt around until he found the necklace's clasp, then unhooked the chain, removed the medallion, and put it in his pack. Maybe it was valuable, or even magical, though it obviously wasn't a medallion of protection against ice. Or machetes. He patted down the creature, but it didn't have any weapons or coins or keys or maps or letters explaining its exact relationship with Nagesh. Did weretigers ally themselves with rakshasas, or let rakshasas dominate them? Or did Nagesh and this hunter have some other relationship, like membership in a shared cult? The weretiger had said "we," which suggested it wasn't a lone agent.

To distract himself, Rodrick said, "I don't suppose you're religious. You Arclords have only one god, don't you? The wizard Nex."

"Nex was *better* than a god, he was—" She stopped abruptly. "I'm not an Arclord."

"No, no, I misspoke. An Arclord wouldn't have needed a knife to kill this poor creature. She would have opened her third eye and projected a blast of mystic mind-energy, or something. You're a devoted servant, though, aren't you? If Nex *were* a god, you'd be a priest—not a *high* priest, but one of the lower levels who gets the work done and keeps the shrines polished—but since Nex was a wizard, and not a god, you've got no one to pray to. You aren't a magic-user yourself, though? No mastery of the arcane? You didn't spend time studying in—oh, what's it called, the magical college in Absalom? The Obfuscatorium?"

"The Arcanamirium. And, no. My interest in the arcane extends only to ancient texts. I've told you, I'm a collector. There are *many* who come from Nex who have nothing to do with the Arclords. They're not even the leading faction in the country anymore."

Rodrick snorted. "A collector. You spirited me out of the city in a smuggler's wagon, which I noticed was *not* stuffed with rare volumes of forgotten lore, then abandoned said wagon without regard for its contents. You have mysterious 'friends' elsewhere on the island, apparently with a ship. Am I to believe you're a group of devoted lovers of ancient manuscripts, then? With the resources to field a secret expedition to Jalmeray for the purpose of stealing what looks remarkably like a treasure map, marked with the same symbol I saw flapping on an Arclord ship during my journey to the island?" He'd finally remembered where he'd seen the eye inside a triangle before, and it only served to cement his suspicions. "Forgive me if I'm skeptical, Grimschaw. I tell lies for a living. You clearly do not, or you'd be better at it."

She rounded on him, glaring. "Who I am and what my purpose might be don't matter. We have an agreement, don't we?"

"Get me on a ship and safely back to Absalom, or some other friendly port, and the map is yours."

She narrowed her eyes and touched her weapon. "I'll take you to the ship, and send you on your way, but you'll give me the map *before* you depart."

Rodrick shook his head. "You have no strength in your negotiating position, I'm afraid, so stop posturing. I'm not going to trust you or your people. A lot of bad things can happen on the open water. Get me to a foreign port, ideally Absalom or points north, and the map will be yours, and not before—that will be an incentive for you to make sure I have a pleasant and uneventful journey." He looked at the corpse of the weretiger. "But in case you're thinking you can sneak up on me unawares, as this beast did, just remember—I'm going to be keeping my eye on you, and on those occasions when I need to sleep, Hrym will be ever watchful."

"Hmm?" Hrym said. "Oh. Right. Be good or I'll shoot icicles through your face."

Grimschaw took her hand from her blade, turned her back, and began marching through the trees again.

"Do you have to antagonize her?" Hrym said, almost quietly. "Usually you try to *charm* women. You were even nice to that sorcerer with the parasitic twin growing out of her back last year."

"Ah, Zaqen. She was a lively conversationalist. A shame she turned on us. I actually quite liked her, aberrant blood and all. But Grimschaw . . . Some people are immune to charm. Trying to flirt with them is like pouring water onto desert sand—they just soak it up and give you nothing back and don't change a bit themselves in the process. She's a woman on a mission, and keeping us alive is a necessary step. Keeping us *happy* isn't."

They walked for hours in silence, and weren't attacked again, though a few times they paused and waited for large things moving nearby to leave the vicinity. At one point, Grimschaw stopped, turned toward them stiffly, and said, "You did save my life from the weretiger. I realize that. I am . . . grateful."

"The pleasure was mine," Rodrick said.

She nodded brusquely, turned, and continued on, slashing with her machete.

Rodrick pondered whether the thanks were sincere. Expressing gratitude had certainly seemed to pain her, which pointed toward its authenticity, but maybe she was trying to lull him, and make him relax around her. But why? A woman armed with a spear and a knife, even a very big one, was no match for Hrym, and Hrym would be watching over him even if he did let his guard down. Rodrick decided vigilance was still the safest bet, even though being on alert all the time was exhausting. Especially as the day faded toward evening, and the jungle filled with flickering shadows the mind could use to conjure any imaginable danger.

Rodrick was no tracker—he could get around in a city, but forests and jungles were not his milieus—but even he could discern that they were finally following a path of sorts, instead of just hacking their way through, and Grimschaw seemed to know where she was going. He tried to take comfort in someone else's certainty, but he vastly preferred his own, which wasn't available at the moment. Eventually they emerged into a small clearing, where a wooden cabin was halfway through being devoured by the forest—its roof was drifted with leaves, and one wall looked to be held up entirely by a net of tangled vines.

"I've camped here before," Grimschaw said. "We should be safe for the night." She went into the structure, and after a moment, Rodrick followed. It was in little better repair inside, but the floors had been swept clear of debris and there was a lantern resting on an overturned half-barrel.

He propped Hrym in the corner, then put his back against the most solid-looking wall and sat down, legs aching from the long walk. His trousers were stained green with sap—plant's blood. Ah, well. Better than human blood. Or tiger blood, for that matter.

Grimschaw opened her pack and removed a few edible odds and ends—round rolls of bread, dried fish and meat, a block of waxy orangeish cheese. Rodrick sighed as she grudgingly passed him a meager portion. "I ate much better in the thakur's palace," he said around a mouthful of terribly dry bread.

"Then you shouldn't have tried to murder the man."

"That's vile slander. I didn't try to kill anyone. What happened was . . . halfway between an accident and an escape attempt." Grimschaw had thanked him for saving her life, so he thought he might as well extend the hand of camaraderie to her as well. "The thakur's advisor, Nagesh, tried to force us to commit a killing for him, to murder some rajah who's visiting the palace soon. He wanted Hrym to ice the man, so he could blame it on foreign agents, that sort of thing. Nagesh promised us rewards and freedom after the job was done, but he was certainly lying, and anyway, we might not be honest, but we're not murderers. We were pretending to go along with the plan, biding our time until we could escape, but we, ah . . . made a mess of things, and left in greater haste than I'd intended. And with more pursuit."

Grimschaw cut a slice of cheese and chewed it thoughtfully. "Vudrani politics are complex, but the thakur doesn't have a reputation for cutting throats to advance his ends. Manipulating people into cutting each *other's* throats, possibly, but hiring a foreign killer is a new direction for him."

"The assassination probably wasn't the thakur's idea," Hrym chimed in. "Most likely it was all Nagesh's idea. He's a rakshasa, you know."

Grimschaw let out a low whistle. "One of the thakur's chief advisors is a *rakshasa*? Are you sure? Information like that could be very valuable to the right people."

"Sell it to whomever you like," Rodrick said. "Consider it a gift. Though feel free to pass along a finder's fee if you discover a buyer."

"I don't know much about the creatures," she said. "Just that they're fiends, exiles or invaders from another plane of existence, and their very natures embody treachery. Are you sure it was a rakshasa and not something more mundane? Another weretiger?"

"When Nagesh was hurt, and let his illusion drop, I saw he has a snake's head," Rodrick said. "Are there were-snakes? There are those stories of an ancient empire of serpentfolk—but Nagesh has backward hands, just like the rakshasas in storybooks."

"Hmm. Interesting. But evidence of rot in the thakur's court is no concern of mine."

"I'm sure it will delight your masters the Arclords, though."

Grimschaw rolled her eyes. "You sing the same song over and over, don't you, Rodrick? Learn a new one."

"I don't suppose you have a deck of cards? Dice? Any interest in carnal—no, no, never mind, I can't imagine either one of us would have much fun doing that. Well, in the absence of ways to pass the time, I think I'm going to sleep." The light was nearly gone anyway, purple deepening to black. "Hrym, keep an eye on her, in case she tries to murder me."

"I suppose you'll expect me to *stop* her, too," Hrym said. "Honestly, the demands you make."

Rodrick wrapped himself in the cloak of the devilfish, tried not to think about insects burrowing into his brain and laying eggs, and drifted off to sleep.

Rodrick was having a lovely dream, making love to the captain from the voyage to Jalmeray, except this time she had four arms like a Vudrani deity, and she knew how to use *every* one, caressing his chest with one while the others—

He opened his eyes to blackness, and there was still a hand reaching into his shirt. He grabbed the wrist, and something struck him in the cheek hard enough to make him loosen his grip. "Hrym!" he croaked.

"Your sword can't help you." Grimschaw's voice was low and, for once, amused. "Look." Light bloomed, blinding him, but he blinked until they adjusted, revealing a globe of light bobbing over Grimschaw's head. She had the map clutched in one hand, and the machete in the other, blade angled perfectly to chop down onto his neck. The two of them were covered by a glittering dome of bluish light. Hrym was still propped in the corner of the shack, outside the dome, and by all appearances doing his very best to rescue Rodrick, with his spears of ice striking the dome and shattering soundlessly.

Grimschaw smirked. "We're surrounded by layers of force that should hold off Hrym's attacks long enough for me to finish my business. Oops—I actually *am* a wizard. Though not an Arclord—I wouldn't have put up with your nonsense even *this* long if I had the powers of my masters. But I'll be among their ranks someday, especially when I deliver *this*." She rattled the map at him.

"You had me entirely fooled." Rodrick wished his voice weren't still such a croak. He preferred to wake up slowly, with lots of languid stretching and then a nice breakfast before he was expected to talk himself out of certain death. "I suppose we'll be going our separate ways, now. It's a shame. I'm sure if we'd met under better circumstances we would have been bosom friends."

"I'm going to chop off your head," she said. "You can't be allowed to live, Rodrick. You've seen the map—*you* could find the Scepter of the Arclords now, or try, and I don't intend to let that happen. Hrym can cover your corpse in a coffin of ice, if he likes, until he rusts away to nothing in this vile land." She raised the machete.

17
Friendless

Before Grimschaw could behead him, Rodrick activated the cloak of the devilfish.

Seeing through the creature's eyes wasn't like seeing through his own, but he was still gratified by her expression of alarm when a lashing tentacle struck her across the face and sent her flying into her own magical barrier.

Sharing an enclosed space with a ten-foot-long creature that weighed a quarter of a ton was unpleasant even if it wasn't trying to smash you with hook-lined tentacles, so he was unsurprised when Grimschaw dispelled the barrier as she scrambled to her feet. She looked at him in horror, and then spears of ice shattered against the walls around her, Hrym's bellowing battle cries—more like very emphatic complaints, really—suddenly audible.

Grimschaw clearly decided escape was a better option than a magical duel with Hrym, and disappeared through a hole in the wall into the night. Rodrick transformed back into himself, not even gasping. Devilfish could apparently survive just fine without water to breathe, at least for a little while. That was good to know.

"Rodrick!" Hrym said. "Are you all right?"

"I am. Slightly poorer than I was a few minutes ago, but intact." He got to his feet, looking into the darkness, and sighed. He doubted she'd attack him again—at least not immediately—but it would be safer to stay awake. He sat down beside Hrym. "She got the treasure map."

"Mmm," he said. "Inconvenient."

"Let's review," Rodrick said. "We're being pursued by weretigers sent by Nagesh, possibly members of some cult. We're probably *also* being pursued by legitimate agents of the thakur, though I doubt Nagesh wants any of them to find us. We've lost our guide, and our way off the island. Said guide is an agent of the Arclords. Oh, and she wants me dead, too—she said she has to kill me because I've seen the treasure map, and I might be able to find something called the Scepter of the Arclords, whatever that is. She was chattier than usual, I suppose because she thought I'd be dead in a moment."

"Scepter of the Arclords," Hrym said. "Have I heard of that before?"

"You'd know that better than I would." Sometimes Hrym knew strange things, information picked up over his centuries of existence, but his memory was a patchwork at the best of times. "I'm sure it's something important. Worth killing for, anyway."

"People will kill for a piece of bread," Hrym said.

"True, but they won't usually voyage in secret to an island controlled by a hostile empire to hire a thief to steal a map that *leads* to a piece of bread."

"That does seem like a lot of work for bread," Hrym conceded. "So, now that you've outlined our current circumstances, friendless and alone in a foreign land, what do we do?"

"Try not to die?" Rodrick said.

"Yes. That's always step one. Do we need to discuss our goals again? Do you want to get revenge on Grimschaw, or try to steal this Scepter of the Arclords?"

"By all ten thousand gods of Vudra, no, I don't. Then I'd have the Arclords after me, *too*. I want to get off this stupid island and forget I ever came here."

"Good boy. Then get some rest, and we'll keep heading south. If all else fails, I'll make a boat of ice and you can *paddle* us back to familiar shores. With a paddle made of ice, I'm assuming."

"That's a terrible plan."

"Of course it is. I'm not the planner, I'm the muscle. But maybe the prospect of sitting in a freezing boat for days on the open sea will stimulate your planning glands."

"There's no such thing as planning glands."

"How would I know that?" Hrym said. "The inner workings of fleshlings are mysterious to me."

Apparently walking doesn't stimulate the planning glands, Rodrick thought as they trudged through the jungle. They'd started walking at first light, and several hours later, they hadn't been attacked or eaten, but they also hadn't found anything to eat themselves. Grimschaw had gotten away with her pack, and though Rodrick still had his own, he'd come to the unpleasant realization that while gold was pretty, it wasn't particularly *edible*. Perhaps some of the things in this jungle were. He saw what looked like fruit, some-times, and berries, but they might well be poisonous. The only animals that came close enough for him to possibly spear with an icicle were small lizards the size of his palm, and he wasn't hungry enough to risk eating one of those. Yet.

"What's the new plan?" Hrym asked, as Rodrick slashed a dangling vine out of the way with the blade. "Pfagh!" Hrym was still bitter about every drop of sap, even though, as a magical blade, he wouldn't be marred permanently. He could just freeze the stuff, and it would crack and flake right off. Rodrick's sympathy had been small to begin with and had shrunk steadily all morning.

"The new plan is: Keep going south, like you said. Hope we stumble upon one of those hunting lodges Grimschaw mentioned. We've got a bit of gold, still, and we might be able to buy ourselves out of this mess." Assuming the guides were honest folk, and wouldn't try to leave Rodrick in a shallow grave—or feed him to giant lizards—while keeping his purse for themselves. "Failing that, we walk until we hit water and then head down the coast in whichever direction seems easiest. There must be fishing villages or *something* down there. A coastline means boats."

"I'm glad you've seen a map of this place," Hrym said. "I'd hate to think we were wandering blindly."

Rodrick grunted. He'd seen maps on the voyage over, but he hadn't paid attention to anything so trivial as *scale*, and the treasure map had hardly bothered with such niceties. Whether this jungle was a dozen miles across or a hundred, he couldn't say. Moreover, he was only somewhat sure they were heading south. He'd been fairly certain in the morning—the light was clearly brighter in *that* direction, so that must be east, and he'd set their course accordingly—but he could hardly proceed in a rigorous straight line in this overgrown nightmare of a place. "If we get lost I suppose we can climb a tree—or better, you can conjure me a staircase of ice—and we'll get above the tree line and look for the twinkle of water."

He tripped over something harder than a root and stumbled, almost dropping Hrym. He got to his feet and turned, examining the jagged thing that had tripped him up. "That looks like a bit of statuary." He nudged the stone with his foot, and frowned. "It also appears to be stained with blood." Continuing more carefully, he found more splashes of blood—and finally a body, apparently human, with its neck broken, very recently dead. A scrap of a black cloth mask still half-covered the dead man's face. Rodrick knelt to see if there was anything on the corpse worth looting—just instinct, really—but the body didn't have any food on it, or any weapons better than his own. No one ever had the latter, really. The body *did* have a ring on its finger, marked with the same circle-filled-with-triangles he'd seen on the weretiger's medallion. A ball of ice that had nothing to do with Hrym began to form in his gut.

Creeping along carefully, turning his head back and forth to search for any sign of life, straining his ears for the least sound, he winced when a woman nearby shouted, "Leave me alone, or die like your friend!"

Rodrick approached the sound of violence—not his usual tactic, but perhaps he was lightheaded from hunger—and peered through the vines and leaves. Half a dozen figures moved about in a clear space that looked like it had once been a plaza or ritual circle, based on the pieces of worked stone scattered around the perimeter. There were five hulking figures, one of them bristling with orange and black striped fur, the others wearing masks, some simply bandannas with eyeholes cut out, others more complex, including one skull mask fit for a carnival. They carried weapons made of stone and metal, and were attempting to surround an unmasked, petite, dark-skinned woman wearing a form-fitting green top and voluminous yellow trousers tucked into boots, her black hair spiraled up into a bun on the top of her head.

She was cute, certainly compared to Grimschaw, and Rodrick always had a weakness for women, especially attractive women who might be grateful to him for rescuing them. When it was five-against-one and the five included a weretiger and a person wearing the face of a skeleton, it was easy to figure out who to root for. "Shall we play hero, Hrym?" Rodrick said.

"I do the work, you get the rewards," the sword grumbled.

Rodrick pointed the blade from concealment and swept it along the ground, freezing the men where they stood, leading to some rather comical expressions and howls of outrage—which were swiftly cut off when the woman began thoroughly brutalizing them. Rodrick stepped out of the leaves and stared at her in amazement. She was a blur, a flurry, a human wind of flying fists and feet, leaping and spinning and twisting and gouging, and when she stopped moving, standing so still she'd never appeared to move at all, the men were all at best unconscious, leaning against one another or crumpled, with only Hrym's icy bonds around their feet and calves holding them even remotely upright.

She dusted her palms together and looked at Rodrick. She then assumed a fighting posture, half-turned to the side, one foot swept back, the other pointed forward, her hands held up before her. He was unfamiliar with the particular stance, but was convinced it could easily lead her to beating him senseless.

"A friend, I'm a friend!" Rodrick couldn't quite bring himself to demonstrate that by putting Hrym away, though.

"You did try to help me," she said, not changing her pose.

Try? He'd held them still for her! Not that she'd needed the help. He could admit that. "Not that you needed it," he admitted.

She nodded. "It *was* rather easier with all of them standing still." She laughed, then, which was a bit alarming given her stance and the beaten and bloody figures a few feet away from her, but it wasn't anything like Hrym's demonic titter—more a full-throated sound of amusement. "My name is Lais."

"I'm Rodrick. And this is Hrym." He gestured with the sword.

She frowned. "You named your sword. I've encountered such things, but it's usually, oh, 'Widowmaker' or 'Demon's Woe.'"

"Ah, well, Hrym named himself, I think. He's a sword of living ice."

"He didn't mention I can *talk*," Hrym said.

Now her eyes widened. "A sword that speaks! Now *that* I've never seen." She gave a bow. "I'm pleased to meet you, Hrym, and if you were the source of the magic that assisted me, then I give my gratitude to *you.*"

"It was my idea," Rodrick muttered. He stepped forward, looking at the men. "Are these bandits?"

"Perhaps." She sounded doubtful. "They must have been looking to attack the foreigners who sometimes hunt in this jungle. One of them jumped out at me back there—you must have seen what was left at him, if you came from that direction. He saw a woman alone and thought I was an easy victim of opportunity, I suppose. After I fought him off, this lot descended on me."

"You handled yourself very well. Are you from one of the Houses of Perfection?"

She shook her head. "No, but my teacher once taught at one of the monasteries, before choosing a life of seclusion and contemplation. He thinks I'll be ready to try for entry to the Monastery of Untwisting Iron in a few months."

Lais had dispatched half a dozen dangerous men with her bare hands—and a little assistance—and she *might* be ready in a few months? Either her master had exceedingly high standards for his students, or the monks of Jalmeray were even deadlier than Rodrick had imagined.

"I'm pleased to keep talking," she said, "but do you mind if we walk away from these men? Such things tend to attract predators."

Rodrick refrained from groaning, but only just. He hated nature. "Please, lead on."

She walked—east, Rodrick thought, though who could say for sure—and he followed. "Do you live near here?"

"Not in the jungle itself, no. There's a village on the southwestern shore of the island, where I was born, but mostly I stay with my master, in the hills on the outskirts of the jungle, just south of here."

"Ah. South. Which is . . . the direction we're walking."

She gave him a sidelong look and a mild smile he interpreted as belonging to the "country person feeling superior to the clueless city fellow" school. "It is indeed."

"This jungle is . . . quite a place. What were you doing in here?"

"Oh, just part of my studies. I'm often sent into the jungle to live for a few days, with no weapons or tools, surviving by foraging." She spoke as if such a task were no more difficult than sweeping a floor.

Rodrick licked his lips. "You know what's safe to eat here, then?" His belly rumbled on cue.

She laughed again. He could get used to that sound. After all the deceit and treachery it was nice to meet someone who seemed so genuine. "Are you hungry? Here." She reached into a pouch at her waist and drew out a gleaming fruit, skin perfect and unblemished. Rodrick had no idea what it was, but he devoured it, only stopping at the stem and seeds, which he spat into the undergrowth. "Oh, thank you, Lais, I needed that." He paused. "You haven't asked me what I'm doing in the jungle."

"I didn't wish to pry. You stepped in to help me, so I'm in your debt. You're not in mine."

In his debt. He liked the sound of that. When it came to sex, he liked his women eager and enthusiastic, but he was happy to exploit a perceived debt when it came to saving his life.

"I assume you were with a hunting group," she went on, "and either got separated or saw your party killed. It's really not quite as safe as the guides pretend."

"Ah. No, not exactly." What could Rodrick tell her that would make her want to help him? A carefully edited version of the truth, perhaps. "I found a treasure map, and came here with an associate to see if we could find where it led. In the process, we fell afoul of . . . well, I think it's some kind of cult. Here, look, I took this off the body of a weretiger that attacked us." He pulled the medallion out of his pack and showed it to her.

She glanced at it, then looked at it more closely, then shuddered and pushed his hands away. "That is the symbol of Vasaghati the Betrayer. The Knife in the Dark. A grim goddess, devoted to corruption and destruction. Her followers infiltrate organizations and sow discord, for the pure joy of destruction—and to reap what profits come from disaster, of course."

"It hardly seems wise to wear a medallion that marks you as a betrayer," he said. "It rather gives the game away."

She nodded. "As you can imagine, it's difficult to be part of a cult devoted to Vasaghati. How could you trust anyone? How could you be part of a group dedicated to *destroying* groups? Yet there *is* a cult. They call themselves the Knife in the Dark, and when they gather for ceremonies or to plot, they wear these signs to mark them. Never tattoos, but always jewelry, things that are easily tossed away when they need to pretend to be someone else. I'm told that, in their gatherings, if they see anyone who *isn't* wearing the appropriate sign, they kill them on sight."

Rodrick swallowed. "Would, say, a rakshasa be a likely devotee of that god?"

Lais made a face like she'd tasted something sour. "Such vile creatures do not worship any gods—they don't like to admit that even a god is greater than themselves—but they might temporarily serve a god to advance their own goals, and Vasaghati is certainly one whose interests would align with those of a rakshasa. Why? Were you attacked by a rakshasa, too? If so, you're lucky to be alive."

"We were, and we are. But we didn't manage to kill the rakshasa. Lais, those men who attacked you—at least one of them was wearing a ring marked by this symbol. The others may have been, too. I didn't look closely."

She whistled again. "I didn't notice. That explains why they attacked me, then—they knew I wasn't of their ilk, and doubtless feared I'd stumble upon their meeting. It also explains the masks. I've heard criminals in the cities sometimes wear masks so they won't be recognized, but there's little chance of running into a casual acquaintance in this jungle. I wondered why they bothered."

"The weretiger you fought wasn't masked, though."

She shrugged. "The members of the Knife in the Dark guard their identities closely, being both secretive and paranoid, but why wear a mask when you can shapeshift? There have been rumors of a dark cult operating in the jungle, taking over some old abandoned temple or ruin not far from here, but I had no idea it was the Knife in the Dark. If your quest for treasure takes you toward them, I would advise you to abandon your goal. They are the foulest of cults."

"Oh, fear not. I've given up my hopes of hunting treasure. My . . . associate . . . stole the map anyway. We had a falling out over the advisability of continuing in the face of such opposition after the weretiger attack, and parted ways rather angrily. She took all the food, too, I'm sorry to say."

She clucked her tongue. "And now you're in the jungle, with no map, and nothing to eat? What do you plan to do now?"

"Get off this island as soon as possible," he said. "I've seen members of this cult, like that rakshasa, and I'm afraid they won't stop pursuing me until I'm dead."

"Getting you across the sea would go a long way toward making you safe," she said. "The Knife in the Dark is a real threat in Vudra, and they're clearly expanding their reach in Jalmeray, but I don't think they're well established in the Inner Sea. Hmm. I'll take you to see my master. He knows many people from the years before he withdrew from public life, and might be able to find you passage."

Rodrick's thanks were fervent and, for once, entirely sincere, but she just waved them away. "I'm pleased to help. It will discharge my debt to you. I don't think my master has ever met a talking sword—it will be pleasant to show *him* something new, for once."

The jungle's heavy growth began to thin out within the hour. Clearly not a jungle a hundred miles across, then. They emerged into a landscape of low, grassy hills, and when they crested the first one, Rodrick took in the vast sweep of the Obari Ocean, not terribly far away. He wondered where Grimschaw's "people" and their camp were, and if, indeed, they existed at all. Not close by, he hoped. Regardless, he didn't intend to let Hrym get any farther away than the end of his own hand until he was safely free from this place. He didn't want to be ambushed again.

Lais led him over one hill and around another, and when she stopped, Rodrick didn't immediately see why—until she pointed out an entrance cunningly (or coincidentally) hidden by rocks.

"Is that . . . ah, I mean to say . . . does your master live in a cave?"

Lais laughed as if he'd made a joke. "Wait here. I'll tell my master about you—it will go better if we don't burst in on him without warning."

"Of course." Rodrick bowed. Lais disappeared through the rocks. Then: "I bet it *is* a cave. He's a hermit, after all. They live in caves, or holes in the ground, or in the desert, don't they? Or up on top of pillars in the middle of nowhere—what are those called, anchorites? I always wondered how they use the bathroom. I suppose the boy hermits just pee over the side, but when it comes to doing anything *else*, I can see how keeping your balance would be an issue."

"You humans and your repulsive bodily functions," Hrym said. "At any rate, her master is hardly a hermit if he has a student."

"Maybe she's a hermit, too. I'm sure there are girl hermits."

"I think when two hermits cohabit they cease to be hermits. Whatever she is, I like her. No nonsense, and not a whiff of treachery." The sword sniffed, always an impressive feat given his lack of a nose. "Someone who's honest and straightforward is a nice change from all this subterfuge and deception."

Though Rodrick had thought the same thing, he said, "Hrym, we specialize in subterfuge and deception."

"Yes, and it's fine when *we* do it to *other people*. I'm just tired of having it done to us."

"I can't argue with you there. And, yes, Lais is a refreshing change from our last traveling companion. I'm fairly certain she won't try to behead me. I just have a sense about these things."

Hrym chuckled. "This whole trip has seen you handed from one beautiful woman to another. First the captain, then Grimschaw, and now—"

"Grimschaw was hardly beautiful. On her best day, she might be severe. I've known men who liked the attentions of unkind, perpetually disappointed women dressed in leather, and I don't begrudge them their pleasures, but such things never appealed much to me."

"Aesthetics again. You fleshlings make everything so complicated. "

"Complication is the spice of—" he began, but then Lais returned, followed by a man. Rodrick had expected a wizened old fellow of the stick-thin variety, but her master was a great round-bellied, short-legged man surely no older than fifty, with a bald head and a placid expression. He wore yellow silk robes, and paused briefly to brush them off after emerging from the hole where he lived.

"Master," Lais said, "this is Rodrick, and Hrym—"

The man's eyes widened and he bared his teeth. "Demon!" he shouted, and rushed at them, hands raised. After a moment of gape-mouthed shock, Lais narrowed her eyes and joined his assault.

Rodrick lifted his blade. Treachery, he thought.

18
Dragon and Demon

top!" Hrym shouted, throwing up a wall of ice in a semicircle around them. "I am *not* a demon! I am *afflicted* by a demon!"

The bluish shadows of Lais and the master struck the other side of the ice wall, and the man even tried to *climb* it before pausing—more miraculously, he made it almost halfway up before sliding down. After a brief inaudible conferral with Lais, the master said, "What's the difference?"

"It's the difference between someone having a leech stuck to him, and someone *being* a leech!" Rodrick called.

Another quiet discussion, and then the master said, "All right. Take down the wall, and let me examine this cursed sword."

"Do you promise not to attack us?" Rodrick said.

"My student says she owes you a debt. As she is in my charge, that debt extends to me. I will not harm you unless you attack me first."

"Hrym," Rodrick whispered, "I know you can't really control it, but if you discover some deep reserve of inner fortitude, *please* use it to keep from having one of your . . . outbursts . . . in the next few minutes."

"Oh, fine, put the burden on *me*," Hrym said, not quietly at all. "Might as well tell someone afflicted with a pox to use his inner fortitude not to get spots all over his face."

"Yes, fine, point taken."

The wall dissolved, splashing their feet. Lais and her master stepped daintily out of the way, but Rodrick just resignedly let his boots get wet. Wet feet were the least of his problems today.

Lais frowned. "You never told me your sword was cursed."

"Tainted," Rodrick said. "I'm sorry I didn't mention it."

"He only just told *me* a day or two ago," Hrym said.

"Lay the sword down," the master ordered.

"You won't . . . hurt him?" Rodrick said.

The master looked at him, face blank, then slowly shook his head. "Your . . . friend . . . is in no danger from me."

Rodrick placed Hrym on the ground, and the master crouched, passing his hands over the blade without touching it. "This taint inside him, though," the man said. "That will eventually consume him. The sword—Hrym, is it? Hrym, your mind will gradually be overtaken by the taint, until there is nothing left of you, and then you will unleash your powers in a frenzy of destruction. I saw the wall you made. You have other powers of ice?"

"I'm more or less a white dragon in sword form," Hrym said. "It's a long story."

"Mmm." The man betrayed no expression. "I would like to speak to your friend, Hrym. Lais will keep you company."

The master took Rodrick's elbow and steered him away, as Lais began chatting with the sword, voice all forced conviviality. "So, how long have you been a magical sword of living ice?" she said.

"Are we out of your friend's earshot?" the monk murmured after they'd walked some little distance away.

Rodrick nodded. "His hearing is no better than a man's, as far as I know."

The monk sighed. "Tell me, how long has he been tainted?"

"Mmm . . . roughly a year, since he was first exposed. There were no signs for a while, not really, just the occasional flash of red light. Then he started to giggle, and talk to himself. Then the flashes and the giggles started to presage what I've been calling 'fits.' Explosions of ice magic and bursts of random chaos. He made a mess in Absalom, and nearly blew a hole in a ship on the way to Jalmeray, and caused some trouble for us in Niswan with an explosion a few days ago. The attacks are coming more frequently."

"How did this happen? Were you fighting at the Worldwound?"

"Something like that," Rodrick said, but the monk's scowl made it clear he wouldn't accept vague answers. The real story was too complex, and didn't paint Rodrick in the best light. The monk seemed an observant sort, so Rodrick chose his words carefully. "I was part of a group, last year, searching for what I was told was an ancient vault that contained a great artifact."

"Lais mentioned you were a treasure hunter. Dangerous work, but it is one way to see the world."

Rodrick nodded. "Including parts of the world no sane person would ever *want* to see. When we arrived at the vault, however, we discovered it was actually the prison of a demon lord. A mad priest was attempting to let the demon free, and Hrym sacrificed himself by freezing the man solid in magical ice—along with Hrym himself. I wasn't pleased with my friend's sacrifice, though, so over the course of several months, I dug Hrym out of the tomb of ice and freed him. By then he'd . . . picked up some of the demon's taint, through proximity."

"Spellstealer," the monk said, and Rodrick started. He'd only heard that name once before, when a druid speculated about Hrym's true origins. "There are one or two surviving examples of such ancient swords in Vudra," the monk said. "We have lost the making of such things, if we ever knew it. Those swords are not intelligent, like Hrym is. They merely soak up magic from other objects, and from casters, temporarily gaining the properties of the spells they steal, though they are not without their dangers—some say they take a toll on a man's soul. How did Hrym come to be as he is?"

"Apparently a white dragon sat on him for a *very* long time, until Hrym soaked up not just the dragon's magic, but also something of its mind. The dragon's intelligence and love for gold, anyway—the rest of Hrym's personality, I think, just developed on its own. The effects seem to be permanent. At least, he's been like this for a very long time."

"That is very interesting," the monk said. "Worthy of study, too. But for now, we have a greater problem. This taint *will* grow, as you have seen already, until there is nothing left of the Hrym you know. I fear that may happen soon. If he truly has the powers you say, and he begins to lash out unceasingly . . ."

"He'd cover this whole island in ice," Rodrick said. "I'm sure the mystics and arcanists in the capital would be able to stop him eventually, but . . . it would take a long, bad time. Fighting Hrym would be easier if he *were* a white dragon—those, at least, can be killed. How do you kill a magical sword?"

"There are ways." The monk's voice was grim, and Rodrick grabbed his arm.

"No. No killing him. If you don't see a way to help Hrym, I'll take a ship out into the deep ocean, where one more ice floe won't do any harm, and stay with him until his mind seems entirely gone." Rodrick knew that point might well come after it was impossible to escape Hrym's icy madness, or even after Rodrick had been killed by accident, but Rodrick only had one true friend in this world, and he intended to *remain* true, just this once.

The monk looked at Rodrick's hand on his arm, but Rodrick didn't release the grip. The monk nodded, then patted the hand in a friendly way. "All right. I think we might be able to heal him—or, at least, give him a chance. Much of the power for the healing will have to come from Hrym himself. Is he strong-willed?"

"He's the most stubborn creature I have ever met." Rodrick released his grip. Also cantankerous and lazy, but those were less comforting adjectives, so he left them out.

"Good." The master strode back to Hrym. "Friend sword! Do you wish to drive this taint from your body and mind?"

"Nothing would please me more. I don't like being unable to trust myself. Distrusting everyone else, that's fine, that's *natural*, but I prefer reliability in my own mind."

"Then I will return in a moment." The monk disappeared into his burrow, and returned shortly afterward carrying a black disk the size of a dinner plate. The monk sat down cross-legged, the disk in his lap. The thing was made of smooth stone, with a groove etched into it, swirling into the center.

"Is that some kind of magic?" Rodrick asked. "Can it cure Hrym?"

The monk grunted. "Magic, yes. Cure, no. But it might enable Hrym to cure himself."

The old man picked up Hrym and placed him across his knees, the blade resting on the disk. Rodrick tried not to grimace. If Hrym had one of his fits now, the monk might be badly injured, and his magical plate broken too. "Rodrick, it's not necessary, but it's possible you could lend your psychic energy to help Hrym. The process is not without its dangers. Even struggles within the mind can have real consequences. Are you willing to try?"

"For Hrym? Anything." That was at least two entirely honest statements in one day. Rodrick would have to be careful such things didn't become a habit.

"Then sit, and touch his hilt."

Rodrick did as instructed.

"I'd like to help, too," Lais said.

"It's very dangerous," the monk began. "You could be hurt, or killed, or have your mind destroyed."

Rodrick's mouth twisted. The monk hadn't gone into that much detail about the dangers when he'd mentioned them to *him*.

"My debt." Lais shrugged, as if that said it all.

The monk shook his head, and Rodrick expected him to begin a speech that was some variation on "Young people today are foolish and disrespectful," but instead he said, "As you wish. Take Rodrick's hand."

She did, giving it a reassuring squeeze.

"What's going to happen?" Rodrick said.

"You're going to fight a demon," the monk said. "And defeat it, if the gods are good."

"Well, the *good* gods are good," Rodrick said. "But there are evil gods, too, like this god of betrayal Lais mentioned, and they're *evil . . .*" He trailed off, not just because no one was paying attention, but because the monk was humming. It was a low hum, just a hair too variable to be called toneless, and it was rhythmic, a single deep repeating syllable. An answering sound emerged from beneath Hrym, as if the disk itself were singing, or vibrating, or resonating along with the monk's hum. As Rodrick listened—he couldn't stop listening, any more than he could stop his fingernails or hair from growing—his own heartbeat and breathing seemed to slow until they sounded in sync with the hum. His surroundings became hazy, the hills around him and the jungle beyond on one side and the sea beyond on the other turning to watercolor paintings of themselves.

Rodrick felt a sense of lightness and disconnection, but rather than rising out of his body, as astral travelers were said to do, he seemed to be sinking *into* himself, down to unimagined depths, to the interior of some vast subterranean inner space. The only things in the world that seemed real as that warm and welcoming darkness engulfed him were Lais's fingers clutching his one hand, and Hrym's hilt in his other. That, and the sound, the hum, the heartbeat of the world—

Then he was somewhere else.

The three of them—Rodrick, Lais, and Hrym—stood on a vast field of snow. Everything was icy white, except in the distance, where the jagged broken peak of a red stone mountain loomed, smoke boiling into the sky, rivers of molten rock running down its sides, a brighter shade of red. "Volcano," Rodrick murmured. Were volcanoes supposed to be blood red like that? He'd heard of them, but never thought to see one. Was he seeing one now? The monk had said Rodrick could lend Hrym his "psychic" energy, which suggested this was a mindscape, or some kind of waking dream. The monk had also said it was dangerous, which meant Rodrick should tread more carefully than he normally would in a dream.

Lais squeezed his hand, and he stopped looking at the volcano to look at her. Not a dream, no, because she was still entirely clothed—and was she *taller* than before? He was sure she was. She'd been quite short, to begin with, head barely to his chest, and now she could very nearly look him in the eye.

"Look what Hrym has become," she said.

Rodrick was still holding Hrym's hilt, though it felt strange now, smooth and curved, and when he looked, he saw why.

Hrym wasn't a sword anymore. At least, not here. Here, Hrym was an immense white dragon, easily twenty-five feet long from snout to tail, and Rodrick was holding one of the talons of the dragon's foreleg. Rodrick waited a moment for panic, or bowel-loosening terror, or overwhelming wonder, but there was nothing like that. He didn't even feel surprise—it wasn't like he'd failed to *notice* he was standing next to a dragon, holding its dagger-sized claw. He just hadn't thought much about it. The dragon was just *Hrym*.

Even sitting on his hindquarters, Hrym still towered over them, and he turned his serpentine neck to regard them. His head was covered in slender horns, oddly frilled or webbed. "Ha," he said. "This is more like it. I'm fully ambulatory. I believe I could even fly. I could get used to this." He looked around the field. "No gold here, though. Can't say I entirely approve of that."

"That volcano," Lais said.

"The taint," Rodrick said. "That's where the demon is. I think we're inside your mind, Hrym."

As they watched, the volcano shuddered . . . and *grew*, rising another ten feet, cracking the ice all around it. Hrym *roared*, a full-throated dragon's fury. "It wants to melt me," he growled. "We'll see about that. You two. Climb on." Hrym crouched down low so they could reach his back.

Rodrick had never, even once, dreamed of riding a dragon, but Lais scrambled up onto Hrym's back like she did it every day. Rodrick followed, surprised to find that Hrym's scales were neither cold nor hot, and that they were easily rough enough for him to climb his way—slower than Lais had—to a place behind Hrym's neck. They got themselves settled, Lais holding on to the dragon's neck, and Rodrick behind, holding on to Lais. It would have been nicer to have her pressed against *his* back, but this probably wasn't the time to think of such things.

Hrym beat his vast wings and they rose into the air, skimming low over the ice, the volcano approaching at a shocking speed, growing larger and larger. There was no sound but the buffeting wind, and Lais's delighted laughter—all right, it *was* fun to fly on dragonback, though the imminent clash with a demonic taint rather spoiled Rodrick's enjoyment—and, in the background, that low, rhythmic, chanting hum the monk had used to send them or guide them to this place.

Hrym landed on the slopes of the volcano, and where his claws touched, ice spread out, covering the red rock, with great hisses of steam rising up everywhere. Hrym roared again, and unleashed a blast of freezing breath, a wave of cold so thick and dense and frigid that it made his usual attacks seem like flurries compared to a blizzard. Everywhere his breath struck, the red rock turned to white ice, and Hrym threw back his great head and laughed. "Is *this* all it takes? Freeze the taint? This will be easy, then."

Rodrick groaned. "Hrym!" he shouted. "*Never* say 'this will be easy!' I'm convinced there are whole legions of gods who lie in wait just to hear variations on that phrase, so they can teach us the folly of thinking things might work out for the best!"

"Ha!" Hrym said. "You worry too much, Rodrick. You always have. This is *my* mind, after all. I think I know it a little better than you do."

MY MIND a voice boomed, seeming to come from the volcano, but also possibly from everywhere else too.

That voice. It had to be the voice of Kholerus, the demon lord whose prison Hrym had been pressed up against for all those long months. The demon had never spoken while Rodrick tried to free Hrym, perhaps because its prison made communication impossible, but he had no doubt the monster was speaking *now*—or whatever fragment of the demon's identity Hrym had absorbed into himself, along with its taint of chaos. It was a voice of hissing fire and cracking stone.

THIS SWORD WILL BE THE VESSEL OF MY COMING, it boomed. *MY TAINT WILL CONSUME HIM, AND CORRUPTION WILL SPREAD TO ALL WHO WIELD HIM, PASS FROM THEM TO ALL THEY TOUCH, UNTIL I AM MULTIPLIED ACROSS THE LAND.*

"That sounds . . . bad," Rodrick said.

"We'd better kill it, then," Lais said.

"How do you fight a volcano?"

"You don't," she said. "You fight the thing that *lives* in the volcano."

She pointed as something came crawling out of the volcano's opening. The creature was, thankfully, a great deal smaller than the imprisoned demon lord Rodrick had glimpsed—which meant it was only twice the size of the dragon Hrym, instead of a hundred times as large. The wormlike thing slithered out, its eyes black, bulging, and multifaceted, like clusters of fish eggs. The demon's mouth was full of grinding mandibles and oozing sores, drooling a flood of pus and spit that struck the molten rivers of rock and sent up foul-smelling clouds of smoke. The demon's long, segmented body followed, endless red-and-black coils that were part serpent, part eel, and part millipede, with hundreds of twitching legs underneath, each tipped by a trio of daggerlike claws.

"Fine," Rodrick said. "Then how do we fight *that*? It looks no easier to kill than a volcano would be."

"I find that going for the eyes is a good approach." Lais leapt from Hrym's back.

Rodrick slid down to the ground, unsure whether he planned to join her or stop her, but Hrym rushed ahead of either of them, spraying ice in torrents and roaring, and attacked the demon head-on. The two of them rolled and fought, Hrym slashing and clawing as he exhaled ice, the demon scrabbling with its countless limbs. Rodrick stared, then noticed Lais running toward the creature's rear end, where a stinger curled lethally, tall as a small tree. When she reached the monster, Lais seized one of its legs—nearly as tall as the woman herself—and *twisted*. To Rodrick's astonishment, she tore the leg free, tossed it aside, and moved on to the next. If the demon lord noticed, the pain didn't seem to count when compared to its ferocious battle with Hrym, but she at least was *doing* something.

But what could Rodrick do? He wasn't a master of unarmed combat, and he didn't even have a *sword*—

Suddenly, he had a sword, a duplicate of the longsword Hrym had been disguised to look like. He blinked. Well, fine, but *armor*—

He slumped under the weight of a full suit of plate mail, of the sort he'd only worn twice, and those times as part of complicated scams, not battles—

The weight lessened greatly, though the armor didn't seem to change; it just got lighter. Rodrick began to smile. This might not be a dream, exactly, but it was *like* a dream, in that thoughts could affect it, to some extent. He should have realized when he'd noticed

Lais was taller here than in reality—some subconscious desire for more stature had translated itself to actuality here.

Well. Let's see what *conscious* desire could do.

The ground abruptly receded as Rodrick grew himself to giant proportions. He wished the helm away, then changed his mind and made it transparent, instead, then made the whole suit of armor into magical ice instead of impossibly lightweight steel. The sword, too, shifted to resemble Hrym in his true form—or his sword form, anyway; maybe this dragon was his *true* form, in some more fundamental sense.

Rodrick towered over the demon lord now, and he swept his sword down in a great arc, bisecting the monster's body. The severed segments sprayed hideous ichors in green and yellow, and its back end thrashed wildly, unwilling to die. Lais somersaulted away from the thing's throes, then got the hang of the trick herself, growing to a size matching Rodrick's. She grabbed the end of the demon lord still connected to its head and began to twist while Rodrick set about chopping its still-living back end into tiny chunks.

NO! the demon boomed, and it tried to grow, too, and to heal its wounds, but it was no match for an onslaught on three fronts. When next it opened its hideous maw to shriek, Hrym shoved his head *inside* the cavernous mouth and breathed ice down Kholerus's throat.

The demon lord's body crystallized, turning blue, and when Rodrick struck it with his sword, the great worm shattered into fragments. Rodrick ground anything that resembled an eye, or a tooth, or a tongue into icy dust as fine as sand, and Hrym raged about, hurling ice at the volcano until it was all just a smooth hill of whiteness blending in with the plain.

Then they stood and stared at one another. "Is that it?" Rodrick said. "Did we—"

The distant background hum stopped, and the white world vanished.

19
Aftermath and Ambush

Rodrick blinked around in the sunlight. He was sitting on the ground again, holding Hrym's hilt and Lais's hand, at least until she slid her fingers free and stood up.

"The taint is cleansed," the monk said. "I felt it disappear. Are you all right, Lais?"

"That was amazing!" she said. "Have you done this sort of battle often, master?"

He shook his head. "Not often. Psychic battles are common among some mystics, but my interest has always been more in the material world."

"I became a giant! We wrestled a demon!"

The monk smiled, all amused tolerance for the enthusiasms of youth. "And bested it, I see. Hrym, how do you feel?"

"I felt fine before," the sword said peevishly. "But it's possible I feel slightly *finer* now. I do notice my lack of arms and legs and wings rather more keenly than I did before."

The monk handed the sword to Rodrick, who took it, grinning widely, as they got to their feet. "I can't thank you enough. Both of you, Lais, and—what was your name, master?"

"Jayin. I am pleased to help prevent the demonic taint from spreading farther." He frowned, a line appearing between his eyes. "Now that the immediate threat is past, there are your other problems to consider. My student tells me you are being hunted by members of the Knife in the Dark?"

"I think so," Rodrick said. "They—"

His eyes widened, and he raised Hrym. A winged creature was swooping down toward them from the sky, big as a person—much *like* a person, but with the face of an eagle, and great spreading wings, more than twice as wide as it was tall. Was this another rakshasa? Did those with the heads of birds actually *fly*? He pointed the sword, intending to knock the creature out of the sky.

His legs went out from under him and he fell onto his back, Hrym bouncing from his grip. The master's bare foot pressed against his throat, and the man looked down at him, just as placidly as ever.

"It's all right, Rodrick, she's a friend!" Lais said.

"Friend?" he muttered. "You're friends with a rakshasa?" Everything was confusing. He'd thumped the back of his head on the ground and sparkles and black motes overlaid his vision. "Or . . . harpy? No, those have the heads of women and the bodies of birds . . ."

"She's a garuda! Her name is Dhyana. An old friend of my master's."

"Garuda," Rodrick murmured. They'd appeared in the storybook he read on the voyage over, too. They were supposed to be as good as rakshasas were wicked. "Noble creatures," he said. "Protectors. Gallant."

"He flatters me." The bird woman now stood beside Jayin, looking down at him. He had no idea what her expression held. It was because of the beak. Beaks were difficult to read.

He groaned. "Could you take your foot off me, please?" The master complied, and Rodrick sat up, rubbing his head. "Are you all right, Hrym?"

"As long as I don't have to meet any more people," he said. "Did it have to be someone with wings? I just *lost* my wings."

"I very much look forward to finding out what I've missed," Dhyana said. "I brought fish. Shall we eat them, and you can catch me up?"

The interior of Jayin's cave was not a cave at all, but a snug little house built into the hill, its entrance made to look natural in order to conceal it. The house was hardly palatial—monks weren't usually great lovers of material things, in Rodrick's limited experience—but it was comfortable, and hardly seemed subterranean at all, apart from the lack of windows, and the many lamps made up for that. The decorations were sparse, just a tapestry depicting a robed figure in meditation beneath a semicircle of mystic symbols, a shrine to some Vudrani deity or another, and a shelf that held a bowl of Andoren pottery—that probably qualified as exotic, here. This room lacked anything that Rodrick would consider a chair, but there were a profusion of cushions on the rich carpets, brightly colored, and the others seated themselves casually, Dhyana arranging her wings neatly behind her as she knelt, Lais sprawling on her side, her master sitting cross-legged. "Lais," he said. "Perhaps some refreshments?"

She bounced up and set a kettle on a small iron stove, then brought out bunches of grapes and bowls of berries and flatbread and bean paste and arrayed them on a low round table. Rodrick did his best not to gluttonously devour everything, at least until the monk said, "Yes, eat, you've had a long day."

Dhyana chatted with Hrym, who rested on a cushion beside her. "So you two are treasure hunters?"

"We seek our fortunes in different places," Hrym said. That was true enough. "This is a beautiful island, but it hasn't been lucky for us."

"To run afoul of the Knife in the Dark is bad luck indeed. They're not a large cult, I don't think, but if so many attacked Lais in the jungle, they must be having a meeting there. Best to avoid the area now."

Rodrick swallowed the last of his bread, washed it down with a cup of cool water, and said, "Have you heard of something called the Scepter of the Arclords?"

The monk and the garuda exchanged a look, and then the monk said, "Why do you ask?"

Rodrick shrugged. "That . . . might be where the treasure map leads. I'm not sure, but I heard it mentioned. I assume the scepter dates from the days when the Arclords ruled Jalmeray?"

"The Scepter of the Arclords is very famous here, a legendary artifact of great power," Jayin said. "The Arclords left it behind when they fled from the island, and the stories say it is still hidden somewhere on Jalmeray. The unscrupulous routinely try to sell jeweled staves covered in glowing runes, claiming they've found the true scepter, but they're all counterfeits, mere trickery and illusion."

Rodrick would have to remember that. Selling false scepters of the Arclords could be a lucrative scam.

"The scepter is reputedly so powerful it would make even Hrym here seem commonplace in comparison," Jayin went on.

"Doubtful," Hrym said.

"What does it do?" Rodrick said.

Dhyana shrugged, with a great rustling of feathers. "No one knows, not really. Even its provenance is unclear. Was it a scepter that belonged to Nex, inherited by his servants, who in time became the Arclords? A magical rod the Arclords used to maintain order among their servants? No one can say, and the Arclords are notoriously closed-mouthed." Her tone became gentle. "This map you found . . . I hope you didn't pay too much for it. There are people who sell fake maps, as well as fake scepters."

"Ah, no. My partner, she's from Nex, and she had me dig around among some old books and scrolls in a forgotten corner of a library. That's where we found the map." Let them think he'd found it *in* Nex. He was trying not to lie outright, just to be on the safe side, but it was like asking a fish not to breathe water. The shame of Nagesh catching him in mid-scam was too fresh, and who knew what powers garudas had? If she could read minds, he was doomed anyway, but couldn't some creatures detect lies?

"Maybe the map really does lead to the scepter," Lais said. "Wouldn't *that* be a find!"

"Do you still intend to seek this treasure?" Dhyana asked.

Rodrick shook his head. "I just want to get away from here. Besides, the jungle is crawling with the Knife in the Dark, and with my luck they'll be camped right on top of the thing."

"This . . . is very troubling." The monk's tone didn't sound troubled, but that didn't mean much. "You told Lais your associate ran off with the map, because you disagreed with her desire to continue your search?"

"I did say that, yes," Rodrick said, still carefully keeping to the letter of truth.

"If your former partner saw members of the cult and survived the experience, they might well be hunting her. When they find her, they will find this map, and will surely be curious about where it leads. If it does take them to the scepter . . ."

"That would be disastrous," Dhyana said. "Anyone who possessed an object of such power could easily use it to gain influence with the thakur and the Maurya-Rahm. The Knife in the Dark could parlay such a find into positions of untold power, and bring about terrible destruction."

Lais stood holding the tea kettle, a cloth wrapped around the hot handle, her eyes wide. "That would be horrible!"

"It must not be allowed to happen," the monk said. "Dhyana, I think you should fly to Niswan and alert—"

The door burst inward, wood shattering, and a tiger nearly the size of a horse charged into their midst, snarling and lashing out with its claws.

The next seconds were a blur of fur, teeth, blood, and howls. Dhyana snatched up Hrym, bellowing in anguish and rage, and Rodrick dove out of the way before the garuda could point Hrym anywhere in his general direction. He didn't like being around the sword's icy wrath, not without the protective power that came with holding the hilt. But Dhyana didn't try to use his ice magic at all, just swung Hrym like an actual sword, something Rodrick had rarely done himself. Hrym's blade was supernaturally sharp as well as supernaturally cold, and the dire tiger's head tumbled from its shoulders, rolling on the floor.

There was no moment of relief, though, because two others followed the tiger in, equally furred, but moving upright like men—more weretigers, prominently wearing the medallions of the Knife in the Dark. Lais hurled the teakettle at one weretiger's face, and he fell like a branch cut from a tree, giving her room to launch herself at the other, fists and feet in a flurry, driving him back against the wall. The garuda still had Hrym in her hand, and she stepped to the fallen lycanthrope and stabbed him neatly through the heart—he still didn't twitch, unconscious unto death.

Before it even occurred to Rodrick to draw his knife—the only weapon he had on him—the fight was done, and Lais and the garuda were kneeling beside Jayin. Rodrick joined them, looking down at the man, or what was left of him. The dire tiger had struck Jayin fast and hard with claws and teeth, and his body was a ruin, face spattered with blood and eyes glazed and lifeless.

Dhyana dropped Hrym and stalked outside, and after a moment Rodrick grabbed Hrym and went with her. There might be more cultists outside, after all. He didn't make a habit of running toward danger, but being in the room with a man who'd done him a kindness and been killed for his trouble was worse than the prospect of fighting devotees of a treacherous god.

The garuda leapt into the air and spiraled upward, flying in wide circles overhead, as Rodrick walked around the hillside, almost in a daze. There were no other assailants, as far as he could see.

Hrym said, "I liked that old man, Rodrick."

"He . . . I . . . yes."

"The old man saved my life. You know that. Probably my soul, too, if I have a soul."

"We're lucky he died *after* doing so, for sure."

"We brought this trouble down on him, Rodrick. The Knife in the Dark was looking for us. He died because of *us.*"

Rodrick kicked at the ground. "We don't *know* that. Lais came upon the cultists in the jungle, too. They said the Knife in the Dark hunts down anyone who might identify them. This could have happened anyway. It can't be laid at our feet!" But everyone who'd seen Lais's face was dead or frozen in place in the jungle, probably food for predators by now. There was no reason anyone would be looking for her.

"You can lie to others all you like," Hrym said quietly. "Don't you lie to me. Don't you lie to *yourself.*"

Rodrick watched Dhyana swoop through the sky in circles. "Yes. Fine. They came for us. So?"

"I think we should avenge him."

Rodrick frowned at the sword. "Avenge? Where's the profit in avenging people?"

"Gold isn't the only thing that matters."

That was like hearing a fish say water was unimportant. "What's gotten into you, Hrym? I thought most humans were interchangeable bags of fluid and gas as far as you're concerned. When Jayin removed the demonic taint, did he fill the hole left behind with some of his own excessive holiness?"

Hrym snorted. "Don't be absurd. You've said there's a circle drawn around the two of us. The only reason that circle isn't broken forever, the only reason I didn't lose myself to the taint of a demon lord, is because of that monk."

"Granted," Rodrick said grudgingly.

"As far as I'm concerned, that lets him into *my* circle—at least a little, at least for a moment. The cult seems determined to find us anyway. Striking them down would avenge the old man *and* protect us."

Rodrick saw some holes in that argument, and would point them out when the time came, but Hrym had raised a troubling point. "How do they keep finding us, anyway? I don't understand. It's a big island, a big *jungle*, and twice now members of the cult have come straight for us. Did Nagesh mark us somehow?"

Before Hrym could answer, Dhyana landed in front of him. She stalked back and forth as she spoke. "The hills are clear, but I saw movement on the edge of the jungle. More may come. I don't intend to wait for them. Lais!"

The student stepped out of the house, face wet with tears, hands stained with blood. "I couldn't help him," she said. "He was dead, dead before he even knew what happened, and I couldn't help him."

"He is beyond help," Dhyana said. "But he is not beyond vengeance. You know I owed Jayin my life, twice over. Without him, I would have died twenty years ago in a cage, or ten years ago when my wings were broken and I was stranded on that terrible rock in the sea. The past two decades of my life were bought and paid for by Jayin's efforts. I have already lived longer than I should have, by rights, and I will gladly give up whatever years I might have left to kill those responsible for his death."

That's me, Rodrick thought, and couldn't suppress a shiver.

"I'll help you," Lais said. "He was my teacher."

"I'm going, too," Hrym said. "I owe Jayin a debt. Besides, if you're armed with me, this might not necessarily be a suicide mission."

"Thank you, friend Hrym," Dhyana said. "You will make a great difference."

"Hrym," Rodrick said carefully. "Are you *sure* you want to—"

"You don't have to go," Hrym said. "You are what you are, and I don't expect you to be anything else. Maybe you can bury the monk, and burn the corpses of his killers. That would be helpful. Dhyana can wield me in battle. I'll explain how I can be used for more than chopping off tiger heads."

Rodrick closed his eyes for a moment. He spent most of his life doing unpleasant things and not feeling a bit guilty about it. Most people were terrible, and deserved more trouble than he gave them anyway. Admittedly, these particular people were good, but they had the kind of hyperdeveloped sense of honor that coincided entirely too often with violent death. Rodrick didn't want any part of that. He was a pragmatist, and an opportunist, and a survivor, and joining an ill-considered vengeance crusade against a murderous cult wasn't pragmatic, opportune, or likely survivable.

"Don't be ridiculous, Hrym." He opened his eyes. "If you're going, I'm going."

"That circle around us," the sword murmured, almost too low to hear.

Rodrick nodded. That much was never a lie.

"I found this on one of the weretigers." Lais held out her hands. A small compass rested in her palm, arrow pointing back toward the house. "At first I thought it was a regular compass, but it doesn't point to the north. Then I thought, maybe it's magical, and it's the way the cult finds their camp in the jungle—it was pointing that way, at first, toward the trees. But when I brought it outside the needle spun around again, and now it's pointing back the way we came." She shook her head. "I don't understand, or know if we can use it."

"Let me see it," the garuda said, frowning. "My people have a sensitivity to magic. If we concentrate . . . yes. There is some enchantment here."

"Rodrick," Hrym said.

"Yes," Rodrick said. "I had the same thought. If you two would excuse me?" Without giving them time to question him, he hurried back into the little house. The stench of blood and bowels emptied in death made him gag. The lovely, spare space had been transformed into a charnel house. Rodrick snatched up his pack and went back outside. He reached in, removed the jeweled scabbard, and began to walk slowly in a circle around Lais and Dhyana. "What's the compass doing?" he asked.

"It's . . . pointing at you. Following you."

Rodrick threw the scabbard on the ground. "It's this. The compass is pointing to this."

The garuda knelt and examined the scabbard, then tapped one taloned finger on a tiny diamond near the hilt. "Not the whole thing. Just this. Only this gem is enchanted." She pried it out with a talon and held the gem in her palm, then looked at Rodrick. "Where did you come by this?"

He wondered again if garudas could detect lies, and chose his words carefully. "I got the scabbard from a member of the cult." True. It had obviously come from Nagesh, who'd had ample reason to keep track of Rodrick's whereabouts, but let them think he'd taken it in battle. "I thought I could use the jewels to finance my escape from the island. I had no idea it was enchanted so the cultists could find it."

"I suppose it's not surprising that they poison even their treasures," Lais said. "Just be lucky it wasn't cursed, too." Tears welled in her eyes. "Though it was cursed, in a way. It brought death to a man of learning and honor."

Rodrick bowed his head. He was uncomfortable with shame. He didn't feel it often, and when he did, it was that much more acute for its rarity. "This is my fault. I brought the cult down on you. Led them to your door."

"You murdered no one," the garuda said. "And your greed in taking the scabbard . . . it's unfortunate, but understandable. I will not pretend you have no culpability. You do. But if you intend to join battle with us, you can make up for your mistake." She picked up the scabbard. "In the unlikely event that we survive, these jewels will pay for a lavish funeral for Jayin, befitting his nobility of spirit, and to finance Lais's studies with some other master."

Rodrick's fortunes were dwindling more every moment. But Jayin had lost far more than jewels. "Absolutely. Take them. It's the least I can do."

"Almost literally the least," Dhyana said. "And now, to battle. Right after I toss this filthy diamond off a cliff."

"No, wait," Rodrick said. Now that he'd committed to joining them, his pragmatic opportunism could be put to use. "Don't be so hasty. There might be better uses for that diamond. As for battle—you just want to run into the woods and look for cultists to kill? Is that the plan?"

"I have fought in many battles," Dhyana said, staring down her beak at him. "Do you think you know more of war than I do?"

"Highly unlikely," Rodrick said. "But I bet I know a *lot* more about deceit and trickery, and if we use those, we can make sure the battle we fight is the battle that counts."

20
Grimmer and Grimmer

I don't see why I can't walk in with you," Dhyana said, once he'd explained his idea. She had the head of a bird of prey, so glaring was her natural expression, but it was especially pointed now. They were lying on their bellies in the grass at the top of a hill, with good sightlines to the jungle and the sea, so they couldn't be ambushed easily. They still had the diamond in their possession, and until it was gone, Rodrick wouldn't be able to fully relax. It should have been gone *already*, but Dhyana wanted to argue tactics.

"You're a garuda, from a culture famed for its nobility and honor," he explained with the illusion of patience. "No one would *believe* you were a cultist of the Knife in the Dark. There's no way we can make a mask that would hide that majestic beak of yours, either. Also, the wings are a problem. Quite distinctive."

"But I think that, because my people value honor, having a garuda join the cult would be a great coup for the goddess. I would be afforded high honors, I'm sure."

"Possibly," Rodrick said. Dhyana had proven her bravery and formidability, but she did seem to think in straight lines, even when twistier cognitions were called for. "At the very least you would excite a great deal of comment, in the way a couple of human cultists would not. And since we hope to take as many of the cultists as possible unawares, the last thing we want to do is draw attention to our arrival."

"I think he's right," Lais said. "It's better for us if you hide among the treetops, Dhyana, watching. You can help us if things begin to go badly."

Dhyana's feathers ruffled, but she nodded. "All right. Let me take the diamond out to sea, and we can leave when I return."

That was Rodrick's idea. Dhyana would take the enchanted diamond and leave it on some little island a few miles offshore, to make the cult think he'd fled on a ship. Let Nagesh's lackeys waste their time plying the waves in a pointless search. "We'll meet you at the edge of the—"

"Wait." Dhyana shaded her eyes. "Someone is approaching." She was gazing east, across the low hills.

"More cultists?" Rodrick said. If he squinted, he could see movement, but no details.

"If they are, they don't have tigers with them, at least. I see a dozen men, dressed in black. The one in front has a spear . . . They're running this way, splitting up into two groups. It looks like they're going to try to flank us."

"The one with the spear," Rodrick said. "Does she have short yellow hair?"

"Yes."

"Grimshaw." Rodrick grimaced.

"Your partner?" Lais said. "The one you told us about, your fellow treasure hunter?"

"She's the one I told you about, yes. I don't know who her friends are—she always claimed she had other resources on the island. It seems she wasn't lying."

"Is she looking for *you*?" Dhyana said. "Why?"

"I saw the map. I know where to find the Scepter of the Arclords, or whatever the treasure turns out to be. I'm sure she's gathered those men to help her find the treasure, and she's obviously decided to kill me along the way, to make sure I don't try to get it first. As for how she tracked me down—"

"Could she have one of the compasses?"

Rodrick groaned. "When we were ambushed, she was the one who cut the weretiger's throat. She had plenty of time, hunched over its body, to find the compass and take it. She was always a secretive one. It wouldn't surprise me a bit if she did."

"Do we flee, or fight?" Dhyana said. "I have no quarrel with this woman, but if you think she will continue to pursue us, it might be better to settle this now."

"She expects to take me by surprise," Rodrick said. "Let's make a surprise for *her* instead. But do me a favor, Dhyana: I don't care what happens to her thugs, but leave Grimschaw alive. I have other uses for her, if Lais is willing to wrestle . . ."

Dhyana stayed in place while Lais crept one way and Rodrick crept the other. Let the flankers be flanked. Or something. Tactics in battle weren't Rodrick's specialty, but some of the same principles he used in confidence games applied, like using your enemy's assumptions against them.

He lay on his belly in the grass and watched the spot where they'd left Dhyana, Hrym firmly in his grasp, waiting for the signal.

It wasn't a very complicated signal. Dhyana sprang up, standing six feet tall, drawing her longbow and firing arrow after arrow to the southwest, where half Grimschaw's party was trying to creep up on her. Garudas were as renowned for their archery skills as for their gallantry, apparently. Shouts and screams greeted the volley, but no arrows streaked back at her. Dhyana had seen men armed with swords and axes, but nothing that looked like long-range weapons, unless you counted Grimschaw's black spear.

Rodrick bounced to his feet, pointing Hrym toward the screams. The attackers were closer than he'd expected, only fifty or so feet away. Three of them were writhing on the ground, arrow-shot, but the other three were trying to flee. Hrym took care of that, gouts of icy wind pouring forth to knock them flat, and Rodrick moved among them, binding the dying and the merely knocked-down alike with shackles of ice. He prodded one of the ones with an arrow in his leg, pressing the toe of his boot beside the wound and making the man groan. "Are you lot from Nex too?"

The man's only response was a lengthy stream of curses, but he had the same accent Grimschaw did.

"Is this all of you?" Rodrick said. "Or do you have more back at your camp?"

"My brothers will *kill* you, they'll come for us, they'll take revenge." The man sounded pretty pleased about the idea, despite his wound.

"So there are more of you, then. Hmm. You must have a ship. Is it nearby?"

"No, Rodrick," Hrym said sharply. "We stick to the plan. No running away. Not this time. I'd be insane and lost if it weren't for Jayin. If you run, you run without me."

"Oh, *fine*. I just like to consider all my options." He looked across the hill toward the other half of the ambush and grinned. Dhyana was rising into the air, holding a wriggling servant of the Arclords in her claws, his legs kicking wildly, sword dropping from his hand in his panic. She took him up about twenty feet and then dropped him, which was a rather efficient way of removing enemies from the field of battle.

Rodrick loped across the grassy hills toward the melee, and saw what he'd most hoped to see: Lais, grappling on the ground with Grimschaw. The latter was hopelessly outmatched when it came to fighting with hands and feet, her jacket flapping open and her face smeared with dirt and grass, but she managed to struggle free and ran awkwardly off toward the jungle without so much as a glance at her writhing band of villains.

Lais didn't give chase, just brushed herself off and waved to Rodrick. He caught up to her, and could tell by her wide smile things had gone well. "Did it work?" he said.

She held out her hand, displaying a more-battered version of the compass they'd found on the weretiger. "It was in the inner pocket of her jacket. She never noticed that I took it. Or that I slipped the diamond into another pocket."

Dhyana landed beside them. "And did you find the map?"

Lais shook her head, smile vanishing.

The garuda made a disappointed sort of cluck. "That's unfortunate."

"I'm sure she's committed it to memory as well as I have," Rodrick said. "I doubt she needs the map to find the site of the treasure, so taking it away wouldn't stop her. But being pursued by the Knife in the Dark should slow her down. If she does decide to take another run at us, we'll see her coming easily with these compasses tracking her every move too."

"Yes, but when the Knife in the Dark finds her, they'll find the *map*, exactly the thing Jayin was worried about," Dhyana said. "I don't expect us to kill *all* of the cult, even with your plan, and if any of them get away, and get their hands on the scepter . . ."

Rodrick nodded. "I've been thinking about that. Our first goal, obviously, is to stop the Knife in the Dark, and take out as many of their number as we possibly can. But after that . . . we should look for the Scepter of the Arclords ourselves."

"Do you still harbor dreams of becoming rich, treasure hunter?" Dhyana said.

"I can say, with total honesty, that I want nothing more than to present that scepter to the thakur," Rodrick said, with actual total honesty. If the scepter was as powerful a legendary artifact as he'd been led to believe, it might be the way to buy Rodrick out of the trouble he was in. Even if he made it back to the Inner Sea, he didn't like the idea of having to duck his head and hide every time he saw someone Vudrani for the rest of his life, for fear it was an agent of the thakur's vengeance. If he could bring a powerful enough offering, and buy enough time to explain things . . .

"Hmm," Dhyana said. "It may be best. If we survive the clash with the Knife in the Dark, we will see how well you remember this map of yours."

"Yes," Rodrick said. "Continued survival is a necessary prerequisite to any and all of my plans." He glanced at the sun. It was getting lower. There might not be much daylight left, and he didn't relish the thought of braving the jungle by night. "So should we get on with it?"

"Should we dispatch the survivors first?" Dhyana asked.

Apparently gallantry and bloodthirstiness could coexist, Rodrick thought. "Do as you like, but Hrym's shackles will hold them for a while. We'll be done with all this, one way or another, before they break free."

"Mmm." The garuda cocked her head. "Then I'll save my strength for war."

"Do you blame me?" Rodrick said, walking with Lais through the jungle. Hrym was sheathed on his back, his distinctive hilt wrapped with cloth to disguise him. Rodrick was wearing yellow robes and a cloak borrowed from Jayin's bedroom, both too short, but he doubted anyone would notice. The clothes didn't smell of blood and gore, not really, but Rodrick kept thinking they did. He was more comfortable in the devilfish cloak, but word of its distinctive texture and ragged hem might have reached Nagesh from those who'd tried to hinder his escape in Niswan, and the cultists might be on the lookout for it. Better safe. He wore a mask—a wide strip of yellow cloth with cut-out eyeholes, tied around his head—but he also had the hood of the cloak shadowing his face. Cutting off his peripheral vision seemed like a bad idea, but he wasn't sure the mask was enough to make him unrecognizable to Nagesh. He hoped the rakshasa was still in the capital, but if he was here with the other cultists, he'd probably recognize Rodrick, mask or not. Lais was attired in her usual way, apart from a mask of red cloth, and they both wore medallions taken from dead weretigers prominently displayed on their chests. "For . . . everything that happened, I mean."

She frowned. "You didn't realize the cultists could track you, and I know you would have prevented my master's death if it had been in your power. The Knife in the Dark was operating so close to our home anyway, and I'd already clashed with them once . . . Well. I wish it had been otherwise, but I don't blame you, exactly. Jayin was a good man. His last command was for us to raise the alarm about this cult before they could acquire the Scepter of the Arclords, so they could be stopped. We're working to stop them, if not exactly in the manner he wished." She glanced at the compass in her hand. It pointed behind them. If the thing gave any indication of how *close* the diamond was, in addition to the direction, they hadn't been able to figure out how to interpret it. If Grimschaw was following, he hoped she was doing it from a great distance.

This was the least planlike part of Rodrick's plan. They didn't know exactly where the cultists were gathered, but it seemed likely the crowd Lais had run into must have been coming from the meeting place or going toward it, so they planned to wander in the general vicinity and hope to find some signs of habitation.

They returned to the site of the fight, and Rodrick's stomach turned at the sight. None of the men they'd trapped had escaped before predators found them. There was little left of any of them except puddles of blood and their boots, still frozen in Hrym's ice. He didn't look to see if any of those boots still had feet inside.

Lais merely said, "That's a relief. If any of them had escaped, they might recognize me, even with this mask."

And Rodrick thought *he* was the pragmatic one. "Still," he said. "That's a terrible way to die. I know you snapped at least a couple of their necks in battle, and I've got no quarrel with that, but some of those men were merely unconscious when we froze them. To wake up to something *eating* you . . ."

"My mother came from the Impossible Kingdoms," Lais said quietly, walking past the frozen boots without another glance. "She told me a story from our homeland. Once there was an orphanage, caring for scores of children whose parents had died in accidents or battles, a place run by monks devoted to a goddess of mercy. The children were taught to read, and to play music, and were educated nearly as well as children of the merchant caste. No one realized it, but the Knife in the Dark gradually infiltrated that orphanage over the years, until none who worked there were genuine followers of the Merciful Mother, but were all secretly followers of Vasaghati. Once they fully controlled the place, they . . ." She shuddered.

"Did they kill the children?" Rodrick said. A cult that organized the murder of scores of blameless young ones . . . people like that might deserve to be eaten standing in their boots.

Her laugh was bleak. "Oh, if only. No. The cultists *taught* the children. They continued to teach them all the things they'd been learning before, but they gave them other instructions, too. They taught the children to worship Vasaghati, until nearly all were made into acolytes of the Knife in the Dark. Their teachers showed them the dark joys of deceit, the thrills of trickery, the sweetness of revenge. Revenge against *everyone*, and against the whole world that had seen them orphaned, left friendless and alone. Those children who were resistant to the teachings had . . . accidents, usually engineered at the hands of other orphans they believed to be their closest friends. Such treachery was good practice, you see. Those well-trained children were then adopted by childless families, or by those who sought to help the less fortunate. The children went to work destroying those families from within, spreading lies and doubts, even sowing the seeds of murder when they could."

Rodrick's mouth was dry. Murdering children was bad enough. Taking children who didn't know better and raising them to *be* murderers . . . he could think of few things more monstrous.

"The cultists who ran the orphanage were only discovered because one child pretended to be a good acolyte, doing unspeakable things to prove his loyalty. He was a brilliant athlete, quick to learn martial arts even at his young age, and when he was nine he was taken in by a wealthy family of the warrior caste, who thought he could have a future serving in the rajah's guard, with proper training. The boy told his new guardians the orphanage was infested by the Knife in the Dark, and when the rajah's ministers investigated, they found the dark goddess's signs hidden away, and some of the younger children confessed. The cult was finally burned out, but the dark monks managed to destroy all the orphanage's records, so it was impossible to find out for sure how many of their tainted students were sent to new families, or where they'd all ended up."

"How long did the cult run the orphanage?"

She shook her head. "Perhaps as long as twenty years. They destroyed those records, too, and all the cultists who were captured told wildly contradictory stories. They wanted to sow doubt, you see, in the minds of anyone who'd *ever* adopted children from that orphanage—to make them fear their own children. The Knife in the Dark claimed to have established similar holds in other orphanages, too. There were investigations, and no other such infiltrations were found . . . but the doubt remained. Which is exactly what the Knife in the Dark wanted. They are bitter, vicious people, Rodrick, either by nature or because their brutal lives have made them so. Every one who is eaten by a monstrous lizard in this jungle could mean tens or scores or hundreds of lives spared in the future, saved from their influence. You must not hesitate to kill these cultists when you can. They have *chosen* evil."

"Don't worry about us," Hrym said. "We'll do what needs doing."

Rodrick nodded. At least they were trying to ambush the Knife in the Dark at one of their secret gatherings—facing them head-on would be much easier than trying to root them out of their secret places, and this meeting robbed them of their main strengths, deception and treachery. Perhaps Rodrick and his allies really could deal the cult a decisive blow today.

And if the *rest* of his plan worked out, then they could still get off Jalmeray with a fat chest of gold after all. It felt strange that getting rich and getting away weren't the most important things on his mind. It may have taken some prompting from Hrym, but Nagesh's efforts to enmesh them in the Knife in the Dark's machinations, and killing the man who healed Hrym, really had made Rodrick angry enough to overlook pragmatism for once. Or at least add other motivations.

A figure dropped from a tree branch in front of them—not a weretiger, this time, but a scrawny man even paler than Rodrick, with greasy brown hair and a long nose dwarfed by a boil growing on one side. A black bandanna covered the entire top of his head and his eyes, with ragged holes cut in the cloth to let him see, but that nose was his most distinctive feature; he should've hidden *that*. The fellow was either a wererat or simply abominably ugly, and he looked like the kind of man who would pick his teeth with a filthy dagger. He wore a ring on his finger marked with the circle full of triangles, and he crossed his arms and grinned, showing them yellow teeth. "And where might *you* two delicious morsels be going?"

21

The Conclave of the Knife in the Dark

Lais went tense, compact violence ready to explode, but Rodrick just returned the ratlike man's grin. He hoped there wasn't a code word—they were counting on the medallions to get them past whatever security the cult had. He put on a Taldan accent, one of his most convincing, touched with haughtiness. "The same place you're going, I imagine."

He nodded. "I'm stuck watching for late-coming stragglers like you. The archaka's address is at sunset, you know."

Rodrick shrugged. "Some of us might have positions that require more care and concealment in order to slip away."

The man snorted. "I'm sure, Your Majesty. Taldans don't have much influence on Jalmeray, last I checked. If you're more than a tourist or a visiting scholar I'll eat my own nose."

"You're making us even later," Lais said, voice low and dangerous, and the rat-faced man blinked.

"Go on then," he said, shuffling aside.

They swept past him without another word, on the theory that cultists of the Knife in the Dark were most likely smug, insufferable jerks whenever they didn't have cause to pretend otherwise.

They stepped almost immediately onto a broken path, gray paving stones broken into rubble in some places by tree roots and still whole, if canted, in others. After a few dozen yards they encountered a stone obelisk, twice as tall as a man and as wide as Rodrick himself, leaned at a precipitous angle across the path.

The monolith was wound heavily with vines, but Rodrick could still make out symbols carved on its face: wavy lines above a spiral, and a delicate leaf that seemed to be dripping water. Had he seen the latter on temples of Gozreh back home? Maybe, but he suddenly realized it was familiar because it looked a bit like the drawing on the treasure map, only the obelisk was a different shape, and there was a leaf instead of an eye. Not the marker for his treasure, then, but a hint of how it *might* appear. He'd keep his eyes peeled for more obelisks. This was roughly the right part of the jungle, if he remembered the map rightly.

"Oh dear," Lais murmured, touching the obelisk. "These symbols are those of a goddess, She Who Guides the Wind and the Waves. This place must have been a temple of hers, but long ago, perhaps during the time of the maharajah, when the jungle was not so thick. See, we're on a hill, and this temple might have had a grand view of the sea, centuries ago. Typical of the Knife in the Dark to pervert a sacred place to their own ends."

They followed the path through crowding trees, stepping over a brightly colored serpent as thick as Rodrick's calf that Lais said wasn't venomous—"Don't worry, it's a strangler, so keep it off your neck and you'll be fine"—and soon reached the temple proper. Rodrick wasn't sure what to expect—maybe another pagoda, or something like the pyramids he'd glimpsed in Osirion—but this structure was clearly wrought with the help of magic and elementals, though more mundane elements had taken their toll over the years. The place was the size of a manor house, with tall fluted pillars and half a dozen small domes on the roof, all seemingly wrought without any joinings, as if carved from a single immense stone. The walls were decorated with friezes depicting She Who Guides the Winds and the Waves, though they were chipped and worn where they weren't crawling with vines. A once-beautiful temple, falling apart: it really was a fitting site for a gathering of the Knife in the Dark.

The space before the temple was a broad plaza of stone, still more or less level, and filled with milling figures. A round depression in the middle of the courtyard, ten paces across and surrounded by a low wall, had likely once been a fountain or sacred pool of some kind, but now it was just a hole, probably with a scum of brackish water at the bottom.

Most of the cultists were human, and most of the humans were Vudrani as far as Rodrick could tell from what he could glimpse around their masks, but he wasn't the only denizen of the lands around the Inner Sea. There were also some weretigers and a half-orc or two. If there were more rakshasas, they were in disguise. No garudas at all, he noted with satisfaction. He glanced skyward. Dhyana was supposed to be up there, somewhere, among the treetops. He hoped she was, and at the same time hoped they wouldn't need her.

Torches had been lit at the corners of the plaza, and up on a sort of balcony in front of the temple overlooking the crowd—clearly the place where the conclave would be addressed by the archaka, whatever that was. Maybe it was some kind of high priest. Maybe Nagesh himself, if Rodrick's luck was especially bad, and he suspected it was.

It was hard to gauge the moment of sunset in the jungle, but he thought they had a little time yet. "Should we mingle?" he murmured.

"I suppose." They moved into the crowd, which wasn't so much a group of people mingling as a group of people glaring at one another, with knots of two or three or five people standing with their heads together here and there, murmuring and shooting glances at other groups. Why would you want to join a cult that was, of necessity, so paranoid?

They walked by a long wooden table laden with trays of fruit and pitchers of water and wine, but no one was holding a single cup or eating so much as a grape. Lais started to reach out toward the table, and Rodrick touched the back of her hand and slightly shook his head. The food was probably all poisoned, a little joke that would also weed out any overly trusting followers of Vasaghati.

A small man with pale hands moved past them with a slight nod of greeting, and for a moment Rodrick thought it might be the conjurer Kaleb, but his teeth were differently crooked and there was a cleft in his chin that the pyromancer had lacked.

Rodrick grimaced. The atmosphere of paranoia was thick here, and could easily infect him if he wasn't careful. There were only fifty so people in the plaza, hardly the hundreds he'd feared. The nine or ten cultists who'd fallen to him and his allies already apparently represented a considerable percentage of the total. If this was even a sizable fraction of the entire population of the Knife in the Dark on the island, they were less fearsome than they liked people to believe.

Of course, fifty was a lot of people for two individuals to fight. Even with Hrym and Dhyana in the equation, it was still worse than twelve to one. They had the element of surprise, true . . . but could you really surprise people who were so primed for betrayal?

The crowd murmured, and someone pointed up to the balcony. Two women dressed in white, with masks of gold cloth, stepped to the rail, looking down on the assembled mass. "The archaka comes! All hail the voice of Vasaghati!"

The response was somewhere between cheers and disgruntled muttering, but that was probably the best that could be hoped for in this crowd. A towering figure emerged from the temple, dressed in black robes, moth-eaten and rotted—a nice touch—and wearing an immense silver medallion bearing the mark of the Knife in the Dark.

He had the head of a snake. It was possible there was *another* snake-headed rakshasa in the cult, but the odds didn't favor it. Rodrick sidled around a bit, until he was somewhat hidden behind a tall half-orc. Lais looked at him questioningly, but he just shook his head and watched the balcony.

"Welcome all," the rakshasa said, voice smooth. Yes. That was Nagesh. "We gather here for the glory of our goddess, the Decay from Within, the Knife in the Dark, the Poisoned Chalice. This temple, once dedicated to She Who Guides the Wind and the Waves, is a suitable shell for us to inhabit. We must thank one of our sisters below, who heard of this place in lore and suggested it for our meeting." He gestured, and a woman dressed in drapes of wrapped white cloth—somehow pristine, despite journeying through the jungle—lifted her hand in a wave. The applause was even less enthusiastic this time. This temple was obviously ideal in certain respects for an evil cult meeting, but the cultists would probably have preferred to meet in a place with taverns and brothels and actual beds, instead of the depths of a filthy jungle.

Rodrick didn't pay as much attention to the crowd's reaction as he did to the waving woman, though. Something about her was familiar—the fall of her hair, the way she smiled beneath her mask, amused and thoughtful . . . Surely he was seeing familiarity where there was none, the way he'd falsely recognized the conjurer Kaleb. The atmosphere here was getting for him.

"But I can't say I much like the decorations," Nagesh was saying. "Even worn down by time, the wall carvings aren't at all to my taste. We've brought along something more suitable." He gestured, and the two women flanking him disappeared inside, then returned with a bulky roll of cloth. Nagesh moved out of the way as they fixed the cloth to the railing, then shoved the roll over the side, unfurling a vast tapestry.

The piece was beautifully wrought, displaying a woman seated cross-legged on a heap of skulls, with thorn vines writhing through the eye-holes and mouths, the same vines twisting up to form a border around the tapestry as a whole. The right half of the woman's face was as beautiful and serene as any other goddess, smiling with secret wisdom, but the left half was a grinning pock-marked skull, and the dividing edge of her face ragged and torn, as if the skin were a mask that had been ripped off hastily. Her garments were similar, beautiful cloth of gold on the right, and shredded rags on the left. She wore a medallion marked with the same circle full of lamprey-teeth triangles that Rodrick wore. She had four outstretched arms: one hand held a bloody dagger, and another held a second bloody dagger, and the other two hands also held bloody daggers. Rodrick was beginning to sense a theme.

"Such is the face of the goddess of the Knife in the Dark, which none of us may safely display, except here, in this place, when for a day and a night we can reveal our truth to one another." Nagesh's voice was kind and companionable, as if each person in the plaza were a personal friend. "We come together today to remind us that though we must often work alone, we are not *truly* alone." Nagesh put his backward hands on the rail and looked down, his snake's eyes seeming to make contact with every face individually as he spoke. "While our goddess allows us great latitude to pursue our own personal glory, we must remember that we ultimately serve *her* glory, and many of us play small parts in a greater whole. Our work on this island goes well. We are poised to sow chaos throughout the highest levels of the nobility, even unto the thakur himself. Once Jalmeray loses the support of the Impossible Kingdoms and becomes isolated from our ancient enemies there, we will be poised to take over this island entirely. Not openly, but absolutely. Can you imagine, brothers and sisters, if the famed Conservatory that trains courtesans and diplomats were secretly dedicated to Vasaghati? We could send the Knife in the Dark into the palaces of every kingdom in the Inner Sea. Imagine the damage that could be wrought then! The world could be broken in two generations, and we, the puppet masters pulling the springs, could live in glory untold!" He lifted his hands aloft, and this time the crowd *did* roar, their voices joined in exultation at the prospect of such a grim and hopeless future. (Rodrick found the vision grim for obvious reasons, but also because a world of people so untrusting would be a very difficult place for him to make a living. How could you be a confidence trickster if you could never gain anyone's confidence?)

Rodrick made a point of cheering just as loudly as everyone else, and Lais took it up, too, just a half a second too slowly.

"There is one minor point of business," Nagesh said, voice comparatively low, and the crowd hushed to hear him. "Some of our hunters are out seeking a man named Rodrick, armed with a magical sword. He is an assassin, hired by a member of the Knife in the Dark in the thakur's palace, to kill a high-ranking member of the Maurya-Rahm. This Rodrick proved an incompetent killer, bungling the job and bringing down the wrath of the thakur. He has since fled, we believe to this very jungle."

Lais turned her head to look at him, eyes wide, and Rodrick gritted his teeth. Nagesh was lying, perhaps because it came to him naturally and perhaps because even the high priest of the Knife in the Dark didn't want the cult to know what his true plans had been . . . but he wasn't lying as much as Rodrick would have wished. Lais would have questions for him, now, and he'd have to think carefully about how to answer them.

Nagesh went on. "Some of you have doubtless heard rumors about this man. I assure you that he does not realize he served the Knife in the Dark—he believed himself a tool of a rival faction within the government. His existence is a loose end, however, and he *has* killed some of our hunters. I have dispatched a larger force, one sufficient to overwhelm him, and have no doubt they will succeed, yet keep your eyes and ears open. All enemies of the goddess will fall! The Knife in the Dark is eternal!"

More cheers. "Now," Nagesh said. "Please enjoy the refreshments." Harsh laughter bubbled in the crowd. "All right, then, in that case, eat what you've brought with you. The priests will send for some of you individually, to discuss your progress with me in the temple, and we will have new instructions for some others, so don't wander off too far—you're likely to be eaten by carnivorous lizards if you do so alone. Later we will have the ritual sacrifice of one of our brothers who failed in his mission last year, and then some chanting, and perhaps our goddess will make a brief appearance—we have prayed for her presence, and may be answered. Some of you were in attendance during her last manifestation, twelve years ago, when she appeared as a mass of poisonous spiders in the shape of a woman and bestowed divine gifts and hideous scourgings at her whim. Even in her absence, remember that I am her chosen one, her voice—her archaka. Until you are summoned or our revels begin, impress one another with your powers of deception. In other words, pretend you're all friends, and have a nice chat." Nagesh returned inside the temple, accompanied by his handmaidens.

Lais grabbed Rodrick's arm and dragged him toward the refreshments table, the one place on the plaza where there were no mingling knots of cultists. The people they passed were engaged in flattering one another, or simpering, or seducing, apparently taking their archaka's suggestion as law.

"What did he mean, that—that *Rodrick* was hired as an assassin? I thought he was a treasure hunter."

"This really isn't the place," Rodrick murmured, watching the crowd. So far none of them were paying any attention to them, but Lais's body language was entirely too agitated. The woman knew nothing of deceit. "They're all distracted, so this would be a good moment for us to strike—"

"Not until I know the truth! I thought you were an innocent, entangled in the Knife in the Dark's plots, but if you're a hired killer taking revenge on your employers, I want no part of you."

Rodrick laughed, as if she'd said something witty, then leaned forward to whisper in her ear. "Lais, I will answer you, but at least *pretend* we're doing what everyone else is doing, or we'll both be killed. Smile, look embarrassed as if I'm suggesting something improper—well, all right, that's good enough, I suppose. Listen. I'm no assassin. I never kill if I can avoid it, and certainly not for money—there are easier ways to get coin. It's true, I wasn't honest with you, but only because I didn't want you to know I was a fugitive from the thakur—for all I knew, you'd try to turn me in for the reward."

"I should have," she said, but at least she smiled as she said it. Though, really, that smile made it worse. Hers was not a face meant for lying.

Rodrick went on. "I was invited—summoned, really—to the thakur's palace. He wanted to buy Hrym from me, to make the sword a gift for a friend of his, a visiting rajah. But then the thakur's advisor Nagesh, who's the snake-headed high priest up there on the balcony, came to me one night and told us that he wanted Hrym to *kill* the rajah, and that if Hrym didn't obey, *I* would be killed. I didn't know it was the Knife in the Dark planning the murder at the time. For all I knew, the thakur was the one who wanted his old friend killed. I tried to come up with a plan to escape the situation, and . . . well, Nagesh is right about that much. I did bungle it, and people thought I'd tried to kill the thakur."

"It was my fault," Hrym murmured, very low, but Rodrick still tensed. Better if no one heard a voice that shouldn't be there.

"I fled, and here I am." Rodrick spread his hands.

"All right," Lais said. "But you haven't mentioned your 'partner,' the treasure hunter who tried to kill you, with her men from Nex."

"Ah. That's . . . more complicated. I'm not an assassin, it's true, but I am *occasionally* a thief." Lais made a sound of disgust. People could be so judgmental. "Grimschaw hired me to steal a treasure map from the thakur's palace, and she helped me get out of the city when the thakur's people began pursuing me, because she wanted the map. But then she decided I should die, since I'd seen the map." That much was true. He'd left out the bit about giving Grimschaw the wrong scroll and trying to cheat her, both because time was short and because those facts could hardly help him win over Lais again.

"How can I ever trust you?" Lais said. "You—"

"Don't keep the handsome ones to yourself, sister," a woman said, gliding up beside them. It was the woman wrapped in folds of white cloth, who'd chosen this site for the meeting, and who'd seemed familiar to Rodrick. "Give us all a chance to practice our skills on such broad-shouldered targets."

He recognized her, now, from her voice and those parts of her face that weren't covered by a mask, especially the ruby stud in her nose. It was Tapasi, the priest he'd been friendly with on the voyage to Jalmeray.

No wonder she'd known about this temple—she was supposedly devoted to She Who Guides the Wind and the Waves. *She* was part of the Knife in the Dark? The idea made him sick to his stomach. Not because she'd fooled him—he was self-aware enough to know horror at being *tricked* by someone would be hypocritical, when he tricked so many people himself. But to be cheated by someone for financial gain, as Rodrick did, was one thing—he could *understand* that. But . . . he'd liked this woman, and she was devoted to bringing about destruction for its own sake. That, he couldn't comprehend.

Unfortunately, Tapasi recognized him just as quickly as he recognized her. She stumbled backward, and raised her voice, shouting, "Rodrick! Rodrick is *here!*"

22
Marked by the Sign of the Eye

Tapasi lifted her hands, crackling with energy—her power derived from a dark goddess, Rodrick now realized—and the crowd turned toward him.

Lais struck Tapasi right between the eyes, then ran *into* the crowd, lashing out and knocking people down as she went. But there were fifty of the cultists, some of them doubtless trained in the same arts Lais knew.

Why couldn't she have a more treacherous mind? If Lais had just acted as horrified about Rodrick's presence as Tapasi had, if she'd leapt back from Rodrick and pretended to be one of the cult, she could have used the invisibility that granted to her advantage. But Lais always acted like exactly what she was: an honest woman, with ample skill for violence. Unfortunately, Rodrick couldn't send shards of ice and clouds of killing frost into the crowd, because Lais was there, too, and though she might willingly sacrifice herself to stop the Knife in the Dark, Rodrick found he wasn't willing to make that choice for her.

Lais snatched a torch from a sconce by the wall and swung the fiery end at the cultists trying to press in on her, clearing enough space for her to kick and punch, but it was just a matter of time before someone risked a burn and the rest overwhelmed her.

Rodrick drew Hrym and called up a freezing mist. Cultists began to slip and fall, but so did Lais, of course, though she still kicked and punched from her place on the ground, and even kept her grip on the torch. Rodrick, moving sure-footed on the ice as Hrym's wielder, reached down and grabbed her free arm, granting her a connection to Hrym and thus the same freedom of movement. A cultist loomed at him from the mist, using some magic to keep his footing—and then shouted as he was lifted off his feet and hauled into the air. Dhyana was getting involved.

That was good. But this wasn't the careful attack from concealment they'd planned, freezing the entire plaza of cultists solid and then hunting down any stragglers or escapees with Dhyana's help. If he could drag Lais to a corner of the plaza and get a good vantage point on the crowd, blast them with ice while they were slipping and sliding, then maybe the plan could be salvaged . . .

Suddenly shouts rose up from the jungle beyond the plaza: "For Nex! For the Arclords!" The roar of tigers and the clash of swords joined the confused shouts of the cultists in the plaza. Rodrick groaned. That must be Grimschaw, with more of her men, trying to follow the treasure map or kill Rodrick or both, and doubtless trailed by the hunters Nagesh had mentioned sending out after him.

"We have to get somewhere safe," he muttered. Lais pulled away from him, immediately slipped in the slick fog, and clutched at his arm again to steady herself. She glared, but didn't break contact again. "Listen, Lais, if we can wait this out, Grimschaw and the cultists will kill each *other*."

"Coward," she spat.

"I prefer to think of myself as a realist."

"And I prefer to think of you as *food*." Nagesh appeared from the mist, untroubled by the ice. "It's such a pleasure to—"

Rodrick slashed the rakshasa across the face with Hrym's blade, and Nagesh stumbled back. The strike would have split any man's head in two, but it just left another thin red line in his flesh, the edges crusted with slivers of ice. The rakshasa roared in pain, and Hrym blasted a torrent of ice, the cult leader disappearing into the fog to avoid being struck.

Rodrick grabbed Lais and pulled her along with him, around the side of the temple and out of the fog. The battle raged here, too, though no one took notice of two more running figures. Grimschaw's black-clad servants of the Arclords were laying about with weapons and magic, fighting off cultists, and vice versa. The groups seemed well matched, with fallen bodies visible from both sides. One facedown corpse, clothed in white, might well have been Tapasi. She'd been so nice to him on the ship, given him advice, told him what to expect in Jalmeray . . . all while hiding her rot. Maybe she'd even been sent by Nagesh to spy on him. He was glad he hadn't succeeded in seducing the woman. At least he hadn't seen captain Saraswati among the cultists.

He chose a direction at random and darted among the trees, Lais finally able to follow on her own as they left the icy fog behind. There were supposedly other ruins in this jungle, and if they could find a place to hide for a while, they could come back later and pick off anyone who'd survived the battle back there. It wasn't cowardice, it was *prudence*, that's all.

After ten minutes, the sounds of fighting now faded into the distance, Lais said, "This is ridiculous. We left Dhyana back there, and you *know* she's still fighting, she wouldn't just run. We can't—"

She tripped on the corner of a large stone sticking up from the ground, the first time Rodrick had ever seen her do anything ungraceful. He paused to offer her a hand up, which she ignored, rising with great dignity. But the moment's hesitation made Rodrick notice the carvings etched on the immense flat stone: the same symbols from the temple the Knife in the Dark had overtaken, the wavy lines, the spiral . . . but underneath those, instead of a leaf, someone had gouged the crude shape of an eye, the stonework chipped and messy. Clearly a late addition—almost vandalism.

"Look at this," he said.

Lais looked down, frowning. She moved her torch closer to the stone for better illumination. "Probably from the time of the Arclords. Their symbolism does favor eyes. Not surprising to find their mark. They defaced a great many things during their time on the island."

Rodrick cleared away the fallen leaves and dirt around the stone, and realized it was an obelisk that had toppled long ago. He stared at it. The shape of the obelisk . . . the combination of the symbols of She Who Guides the Wind and the Waves with the eye of the Arclords . . . This exact configuration had been drawn on the treasure map he'd stolen from the thakur's library.

The Scepter of the Arclords was here. He'd inadvertently led Grimschaw almost directly to her target.

Someone shouted, not nearly far enough away, and Lais looked around. She pointed to what looked, at first, like a tumble of vine-encrusted rocks, but upon closer examination proved to be an arrangement of fallen stones that formed a sort of natural cave. Rodrick and Lais brushed the vines aside to duck inside . . . and instead of finding a dirty hidey-hole, discovered a set of muck-encrusted stairs leading into the ground.

"It must be the remains of another temple," Lais said. "Or maybe part of the same temple complex?"

"Either way, it makes a suitable sanctuary." Rodrick led Lais down the stairs, which descended for thirty steps before leading to a cobwebbed stone corridor that gloomed off into darkness.

Heaving a great sigh of relief, Rodrick slid down to the floor. "All right," he said. "We should be safe for the moment."

"Did we come into the jungle seeking safety?" she said bitterly. Her face was drawn in the light from the smoky torch. "I came to kill cultists, not run from them. The thakur's justice doesn't extend to the heart of this jungle, not usually. We must cut out the rot ourselves. I just wish I knew whether or not *you* were part of that corruption."

"It's fairly clear the head of this cult wants us dead," Hrym said.

Rodrick nodded. "Be practical, Lais. Maybe Hrym and I aren't as blameless as we pretended, but we've got the same enemies as you do at the moment."

"You're thieves and liars."

"The way you say it, those sound like bad things," Hrym said.

"You deceive, and insinuate yourselves, and take advantage! How is that different from the Knife in the Dark?"

"We just want gold," Hrym said. "I won't pretend we always steal from those who deserve it, but we don't kill people if we can avoid it. We're no heroes, but you saw Rodrick fight the demon to save me. Would a treacherous man bother to do that?"

"You're Rodrick's livelihood," she said. "How can you think he cares for you? You're just another thing he can *use*."

"I can't convince you," Rodrick said. "There's no reason you should trust me. Certainly not my words. But if you can believe anything, believe this: Hrym and I would never turn a child against her parents. We would not teach hate and evil. We don't revel in destruction for its own sake. Words aside, you *can* trust actions, can't you? I saved you from that crowd. I could have fled, and tried to save myself, but I owe *you* a debt, after all this, and I mean to repay it."

She scowled. "That's true. You've saved me twice, now, when it would have cost you little or nothing to let me die." She sighed. "You're not good. But perhaps you aren't as bad as the Knife in the Dark."

"High praise," Rodrick said, though her words stung him more than he liked to admit. "I really do think Grimschaw's warriors and the cultists will reduce one another's numbers significantly. We'll stay here a while, then we can take out any stragglers."

She nodded, and they waited in less-than-companionable silence for a while—until they heard the flutter of wings and low muttering above. Lais widened her eyes, thrust the torch into Rodrick's hand, and hurried up the stairs.

She returned a moment later, followed by Dhyana, holding her bow. She gazed down at Rodrick. "Well," she said. "This isn't going as we planned." She wasn't shouting at him, so maybe she hadn't heard Nagesh's speech about Rodrick being an assassin.

"Plans usually don't," Rodrick said. "How did you find us?"

"I saw a torch moving through the jungle, and when the fog dissipated and I couldn't find the two of you, I realized it might have been yours, and came to see. Why did you run?"

"My strong sense of self-preservation had a hand in that," Rodrick said. "Are the cultists and Grimschaw's people still fighting?"

Dhyana nodded.

"Then let's wait a bit for them to reduce one another's numbers further, and we can ambush whoever's left."

"Not brave, but not a bad plan." Dhyana moved deeper into the corridor, and Rodrick pointed Hrym up the stairs, conjuring a wall of ice to block entry from above. Might as well discourage other visitors.

Lais stood beside Dhyana, peering into the darkness down the passageway as far as her torchlight would let her. Rodrick waited for her to tell Dhyana about his deceit, but she didn't mention it. He doubted the garuda would take the news as well as Lais had. Apparently Lais felt she owed him enough to keep his secret, at least for now.

"We can rest a bit if you need to," Rodrick said. "But soon, I want to go looking for the Scepter of the Arclords."

Lais spun around. "What? It's *here*?"

"I think it's somewhere in the vicinity, yes. That eye scratched on the obelisk outside, below the symbols of your goddess of the waves—those same symbols were all drawn on the map I saw, to mark the treasure's location." Rodrick suddenly regretted not kicking dirt over the obelisk. If he'd seen it, Grimschaw might, too. Then again, she probably had plenty to occupy her just now. "Of course, someone else might have looted it before us. But if not . . ."

"We should search now." Dhyana rubbed her hands together with fervor. "If we have the scepter, we may be able to use its power to strike our enemies down in one blow, the cultists and Grimschaw's fighters alike."

"Do we even know for sure the scepter is a weapon?" Lais said. "I thought no one knows *what* it does."

"Why else would it have such a fearsome reputation?" the garuda said. "It *must* be a weapon, and one of great power."

Rodrick wondered. If it was a weapon so powerful, why did the Arclords hide it when the Vudrani came to reclaim the island, instead of using it to fight the newcomers off? But he'd already observed that Dhyana thought in straight lines. Weapon or not, the scepter was *valuable*, and probably instrumental to getting him off the island in one piece, and rich besides. "I'm sure you're right," he said, "but we won't know until we get it. Shall we search?"

This underground temple certainly hadn't been looted *recently*, being full of drifted dirt, spiders, and snakes, a nest of which slithered away when Dhyana strode down a side corridor with the torch. "Those are poisonous," Lais said, and Rodrick gestured with Hrym and froze the serpents before they could demonstrate their toxicity.

"Another temple full of vermin," Rodrick said. "At least these don't wear masks and robes."

"Do you think there will be gold in here?" Hrym said. "If there's a secret vault where the scepter is hidden, there might also be gold. What's the point of a vault if there's no gold? That's why vaults even *exist*."

After exploring a few passages that led only to dusty old sleeping chambers for long-dead priests, they followed a corridor that ended in a large room, the ceiling disappearing in shadow, perhaps built into a natural cavern. Rows of mostly broken benches filled the room, and something that might have been an altar stood beneath a twenty-foot-high statue of some unfamiliar Vudrani deity, its face broken, with holes where its eyes should have been. There were a few torches on the walls, old but still serviceable, and Dhyana lit a couple of them.

"She probably had jewels for eyes," Dhyana said. "Looters *have* been through here, it seems. The scepter might be long gone, in that case. It would be unfortunate if the scepter is hidden in some dead treasure hunter's attic. Someone is following us." She said the last in the same low, conversational tone as the rest, and at first Rodrick thought he'd misunderstood her, but Lais picked it up immediately.

"That would be a shame. How many?"

"Just one, I think. Trying to be stealthy, but I have good hearing." Dhyana drifted toward the left side of the room, torch held aloft. "I'll look for this sign of the eye you mentioned over here," she said. "Lais, perhaps you could check the other side of the room?"

"I'll look by the statue," Rodrick said, taking one of the new torches. The two women seemed to have a plan to deal with whoever was following them—some creature that had made this hole in the ground its lair, hidden away in some dusty side corridor they'd failed to check thoroughly enough? Rodrick would happily stay out of the way and let them deal with the trouble.

He took the torch, then walked around the statue to its backside, not really looking for anything—but then he saw, scratched into the stone at the base of the statue, a little curved line scored into the rock. He crouched, running his finger over the old grooves, and, yes, it was the shape of an eye like the one on the obelisk, the whole thing no larger than the palm of his hand.

There was the sound of a scuffle, and Rodrick came around the statue to find Lais leading Grimschaw, the latter's arm twisted up uncomfortably behind her. Lais didn't appear to be working hard to hold the woman, but Rodrick suspected that if she applied the least bit of pressure, Grimschaw's arm would be broken or dislocated. Dhyana followed behind, holding Grimschaw's spear.

"Hello, Grim," Rodrick said lightly. "Funny we should both end up here. How'd you get past the ice wall?"

"The ice is strong, but the stones were old. I made another opening."

"Wizards," he said. "They get in everywhere."

"Should we kill her?" Dhyana said. "She did attack us, but she also fought the Knife in the Dark, or at least, her people did." Clearly the garuda was having trouble sorting Grimschaw into her usual black-and-white worldview.

Grimschaw stood as straight and haughtily as she could manage, considering the grip Lais had on her arm. "A good trick, putting that jewel in my pocket so they could track me," she said. "I lost five good men when the hunters first found me."

"They couldn't have been all that good, then," Rodrick said. "I suppose you followed us from the temple? Abandoned your people?"

"They knew their sacrifice was not in vain," she said. "Their mission was to help me find . . . the treasure. I was going to wait and see if you emerged with it, then take it from you, but when you tried to shut me out with ice . . ." She shrugged. "I wanted to keep an eye on you."

"'The treasure.' So coy. You mean the Scepter of the Arclords. They know about it. Out of curiosity, what does the scepter *do*, anyway?"

Grimschaw sniffed. "That's something only the Arclords need to know."

"Oh," Hrym said. "She doesn't know, either. That's disappointing."

"You work for the Arclords?" Dhyana said. "You're not just a treasure hunter?" She didn't quite point the spear at Rodrick, but it twitched that way. "And *you*? Do you, too, work for the enemies of Jalmeray?"

If Rodrick's hands hadn't been full of sword and torch, he would have raised them in a placating manner. "I didn't know she was a servant of the Arclords when we met." He'd suspected, but he hadn't *known*. "I am absolutely not aligned with those wizards. I'm not fond of Grimschaw at all, either. I'm not saying we have to kill her, but we can freeze her in place. You might want to gag her, too. I find not being able to talk or move the arms has a calming effect on wizards, and keeps them from causing so much trouble."

The garuda drew a knife and cut off strips from Grimschaw's clothes and armor, ignoring her squawks, then shoved a thick wad of leather into her mouth to silence her. Hrym provided shackles of ice for Grimschaw's hands and wrists, and they sat her on the remains of a broken bench.

"We should continue our search," Dhyana said. "We must not let the scepter fall into the hands of the Arclords *or* the Knife in the Dark."

"Oh, I think I found it," Rodrick said. He led Lais and Dhyana around the statue and pointed out the eye. The garuda looked doubtful, but when Rodrick put his shoulder to the statue and started trying to push it, she lent her strength. They shouldn't have been able to shift so much stone easily, but it slid forward four feet as if it were no heavier than a sea chest, cunningly counter-weighted in some way, moving on almost invisible tracks. There was an opening underneath, with stairs leading down. "Aha," Rodrick said. "This could be—"

Shadows moved at the bottom of the steps, and then creatures swarmed out, more than a dozen things the size of cats. Some were roughly human in form, the color of blood-flecked ash or clay, and others had tiny wings and horns. Still others had leathery flesh, and what seemed like masks grafted to their tiny faces, but those masks were snapping jaws made of metal and bone. They leapt, hissing and spitting, the ones with monstrous jaws opening and dripping acid that smoked when droplets struck stone.

23
The Scepter
of the Arclords

Lais leapt back and clambered up the statue as easily as if climbing a tree, and Dhyana beat her wings and rose into the air. Nice for *them*. Rodrick swung Hrym to try to freeze the creatures as they emerged, but only caught a handful in bonds of ice. The rest were scattering throughout the room, the more humanoid among them shouting in eerie, piping voices, "For Nex! For the Arclords!"

Of course. The Arclords were famed for their construction of golems and other constructs, like these homunculi—Tapasi had told him that. It made sense that the Arclords had left a nest of the vile creatures to guard their treasure. At least this meant the scepter probably hadn't been looted already. A few of the creatures darted at him, and he swung Hrym, flinging ice at them, and one of Dhyana's arrows caught another—though it simply pulled out the shaft with its tiny hands and continued coming.

Grimschaw grunted loudly around her gag, and Rodrick looked over to see two of the horned creatures climbing her body, hissing as they went. Dhyana howled above, and Rodrick saw a swarm of the winged homunculi harrying her. Lais was clinging to the statue's face, shaking one leg wildly and trying to dislodge a homunculus that stabbed at her ankle with a knife the size of a toothpick.

He couldn't help Dhyana or Lais, and he didn't *want* to help Grimschaw, but he'd have to deal with the creatures climbing on her eventually. He darted toward her, swooping the sword around in an ice-spraying arc to suppress further ambushes. Once he was within reach of Grimschaw he dropped his torch and pulled one of the homunculi off her chest, where it tried to cling, leechlike. The texture of its flesh was grotesque, slick and yielding, and when it hissed at him he tossed it onto the torch, where it burst immediately into flame. He tore off the other creature and hurled it at the ground, where it splattered, though that didn't stop its tiny hands from clutching and waving a miniature knife.

More were coming out of the vault. How many of these things *were* there? Had they bred over the centuries? Could constructs do that?

Grimschaw's muffled voice sounded like she had something to say, so he reluctantly pulled out her gag. He assumed she was going to demand he set her free so she could fight, and was trying to decide if he'd comply, when she shouted some ear-twisting word that made his head hurt. Suddenly lengths of whitish-gray rope appeared throughout the room at knee level, immense spider webs stretching from benches to pillars to the base of the statue, covering the chamber's floor in a complex web. Rodrick leapt onto the bench to keep from being caught in the strands, and heard howls of outrage as the homunculi were bound up in sticky strands.

"The torch," Grimschaw said. "Burn the webs."

Rodrick reached down for the torch, careful to avoid the nearest wrist-thick strand of webbing, then touched the flame to the web. It flared so brightly it made him blink, and flames raced along the strand, met at the first intersection of webs, then burned along in both directions, until within moments the entire complex net of webbing was alight. The trapped homunculi burned and howled as the strands turned to ash, some running a few steps before falling over. A few of the flying creatures weren't caught in the spell, but Dhyana took them with her arrows, making them fall into the flames, where they perished.

"Be glad they weren't golems," Grimschaw said. "Those seldom burn as easily as homunculi, and my magic would be largely useless against them." She shook her head. "Homunculi aren't meant to do battle—even the snapjaw homunculi, the ones who spat acid, are fairly weak. For the most part such creatures are used as familiars and messengers."

"These were sufficiently warlike," Rodrick said.

Grimschaw grimaced. "When homunculi get too far from their masters, or their masters die, they go mad, attacking anyone who invades their territory. This was a desperate sort of trap to make, I think—a great many Arclords and their servants must have sealed their homunculi away beneath that statue, knowing they would become ferocious in time and provide *some* protection. Or perhaps their masters simply expected to return, before they were driven from the island." She shook her head. "You clearly need my help. You should—"

Rodrick stuck the gag back in her mouth. "Sorry. You only saved us because it was the way to save yourself. I couldn't trust you any less if you were a member of the cult, Grimschaw."

"Shall we go down?" Lais said, standing near the edge of the opening. "No more of those creatures have come out. Maybe it's safe."

Dhyana nodded, lifting her bow. "Rodrick should go first, with Hrym. If there are other surprises, ice will do better in those quarters than your fists or my bow."

Leading from the rear was more Rodrick's style, but he nodded assent and went down the stairs, holding a torch ahead of him. What he could see of the chamber below was rough-hewn, perhaps cut hastily with magic, and the walls seemed more like those of a cave than the worked stone of the temple above. A secret room the Arclords made in an abandoned temple to hide something precious. There were unlit torches on the walls by the door, and

Rodrick touched them with his flame, flooding the small chamber with light.

There were only two things of note in the room. One was a human-sized statue of a Vudrani god, one he didn't recognize, sitting cross-legged, with four arms, one holding a stone knife, one a stone hatchet, one a short sword, and one a small round shield. The god's face was serene and human, apart from his boar tusks.

The other item interested him more. A stone pedestal stood beside the statue, against the room's back wall, and on it rested a staff four feet long. The Scepter of the Arclords was not the confection of jewels and mystic runes Rodrick had expected, but was made of gleaming silver metal, one end tipped with a spike flanked by curving, sharp ornaments shaped almost like wings, the other end capped by a pair of smaller sharp curves, coming together to nearly form a point like a spear's. There were three eyelike blue gems arranged at the top, and a single smaller gem at the bottom. Rodrick took a step forward—and the blue eye-gems rolled toward him and blinked in unison.

He took a step back.

Lais and Dhyana joined him, and he said, "I think . . . I think the scepter *looked* at me."

"What's wrong with that?" Hrym said. "I look at you. Are you saying objects shouldn't look at people? What, we aren't good enough? You there, scepter—do you talk? I could do with some non-human conversation."

"I do not recognize that god," Lais said, nodding at the statue. "Do you, Dhyana? What would a statue of one of our gods be doing down here in a chamber the Arclords made, anyway? It doesn't make any sense."

The scepter's eyes rolled again, this time toward the statue.

The statue blinked its eyes, smiled with its tusked mouth, and began to stand up, stone dust sifting down.

"Golem!" Rodrick shouted, and pointed Hrym, throwing up an ice wall between the statue and themselves. "Get the scepter, quick!" Lais darted forward without hesitation and Rodrick thought better of his suggestion. "No, wait, what if it's a trap—"

Lais grabbed the scepter with no apparent ill effects, but she gave Rodrick a considering look before darting up the stairs, Dhyana after her.

The ice surrounding the golem cracked under a massive blow from the other side, and Rodrick yelped and backed up the stairs. "A wall, another wall, a *thicker* wall," he said, and Hrym complied, sealing off the back half of the room behind a barrier of ice. The golem pounded on the ice with monstrous thuds. "How can it be strong enough to break your ice?" Rodrick said.

"It doesn't feel pain, and it won't stop hitting until it shatters itself into dust." Hrym said. "Those are very bad qualities in an enemy!"

They hurried upstairs, where Lais and Dhyana stood holding the scepter, looking around the room wide-eyed and scowling, respectively. Grimschaw was gone, the shackles in ruins, the gag on the bench. "You didn't shove the gag in deep enough," Dhyana said. "She must have spat it out and worked some spell to free herself."

"I doubt she went far," Rodrick said. "Not without the scepter." He nodded toward Lais, who held the scepter, its eyes still rolling wildly. "We'll keep our eyes open, but we should go. If we can get back to Niswan—"

"But you left Niswan in such a hurry." Nagesh's voice came from the shadows, smooth and amused. "You're so eager to go back?"

"Oh, this is wonderful," Rodrick said.

"Nice of you to leave a wall of ice standing in the jungle to mark your location," Nagesh said. A swift arrow flew from the shadows and splashed when it struck Dhyana, the garuda howling as her feathers smoked—he'd conjured or hurled some sort of weapon made of acid.

Nagesh's voice came from another place in the darkness; either he was moving around, or he knew a trick for throwing his voice. "I don't know how you set these slaves of the Arclords upon me, but their attack, combined with your fog, served to spoil the conclave. Those not dead have fled. Vasaghati's cultists are seldom bold fighters, and their skills leave a great deal to be desired when it comes to working together. But *I* am here, still. And I am *enough.*"

"We have the Scepter of the Arclords!" Dhyana shouted, and Rodrick groaned. Always thinking in straight lines, never keeping anything back. Admirable qualities, in a way, but badly misplaced now. "Leave this place, or we'll use it against you!"

"Oh *really*," Nagesh said. Rodrick still couldn't pin down where his voice came from. "How very interesting. That scepter would be a fine prize."

"You will never use it to further the goals of Vasaghati!" Dhyana cried.

"Hmm? Oh. Yes. Of course. My goddess. To be perfectly honest, and since none of my fellow cultists are here, I must admit that I'm less interested in the Lady of Knives than I am in *myself.* I'd make a better god than she would, anyway, though it does amuse me to rot out *her* cult from within, and turn it into my own. But listen to me—I've given too many speeches today, and clearly I've gotten into the habit. You were going to use the scepter against me, weren't you? Well, go ahead. I'm curious to see what it does."

Reading garuda features was difficult, but Rodrick thought Dhyana was annoyed. He was annoyed, too. It was fine to bluff, but it was always better to have some idea what you'd do if your bluff was *called.*

Dhyana tried to brazen it out, stepping forward with the staff held aloft—and then gasped as a blindingly white bolt of lightning cracked out from the darkness and struck her, knocking her into the stone benches and onto the floor, where she shuddered and trembled.

The scepter, dropped when she fell, rolled away along the canted floor—more than the floor's slight slant could account for, especially with that elaborate ornamental head, which should have kept it from rolling at all. Was it moving *itself*? Rodrick supposed he shouldn't be surprised. Its eyes moved, so why not the rest of it?

"Decisions, decisions," Nagesh said. "Should I kill you with acid and lightning from the shadows, or enjoy the earthier pleasures of biting you to death?"

Enough. Rodrick started swinging Hrym, firing sprays of ice into all the shadowed corners of the room, and was rewarded with a curse from one corner. "Get the staff!" Rodrick cried.

"Already done," Nagesh said, suddenly visible in the light of a toadlike fire elemental who burst into luminescence beside him. At a glance from the snake-headed rakshasa, the elemental swelled into a ten-foot-high giant, like the volcano from Hrym's mindscape made into a man.

The rakshasa had an ice-encrusted arm where Hrym's magic had struck, but his other hand held up the scepter, its eyes staring directly at Rodrick.

Rodrick ignored Nagesh for the moment and focused on the fire elemental, sending spiraling clouds of snow and spears of ice at it, buffeting the thing back. Dhyana tried to take flight, but stumbled to her knees, then looked around blankly before falling forward on her beak, apparently still disoriented from the lightning strike. Lais rushed to her, murmuring and trying to rouse her. Rodrick couldn't spare them his concern. He pushed forward, driving back the elemental step by step.

The rakshasa didn't seem to pay any of them any mind. "Perhaps I *should* try to catch the goddess's attention," Nagesh said, holding up the scepter and looking at it admiringly. "I'm sure she knows what this thing does. Maybe I can convince her to let me be the one to do it. Mmm. Or perhaps I could change my appearance, pretend to be Nex himself, returned at last, to take my rightful throne again . . ."

Then the rakshasa stumbled, dropped the staff, and fell forward. Rodrick was busy trying to drive back the elemental, and could only spare glances, but he saw Grimschaw on the rakshasa's back. She was wearing some kind of fist weapon—spiky brass knuckles, more or less—that glowed with crackling magical energy every time she punched Nagesh in the back of the head. One blow should have filled his brain with holes, but based on Rodrick's own experience with Nagesh, she was probably doing little more than combing his hair. Still, if Nagesh was paying attention to Grimschaw, he *wasn't* paying attention to Rodrick.

The elemental diminished in size, its limbs turning to steam and smoke, as it succumbed to Hrym's onslaught. Good. Once it was extinguished, Rodrick could turn his attention to freezing Grimschaw and Nagesh both—

She ran past him, to where the scepter had rolled—it seemed almost to be trying to return to its hidey-hole. He glanced at Nagesh, who tried to push himself up on his hands and knees but then slumped back down, tongue flickering out weakly. One or two of Grimschaw's punches must have done actual damage. The wizard snatched up the staff and turned on Rodrick, holding the artifact aloft. "I have it! The Scepter of the Arclords is mine! And unlike you fools, *I* was told how to use it!"

Something boomed and cracked from the direction of the huge statue. Rodrick spared a glance in that direction—the elemental was the size of a small dog now, and shrinking fast, but if he left it alone it could flare back to full size—and saw the stone golem emerged from the hole, plodding along implacably. It must have smashed its way through the wall of ice. Things *did* keep finding ways to get worse, didn't they?

The golem didn't pay any attention to Rodrick. It only looked at Grimschaw, wielder of the scepter. "No!" she shouted, turning to face it. "No, the Arclords sent me, I'm *supposed* to take it!"

The golem hurled its stone axe at Grimschaw. She lifted the scepter and opened her mouth, but whatever she was going to do, or say, or cast, she didn't have the chance. The axe struck her head with a sound like . . . well, like an axe burying itself in someone's head. It was a sound Rodrick had, unfortunately, heard before.

Then the golem just stood there. Rodrick looked at the scepter, which had fallen from Grimschaw's grasp and was rolling across the chamber again, back toward its pit. Definitely moving under its own power. Apparently the guardian didn't much care about anyone else's presence, as long as no one touched the scepter. When the staff rolled past it, the golem turned and began to follow it back toward the vault.

The scepter was Rodrick's only chance at real freedom. He didn't know much about golems, but he knew they were largely immune to magical spells, and clearly it was strong enough that Hrym's ice couldn't contain it for long.

But Hrym was a *sword*. He was many other things, too. But he was definitely also a sword.

Rodrick ran toward the golem, raised Hrym high, and swung at the golem's head.

The magical blade, which he'd seen cut stone pillars in two, just bounced off.

The golem turned toward him, raising its weapons. Rodrick fell back on what basic sword fighting knowledge he had. He'd learned a lot of flashy flourishes, things that looked impressive, but knew very little when it came to actually defeating an enemy, and he barely parried the golem's strike with its short sword. Fortunately, the stone blade sheared right off when Hrym struck it—at least the golem's weapons weren't impossibly durable. Rodrick remembered one move, a sort of spinning curtsy with blade extended, which in theory could hamstring a man . . .

He made a very pretty pirouette, ducked low, and swung, but the sword just bounced off the golem's legs with a clang. The thing kept coming, hefting its remaining weapons, as implacable as a flow of lava or an avalanche.

Rodrick had to dance away, parrying bows that came slowly, but with enough force to make his arms go numb under the impact. This was a not a sword fight he was going to win, and if Nagesh got his wits about him and decided to bite Rodrick on the back of the head . . .

Hrym sighed heavily and began to gush forth torrents of ice. The golem was, alas, not blown backward the way a person would have been, but as the ice built up around it, the creature's legs slowed. "Hrym, it's shattered two walls of ice, this won't work!"

"This time, I'm not giving it room to move!"

As the golem lifted its arms, the ice climbed its body, holding its limbs in place, layers of ice piling up thicker and thicker to hold it there. Rodrick backed away, giving Hrym more space to pile on layers, until he stood before an immense boulder of bluish-white ice, with a barely visible gray smudge of golem at the center.

"I don't think that will hold forever," Rodrick said. "The thing will get out eventually.

"Then let's run away *very promptly*," Hrym said.

"What if it keeps coming after us, to get the scepter?" Rodrick said.

"Golems are not famed for their investigative skills," Hrym said. "I doubt it'll be able to track us down."

"There could be, I don't know, some magical link between the golem and the scepter . . ."

"Were you planning to keep the thing?" Hrym said.

"Of course not!" The scepter was a means to an end. One animated magical weapon was more than enough for Rodrick.

"Then even if the golem *does* pursue, which it will do at a typically slow golem's pace, it won't be our problem when it arrives, will it?"

Rodrick relaxed. "You make a good point." He looked toward the secret room, and Lais was there, bending to pick up the scepter before it could roll down the stairs. "We fought for this," she said, sounding tired. "We may as well keep it." Rodrick nodded, and looked toward Dhyana, who was sitting up, clearly shaken but alive.

He turned to spray Nagesh with ice, to at least slow *him* down, too—but the rakshasa was gone. Rodrick groaned. Defeating *both* his enemies, Grimschaw and the rakshasa, was clearly too much to hope for. Maybe the wicked advisor would be eaten by an immense lizard in the jungle. There was always hope.

"We should get away," Rodrick said. "Even if the golem doesn't get loose, there might still be Knife in the Dark nearby. Or even more of Grimschaw's crew." He didn't look too long at her corpse. She'd hated him, and to be fair, he'd given her reason. The fact that she was an objectively terrible person didn't change the fact that he'd tried to cheat her, and that deception had led her on a winding path to the moment of her death. He didn't usually feel bad about cheating people, *especially* when they were terrible people, but Lais and Dhyana's upright company, and the bad example of the Knife in the Dark, made him more than usually sensitive to his own moral failings.

"Where do we go now?" Lais said, sounding immensely weary. "My master is dead. I have no home anymore."

"I think," Rodrick said, "that we should go to Niswan, and as fast as we possibly can."

"To get the Scepter of the Arclords to safety?" Dhyana said.

"Partly that," Rodrick said. "And partly so I can face justice."

"Wait a minute," Hrym said. "So you can do *what*?"

24

The Audacity of Truth

The escape from the temple was uneventful, with no further attacks from Nagesh. Maybe he'd fled. A lizard-thing much bigger than a horse crouched in the Knife in the Dark's plaza, feasting on corpses with such devotion that it paid the living no mind at all as they crept past in the dark. They tore a cloak from the body of a fallen servant of the Arclords on the far side of the temple and wrapped the scepter inside it, mostly to stop the sense that the rolling eyes were gazing at them.

None of them wanted to travel far in the jungle at night, but they wanted to get away from the temple in case Nagesh or any of the other Knife in the Dark cultists returned. At first, Lais and Rodrick had to support Dhyana as they walked, and he was shocked at how light she was, though he recalled reading somewhere that birds had hollow bones, and perhaps garudas were similar. After a while she shook them off, though, seeming to recover more fully from the effects of Nagesh's attack.

They camped in the first reasonable clearing they found, where a great tree had fallen and smashed down many of its smaller neighbors. After seeing the immense lizard eat the dead, Rodrick was too nervous about being in the jungle to sleep, and so Lais assigned him first watch, leaving him seated on a log peering into the darkness. Nothing made him sleepier than guard duty, and Hrym frequently hissed at him to keep awake. When Lais took over, he nodded off immediately.

They rose at first light, woken by a chorus of shrieking birds. "Such a racket," Rodrick said. "How do you stand it?"

"I love the sound of birds," Lais said. "If they were quiet, I'd be worried, because it would mean they were frightened of a nearby predator."

After that, Rodrick went tense whenever the cacophony of birdsong lessened. They made their way out of the jungle to the hills and reached Jayin's house, finally taking the time to bury the man and burn the monsters who'd killed him, along with the bloodstained cushions and rugs. Once that was done, and Lais's tears dried, they ate and discussed their plans.

Dhyana wanted to just walk up to the doors of the palace, but Rodrick convinced her that a bit more subtlety was in order, given the circumstances. He came clean with her, too, about how he was wanted by the thakur's men, partly because he felt he owed her the truth, partly because he was sure Lais would tell her if he didn't, and partly because it was necessary for the success of his plan. It wasn't the best plan he'd ever had, but he felt it was the one he had to follow.

The garuda touched her bow thoughtfully after listening to Rodrick's revelations. "I will not drop you into the sea, but only because you helped avenge Jayin's death. The lies will stop now. I will have only honesty between us."

"I can agree with that," Rodrick said. He'd been thinking a lot about truth. Lies were a valuable tool, but he could admit there were some times when truth worked better. "I'll set out for Niswan in the morning."

The next day, Lais took him to the fishing village where she was born, and convinced a man she knew to sell Rodrick his horse, a placid old mare that would at least be faster than walking, especially since he didn't intend to cut across the jungle again, and would have to go the long way around. He kissed Lais's cheek, which she tolerated, and then set off riding. Traveling without

Hrym on his back or on his hip was quite strange, but he didn't dare proceed with this plan armed with such a weapon. Besides, if everything went horribly wrong, and he was murdered on his journey or soon after his arrival, Lais would take care of the sword.

Rodrick traveled for days in fear of being stopped by the thakur's men, or survivors of the Knife in the Dark, or Nagesh himself, or even simple bandits, since he was armed only with a knife he'd borrowed from Lais. Well, and the cloak of the devilfish, though he'd hate to have to use that. Transforming into a monstrous sea creature would almost certainly scare off his horse.

As if to make up for the horrors of recent days, his journey was largely uneventful. He rode north along country lanes, past fields and small villages and the odd temple. He didn't push the horse too hard, because he had no idea how he'd find another, and he slept in hedges and beneath trees not far from the road, subsisting on the dried fish and bread Lais had put in his saddlebags. He had entirely too much time to think, and no one to talk to, and he was beset by doubts in a way he never was when he had a pitcher of wine and a warm bed and someone to share both with.

But what other course could he take that wouldn't have him pursued for the rest of his days by a murderous cult *and* a hostile government? The former was a lost cause, but he could perhaps mitigate the latter. It just meant risking execution. How did the Vudrani even execute people? Burned alive? Stepped on by an elephant? Maybe a life being hunted *would* be better than risking that, but he'd committed to his course of action now.

On the afternoon of the fourth day, he trotted across one of the many bridges spanning the River Sald, wondering if it was the same one the late unlamented Grimschaw had smuggled him across in her cart.

He kept his hood up as he rode into Niswan, but no one paid him any mind. He wasn't surprised. Oh, if they knew who he was, or had reason to suspect he'd returned to the city, he'd be surrounded by guards and genies and possibly even good citizens with wrath in their hearts, but he'd fled the city over a week ago, and no one would expect him to return here. He was probably unrecognizable with four days' growth of beard anyway.

He wondered if he could stroll down to the docks and get passage on a ship, or if the captains were still under orders to look out for him. He wondered if Saraswati was there on her ship. Wondered if she, in turn, was wondering where Tapasi was, and who would call up favorable winds for the ship when the treacherous priest never showed up for work.

Ah well. Fantasies of escape were all well and good, but he had the realities of captivity to deal with. He rode his horse up the red stone walkways, through the High-Holy District, marveling again at the beauty of the architecture, the colorful garb of the people, the scents and sounds. Maybe all for the last time.

He did pause for food from one of the booths, spiced fish served in a huge leaf, because hot food was a pleasure after his long and lonesome journey, and if things went badly he'd likely be forced to subsist on bread and water until his demise. He didn't think that outcome was likely, or he wouldn't be here, but it was a poor gambler who didn't know the consequences of a bad toss.

Eventually there was no reasonable cause for further delay. He offered the reins of his horse to a startled priest at a temple to She Who Guides the Winds and the Waves and murmured, "Please accept this donation."

Then he strolled to the palace, bowed to the guards standing with their pikes by the arches that led to the inner garden, cleared his throat, and shouted, "I come with dire news!" The guards frowned at him and stepped forward, and a few of the young people from the inner garden drifted forward to see what the foreign madman was ranting about.

"I have discovered a plot by the Knife in the Dark that extends into the very palace, as high as the advisor Nagesh! I must speak to the thakur immediately!"

The guards growled. "Move along, or we'll move you along."

He shouted more loudly, and with all the certainty he could muster. "I am Rodrick of Andoran! Falsely accused of violence against the thakur! Threatened by the Knife in the Dark! I have come to make the truth known, and to await the thakur's justice!"

The guards looked at one another—one muttered something about a sword, probably noting Rodrick's lack of a magical one— and the other nodded slowly. "I think that's him. He didn't have that fuzz on his face before, is all." The guard took Rodrick's arm in an iron grip. "Go and fetch Nagesh," he said to his partner. "He wanted to be notified right away if this man was seen."

"Nagesh is a member of the Knife in the Dark, a high priest of Vasaghati, and a rakshasa!" Rodrick shouted. "I have proof!" That last bit wasn't strictly true, but it was a very small lie, in service of the greater truth. The whole point of turning himself in with all this public shouting was to make sure Nagesh couldn't just make him quietly disappear. "Take me to the thakur! If I die before he speaks to me, it means the Knife in the Dark killed me so I couldn't tell your ruler what I know!"

The young courtiers murmured, and one stepped forward, a familiar-looking woman with eyes that managed to be both large *and* piercing, and dark hair framing a foxlike face. (Why did Rodrick have to think of her that way? Did rakshasas ever have the heads of foxes?) He'd spoken to her at the feast the night of his arrival, which seemed so long ago. Kalika, that was her name. Nagesh hadn't liked her much, and Rodrick hoped her appearance now meant the feeling was reciprocated.

"Guardsman," Kalika said. "I will take custody of this man, and escort him to a secure room until the thakur can decide what to do with him." She pointed to the other guard. "And you, tell Nagesh nothing." She sighed. "I'm sure word of this commotion will reach him anyway, but not from your lips, please."

"I . . . I don't think . . ." the guard holding Rodrick said.

"Do you know who my father is?" Kalika said.

The guard lowered his eyes and nodded, then dragged Rodrick along after her as she walked purposefully through the inner courtyard, surrounded by murmuring courtiers, and on into the palace. She caught a passing servant's eye and whispered into his ear. The eunuch widened his eyes and rushed away so quickly he was very nearly running.

Rodrick walked down the corridor with as much dignity as he could muster. He supposed he should have been terrified, but as usual once he'd committed to a course of action, he was relatively calm. He'd made his gamble, more or less. Now it was just a question of seeing how the dice fell. He said, "I appreciate you not turning me over to a rakshasa, Kalika. Though I confess, unlike the guard, I don't know who your father is. Care to enlighten me?"

"Just a humble member of the Maurya-Rahm," she said. "He serves our country by acting as chief minister of justice." Ah. That explained her interest in foreign legal systems at dinner. It must be a family hobby. "If you are to be executed," she said conversationally, "it will be my father's voice that pronounces sentence and his hand that signs the death warrant. I have been interested in your case, perhaps only because we spent time conversing after your arrival, and I was angry at myself for not perceiving your true intentions. You're a truly incompetent assassin, but I'm curious about how you came to be an assassin at *all*. Did someone hire you in the city after you arrived, or was there a deeper, older plot that led to your name coming to the thakur's attention, and your summons to the island? Well, the truth will out, and these outrageous lies about Nagesh cannot save you from the fate you deserve."

The guard chuckled, and Rodrick glared at him, then looked back at the woman. Outrageous lies. That wasn't promising. "If you think I'm guilty, why did you keep them from handing me over to Nagesh?"

"Accusations as dire as the ones you made must be investigated, no matter how absurd. My father taught me that extraordinary claims are not to be dismissed out of hand—they merely require extraordinary evidence. We'll soon have the truth."

"I look forward to it."

She frowned at him. "You almost sound as if you mean that. How interesting." She pointed to a door, and the guard opened it up and shoved him inside. It was a windowless, bare space, but not cramped, probably meant for storage. A servant was already waiting there with shackles—that eunuch had moved quickly, and spread messages as he ran, clearly—and Rodrick submitted without complaint to his captivity.

"I will wait with you," she said, which spared him having to ask for her company. He was quite sure Nagesh had partisans in the palace, either fellow members of the Knife in the Dark or just people personally loyal to him, who would be happy to make sure Rodrick had an "accident" while "trying to escape." The guard shoved him to the floor, his back against the wall, and stood looming over him, spear ready to stab down at any moment. Maybe in the right light, Rodrick could read that as flattering. People usually didn't find him all that impressive or dangerous when he didn't have Hrym in his hand.

Kalika looked at him coolly, and he smiled. "Thank you for not having me dragged to a dungeon."

"I want to see how this works out, and I don't like sitting around in dungeons, so." She shrugged. "This is for my comfort, not yours."

"What happens next?"

"Who can say? I have sent messages. They will be answered. Whether the answers are to your liking, or even mine, I cannot say."

They sat in silence for a while longer. "Would you like to hear my side of things?" he said. He'd rehearsed it enough, as often as he'd rehearsed any lie, but it wouldn't hurt to run through it again.

"No need. You will not be summarily executed. There will be a trial, or at least a hearing. I will have the opportunity to hear your tales then."

"So we should stick to light conversation about the weather?"

She snorted, and the door swung open, a eunuch bowing as he entered. "If you will accompany me? The thakur wishes to see the prisoner."

The guard dragged Rodrick up by the elbow, then shoved him out into the hall. Walking with ankles shackled was an awkward affair, but he didn't have to manage long. There were four more guards, and a pair of djinn. Two of the guards grabbed his arms and dragged him along the hall, his toes scraping on the floor, at a pace faster than he could walk shackled.

He expected the garden again, but this was apparently a more formal and serious matter, because he was taken to a round room with a high ceiling, two rows of benches, and a mosaic on the floor of a Vudrani god holding a set of scales and a sword. A huge stone chair, flanked by two smaller chairs, dominated the space beyond the benches. Rodrick was dragged along the aisle between the benches, then shoved down on his knees just before the large chairs, inside a red circle four paces across, which reminded him uncomfortably of a target for archery practice. The djinn stood on either side of him, swirling lower bodies ruffling his hair.

A moment later, the thakur came in through another door, trailed by an old man in robes that Rodrick took for a priest, probably of whatever god of justice adorned the floor he knelt on.

The thakur took the central seat, and the priest the seat on his left. Kalika lounged by the wall, off to one side, apparently of high enough status to remain but not high enough to sit in the other empty chair.

"I understand you have a story to tell me," the thakur said. His face was perfectly expressionless. "Tell it."

Rodrick took a breath and began. He told the thakur how Nagesh had threatened him with an elemental in his room and demanded that Hrym commit an assassination, or see Rodrick killed. He explained his fear that the thakur might be part of the plot—the man's face didn't change at that, either—and his attempt to find a way to escape. He explained about Hrym's demonic taint, and how his outburst had spoiled his plan, adding profuse apologies for inadvertently putting the thakur in danger. (The thakur showed no response to the explanation about how Hrym had acquired the taint, but Kalika rolled her eyes and shook her head disdainfully.) Rodrick began to warm to the story when he talked about slashing Nagesh in the face and startling or hurting him enough to make him reveal himself as a rakshasa.

He almost glossed over the precise details of his escape, because he didn't want to mention Grimschaw. He couldn't talk about her without admitting the theft from the library, and that was a crime for which he had no excuse at all, apart from avarice. But he quashed his misgivings and told the truth about that, too, getting more disgusted looks from Kalika. Maybe his honestly about the theft would incline the thakur to find the rest of his story more plausible.

Having crossed that hurdle, the rest came out in a rush—being attacked by weretigers bearing the mark of the Knife in the Dark, meeting Lais, Jayin's cleansing of Hrym's taint and his subsequent death, all of it up through the fight in the jungle, finding the location of the treasure, facing the golem, Grimschaw's death, Nagesh's escape . . . and the discovery of the Scepter of the Arclords.

Kalika laughed openly at that.

"It's true," he said. "I have it, or rather my friends do, but we want nothing more than to place it into your hands, Thakur. Perhaps it will make a suitable gift for your friend the rajah, as it is even more wondrous than Hrym."

The priest's eyes widened. "It must be the truth."

Now the thakur looked annoyed, and at his glare, the priest ducked his head and looked abashed.

The thakur shook his head. "Many have believed the scepter was in their hands over the years, but none of them have ever been correct." He sighed. "You are kneeling inside a circle of truth, Rodrick. A magical ward created by this priest. No falsehood may be spoken inside that circle." Another look at the priest. "We don't generally tell people that before we're done taking their testimony. The looks on their faces when they try to lie and cannot is usually quite amusing."

Rodrick was glad he hadn't decided to embellish his tale or make himself seem more heroic than he was.

"You have spoken no lies today," the thakur said. Kalika didn't gasp, and so Rodrick didn't let himself look smug. "But the circle is not absolute proof against falsehood. There are counter-magics that can overcome the compulsion to speak truth. Or the mind of the witness can be tricked—the circle knows nothing of *absolute* truth, if there is such a thing, but only judges the speaker's understanding of truth, and so one can speak any falsehood if they merely believe it to be true. The circle also knows nothing of omissions, and you have a reputation, Rodrick, as someone capable of making words dance to the tune you choose. For these reasons, and others, we do not rely on the circle absolutely in order to render judgment. We must investigate your claims against Nagesh. As for these other claims . . . have you any proof? Any corroboration?"

"I do," Rodrick said. "Those who helped me fight the Knife in the Dark, Lais and Dhyana, did not join me here today, because I did not want them to be harmed if Nagesh reached me before I could speak to you. But I know how to get a message to them. I can tell you, but let me assure you, even if you deem me guilty of some crime, they are guilty of nothing."

"These friends have this supposed scepter, you say?" At Rodrick's nod, the thakur sighed. "You will be confined until I know the truth of this to my satisfaction, Rodrick." He gestured. "Take him away, and question him about how to reach these friends of his."

The djinn moved aside, and human guards seized him and pulled him away. There was no indication of how long the thakur's investigations, or deliberations, or both would take, or if Rodrick could expect mercy or decapitation at the end of it all. No wonder he'd never fed himself to the maw of justice before. The process was terrifying.

25
In the Cells

They did take him to a dungeon, this time. Rodrick had seen a dungeon or two in his day, and this one was quite pleasant, by those standards. There were no rats. No filthy dung-smeared drifts of hay full of lice for bedding. No skeletons hanging by their wrist bones from shackles on the wall, though he suspected that was something torturers liked to stage for intimidation value rather than something that really happened naturally. The basement was on the dark side, and the cell was bare stone, true, but the walls were clean, with no bloodstains or scratched pleas for the blessed release of death left behind by prior inhabitants. Rodrick sat on the floor in the corner with his back against a wall, looking at the thick steel bars that penned him in. Captivity had never suited him, but he'd brought it on himself.

After an uncountable interval, Rodrick was given a cup of brackish water and a bit of bread—no weevils, this was a lovely dungeon—and a hard-boiled egg. He ate, contemplating the flickering shadows in the light of the single torch in the hallway. He was considering trying to sleep on the stones when Kalika appeared, escorted by a hard-eyed guard with a scimitar big enough to fell a tree hanging at his hip, incongruously carrying a three-legged wooden stool in one hand.

Kalika waved the guard away imperiously, and he sighed like he'd lost an old argument for the thousandth time, then set down the stool before Rodrick's cell and walked off some little distance.

Kalika sat, taking her time about arranging her scarves and neck-laces just so, then looked in at Rodrick. "I am here unofficially, because, as I said, I've taken an interest in your case. I thought I'd share some of the recent developments."

"News is welcome, as long as it's welcome news. If I'm going to have my head struck off in the morning, though . . . Actually, I suppose it's better to know, even if it will fill my final hours with anxiety instead of hope." His final hours would actually be filled with desperate attempts to escape, in that case, but he wasn't hopeful about his chances for success.

"I understand a message was left at that horrid tavern in the foreign quarter you mentioned, telling your friends to present themselves at the palace. They will be questioned sharply, if and when they arrive . . . though if one of them really is a garuda, that helps your case. I suppose it's possible for garudas to lie, but they set great store by their uncompromising honesty. One wonders how a trickster like yourself made an alliance with one of those."

He shrugged. "At first I lied very well, and then I stopped lying. I can't say Dhyana likes me much—I think she prefers Hrym by a wide margin—but she purely hates the Knife in the Dark, and I helped kill a number of them." Indirectly, mostly, but it still counted. The cult would certainly hold him responsible, so he might as well take the credit where it did him good.

"On that score . . . The thakur sent a couple of the court wizards to investigate the site of this supposed temple. This is all secondhand, mind you, from . . . call them friends of mine . . . who overheard, but I'm told they found the temple, and the banner of Vasaghati you mentioned, and a great many dead, mostly eaten by creatures from the jungle but identifiable for all that. They also found a second temple with a secret room devoid of treasure, and the remains of several constructs of the sort the Arclords were known to create, including a stone golem . . ." She shook her head.

"A story as outlandish as yours seemed like it *must* be a lie, but it seems at least some of it was true."

"Ah, but that's the sign you're an amateur liar at best," Rodrick said. "Professionals often do their best to make their lies simple and clear." He recalled a couple of elaborate impostures that were more complicated than they needed to be, just because it was more interesting that way, but there was nothing that said his advice about how to lie had to be entirely truthful. "You'll find that, the more complex the lie, the faster it falls apart. No, it's *reality* that's absurd and overcomplicated. What sort of complicated lies is Nagesh telling? How is he explaining away his absence from the palace? I *know* he was gone for some time—he was at the temple. Or can rakshasas teleport, too?"

She looked at him thoughtfully. "He was out searching for you, as he found your attack on the thakur in his presence a source of personal shame. Or so he explained when he returned to the city, which he did rather more quickly than you did—of course, he had access to a flying carpet."

"See?" Rodrick said. "He told an excellent lie, because almost every word is true, just not in the way you'd expect. He *was* searching for me, after all."

She adjusted her bracelet. "I probably shouldn't tell you this, but . . . Nagesh is gone. He vanished soon after you turned yourself in, after a servant loyal to him reported your arrival and my involvement. Nagesh was not seen to leave the palace, but if he is . . . what you claim . . . he would be able to escape with relative ease. The powers of rakshasas vary, but even the least of them are capable of great stealth. His flight is taken by many as evidence of guilt, though of course that is not definitive."

"Better and better," Rodrick said. "I'd prefer to see him strung up by his feet and beaten with sticks, but running away will do—I'm sure your people will track him down eventually. Given all that's happened, when my friends arrive and confirm my story, as they will, do you think I'll be set free?"

She shook her head. "It's nice to see you so hopeful. You *stole* from the thakur, Rodrick, crept into his library and absconded with a scroll of great antiquity and value."

Rodrick scowled. "I didn't creep anywhere. A librarian showed me to the shelf! And the scroll may have been old and valuable but no one had looked at it in centuries. No one would have even noticed if it was gone if I hadn't come clean."

"Ah, but you did confess. The punishment for a common thief is the loss of a hand. But stealing from the thakur . . . I'm not sure, but it would not surprise me if the loss of your life was deemed a reasonable punishment."

Rodrick tilted his head back and looked at the dungeon ceiling. This was just marvelous. "The thakur isn't inclined to be merciful because I killed so many of the Knife in the Dark and exposed the treachery of his close advisor?"

"I can't presume to speak for the thakur. I don't sit in on his counsels, I just know people who do. But . . . News of Nagesh's potential treachery left the thakur shaken. Some of the recognizable corpses at the temple were known to people in the palace, though fortunately none were so highly placed as Nagesh. A teacher at the Conservatory, relatively new, but considered a rising star. A monk at one of the better monasteries, not high-ranking, but still, his presence indicates a troubling potential for deeper blight. A maid employed by one of the oldest families in the city, privy to who knows what secrets spoken unthinkingly in her presence. You may have undone innumerable plots by helping kill those cultists. And what you said, about the cult's attempt to stage a coup and take over the whole island, to make it a machine for pumping the toxin of the Knife in the Dark out into the wider world . . . that did carry weight. Will it be enough to spare your head? I couldn't say."

"Hmm. And giving the thakur the Scepter of the Arclords? Does that bring me a little *more* goodwill? Enough to tip the balance toward life and freedom?" Rodrick didn't expect to be given a palace, though in normal circumstances he thought that would be reasonable considering all his service, but a fast ship laden heavily with gold seemed plausible.

She sighed. "You seem so smart, sometimes, and then, at other times . . . Rodrick, scholars debate whether the Scepter of the Arclords even *exists*. It's a fairy tale the Arclords tell themselves—a great treasure left behind, one that could restore them to primacy in Nex and even allow them to retake Jalmeray, perhaps even a way to call back their beloved old vanished archwizard himself! It's nonsense. I don't doubt you found *something*—perhaps a staff that grants clairvoyance, based on the eyes you say decorated it—but I think wishful thinking led you to believe it was something more."

"Oh, thank goodness you're here to set me straight," he said. "I don't have any experience at *all* with wondrous weapons of untold power and deep magic. How would I ever recognize such a thing if it came into my hands?" It was hard to tell in the dim light, with her dark skin, but he thought perhaps she blushed. "If it's real, that would help my case, wouldn't it?"

"Yes, and if you had wings, you could fly."

The guard grunted, and Kalika turned her head, then widened her eyes, leaping from the stool and stepping back. Rodrick went to the bars and tried to look down the hall, but he saw only shadows from his vantage, and the shape of the guard slumped on the floor.

"You fool!" she said. "What are you doing here?"

Nagesh came forward, in his human disguise, his clothes disheveled, his grin wide but his eyes hunted. "I'm here to kill. I knew Rodrick would be brought here eventually, so I hid myself away—I know *all* the places to hide, and I can go unseen at will. I wanted Rodrick, but the daughter of the minister of justice will be good, too. In fact, I believe I can make it look like *Rodrick* killed you—that might be better. Or I could dispose of you entirely, and take on *your* face, and continue to move in the corridors of power . . . yes, that might be good, they say you have a very promising future."

"Someone already *had* that idea, worm." Kalika's voice was imperious and cool, and not at all terrified. "You struck one of my loyal guards, and for that you will suffer, even more than you will suffer for your terrible failure to the Lady of Knives."

Nagesh hesitated. "What—do you claim—"

"I serve the Knife in the Dark." She looked at Rodrick with such disdain and hate that he backed away from the bars. "When your failures became apparent, I was sent to step in."

"You were not at the conclave—"

"Some of us are too *important* for such charades, *ghoshta*." She spat the word like an insult, and Nagesh flinched.

"I am *darshaka*," he said, but it was really more of a whine.

Kalika snorted. "Perhaps in *this* life, but your failures will be known, and in your next incarnation you will be lucky if you are not made *pagala*." Nagesh flinched again. She glanced at Rodrick. "There are castes among the rakshasas, Rodrick. This one before me is not the lowest, but he is far from the highest. All rakshasas have appallingly high opinions of themselves." She drew herself up—and kept drawing herself up, seeming to grow two feet in height. Her human features melted away, revealing a regal figure with the head of a snow-white tiger, draped so heavily in gold and gems that her rich robes were barely visible underneath. A medallion of the Knife in the Dark was prominent among her necklaces, now. "But in this case, he will bow to a *mere* weretiger, knowing that I am exalted in the eyes of the goddess I serve, and that he *pretended* to serve."

Rodrick swallowed, but managed not to whimper. Her attention was mostly on Nagesh, at least. Maybe while she was tormenting him a guard would appear, and . . . and . . . be knocked unconscious or killed like the other guard. Oh, why had he ever let Hrym leave his hand? Truth was a terrible option.

"I—I am loyal—" Nagesh said.

Kalika snorted. "Rodrick told us all about your plans to take over the cult, fool, not that we ever believed your devotion was true. Rakshasas are loyal only to themselves. Our Lady knows that. She indulged you, though, and why not? To attempt to betray the goddess *herself* is a powerful form of treachery, and she adores betrayal in all its forms. The depths of your vileness only made her stronger."

Kalika stalked toward Nagesh, who was trying to maintain his composure, but doing a poor job of it. "The plans we have for this island are too important to leave in disloyal hands, so I came from Vudra and slew this Kalika and took her place. I am the new archaka of Jalmeray—the *true* archaka—come to shepherd things to completion, and keep watch over you. But now it's all a shambles. Reveal yourself, Nagesh. You should wear your true face when you face our Lady's judgment."

The advisor's features shimmered, revealing his snake's head. His snout showed scars from where Hrym had struck him, which gave Rodrick some comfort. Not much, but when you were about to be murdered while defenseless in a cell, you took what comforts you could.

The regal weretiger interlaced her fingers, long claws curving over the backs of her hands. "Do you have anything to say in your defense, Nagesh?"

He knelt, bowed his head, and said, "I . . . I *do* serve the goddess. Rakshasas respect power, surely you know that. And . . . none of this is my fault. It's this man, this *Rodrick*—he ruined everything! It would have been such a marvelous thing to kill the thakur's childhood friend. Every rumor would have said the thakur planned the murder, that he summoned this man to the island for that very purpose! The dead man's family would have sought revenge, and chaos would have bloomed everywhere! But he *ruined* it!" Nagesh lifted his snake's head and stared at Rodrick with infinite hatred, forked tongue flickering wildly.

They said you could judge a person by the quality of their enemies. Rodrick had made a particularly vile one, which spoke well of him. Perhaps someone would mention that at his funeral, if these two left enough of his body to bury.

"But you chose the tool," Kalika said. "The fault is yours." She looked at Rodrick. "I think I've heard enough. Haven't you?" She showed a mouthful of tiger's teeth, and Rodrick put his back against the wall.

26
The Thakur's Justice

I've certainly heard enough," a voice said gruffly, and suddenly a dozen men appeared as if from thin air, armed and armored, plus two women in dark robes. One man with gray in his beard wore a breastplate but no helmet, and held a spear that he used to prod Nagesh in the side of the head. The snake-headed rakshasa gaped and trembled, and when he started to rise, several crossbows moved to point at various vulnerable points on his person. "No need to get up," Kalika murmured. "Every crossbow bolt pointed in your direction has been blessed, and the weapons wrapped with enough spells to penetrate even the defenses of your kind." Nagesh sank back down, head lowered.

The graybeard walked over to Kalika, who was tall enough to look him in the eye, and then kissed her on her cheek. Rodrick goggled. Were these more members of the Knife in the Dark? How vast *was* this conspiracy? Was anyone in the palace *not* some monstrous beast in disguise?

"Do drop that illusion, daughter," the man said. "It's horrible."

"I think the fur's very pretty." She shimmered, and was a human again. "It's just like that tigerskin rug you used to have in your office, when you were captain of the guard." She smiled. "See, I told you Nagesh was lurking around somewhere. And I got a confession out of him, as promised."

Rodrick approached the bars. "Wait. You're *not* a weretiger? This was a trick to catch Nagesh? But how? I thought he could read thoughts!"

She sniffed. "We have some experience dealing with such creatures." She held up her finger and tapped one of the thick rings there. "This ring shields my thoughts from intrusion."

Rodrick sighed. "I could have used one of those. But I suppose such things are easier to acquire for wealthy nobles."

The old man looked at him and snarled, "Quiet, thief."

"Oh, Father, he's not so bad. A thief, yes, and a liar at times—but it's not as if *we* never use trickery to advance our goals. Pretending to be a high priest of the Knife in the Dark is a fairly big lie."

"You used me as bait," Rodrick said. "Me! Bait!" He didn't like that at all. He much preferred using others as bait. "What if Nagesh had killed me?"

"It would have spared me passing a sentence on you," Kalika's father—ah, yes, the minister of justice—said. "My daughter was well warded, and he would have had trouble harming you. Besides, you were in a cell."

"Oh, so iron bars provide proof against death by rakshasa magic? How wonderful, I had no idea."

"You aren't helping yourself, Rodrick," Kalika said. "Silence might be best now."

The guards hauled Nagesh away, the crossbowmen keeping their weapons aimed at him as they went, making a strange procession. "Where are they taking him?" Rodrick said. "There are plenty of cells right here. Put him in this one. I'm happy to let him take my place."

"He's going to some cells that are . . . less nice," Kalika said. "These are the ones for prisoners whose spirits we don't need to break, or for nobles. We have other facilities for those who possess the special skills that rakshasas do."

"I am glad of my accommodations, then," Rodrick said. "But will be even gladder when I am set free and given a room with a bed. Who has the key?"

"Your trial is set for tomorrow morning," the minister of justice said. He turned and walked off, followed by the remaining guards.

Rodrick stared after him, gaping, and Kalika shrugged. "You're no longer accused of attempting to kill the thakur. But there are still those other crimes."

"The *map*?" Rodrick said. "Really? After all my service, after serving as the lure to trap Nagesh, I'm still to be put on trial for *theft*?"

"We believe in justice," she said, and left him alone with his thoughts, an absolutely terrible place to be.

Breakfast was another egg and a lump of bread, and then he was shackled and dragged through the palace, back to the room with the circle of truth, though this time he was shoved onto a stone bench. The room was filled with Vudrani—all eager to watch the show, he supposed. He didn't see Kalika, nor did he see Dhyana and Lais and Hrym, so it seemed a daring last-minute rescue wouldn't be forthcoming.

The thakur sat in the central chair, the minister of justice on his right, the priest on his left. "We have heard Rodrick's testimony," the minister of justice said. "He admits to stealing from the library, and selling what he stole to our enemies the Arclords." Murmurs of outrage filled the room, and Rodrick hunched his shoulders.

"We have questions," the minister of justice said. "Put him in the circle." A guard grabbed him by the arm and roughly shoved him into position. No djinn guardians, this time. He supposed as an accused thief he didn't rate as many precautions as an accused assassin.

"Some have suggested that Nagesh coerced you into stealing the map for his own reasons, as he coerced you into other crimes, from which you have been absolved," the minister of justice said. "Did he?"

It was a pretty lie. They would believe anything of Nagesh today. But he was in a circle that allowed no falsehood to be spoken, and he could think of no circumlocution to suggest that the minister of justice was right without saying it straight out. In a strangled voice, he said, "No."

"Then you undertook the theft solely because you were hired to do so by a servant of the Arclords of Nex?"

It was more nuanced than that, but he said, "Yes," hoping he'd be given a chance to explain.

"Very well. Does the accused have anything to say in his own defense?"

He cleared his throat. "I do. I did steal the scroll, in exchange for gold. But I didn't knowingly sell it to an enemy of the island—I didn't know she was working for the Arclords, as I believe I mentioned once in this circle before. After I realized she was an agent of the Arclords, I did my best to keep her from *getting* the scroll." Technically true. He hadn't tried to keep it from her *because* she was associated with the Arclords, but a lot of people heard "after" and mentally replaced it with "because," so the statement would probably serve.

"Your motives don't matter, or your later misgivings," the minister of justice said. "If you were from this island, your conspiracy with an Arclord agent would count as treason, but as an outsider, the crimes don't rise to *that* level. For that, you are fortunate."

Was he? What could they do to traitors that was worse than death? Actually, never mind. He didn't want to know. There were probably many things. "The scroll was a treasure map, and I have offered to return what we found—"

"Ah, yes, this so-called Scepter of the Arclords." Another murmur in the crowd, this one surprised, perhaps even a little worried. The minister held up his hand for silence, and was obeyed instantly. "The staff you found is trash, a mere stick enchanted to seem wondrous. One of many such false treasures. Confidence tricksters—much like you, Rodrick—sometimes hide such things away and sell false maps to the treasure. Many fools have been tricked that way."

Rodrick kept his face impassive, but had to suppress a groan. The map had seemed genuine, certainly very old, and it had fooled Grimschaw, too. How long had people been perpetrating this scam? The scepter had seemed quite eerie and remarkable, but it could have been an illusion. After all, it hadn't *done* anything particularly magical. He'd enchanted enough ordinary swords to look like Hrym to know how convincing such illusions could be.

The crowd made sounds of relief. Good for *them*; Rodrick had lost one of the few bargaining chips he'd expected to have.

"Anything else?" the minister of justice said.

"I exposed Nagesh!" Rodrick said, unable to conceal his irritation. "I helped bring down the Knife in the Dark! I—"

"Not relevant to the charge," the minister of justice said, cutting him off. "Those actions do not bear on your theft."

The thakur cleared his throat, and the minister of justice nodded, not taking his eyes off Rodrick. "However, since you brought it up, you may as well know: You are to be awarded a medal for your services to Jalmeray, one of only three foreigners to ever receive such an honor. There will also be a bust of you, cast in gold and placed in a suitable location in the palace, perhaps in the room where you stayed as the thakur's guest." His voice was as flat as if he'd just delivered an execution order.

Indeed, his voice was just that flat when he said, "In light of your confession, and your failure to provide any useful mitigating testimony, the situation is clear. You are guilty of stealing from the thakur, and you will be executed at dawn."

There was no uproar at the sentence, only silence. Rodrick tried not to gape. Dawn. Less than a day away. What could he do in a day? Could there be an appeal? He'd made a point of learning the essentials of the legal systems of Andoran and Absalom and a few other countries where he did business, but he had no idea how things were done here. He'd have to take a leap and hope for the best. "I . . . Thakur, I request mercy."

The minister of justice glanced at the thakur, who inclined his head a fraction.

"Mercy is granted," the minister said. "Your death will be painless."

Now Rodrick did gape. "I—that's not the mercy I had—" He took a breath. He didn't know what he could do to save himself. Maybe nothing. Maybe the bill for everything bad he'd ever done had finally come due. Karma. But he could speak up about one thing. "Thakur . . . I appreciate your mercy. If I may ask, what will happen to Hrym?"

The thakur just raised an eyebrow, and the minister of justice scowled. Rodrick hurried on before the man could order him hauled away. "I left Hrym with some friends of ours, and he is utterly blameless in all this. He did not join me when I stole the scroll, and in fact he counseled against it. If . . . if you intend to keep him, I hope you will keep him well, in comfort, and if not, let him go with whomever he chooses as a companion. I know I have no right or standing to make this request, but if a condemned man's last wishes carry any weight in this land, I want to make mine known."

The thakur might have nodded, but it was so scant Rodrick could barely see it, and he wondered if it were mere wishful thinking.

"Take him away," the minister of justice said.

Rodrick wasn't dragged to the dungeon, but instead taken to what looked like a study, with a writing desk, a shelf of books, and several comfortable chairs. The guard shoved him into one of those chairs and then left the room. Rodrick considered running for it. There was only one door, doubtless guarded, and he was shackled besides, but if he could find something here that might be used as a weapon . . .

The door opened, and the thakur entered, alone, and sat in a chair on the other side of the desk. He waved his hands, and Rodrick's shackles fell to the carpet with a rattle. Rodrick rubbed his wrists as several very dangerous ideas passed through his mind. None were more dangerous than certain death at dawn, though. "You don't mind sitting here with a condemned man, Thakur?"

The thakur smiled, and glanced upward. A faint disturbance in the air marked a djinni, and Rodrick dismissed those dangerous ideas. Death by djinni right now was unappealing. Dawn was a long way off, comparatively. A lot of things could happen before dawn. Though he wouldn't bet on the monkey learning to talk.

The thakur lifted a long wooden box from the floor and set it on the desk, then lifted the lid. The so-called Scepter of the Arclords was inside, its eyes rolling. "Do you know what you've brought me?"

"A fake?"

The thakur shook his head. "Oh no. It's genuine. Only two people besides you and I know that, now, and they only know because I needed my archwizards to authenticate it. This is the true Scepter of the Arclords, sought after for centuries, a relic of such power that it could shift the balance of power between Jalmeray and Nex, and cause ripples throughout the rest of the Inner Sea— perhaps even in the Impossible Kingdoms."

Rodrick beamed. The scepter was real! Maybe he'd get his freedom and *more* than his weight in gold.

"You thought you were giving me a gift," the thakur said mildly, "but this is a nest of vipers."

Ah. So much for the gold.

"If the Arclords heard we had this in our hands, they would be outraged," the thakur said. "Even those in Nex opposed to their faction would be unhappy to hear we possess a staff that, by some accounts, belonged to Nex himself. Factions in Nex might join together and attack us in force. Oh, we could fight them off . . . but it would be bloody, messy, and costly. Nor are the only dangers from the people of Nex. There are those in the Impossible Kingdoms who would see possession of the scepter as an opportunity to gain a further foothold in the Inner Sea—they might want to use the scepter as a pretext to invade Nex itself, to claim it gives them, or even *me*, the authority of the departed wizard. I am quite happy ruling Jalmeray, Rodrick. I have no desire to be used in some rajah's territorial ambitions—nor do I wish to be put in a position to *refuse* to do so, lest my lack of fervor for invasion be perceived as weakness. And those are just some of the potential problems this damnable scepter brings. There are factions you've never heard of, on both sides of the ocean that surrounds us, who could make the scepter central to their plans."

"I take it you won't be giving it to your friend the rajah," Rodrick said.

The thakur chuckled, a musical sound. "No. I will, in fact, be burying it somewhere very far away, where, with luck, it will never be found again. I have spent a long time trying to convince people this thing was only a story the Arclords told themselves." He snapped the lid shut, and Rodrick could understand why. The scepter was certainly watching, and it gave the impression of listening, too.

"So are you planning to give Hrym to your friend instead? I assume Hrym is here, now. If you have the scepter, then Dhyana and Lais came to you."

"They did. Hrym is here, but I don't *have* him. He is a free . . . person. He will not be forced to go anywhere he does not wish to go. He actually offered himself to me, you know, if I would spare your life."

Rodrick perked up. Living without Hrym would be dreadful, but it would be better than dying. After all, if he was alive, he could always steal Hrym back.

"I declined his offer," the thakur said. "Instead, I have acquired a relic I am assured comes from the Silver Mount itself in Numeria, a toothed wheel that sings when you spin it, though not very well. I purchased the wheel from a man in Almas who deals in such trinkets. My friend will be very pleased with it. Not as pleased as he would have been with Hrym, but . . ." The thakur shrugged. "I was quite impressed that you chose to speak on Hrym's behalf in court today."

"I thought I should try to save *someone*," he said bitterly.

The thakur nodded. "In fact, you saved many someones. You helped deal a blow to the Knife in the Dark—perhaps even a decisive one, though with that cult, it's hard to tell. Your friends, and Kalika, too, spoke out strenuously on your behalf. They would all rather see you paraded through the streets like a hero than put to death."

"I'd prefer that, too, if it's an option, sir." Hope was stirring again.

"Ah, but if I let an outsider steal from me without consequence, no matter what other heroic acts he performed, what does that tell my people? My minister of justice is a hard man, but fair, and he believes in the law. He sees no contradiction in putting a medal around your neck and then cutting your head off that same neck. He thinks both are justice."

"Remind me never to turn myself in again," Rodrick said.

Another chuckle. "I am a ruler, Rodrick, but I am also a poet. I can rarely afford to be sympathetic in my position, but there are times . . . You put the Scepter of the Arclords in my hands instead of trying to sell it or trade it to some other faction for favors. Oh, I know you tried to *use* it, that you thought by giving it to me you might save yourself, but you could have used it in ways that were destructive to me and all I hold dear. You did not. And so . . . I am inclined to mercy. Even more mercy than a painless death. Here's what will happen. A rumor will be started that you were executed at dawn, in private, as a kindness in recognition of your service, but no official statement will be made either way. At the same time, a very small note will be made in a file that will be shelved where no one is ever likely to read it, noting that your sentence was commuted by the thakur's order from death to exile."

Rodrick nearly fell out of the chair from relief. "Thank you. Thank you, thank you, thank you." He paused. "Though it was a bit cruel to make me think you were going to have me killed all this time."

The thakur's voice hardened. "Perhaps that fear will make you think twice before you next decide to *steal from a sovereign*. Really, Rodrick. There's such a thing as being too sure of yourself." His tone eased. "You—and Hrym, since I assume he wants to stay with you—will be put on a ship tomorrow morning and taken to some foreign port, and you will not be allowed back on these shores unless I choose to summon you. I'm afraid the medal you're being awarded hasn't been struck yet—I'll have it sent to Absalom, to the inn where you were staying when we first contacted you. Here." He tossed a jingling leather bag to Rodrick. "This is payment for bringing me the scepter, and for other services." The thakur glanced upward, and the disturbance in the air materialized into a djinni. It drifted across the room and opened the door.

Lais came in, all boundless energy and smiles, and Dhyana, too, with Hrym on her hip. Lais leapt at him as he stood and gave him a hug. "I'm to enter the Monastery of Untwisting Iron!" she said. "All my expenses paid! The thakur put in a word for me personally!"

"That's marvelous," Rodrick said, hugging her back. Very strange to hug a woman and think thoughts that were truly nothing more than brotherly.

"I am to be made a member of the thakur's household guard," Dhyana said severely. "Be glad I did not hold that position when you had your little accident with Hrym, or I would have spitted you on a spear."

"Dhyana, I'm so pleased for you. And, yes, I'm also pleased you didn't get the job sooner."

"And I," Hrym said grandly, "am stuck with you, I suppose, you scoundrel. I can't believe you got us exiled. I like it here. The place is *full* of gold."

"You may visit with your friends here for a while," the thakur said. "Then they must be about their business. I have set aside a room for you, in a private part of the palace, where you aren't likely to be noticed. You will *stay there* until it is time to leave. Do not think to pick up any further trinkets and take them with you when you depart. Is that understood?"

"My thieving days are over," Rodrick lied.

27

The Knife in the Dark

The thakur didn't stay long, but Rodrick had more than an hour with Dhyana and Lais, the latter doing most of the talking, excited about her plans and hopes and goals. Dhyana spoke little—after everything, she still didn't like him much—and Hrym mostly complained about them leaving nearly as poor as they'd been when they arrived, but after a week of not hearing Hrym's voice at all, his complaints were like music. Eventually Lais and Dhyana had to go, and a guard led Rodrick, with Hrym on his hip again—though with no jeweled scabbard, alas—toward their private rooms.

These quarters were lavish, even more so than the apartments he'd been given earlier, and included a gold-rimmed bathtub with magically warmed water. He took a long soak, Hrym propped against the wall and complaining about the steam. "We didn't do badly," Rodrick said. "We're getting out of here alive. We don't have to swim to Absalom. Not as rich as we could have been, no, but I looked in the purse the thakur gave me, and it's all gold, and good weight. We won't have to work again for a little while, and you can sleep on a bed of gleaming."

"The last time you got me into a mess like this, we ended up saving the world from a demon lord," Hrym said. "This time, we merely saved an island nation from a murderous cult. Perhaps next time we can do something even smaller, and just save a city, or a village."

"I don't want to save anything. No more grand excursions. Next time a supernatural creature appears before me with an invitation, I will politely decline."

"It's good to be back with you," Hrym said. "I spent a week in the company of Dhyana, who wouldn't lie even if doing so would save her life, and with Lais, who's so sweet and earnest she would make my teeth ache, if I had teeth. I'm sick of the company of the noble and upright. Though I *was* touched that you spoke up in court to try to save me. As if I could be taken anywhere or destroyed without my consent. If the thakur had tried to give me away like a piece of silverware I would have wrapped his whole palace in ice."

Rodrick laughed. He suspected the thakur had access to magics that could overwhelm Hrym given sufficient time, but was glad it hadn't come to that. "I will try not to be earnest in your presence. Except in my insults. Those will be as earnest and heartfelt as ever."

After his bath, Rodrick toweled and dried off, then wrapped himself in a robe, picked up Hrym, and went into the bedroom. He'd be hustled out of the palace before dawn, and he'd hardly slept well last night in the dungeon. A long nap, then a hot meal, then a full night's sleep before the journey. Maybe he'd end up on Saraswati's ship again. She *had* made the voyage over more enjoyable, and maybe she'd forgotten about the cracks in her hull.

A tall woman was standing by the bed, her back turned to him, seemingly examining a tapestry. Her hair was long and black, her clothing rich and embroidered with gold.

Rodrick frowned. Was this woman meant as a gift from the thakur? He didn't like the company of women he didn't win with his own charms. "Sorry, miss, but I think you have the wrong room."

The woman turned toward him. His eyes blurred when he looked at her. Did she have four arms, or six, or two—or only one, with the other a ragged, bleeding stump? Was she beautiful, or was her face a skull, and why did it seem to flicker from one to the other, her eyes sublime and placid pools in one moment, and empty sockets writhing with worms the next? Rodrick fell to his knees, his head pounding, and stared at the designs on the carpet. It was easier to think when he wasn't looking at her. A little.

"You broke up my conclave," she said, and how was her voice both sweet music and the buzzing of flies? "I was going to appear there, this year, and watch my servants turn on one another, snapping and tearing, as they tried to please me. I thought I might dance among them. Sometimes I like to dance. But you were there, in the deep jungle, pretending to be one of mine—an imposter among those skilled at imposture. You played three sides against each another, and brought down disaster, to get what you wanted: to go free with a bag of gold. All this, and you managed to defeat and expose my most powerful follower in the palace, who was also my archaka. This you did in mere days. Undoing the work of years, in days."

This had to be a trick. A wizard, casting an illusion. It couldn't be—it couldn't *really* be—

"I am not angry." The voice was, if anything, amused. "Nagesh allowed himself to be exposed, so he failed me by definition, and deserves the death he has already received at my hands. He bleeds out even now, deep in a black cell, as yet undiscovered, and the palace will think he was killed by a member of the Knife in the Dark, and know fear again. I could not let him live, you see, to give away my secrets—he would betray me as rapidly as any other. Such is the nature of all my followers, and Nagesh even more so. But you. *You* have done my work for years, haven't you?"

He knew she was standing before him, over him, reaching down with long fingers to touch the top of his head. Her touch was warm and comforting; her touch was repellent and foul. "You have wormed your way into hearts and homes and minds, only to betray them, to slip off into the night and leave those who considered you friend or mentor or partner penniless, bereft, and confused. You have served me by your actions, showing the world a smile that hides a lie. You never served in my name, and you acted without hope of gaining my favor—which makes your actions more pure, in a way."

He struggled to speak. "I'm not . . . I'm not like Nagesh . . . I don't . . ."

"Oh, you have some similarities. He did not wish to serve me in his heart, either—rakshasas do not willingly serve any god—but he did my work just the same. And now I have no champion in the Inner Sea. I have enough to occupy me in the Impossible Kingdoms, but . . . I may look upon you, from time to time, Rodrick of Andoran. You are not so different from many men, I think. Doing whatever you wish, to enrich yourself, though with great élan. But you have passed before my eyes, into my sphere, and so called my attention down on you. That is all some men need, to become great—the attention, however glancing, of someone like me. Perhaps I will have work for you, in the future. And rewards, of course, for work well done. I know how you like your rewards."

Her fingers reached down again and touched his chin, trying to tip his head back. He resisted, but just for an instant. Then she was irresistible. He gazed up at her face, and it was not blurry, now: half beautiful woman, half grinning skull, the edge between them ragged and bleeding. "I feel what you are. You have loyalty to no one, except your sword . . . it's unfortunate that you have even that much. But perhaps something may be done about that. My followers are often called upon to betray those closest to them. Sometimes they are even brought to betray themselves."

She leaned forward and kissed his forehead with her bloody half a mouth.

Everything went black.

"Rodrick!" Hrym said. "Rodrick, what's wrong with you? Are you all right?"

He opened his eyes. He was on the floor, carpet rough against his cheek. He sat up, blinking. "Is she gone? Hrym? Is she?"

"Who?"

"Vas . . . a woman. There was a woman . . ."

"Rodrick, what's wrong with you? We came into the room, and you started talking to yourself, and then you knelt, and then you just fell over. I was shouting at you, but you didn't seem to hear. If I didn't know better, I'd think *you* were tainted by a demon."

Rodrick laughed, but it was almost a sob. He struggled to his feet. "We're leaving, Hrym. Right now. We have gold, we have my pack and cloak, we can get to the docks, they won't try to stop us—"

"Are you mad? You want to try to escape again? Why? We're being sent away as heroes, at least by our standards, in a few hours. If the wrong people see you walking around before then you'll be killed on sight. Calm down, man."

Rodrick took deep breaths. All right. Calm. Calm. If that woman had been . . . who he feared, running wouldn't help. She could be anywhere, couldn't she? The only way to defeat her . . . Could he root her out of his heart? Make it an unwelcome habitation for her? "Hrym. We . . . we have to make some changes."

"What are you talking about?"

"The way we live. The . . . the cheating. The lies. I don't know . . ."

Hrym's voice was concerned. "Don't tell me you meant what you told the thakur, about your thieving days being over. I know you saved yourself this one time by telling the truth, or at least large parts of it, but if you intend to do honest work, by which I mean anything that *resembles* work, I may have to take back my decision to travel with you. We are what we are, Rodrick. Why try to change it now?"

"The Knife in the Dark," he said. "They lie. They trick. Are we like them?"

"No. Of course not. We just want gold, and a pleasant time, not chaos and destruction. When pushed, we've even been known to do good. We avenged Jayin. We *are* different than Nagesh, Rodrick."

"In kind, though? Or degree?" He was starting to think more clearly, but the thoughts were still not easy.

"What do you want to do, then?" Hrym said. "Pledge yourself to Iomedae and become a paladin? Don't think you're carrying me into battle at the Worldwound. I've turned down that opportunity before."

"I . . . No. No." He scrubbed a hand through his hair. Could there be a middle path? Somewhere between honesty and treachery? "But I'm going to be a lot more careful about who we try to swindle. They say you can't cheat an honest person, but we both know you *can*, and we often have. It's just a little harder. You can exploit goodwill almost as easily as ill. I think, going forward, I'll try to focus on stealing from those who deserve to be stolen from instead. I . . . I'd like to see if it's possible to use the things we can do against those who *deserve* it."

"There should be no shortage of targets, then," Hrym said. "But I'm not signing on for charity work. You always pick the targets, you make the plans, that's your strength. But our goal must remain the same: a pile of coins as big as a mountain, for me to slumber on."

"The wicked are often rich," Rodrick said. "I think we'll be fine."

He went to the bed and pulled back the bedspread. There was a medallion there, black metal, marked with a circle full of inward-pointing triangles. He tore the sheet from the bed, sending the medallion spinning across the floor, then snatched up Hrym and brought the blade down hard on the medallion, freezing and shattering it on impact.

He heard laughter in his head. Laughter that was somehow half sweet music, and half the buzz of flies.

About the Author

Tim Pratt is the author of the Pathfinder Tales novels *Liar's Blade* (also featuring Rodrick and Hrym), *City of the Fallen Sky*, and *Reign of Stars*, as well as several Pathfinder short stories available for free at **paizo.com/pathfindertales**. His creator-owned stories have appeared in *The Best American Short Stories*, *The Year's Best Fantasy and Horror*, and other nice places, and he is the author of three story collections, most recently *Antiquities and Tangibles*, as well as a poetry collection. He has also written several novels, including contemporary fantasies *The Strange Adventures of Rangergirl*, *Briarpatch*, *Heirs of Grace*, and *The Deep Woods*; the Forgotten Realms novel *Venom in Her Veins*; the gonzo historical steampunk novel *The Constantine Affliction* (under the name T. Aaron Payton); and, as T. A. Pratt, eight books in the urban fantasy series about ass-kicking sorcerer Marla Mason: *Blood Engines*, *Poison Sleep*, *Dead Reign*, *Spell Games*, *Broken Mirrors*, *Grim Tides*, *Bride of Death*, and the prequel *Bone Shop*. He edited the anthology *Sympathy for the Devil*, and co-edited the *Rags & Bones* anthology with Melissa Marr.

He has won a Hugo Award for best short story, a Rhysling Award for best speculative poetry, and an Emperor Norton Award for best San Francisco Bay Area-related novel. His books and stories have been nominated for Nebula, Mythopoeic, World Fantasy, and Stoker awards, among others, and have been translated into numerous languages.

He lives in Berkeley, California with his wife Heather Shaw and son River, and works as a senior editor and occasional book reviewer at *Locus, the Magazine of the Science Fiction and Fantasy Field*. He blogs intermittently at **timpratt.org**.

Acknowledgments

Thanks as always to my wife Heather Shaw, who is the best partner I could ever hope for. My editor James Sutter has been supportive, as usual, of all my weird ideas. My agent Ginger Clark always makes sure the wheels of publishing turn smooth. My son River—who just turned seven!—has reintroduced me to the joys of running games with his enthusiasm and excitement. My gamer friends Jeff Martin and Katrina Storey are always a great help when I need to enthuse or geek out about Pathfinder-related things. Finally, thanks to the local Pathfinder community for being so welcoming, especially Mitch Anderson, who's invited me to speak at a couple of gaming days at the fantastic Oakland, California shop Endgame.

Glossary

All Pathfinder Tales novels are set in the rich and vibrant world of the Pathfinder campaign setting. Below are explanations of several key terms used in this book. For more information on the world of Golarion and the strange monsters, people, and deities that make it their home, see *The Inner Sea World Guide*, or dive into the game and begin playing your own adventures with the *Pathfinder Roleplaying Game Core Rulebook* or the *Pathfinder Roleplaying Game Beginner Box*, all available at **paizo.com**. Those interested in learning more about Rodrick and Hrym should check out their earlier adventures in the Pathfinder Tales novel *Liar's Blade*.

Absalom: Largest city in the Inner Sea region, located on an island in the middle of said sea.

Abyss: Plane of evil and chaos ruled by demons, where many evil souls go after they die.

Almas: Capital city of Andoran.

Andoran: Democratic and freedom-loving nation north of the Inner Sea.

Andoren: Of or pertaining to Andoran; someone from Andoran.

Arclords: A powerful faction within Nex, which led the country for a time before being ousted from power.

Avistan: The continent north of the Inner Sea.

Bloodline: The unusual ancestry from which a sorcerer draws his or her magical power.

Brevoy: A frigid northern nation famous for its swordlords.

Bugbear: Large, humanoid monster related to the goblin. Extremely violent and ill tempered.

Chelaxian: Someone from Cheliax, or of its predominant ethnicity

Cheliax: A powerful devil-allied nation north of the Inner Sea.

Chelish: Of or relating to the nation of Cheliax.

Coins: Mercantile district in Absalom.

Demon Lord: A particularly powerful demon capable of granting magical powers to its followers. One of the rulers of the Abyss.

Demon: Evil denizen of the plane of the afterlife called the Abyss, who seeks only to maim, ruin, and feed on mortal souls.

Devilfish: A semi-intelligent, seven-armed octopuslike creature with hook-lined tentacles.

Devilkin: A mortal with a devil somewhere in his or her ancestry.

Djinn: Race of generally good-natured genies that often appear as large humanoids with lower bodies made of mist and wind.

Druid: Someone who reveres nature and draws magical power from the boundless energy of the natural world (sometimes called the Green Faith, or the Green).

Eagle Knights: Military order in Andoran devoted to spreading the virtues of justice, equality, and freedom.

Efreet: Race of evil genies that often appear as large humanoids with horns and burning skin.

Elemental: A being of pure elemental energy, such as air, earth, fire, or water.

Elves: Long-lived, beautiful humanoids identifiable by their pointed ears, lithe bodies, and eyes without visible whites.

Garuda: Race of birdlike humanoids renowned for their honor and nobility.

Garund: Continent south of the Inner Sea, famous for its deserts and jungles.

Genies: Magical humanoids creatures associated with the elements, and residing on the elemental planes of the multiverse.

Gho Vella: Small island near Jalmeray that acts as a refuge for those cursed and afflicted by magic.

Gillmen: Race of amphibious humanoids descended from humans after their home island of Azlant sank into the sea.

Gnomes: Small humanoids with strange mindsets, big eyes, and often wildly colored hair.

Golems: Magical constructs created for use as servants and guardians.

Gozreh: God of nature, the sea, and weather. Depicted as a dual deity, with both male and female aspects.

Grand Sarret: Small island controlled by Jalmeray and famous for its school training courtesans and diplomats.

Gray Corsairs: Naval division of the Steel Falcons, the Eagle Knight branch focused on abolitionist military activities. Often focused on raiding slave ships.

Half-Elves: The children of unions between elves and humans. Taller, longer-lived, and generally more graceful and attractive than the average human.

Homunculi: Small, devil-like constructs often used as familiars and servants by spellcasters.

Houses of Perfection: Prestigious monasteries in Jalmeray legendary for training fighting monks.

Impossible Kingdoms: Vudra.

Inner Sea: The vast inland sea whose northern continent, Avistan, and southern continent, Garund, as well as the seas and nearby lands, are the primary focus of the Pathfinder campaign setting.

Irori: God of history, knowledge, self-perfection, and enlightenment.

Jalmeray: Island nation in the Obari Ocean, heavily influenced by the customs and cultures of distant Vudra.

Kaina Katakka: Smaller island near Jalmeray, said to be haunted.

Katapesh: Mighty trade nation south of the Inner Sea. Also the name of its capital city.

Kellids: Human ethnicity from the northern reaches of the Inner Sea region, often regarded by southerners as violent and uncivilized.

Khiben-Sald: The legendary maharajah who first established Jalmeray as the westernmost of Vudra's Impossible Kingdoms.

Mammoth Lord: The ruler of a following of Kellid tribes in the Realm of the Mammoth Lords.

Marids: Race of genies that usually appear as blue-skinned giants.

Maurya-Rahm: The system of powerful advisors which rules Jalmeray in the thakur's name.

Mwangi Expanse: A jungle region south of the Inner Sea.

Nex: Nation in Garund formerly ruled by an immensely powerful wizard of the same name.

Niswan: Jalmeray's capital city.

Obari Ocean: Ocean east of Garund.

Ogres: Hulking, brutal, and half-witted humanoid monsters with violent tendencies, repulsive lusts, and enormous capacities for cruelty.

Osirian: Of or relating to the region of Osirion, or a resident of Osirion.

Osirion: Ancient nation south of the Inner Sea renowned for its deserts, pharaohs, and pyramids.

Paladin: A holy warrior in the service of a good and lawful god. Ruled by a strict code of conduct and granted special magical powers by his or her deity.

Pharasma: The goddess of birth, death, and prophecy, who judges mortal souls after their deaths and sends them on to the appropriate afterlife; also known as the Lady of Graves.

Quantium: Nex's capital city.

Rakshasa: Evil spirits capable of disguising themselves as humanoids in order to sow chaos and destruction. In their natural forms, they appear as animal-headed humanoids with backward-facing hands.

Segang Jungle: Large jungle in southern Jalmeray.

Shaitans: Race of genies associated with the element of earth. Often appear as giant humanoids with stone skin.

She Who Guides the Wind and the Waves: A Vudrani name for Gozreh, particularly her female aspect.

Shory: Ancient empire, now long since fallen to obscurity, most famed for its flying cities.

Sorcerer: Someone who casts spells through natural ability rather than faith or study.

Sothis: Capital city of the desert nation of Osirion, on the northeastern shore of Garund.

Steaming Sea: Sea north and west of the Inner Sea, east of the continent of Avistan.

Stonespine Island: Island in the Obari Ocean owned by Katapesh, and famous for the slaver port of Okeno.

Taldan: Of or pertaining to Taldor; a citizen of Taldor.

Taldane: The common trade language of the Inner Sea region.

Taldor: A formerly glorious nation that lost many of its holdings due to neglect and decadence.

Thakur: The ruling monarch of Jalmeray.

Tian Xia: Continent on the opposite side of the world from the Inner Sea region.

Veedesha: Small island off the coast of Jalmeray that was once a prominent port, but has since been abandoned.

Vudra: Continent far to the east of the Inner Sea.

Vudrani: Someone or something from the continent of Vudra.

Wizard: Someone who casts spells through careful study and rigorous scientific methods rather than faith or innate talent, recording the necessary incantations in a spellbook.

Worldwound: Constantly expanding region overrun by demons a century ago. Held at bay by the efforts of crusaders.

With strength, wit, rakish charm, and a talking sword named Hrym, Rodrick has all the makings of a classic hero—except for the conscience. Instead, he and Hrym live a high life as scoundrels, pulling cons and parting the weak from their gold. When a mysterious woman invites them along on a quest into the frozen north in pursuit of a legendary artifact, it seems like a prime opportunity to make some easy coin—especially if there's a chance for a double-cross. Along with a hooded priest and a half-elven tracker, the team sets forth into a land of monsters, bandits, and ancient magic. As the miles wear on, however, Rodrick's companions begin acting steadily stranger, leading both man and sword to wonder what exactly they've gotten themselves into . . .

From Hugo Award winner Tim Pratt, author of *Liar's Island*, *City of the Fallen Sky*, and *Reign of Stars*, comes a bold tale of ice magic and situational ethics set in the award-winning world of the Pathfinder Roleplaying Game.

Liar's Blade print edition: $9.99
ISBN: 978-1-60125-515-0

Liar's Blade ebook edition:
ISBN: 978-1-60125-516-7

PATHFINDER TALES

Liar's Blade

Tim Pratt

Count Varian Jeggare and his hellspawn bodyguard Radovan are no strangers to the occult. Yet when Varian is bequeathed a dangerous magical book by an old colleague, the infamous investigators find themselves on the trail of a necromancer bent on becoming the new avatar of an ancient and sinister demigod—one of the legendary runelords. Along with a team of mercenaries and adventurers, the crime-solving duo will need to delve into a secret world of dark magic and the legacy of a lost empire. But in saving the world, will Varian and Radovan lose their souls?

From best-selling author Dave Gross comes a fantastical tale of mystery, monsters, and mayhem set in the award-winning world of the Pathfinder Roleplaying Game.

Lord of Runes **print edition: $14.99**
ISBN: 978-0-7653-7451-6

Lord of Runes **ebook edition:**
ISBN: 978-1-4668-4263-2

PATHFINDER
TALES

Lord of Runes

A NOVEL BY **Dave Gross**

When the aristocratic Vishov family is banished from Ustalav due to underhanded politics, Lady Tyressa Vishov is faced with a choice: fade slowly into obscurity, or strike out for the nearby River Kingdoms and establish a new holding on the untamed frontier. Together with her children and loyal retainers, she'll forge a new life in the infamous Echo Wood, and neither bloodthirsty monsters nor local despots will stop her from reclaiming her family honor. Yet the shadow of Ustalavic politics is long, and even in a remote and lawless territory, there may be those determined to see the Vishov family fail . . .

From *New York Times* best-selling author Michael A. Stackpole comes a new novel of frontier adventure set in the world of the Pathfinder Roleplaying Game and the new *Pathfinder Online* massively multiplayer online roleplaying game.

The Crusader Road print edition: $9.99
ISBN: 978-1-60125-657-7

The Crusader Road ebook edition:
ISBN: 978-1-60125-658-4

PATHFINDER TALES

THE CRUSADER ROAD

MICHAEL A. STACKPOLE

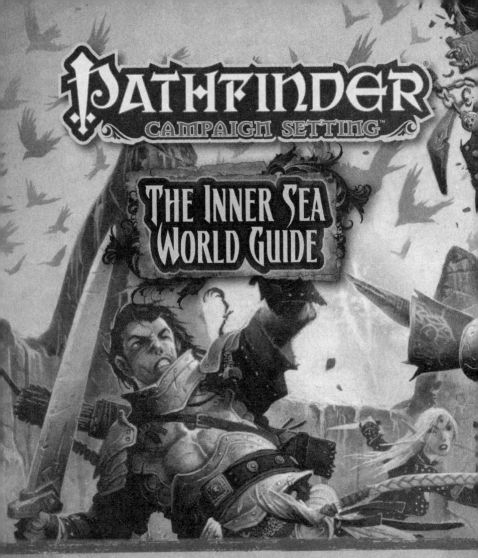

PATHFINDER
CAMPAIGN SETTING

THE INNER SEA WORLD GUIDE

You've delved into the Pathfinder campaign setting with Pathfinder Tales novels—now take your adventures even further! *The Inner Sea World Guide* is a full-color, 320-page hardcover guide featuring everything you need to know about the exciting world of Pathfinder: overviews of every major nation, religion, race, and adventure location around the Inner Sea, plus a giant poster map! Read it as a travelogue, or use it to flesh out your roleplaying game—it's your world now!

EXPLORE YOUR WORLD!

paizo.com